PRAISE FOR
H. MITCHELL CALDWELL

COST OF DECEIT

"Readers will cheer this polished, highly enjoyable legal thriller. Caldwell gradually raises the tension level until the plot verges on thriller. Fans of courtroom drama will savor this peek into the inner workings of an attorney's mind while puzzling over the alleged villain's guilt."

— EDITOR'S PICK, BookLife

"The dramatic dynamic of the trial is comparable to the action that occurs outside the courtroom as one proceeding gives way to another and tensions rise. A most enjoyable read from start to conclusion. 5 STARS."

— Philip Zozzaro, Los Angeles Book Review

"H. Mitchell Caldwell's COST OF DECEIT is a well-structured and easy-to-read legal thriller with believable characters, an engaging story and insight into the criminal court system."

— *Indie Reader*

COST OF ARROGANCE

"A complex courtroom drama, anchored by sharply drawn characters. In Caldwell's legal thriller, a law professor decides to represent an inmate on death row and finds it to be a daunting case. Caldwell's work shines in his ability to make the intricacies of the law accessible to laypeople while still satisfying those with legal experience."

— *Kirkus Reviews*

"This book is a must-read for any fan of courtroom thrillers. There is no stone left unturned when Jake Clearwater takes on a case. Author Caldwell certainly knows his subject matter and I look forward to reading more courtroom fiction by this author."

— Kristi Elizabeth, *San Francisco Book Review*

"As a former prosecutor myself, I appreciated how the book accurately portrays trial proceedings, including a realistic approach to cross-examination and an insightful view of the different ways prosecutors and defense attorneys approach a case and present their evidence."

— Darren Shulman, Ohio Lawyer, *Ohio State Bar Association Journal*

"A gripping novel about a former top prosecutor turned esteemed law professor who takes on a case to challenge the death sentence for a vicious, confessed, and convicted murderer. The trial details are accurate and dramatic reflecting the author's real-life experience as a prosecutor who now teaches law. I lost a night's sleep—I couldn't put it down."

— John Sharer, trial lawyer, Gibson Dunn & Crutcher, member of the American Board of Trial Advocates

"Pepperdine/Caruso law professor H. Mitchell Caldwell has written a chilling legal thriller around the retrial of a convicted murderer facing the death penalty."

— Norm Goldman, *Bookpleasures.com*

"Caldwell's strong and charismatic protagonist Jake Clearwater is the new Perry Mason, and I can't wait to read the next entry in the series. Highly recommended!"

— Eric Petersen, *The Internet Review of Books*

COST OF DECEIT

for Julie, Louie, Stephanie, and Kelly

COST OF DECEIT

A JAKE CLEARWATER LEGAL THRILLER

H. MITCHELL CALDWELL

COST OF DECEIT
Published by Nine Innings Press
First Edition March 2023

Copyright © 2023 by H. Mitchell Caldwell

HMitchellCaldwell.com

Cover design: Eric Labacz

ISBN: 978-1-7375123-3-2 Paperback Edition
          978-1-7375123-4-9 Hardcover Edition
          978-1-7375123-5-6 Digital Edition

Library of Congress Control Number: 2023901490

Author services by Pedernales Publishing, LLC
www.pedernalespublishing.com

10 9 8 7 6 5 4 3 2 1

Printed in the United States of America

CHAPTER 1

HIGH AND MIGHTY

The studio's lights were no longer a distraction as I took my seat opposite Lisbet Boget, one of LA's local news anchors. She turned to me and began, "Once again we've got prominent trial attorney Jake Clearwater here with us. Mr. Clearwater, share with us your thoughts on the opening statements by both sides in the Max Cort murder trial."

"Thank you, Lisbet." I nodded to her and turned to the camera. "Prosecutor Wills methodically and competently laid out his case against Lt. Cort. He went witness-by-witness, summarizing their anticipated testimony. No surprises. If anyone was expecting theatrics from the prosecutor, they were disappointed. Mr. Wills has an understated delivery—just the facts. Not much embellishment. He did emphasize that Christie Cort's last known contact was with her sister, Mary Lynn Holder, at 8:30 p.m., February 3. Lt. Cort reported her missing nine hours later when he returned home from work."

"And what of defense counsel, Merci MacPherson?" Lisbet asked.

"In contrast to the prosecutor, Ms. MacPherson was high energy throughout her opening statement. It's easy to understand why she is considered one of the top defense attorneys in the country. She is compelling. Her presence demands attention. She declared that the state will not be able to prove Lt. Cort murdered anyone. She spent much of her time emphasizing that there is grave doubt that the supposed murder victim, Christie Cort, is even dead. She suggested that Ms. Cort is an unhappy wife who chose to run away and assume a new life with a new identity. Ms. MacPherson acknowledged that while her client is not a good husband and perhaps not even a good person, that does not make him a murderer. Her acknowledgment of Cort's failings, at the very outset of trial, is in my view an excellent strategy and removes any necessity to attempt to fend off any personal attacks on his character."

Lisbet asked, "But doesn't acknowledging that Max Cort is an abusive husband portray him as someone perhaps likely to kill his spouse?"

I nodded my understanding. "I hear your reasoning. However, from MacPherson's opening statement, it appears that her strategy is not to defend Cort's character but to hammer away on the fact that being an abusive husband does not equate to murder, and that Christie Cort is a runaway wife hiding out somewhere."

I could see by Lisbet's pained expression that I wasn't giving her the dramatic, live-TV take she had hoped for, so she asked, "Turning back to the prosecutor's opening argument. I sense from your comments, Professor Clearwater, that you were," she grappled for the word, "*underwhelmed* with his argument."

I grinned and looked directly at the anchor. "Just to be clear, the lawyers were not making arguments today, but rather opening statements." I turned back to the camera. "Counsel are not permitted to argue their case during opening statements, although many lawyers do precisely that. Opening statements are for the lawyers to give a factual overview of their case." I took a breath and mildly admonished myself. I was not teaching a trial advocacy class to law students; I was talking to a TV audience that couldn't care less about the more technical aspects of opening statements. "As for the prosecutor's opening statement, 'underwhelmed' is too strong a word. I would describe it as workerlike. He did what he needed to do, but given this trial with all its attendant notoriety, it lacked much artistry." Again I paused. "Let me go back to my earlier characterization of the prosecutor's opening statement. It was methodical and competent."

"Faint praise indeed," Lisbet offered, with a grin and a nod. "Last week during jury selection you raised questions about some of Prosecutor Wills's decisions concerning several jurors. Am I sensing that you, as a former prosecutor, are not giving him high marks thus far?" She was hunting for something provocative. I wasn't going to play.

Shaking my head, I replied, "Not at all. Mr. Wills is one of the premier trial prosecutors in the LA District Attorney's office. He would not have been selected for this trial if he were not up to it." I leaned toward Lisbet with my palms up in a "please understand" way, to emphasize the point. "And let me add, every trial lawyer has their own way of doing things. His way has obviously been successful, as evidenced by being selected to prosecute this high-profile case." I hesitated, picking my words carefully. "However, in contrast to Merci MacPherson's opening statement, it was not commanding, and it lacked a sense of urgency."

Lisbet gave me a knowing look. "Thank you, professor." She turned away from me toward the camera and, in a practiced voice, said, "That concludes our coverage of the Max Cort murder trial for tonight. We'll return to more news after the break."

With that, my interview ended. I pinched off my mic, nodded

at Lisbet, and walked off the set. Lisa was waiting behind the crew. She had been good enough to come with me to the station tonight. She gave me a halfhearted hug; her manner was subdued. I immediately sensed that she was upset with my criticism of the prosecutor. She had commented to me the evening before that I had been somewhat critical of the prosecutor. And even as I was offering my thoughts while on the air tonight, I felt I had pushed the envelope too far.

I acted as if I hadn't noticed her pique and, with an air of nonchalance, said, "Our work here is done. Now off to that dinner I bribed you with."

As we drove to Roy's off Topanga, Lisa's disappointment radiated from her. Finally she broke, and in a tight voice, said, "Jake, you know I love you and respect you, but it was beneath you to so blatantly criticize another lawyer, especially in this case. You've admitted that a murder case without the body of the victim is extremely difficult." She took a breath, working to maintain her composure. "I've got to think that prosecutor is under intense pressure already, without you piling on." When I didn't react, she went on. "It is beneath your character."

Lisa St. Marie was my confidant and lover. We had been together better than a year and a half. I let out a breath and kept my eyes on the road. My discomfort with my role as a TV commentator had grown over just the first days of trial. It was one thing to critique my law students in the relative privacy of the classroom and a whole other thing to call out a lawyer in public. When the station manager contacted me after last summer's Durgeon trial to comment on the Cort murder case, it seemed harmless—stimulating even, to be involved in such a publicized trial. I was now rethinking my position. Maybe I made a mistake in agreeing to this commentary gig.

Without taking my eyes off the road, I offered my less-than-convicted rationalization. "I insisted when I took the job that as a condition of my participation, I would be given free rein to be completely candid and honest in my evaluation." *How lame was that.*

I turned to Lisa, who was looking straight ahead at nothing. At the risk of digging my hole even deeper, I said, "Maybe I took this little sidelight too seriously. I know the prosecutor is doing his best, but especially when contrasted with someone like Merci MacPherson, he was underwhelming, to borrow a phrase from Lisbet." I paused, waiting for a reaction. When none was forthcoming, I ventured on. "His opening statement and some of his decisions last week during jury selection were just not what I would have expected." Again I paused, still no reaction, no eye contact. In an effort to salvage the evening, I said, "Wills is a top prosecutor, and prosecutions generally result in convictions. Just for the record, I believe Cort murdered his wife and should be locked away for the rest of his life."

Without looking at me, Lisa snapped, "You were not very pleased when that TV commentator critiqued your every move during the Durgeon trial." *Indeed, I wasn't.*

The previous summer, I took on the defense of Duane Durgeon in his capital case. The startling and newsworthy events in that trial, in which I had received some notoriety, led to me being contacted to comment on the Cort trial.

Lisa was right to be irritated. We both knew it. "Tell you what, Lisa. I'll quit this commentary business as soon as this trial is over and stick to my real job as a lowly law professor."

She turned to me and gave me a slow contemplative nod, not completely assuaged. Finally, while studying my face, she said, "I'm glad. I like the lowly law professor. But I'm not so sure about the high and mighty TV commentator." *High and mighty? Shit.* She gave me a weak smile, the kind an indulgent teacher gives a rowdy nine-year-old, leaned over the console, and gave me a perfunctory peck on the cheek. We both took a breath as we pulled into the parking lot at Roy's. Now that Lisa had kind of forgiven me and lightened up, our dinner stood a good chance of being pleasant.

CHAPTER 2

NO BODY

When I was first approached by the media to be a commentator, it was via Jeremy Kaye, the general manager of Channel 6 in Los Angeles, four months after last summer's Durgeon trial. He and his station had covered the closing days of that trial, even though it was in San Arcadia, a hundred miles north, on the outer edges of Channel 6's coverage. The beatings and general chaos surrounding that trial, coupled with the real possibility of a death sentence, had drawn a lot of attention. As a result, Kaye tapped me for the Max Cort case—a no-body murder trial.

That's right, a no-body murder trial. Christie Cort, the wife of a sheriff's lieutenant, disappeared sometime between eight thirty on the evening of February 3 and five thirty the following morning. And now, nearly a year later, her husband, Lt. Max Cort, was standing trial for her murder. The Cort trial had it all: a no-body case, a high-ranking cop defendant, a victim who had once posed for *Playboy*, infidelity, the defendant's stripper girlfriend, and now a celebrity defense attorney, Merci MacPherson.

MacPherson's appearance had been a complete surprise. As a much-in-demand criminal-defense trial attorney, she commanded legal fees in the high six-figure range. It was reported that she had never lost a jury trial. *Maybe a bit of hyperbole. Didn't everybody take a hit from time to time?* There was no way a cop, even a lieutenant, could afford MacPherson. Her representation of Cort was a mystery. *I wondered if there was a silent benefactor somewhere in the shadows.*

As for the offer to be a commentator, I was surprised and mildly pleased, but I declined. I was still beat down after Durgeon, and thoughts of watching and critiquing what figured to be a gut-wrenching trial seemed ill-timed. Beyond that, my spring classes were set to start in just over five weeks, and Lisa was looking at another semester as an overworked vice principal. The two of us needed a break, a little R and R: snorkeling, surfing, and just lazing in the sun. More importantly, we needed some time to ourselves. Maybe a week in Cabo over Christmas would serve. If not Cabo, there was Hawaii—in particular, Lanai.

Following my initial rejection of his offer, Kaye had insisted on coming to my office at Pacifico Law School to press further. *He didn't take No easily.*

I tried to fend him off, reasoning, "Mr. Kaye, I need to get away from trials for a while. All I'm thinking about now is a vacation with my significant other."

Undeterred, he pressed further and said we could work around a vacation and my teaching schedule. "Professor Clearwater—may I call you Jake?"

"Sure." I shrugged.

"Your trial up north in San Arcadia generated a lot of interest, especially in those final days. Your closing argument, when you co-opted the prosecutor's points, has been dissected and discussed by some prominent LA media commentators. You are someone our viewers would like to hear from."

"Jeremy," *I guess it was to be first names,* "I'm flattered, but as a full-time law professor, I don't see how I would be able to teach my classes, sit in on a trial, and provide nightly commentary."

He was ready for me. "I've given that some thought. Jury selection starts January 20, five weeks from now. You could take your vacation, and then sit in on the Cort jury selection and the start of testimony before your classes begin."

I started to respond, but Kaye cut me off with a wave of dismissal. "I understand the concern about your classes. Of course, you would not be able to sit in on the trial once your classes begin, but since the trial will be televised, we could provide you with edited recordings of the proceedings each afternoon. Once you reviewed them, you would go on live at 6:00 p.m."

I leaned back in my chair and gave him an appraising look. "Jeremy, you've really put some thought into this." *I was being both ambushed and seduced. An unlikely combination.*

"Yes, I have; it shows how much I value your participation." He nodded enthusiastically. "I've even had my staff look at your teaching schedule. You are off at eleven o'clock on Mondays and Wednesdays and at two on Fridays. You have no classes on Tuesdays and Thursdays. I am convinced this could work." He pointed out that after a week's vacation, there would be plenty of time to get up to speed on the background of the trial before things got underway.

TV commentator? I had watched others do it, most notably during the Durgeon trial, where my every move was scrutinized. As I was weighing the ups and downs, Kaye interjected, "Of course, you would be well compensated for your time." I had not even thought about money. I had just naively assumed I would be doing this as a sort of public service. Kaye, watching me waver, threw in what he thought was an added incentive. "Many lawyers would kill for this opportunity. Think of the exposure this would generate for you."

I didn't want or need exposure. I didn't want future clients. I wasn't looking to take on any more cases. I was a law prof, not an attorney looking for business. Durgeon was a one-off. The money, however, would mean Lisa and I could fly first class to wherever. I certainly was not averse to being paid.

"Jeremy, I need some time to think it over. You've made an intriguing pitch, but I need some time."

"Of course. But keep in mind, jury selection is scheduled to start in five weeks. How about forty-eight hours to get back to me?" *Assertive on the edge of aggressive. No, just aggressive.*

After discussing the offer with Lisa, who, in my defense, was fine with it, I accepted. We did fly first class and enjoyed a week on the islands. And it was glorious. Sitting on the beach in Lanai with a beautiful woman in a skimpy bikini was living the dream. When I returned, there was a four-inch three-ring binder of the media coverage surrounding Christie Cort's disappearance and the ensuing events culminating in the arrest of Lt. Max Cort for his wife's murder.

Trial Tip #1: Direct Examination

Advocates should begin direct examination by personalizing their witness, giving the jurors some context to better understand events from the witness's perspective. Keep in mind that one of the critical tasks we ask of jurors is to gauge the credibility of each witness—who can be trusted and who can't. Understanding the background of each witness is helpful to the jurors in assessing witness credibility.

CHAPTER 3

THE SISTER

February 4, 2015, nearly a year before his trial, Los Angeles County Sheriff's Department Lt. Max Cort called to report his wife missing. He had returned home around 7:00 a.m. from his 7:00 p.m. to 5:00 a.m. shift at the sheriff's substation at the west end of the San Fernando Valley, and found that his wife of six years had disappeared. Cort immediately called Christie's sister, Mary Lynn Holder, asking if she knew where Christie was. Mary Lynn had no idea. Cort then called his substation and requested assistance. The residence was searched, with Cort's acquiescence. Christie's Lexus, her passport, some $1900 from her bureau, and a few other personal items were missing. A later, more-detailed search by the forensic techs found a small bloodstain on a throw rug in the den leading to the garage.

Press coverage noted that Mary Lynn responded to Cort's early morning call and arrived shortly after the first responding sheriff's deputy. When she saw Cort on the front porch talking to the deputy, she ran at him and began striking him and screaming, "You monster, what have you done to her?" As she was being restrained, she scratched Cort's face, drawing blood.

The sheriff's department issued a region-wide alert for Christie and her vehicle, including a detailed description and photograph of Ms. Cort, along with the particulars of the vehicle. Christie, at thirty-two, was a striking platinum blond who, nine years earlier, had been featured in all her glory in *Playboy*. Two days after her disappearance, the detectives on the case, led by Det. Sherri Ossoff, still had no leads. Suspecting that Christie might have been kidnapped, Det. Ossoff called in the FBI.

Working through the coverage, I learned that there was no ransom call or any leads as to Christie's whereabouts. Five weeks after she had gone missing, the FBI bowed out of the investigation. Once kidnapping had been ruled out, Det. Ossoff and her team began to focus their investigation on Lt. Cort. In the midst of a follow-up interview, Cort disclosed that during the early morning of February 4, he had been with his girlfriend, whom he refused to identify. Not surprisingly, two things happened. He was suspended with pay pending the resolution of the investigation, and he quit cooperating with the investigation.

Meanwhile, the sister, Mary Lynn, had remained adamant that Cort was responsible for Christie's disappearance. She claimed that Cort was an abusive husband and that on one occasion, three months before Christie's disappearance, she had seen Cort strike Christie in the face. She also reported that she was present when Christie brought up the possibility of divorce with Cort. Cort yelled at her and said, "A divorce would fuck my career. You fuck with my career, you fuck with my life, and I'll fuck with your life."

Mary Lynn also reported that she had long suspected Cort of infidelity. To confirm her suspicions, a couple of months before Christie's disappearance, she had parked across from the sheriff's substation during one of Cort's late-night–early morning shifts. She saw him drive away from the station around 1:00 a.m. and followed him to an apartment two miles from the station, to what she suspected was Cort's girlfriend's apartment.

Following the lead, Det. Ossoff contacted the occupant, Willow Merkle, who denied any involvement with Cort and refused to answer any further questions. Ossoff questioned Merkle's employer at the Rocks, a strip club where Merkle danced, and learned that Cort had been a regular patron at the club in the months prior to Christie's disappearance.

With Cort not talking and Merkle refusing to be questioned, the investigation was at a standstill. Only two pieces of evidence, the blood found at the scene, which tested positive for Christie's DNA, and Mary Lynn's insistence on Cort's culpability, kept the case alive. Media interest, however, only amplified in the months following Christie's disappearance. Even though there seemed to be little hard evidence, the scandalous details of the case continued to garner attention. Cort's high rank in the sheriff's department, Christie's stunning beauty and *Playboy* notoriety, and Cort's stripper girlfriend made for colorful fodder. The lead in one of the more brazen grocery-store scandal sheets blazed, "Playmate Murder: Stripper Girlfriend." Another paper referred to the case as the "Bunny Murder." The whereabouts of Christie or her remains was still a mystery. Had she been killed and her body secreted away, or had she run away from her abusive husband?

Despite the lack of additional information, the sheriff's department persevered. Using ground-penetrating radar and cadaver dogs, they conducted a grid search that encompassed a five-mile radius of the Cort residence, which included intruding on some of the Corts' neighbors. The area was primarily rural, with open spaces dotted with citrus and avocado orchards. The search revealed no anomalies. Airline and train records from travel originating in California, Nevada, and Arizona were checked. The internet was scoured for any indication that Christie had run away. There was no activity on any of her credit or debit cards.

Nonetheless, Det. Ossoff mustered what she had and recommended to the DA that murder charges be brought against Cort. The filing package included Mary Lynn's claim of Cort's spousal abuse, Cort's statements overheard by Mary Lynn that he could not divorce as it would scuttle any chances of future promotions within the sheriff's department, Cort's affair, and a match of Christie's DNA with the blood found on the rug in the Corts' residence—all coupled with Christie's five-month disappearance.

The DA and his filing committee pored over the case for a week before rejecting Ossoff's recommendation, determining there was insufficient evidence to pursue a murder charge against Cort. That decision was met with skepticism in the press. There was strong public outrage. The salacious details of Cort's life rendered him a pariah. His infidelity, linked with Mary Lynn's claim that he had abused his beautiful wife, had cast him as a villain. Now, with the failure to charge him, Cort was seen as a villain that had literally gotten away with murder. He was reinstated to his position.

But then the 2015 summer drought continued into August when water levels at the Hondo Reservoir dropped, and Christie's Lexus became visible twenty feet beneath the surface. The reservoir was six miles from the sheriff's station, just outside the five-mile search radius. Christie's body was not in the vehicle. The sheriff's CSI team, following a thorough examination, found no forensic evidence in the car, concluding that no blood or other trace evidence would have survived after months in the reservoir. However, a necklace with a broken latch was found in the wheel well of the trunk. Mary Lynn identified the necklace as a family heirloom given to Christie by her mother. The reservoir was dredged—but no body.

With the discovery of Christie's car, the district attorney reopened the case and charged Max Cort with his wife's murder. Cort was taken into custody. Shortly thereafter, celebrity and much-ballyhooed lawyer Merci McPherson announced at a press conference she would defend Cort. He was able to make the $2 million bail. It was unclear as to the source of the funds for the bail or MacPherson's expensive services.

Five months later, on January 20, 2016, following the preliminary hearing and assorted pretrial skirmishes, the trial was underway. It felt strange sitting in the press section, watching a trial instead of being one of the combatants. MacPherson, in a cream pantsuit that accentuated her long, slim body, planted the defense's "runaway wife" theme through her engaging and adroit voir dire, the Latin term used for questioning potential jurors.

She was not put off by the discovery of Christie's vehicle. Her charming demeanor and her striking appearance commanded the courtroom. Judge Walter and Prosecutor Wills may as well have been floor lamps in a forgotten part of a house. The prospective jurors, usually fighting anxiety and reticent to answer questions during voir dire, fell over themselves responding to MacPherson. They couldn't take their eyes off her.

Several times during questioning, MacPherson worked her way from in front of the jury box over to Cort's side and touched him gently, encouraging the jury to emotionally engage with him, as she did, on a human level. The subliminal message, of course, was that since she could touch him, he must not be toxic. MacPherson was an advocate of the belief that goodwill engendered by counsel may well transfer to the counsel's client. It was a theory to which I also subscribed.

Voir dire was round one, and MacPherson was well ahead on points. As defense counsel, she only needed one juror, and by my reckoning, she had earned critical goodwill with a handful. In my time as a prosecutor, I worked during voir dire to identify those one or two prospective jurors that I viewed as potentially adverse to my position—that one person or persons who might be likely to hang the jury 11–1 or 10–2—and then did my level best to excuse them. Getting twelve folks to render a unanimous verdict is a difficult task. Given MacPherson's early efforts, prosecutor John Wills was in a tough spot.

CHAPTER 4

A NEW SEMESTER

Monday morning, January 25, Lisa had stayed over and got up early with me. Armed with a mug of coffee, she sat on the sand while I did my thrice-weekly swim around the Malibu Pier. It was my primary mode of exercise. Some mornings it was tough to brace against the chill of the Pacific, but I had been diligent. I had taken up these swims when I first moved to Malibu. By seven o'clock, Lisa was well on her way home to San Arcadia while I showered for my criminal law class. Following class, I would head downtown to watch the recordings of the day's trial.

Lecture Hall A, a stadium-style classroom, held up to eighty students. I much preferred the more intimate seminar-type rooms, but with sixty-five students, this would have to do. Since this was our first class, I had no history with them, nor they with me. As I entered the lecture hall, the level of student anxiety was palpable. I flashed back to my first year in law school, praying that I would not be called on. I shook off the reverie and, without preamble, broke the seal on the class. I gestured to a male student in the second row. "Your name?"

"William Boland."

"Do you prefer William or Bill?"

"William, sir." Once I had a name, I would remember.

"William, take this hypothetical." I stepped toward him. "Defendant walked into a Circle K, otherwise known as a Stop 'n Rob, pulled out his handgun, and demanded the clerk put the cash register contents in a bag. The clerk complied, and as the defendant drove off, he slammed into a kid riding his bike in the parking lot. The child died from his injuries." I paused to let the facts sink in. "William, what is the most serious crime we can charge?"

He shrugged and said, "Well, he ran over a kid. That's pretty serious."

I nodded. "Is a traffic accident necessarily a crime?"

"Not necessarily, but maybe here since he had just robbed the store."

"So to be clear, are you suggesting that this collision may be a crime?" I was looking for some clarity.

He hesitated. "I don't believe it is. But since he just robbed, and he was trying to get away, maybe." *Not much clarity.*

"William," I said, throwing him a lifeline, "can we charge this defendant with robbery as well as with murder?"

William sat with that for a minute. "I was leaning in that direction, Professor Clearwater. From the readings you assigned, could this be felony murder?" *A bit slow, but we were starting to get traction.*

"William, let's lean a little harder." I walked back down the aisle. "For felony murder, do we need to show that the defendant intended to kill?"

"I don't think so." *And with that equivocal response, it was past time to move on.*

"William, let's get some help from co-counsel." *I didn't want to scar the kid for life.* Fifth row, my left. A woman had her hand up. *Maybe my first gunner.* Gunners are common in law schools everywhere. We reserve that distinction for students who want to command attention. They want everyone to know that they believe they are the smartest person in the room. Given half an opportunity, they delight in criticizing another student and, if they are feeling particularly robust, trying to show up the professor.

I nodded at her. "Your name?"

"Maribeth Clemons."

"Okay Maribeth, can we find someone guilty of murder if they had no intent to kill or inflict serious injury?"

"I believe so. Like the guy you just questioned said, we can use felony murder. From what I understand from the readings, felony murder is applicable even without any intent that someone should die."

"Good start." *Reasonable demeanor, maybe not a gunner, maybe just a well-prepared student.* "Can a traffic accident that resulted in someone's death be felony murder?"

She nodded. "One of the things I pulled from *People v. Reid,* one of the assigned cases, was that the death must have occurred in the perpetration of a felony."

"I'm with you so far. What did *Reid* tell us about the type of felony that might bring us within the scope of felony murder?"

She thought. "It would have to be a particularly serious felony."

"Isn't every felony by definition serious?"

She nodded. "That makes sense. Maybe I meant to say that the felony had to be dangerous." She stared at me, hoping she was on track. *She was.*

"Good. First rule of felony murder is that the underlying felony must be dangerous." I nodded at Maribeth. "Why must it be dangerous?" *Keep pushing.*

Without hesitation, "We are talking about murder. Just intuitively that makes sense."

"Let's build on that." It was time to tease out some law. "Let me start with the underlying rationale for the felony murder rule." I drifted back to the front of the class. "The purpose of the rule is to deter felons from killing anyone while they are committing their life-threatening felonies."

I saw a number of confused looks and selected one. "Your name?"

"Teagan Curtis."

"Teagan, you look confused by the reason behind the rule. How come?"

She took in a breath. *Definitely not a gunner.* "I suppose I thought the reason for the rule was odd. I thought the reason would be to deter criminals from committing felonies, not from killing during the felony. I was surprised."

"It is odd, isn't it? I completely agree with you. However," I emphasized with a hand gesture, "we would both be wrong. The rule was developed centuries ago, going back to English common law; it recognizes that some people are going to rob, burgle, rape, and commit other felonies, no matter what." I shrugged. "It's just what they do. With this felony murder rule, we are acknowledging that hard reality. We can't stop those who are hell-bent on committing their felonies, so the next best thing is to deter them from leaving bodies behind when they do commit their felonies."

William leapt back into the discussion without being called. "So the felony murder rule is not to deter felonies but to deter felons from killing while they're committing their felonies."

"I could not have said it better myself." *Isn't that what I just said?* "What do you think of that, William?"

"I don't know, seems somewhat odd. Seems as if society should be trying to deter felonies."

"Oh we do—with lengthy prison sentences."

He nodded understandingly.

I continued. "Now that we have the rationale down, let's turn back to how the rule works. Maribeth, back to you." Once again, I moved up the middle aisle toward her. "We have established that the rule requires that the underlying felony has to be dangerous. What else is required?"

"You mentioned earlier that the death has to occur in the perpetration of the felony."

"The perpetration?" I stayed with her.

She was right with me. "The robber was driving away from the robbery when he ran over the child. That seems to be in the perpetration."

I turned to Teagan. "You agree?"

She thought briefly and then answered, "That makes sense, but what if the robber runs over a kid two miles away? How far does the perpetration extend?" *Now we are getting somewhere.*

A flurry of hands. They were warming to the task. The pump had been primed. We continued on for the balance of the class. It seems I had the makings of a fine group. I was particularly pleased that no one had mentioned my television commentary. Perhaps as first years, they didn't have the time, or they just didn't give a damn.

That evening, having reviewed the recordings of the day's trial proceedings, I sat just off the set, waiting for my cue to join Lisbet up front. After I was motioned up and while we were waiting for the commercials to play out, she leaned toward me and whispered, "Jake, your observations have been very helpful. We all appreciate you being here and making sense of this trial."

"Thanks, I appreciate that. This commentary business is foreign turf to me."

She gave me her Hollywood smile. *Dazzling teeth. Rosy cheeks.*

The red light came on, and she was all business. "Once again we have Professor Clearwater with us to discuss today's testimony in the Cort murder trial. Professor, please fill us in."

"Thanks, Lisbet. Today we got into testimony. Prosecutor Wills put Mary Lynn Holder on the witness stand, and the case against Lt. Cort began to play out. As many of you who have been following the trial know, Ms. Holder is Christie Cort's sister and she has been adamant from the day Christie disappeared that Lt. Cort killed her. During direct examination, Prosecutor Wills was able to establish the deep relationship between the sisters, who are only separated by a year in age. Extremely close, the two spoke daily on the phone and usually saw each other at least twice a week.

"With Holder on the stand, Wills further solicited her observations about the relationship between Christie and the defendant. She testified that shortly into the six years of marriage, Christie was unhappy and wanted out of the relationship, but that Cort insisted they stay married for the sake of his career. Over strong objection from defense attorney Merci MacPherson, Holder testified that Christie told her that Cort was obsessive about being promoted within the sheriff's department. She related the vile threat that was loaded with foul language I cleaned up for the television audience. Holder also described in detail an incident prior to Christie's disappearance, when she saw Cort strike her sister."

Lisbet was indignant. "He hit her?"

I nodded and went on. "Mary Lynn testified that she tried to get at Cort but was pulled back by her sister. When pressed as to why law enforcement was not called, Mary Lynn explained that Christie wouldn't let her. Christie insisted that getting law enforcement involved would make her life even more unbearable. When asked the last time the sisters spoke, Mary Lynn replied it was on the evening of February 3, around eight thirty. She then tearfully testified that she has not heard from Christie since that last call."

Lisbet interrupted. "So the sisters' last conversation was during the evening before Christie's disappearance!"

"That's right."

"Sorry for the interruption, Professor, please go on."

"Right. Wills then directed Mary Lynn's testimony to the necklace found in the wheel well of Christie's car. Mary Lynn identified the necklace as a gift from the sisters' mother. When she was shown the necklace, she again became emotional and, through tears, said that Christie treasured the necklace and never took it off.

"The prosecutor then turned to Mary Lynn's surveillance of Lt. Cort. She was convinced that Lt. Cort was having an affair. Aware that he worked the 7:00 p.m. to 5:00 a.m. shift, she believed that Cort would leave the sheriff's substation during his shift to meet with a girlfriend. She testified that months prior to Christie's disappearance, Mary Lynn parked on the street opposite the sheriff's station at midnight. On her third consecutive night of surveillance, she saw Cort drive off around 1:00 a.m., and she secretly followed him to an apartment several miles away, where Cort entered and stayed for more than an hour. The woman living at that apartment was later identified as Willow Merkle. Asked if she shared this information with her sister, Mary Lynn responded, 'Yes. But Christie said there was nothing she could do. Max would hurt her. Badly this time.'"

"Sounds like it was an emotional day of testimony," Lisbet offered. "A good day for the prosecutor?"

"It was. Prosecutor Wills did a fine job of sitting back and keeping the focus on Holder. And when defense counsel MacPherson tried to break up the narrative flow of her testimony, Wills skillfully fought to keep it on track." *No criticism of Wills, only praise.* "Tomorrow, Ms. MacPherson will have her opportunity to cross-examine Holder. That promises to be memorable."

CHAPTER 5

TENURE

When I got home to Malibu following the telecast, I heard voices coming from the deck of my landlord's beach house. I climbed up the outside stairs and was greeted by Lisa and a small crowd. Lisa gave me a hug and kiss. I had not expected her. It was a weeknight, and she lived in San Arcadia, two hours north.

"Surprised?" She smiled.

"And delighted," I said, and kissed her again. I took her hand, and together we moved to the familiar faces. I was greeted by Dean Chauncey, his wife Shelby, Howard Alexander, and, of course, my friends and landlords, Tony and Eve Martin. When I started at Pacifico, Tony was my faculty mentor and best friend. He's tall and thin and can eat and drink without any seeming consequence. Eve is a foot shorter with a vivacious personality that more than compensates for Tony's taciturn demeanor. Tony had been born rich, and he spent his money carefully enough to afford a sleek, contemporary-style beach house on the sand just a few steps from the Malibu Pier. When Tony and Eve offered to rent me the third level of their house for a fraction of what it was worth, I became their housemate, and over the past year and a half, Lisa had grown our friendship of three to four. Evenings, even in February, on their deck barbecuing was the thing to do.

But tonight was different; I'd had no idea a party would be underway. Tony stepped forward, and I flashed him a what-the-hell look. He said, "I thought we would surprise you, and it looks like we did. This is the dean's idea."

Dean Chauncey stepped around Tony with a bright smile. He was a take-charge guy, big and a little rough around the edges. Still, he was a superb administrator who, with few exceptions, was popular with the law faculty. He greeted me, sticking out his hand. "Tony invited us over to deliver glad tidings." And with no further preamble, he said, "Your application for tenure has been approved."

He stuck his hand out and we shook again. "Congratulations, well deserved," he said.

The small gathering had leaned into the announcement and clapped. I was momentarily speechless. "Thank you, Dean." Gathering my thoughts, I gestured to Tony and Howard. "Thank you, Tony and Howard. You two shepherded me through the process from day one." I gave a slight head bow. Eve handed me a glass of chardonnay, which I raised to the group. "A heartfelt thank you to my true and loyal friends."

"Jake," Chauncey picked up, after my short toast. He clearly had more to say, and he was going to say it. "You've had a remarkable four and a half years at Pacifico, and this acknowledgment from the tenured faculty and the Board of Regents confirms your accomplishments on behalf of our proud school." He paused, and with a broad grin, said, "And don't get any ideas about leaving us and moving back to the courtroom." That elicited mild laughter.

"Thank you, Dean."

"Now that you are in the club, please refer to me by my first name."

Again raising my glass, I said, "You got it, John." He clapped me on the shoulder.

Speeches done, I joined Tony and Howard as they hovered near the barbecue. Tony said, "Chauncey's idea. He wanted to give you the news in front of people who most mattered to you."

"A grand gesture," Howard added. Apart from Tony, Howard was my closest and most loyal friend. Howard was Pacifico's faculty star. He taught Constitutional law, wrote textbooks, and cranked out law review articles on some of the most perplexing issues of the day. He was in the upper pantheon of legal thinkers. Along with his glittering credentials, he was quirky and unconventional, down to his preferred mode of dress. He taught classes in checkered sports coats and op-art ties. The students loved his out-of-nowhere anecdotes and his quasi-celebrity status. He frequently appeared on the Sunday-morning talk shows. He was on a first-name basis with Chuck Todd and Jake Tapper. He was the best of everything at Pacifico.

Spatula in hand, Tony announced that the grilled chicken breasts were ready. Side dishes were laid out, and everyone served themselves buffet-style. Chauncey, as usual, carried the conversation, and that was fine with all of us. He knew a lot about a lot, and he was a terrific storyteller. Eve took the chair next to me and whispered conspiratorially, "You're not at all surprised at getting tenure, are you?"

"I figured with Tony and Howard on my side, it would happen."

"You looked good on TV tonight. They treating you okay?"

"Nice folks. It's going well. The prep and commuting downtown are a bit tiring, but I knew that going in. And for once, I'm enjoying watching others try a case."

"No urge to join the battle?" she prodded.

"I'm fine sitting on the sidelines." I shrugged. "But when I see glitches, I twitch."

"Twitch?"

"Yeah, almost like a conditioned response."

"From your televised comments, I assume the prosecutor, whatever his name, is the one inducing the twitches?"

"That would be a good guess." I leaned to her. "But I promised Lisa I would go easy on the prosecutor."

Eve got up to mingle, and Chauncey took her seat. "You've got some great and powerful friends, Jake."

"Very true."

Chauncey took a drink of wine and squared up with me. "I know you are terribly busy with classes and with your commentary, but I need some help."

"Whatever I can do." *Words that should never pass my lips.*

"For reasons I can't go into, I had to terminate the adjunct prof who was coaching our interschool trial team. And as you know, we don't have many profs who know their way around a courtroom." He paused and reconsidered. "In fact, you are the only one with significant trial experience." Wrapping his arm around my shoulder, he asked, "Would you give the team a hand preparing for their tournament? It would only involve sitting in on a couple of practice rounds and giving them some feedback."

For the second time that evening, I was speechless and hesitant. "I'm a bit busy right now."

"I'm fully aware of that. But I'm in a tough spot. Like I said, you're the only one on the faculty that is qualified, and it would take too much time to vet another adjunct."

I don't like to assign motives, but perhaps this is why he came to give me the tenure news in person. I didn't see a way out. *When stuck in a no-win situation, be gracious. It's going to happen anyway, so accept and make the best of it.*

"John, happy to help out."

I lied.

CHAPTER 6

MARY LYNN IS OVERMATCHED

Tuesday morning knockout. Mary Lynn Holder was a welterweight. Merci MacPherson was the metaphorical heavyweight champion. It was ugly. Mary Lynn started out swinging during MacPherson's cross-exam—I think she thought she could get the better of MacPherson. She couldn't, and she didn't. MacPherson, without ever raising her voice, established that Mary Lynn's hatred of Cort compromised her description of the relationship between her sister and Cort. MacPherson did it with small cuts that grew bloodier and bloodier as Mary Lynn tried to fend off the onslaught. Amazingly, throughout the entire cross, MacPherson was never a bully. But by the end of the cross, Mary Lynn's credibility was battered and bruised.

I toned it down a bit when I went on the air that evening, but I'm certain the viewers received the thrust of what MacPherson had done to Mary Lynn. As Lisbet listened to my account, her perfect brow furrowed. There was no question that she was concerned for the state's case. Any semblance of Lisbet's journalistic objectivity was nowhere to be seen. She, like most folks, believed Cort was an awful, abusive man who was guilty, if not of murder, then of being evil. *But evil isn't a crime.*

"Was the afternoon session any better for the prosecution?" *She was hopeful.*

"Yes, it was. After Mary Lynn, Prosecutor Wills then called Det. Sherri Ossoff." I laid out the detective's testimony, starting with Christie's call to her sister at eight thirty the night before and ending with Cort's report of his missing wife when he returned home from work. I summarized Ossoff's testimony about the missing money, passport, car, and personal items.

"What did the detective say about the search for Christie?"

"She went into detail in describing the efforts to find Christie's body. She explained that the search for a possible burial site encompassed an area within several miles of the Cort residence."

Lisbet asked, "Why only within several miles of their home?"

"Ossoff explained that the detectives had established a relatively short window of time that Cort was absent from work—from approximately 1:00 a.m. to 5:00 a.m. Given that, there would not be sufficient time for him to drive very far to bury or otherwise dispose of the body."

"Makes sense." Lisbet nodded.

"Wills had Ossoff use a map of the five-mile radius around the Cort residence. The sheriff's station was within the eastern portion of the radius, and the search area was primarily rural, with few residences and a lot of orchards. Using the map and under close questioning by Prosecutor Wills, Ossoff described how the sheriff's search-and-rescue team did a grid search within the radius."

"A grid search?"

"A thorough systematic search of the designated areas. Ossoff explained that they were looking for signs of recent disturbances. The searchers used ground-penetrating radar as well as cadaver dogs."

"Ground-penetrating radar?" Lisbet asked.

"That's a fairly new technology that can actually detect anomalies beneath the surface."

"I wasn't aware of such technology," Lisbet said. "I take it that nothing turned up?"

"There were several possible sites that, when dug up, did not pan out."

"How about the reservoir where Christie's car was found?" Lisbet asked.

"Wills asked the detective that very question. Keep in mind the reservoir was not initially searched, as it was outside the original search parameters. But after Christie's car was found, it was thoroughly searched for Christie's body."

"Sounds pretty exhaustive."

"It was. And there was one other intriguing note from Ossoff's testimony. She confirmed that a bike was found in the Cort garage. I was initially puzzled why the detective brought this up, until it occurred to me that the prosecutor was thinking that Cort might have used a bike for transport back to his residence after he dumped Christie's car."

Lisbet gave me a questioning look. "Why would it matter?"

"If Cort dumped Christie's car, he would need some transport back to his residence."

"I see," Lisbet said, nodding.

"Wills's questioning then turned to the other end of the search."

"What do you mean?"

"Looking for evidence that Christie had not run away," I answered. "The sheriff's team set about to determine the plausibility of her leaving on her own. Bear in mind that her passport and at least $1,900 in cash were missing at the time of her disappearance. The search team, in addition to posting photographs nationwide, scrutinized banking and credit-card activity in the six months following her disappearance. Additionally, a search of tickets for all airlines and trains originating from anywhere in California, Arizona, Nevada, and Oregon came up empty. Ossoff explained that Mary Lynn's phone and internet, as well as Christie's parents' phones and internet, were searched for any possible contact. Nothing."

Lisbet added, "Given Christie's stunning good looks, it seems it would have been difficult for her not to have been noticed." *Odd observation.*

I hesitated, then said, "Fair point, but of course there are devices to help conceal one's appearance—wigs, dyes, glasses, skin coloring, padding, bulky clothing, and so on. There are ways, but I agree that someone who looks like Christie has more of a challenge."

"Not having a body certainly helps the defense, but not finding any evidence that she ran away seems to help the prosecution," Lisbet concluded. *She certainly has a flair for the obvious.* I nodded agreement as she went on. "Was there time today for the defense counsel to cross-examine Det. Ossoff?"

"No, that will happen Thursday. Tomorrow the court will be dark due to a conflict with the judge's schedule. I suspect that when they reconvene, MacPherson will concentrate her efforts on establishing that Christie ran away and is now hiding." I added as an aside, "The cross-examination of Det. Ossoff may go a long way in deciding the outcome of this trial."

Lisbet mused and sat back in her chair. "Lots to think about. Thanks Jake, we look forward to hearing from you Thursday evening about that cross-examination."

That evening, I FaceTimed Lisa and asked about her first day of the new semester. I knew she was somewhat apprehensive about it.

Lisa was, in all likelihood, the most beautiful middle-school vice principal in America. Let me expand that—the most beautiful school administrator in America. My comments are not meant to demean her experience and skill set as a school administrator, but to call attention to her beauty. And just to round things out, on the side, she was an artist. I am not talking about a weekend hobbyist; I am talking about a brilliant watercolorist whose works commanded four and five figures. I'd been to two of her shows, and her works sold out and generated thousands of dollars. She was a celebrity in the Southern California art world.

She slid me a frustrated look. "The usual gymnastics," she sighed. "Parents want their kids in with different teachers. Some teachers don't want certain students in their classes. My principal, in trying to please everyone, leaves it to me to best accommodate the requests." She paused and added, "Two fights. One involved a new kid being bullied by one of my problem boys. The other was between two girls—mind you, thirteen-year-old girls—who it appears are dating the same boy. Things just boiled over."

"Ah, the joys of adolescence. I'm sure you straightened things out."

"I'm still working on it. I haven't left the office since seven this morning."

"I wish I was up there. I would take you out for drinks and then back to your place for a stress-relieving massage."

That earned a tired laugh. "Jake, I know about your massages." Lisa groaned. We both laughed.

CHAPTER 7

A TARGET-RICH ENVIRONMENT

It was raining Wednesday morning, so I opted out of my swim and slept an extra hour. Ocean swimming after or during rain is hazardous. The rain washes all kinds of crap into the ocean. Swimming in a bacterial soup, not a good idea. The courtroom was dark because Judge Walter had a can't-miss day-long meeting. I taught my criminal law class, caught up on paperwork, and read most of Michael Connelly's new Harry Bosch novel. Detective Bosch was at it once again, delightfully irritating the LAPD brass. *Who doesn't love a good smartass?*

I had no classes on Thursday, so I decided to go downtown and watch the trial in person. I was curious how Det. Ossoff would hold up under grilling by MacPherson. This was a critical juncture of the trial. Was Christie alive and out there somewhere, or was her body buried or otherwise well concealed? MacPherson had a target-rich environment to exploit on cross.

Judge Walter emerged and gave his desultory morning greeting. *What a charmer.* If there is such a personality trait as anti-charismatic, Walter fit the bill. I would bet my left arm that he had never tried a case before he was appointed to the bench. In practice, he had to have been in probate or bankruptcy, areas of the law in which you'd rarely see the inside of any courtroom. I made a note to Google him when I got home. With a complete lack of self-awareness, Walter cleared his throat right into his microphone, sending stifled spasms of hilarity throughout the courtroom. Unabashed and probably oblivious, he recalled Ossoff back to the stand and reminded her that she was still under oath. MacPherson, dressed in a pink silk skirt suit, stood and, without notes, began.

"Detective, let's keep this short. You can't tell these jurors whether or not Ms. Cort is living in Akron, Ohio, can you?" *Whoa, what a startling and brilliant start to her cross-examination.*

Ossoff leaned back and forced a smile. "I certainly don't think so. We went to great lengths in establishing that she had not run away and had not started a new life somewhere."

MacPherson patiently took in the answer and continued. "Detective, let me try my question again. You can't tell us whether Ms. Cort is living in Akron, Ohio, or anywhere else for that matter, can you?"

Ossoff shrugged. "Not with absolute certainty. But I'm confident she was killed and her body was concealed."

MacPherson ignored the answer and asked, "Detective, you can't tell us whether Ms. Cort is living under a different name in Boise, Idaho, can you?"

"Ms. MacPherson, since we have not seen Ms. Cort's body, there is no way we can say with absolute certainty that she is deceased"—Ossoff paused for emphasis—"but I can tell you my department took extraordinary measures and exhausted every mechanism possible in verifying that Christie Cort didn't run away and is not hiding somewhere."

"Yet, here we are, Detective. You can't sit on this witness stand and testify under oath that she is deceased?"

Wills was on his feet. "Asked and answered several times, Your Honor."

"I'll allow it. Overruled."

With exaggerated patience, MacPherson repeated the question.

Ossoff responded. "I'll repeat my previous answer. I can't say with one-hundred-percent certainty, but I can tell you that beyond any reasonable doubt in my mind, she is deceased."

"Objection, misstates the burden of proof!"

"Ms. MacPherson, move on."

"Very well. As an investigator, you are aware of and most likely have investigated situations where people simply abandon their lives and disappear among the three hundred and forty million people who live in this country, isn't that correct?"

"Can't say that I have."

MacPherson moved to the far end of the jury rail nearest Ossoff and asked, "Detective, would you agree with me that the circumstances of Christie Cort's life could well have made her a likely candidate for such a feat, to simply abandon her life and seek to start over somewhere else?"

There was a moment's pause as Ossoff considered, then answered. "Ms. Cort was close with her sister and her parents. I don't think she would leave them wondering whether or not she was dead." Then she added, "That would be extremely cruel, and from everything I've learned about her, I don't think she was a cruel person."

"I appreciate your opinion, but let's explore Ms. Cort's circumstances prior to her disappearance, shall we?"

Ossoff put up her hands. "You're asking the questions, counselor."

"Indeed, I am." MacPherson smiled. Even when she was mixing it up with a witness, she was charming. "We've heard testimony that Ms. Cort had been physically struck by her husband. Would you agree that an abused woman might be motivated to run away and leave an abusive spouse?"

Ossoff shrugged. "Perhaps. But there are certainly options short of simply running away and leaving loved ones wondering if you're still alive." *Ossoff was holding her own.*

"So that is a yes, that an abused spouse might be motivated to abandon her life and take off?"

"'Might' being the operative word." *Ossoff wouldn't give in.*

"Let's add another layer to Christie's circumstances. If she learned that her husband was involved in an extramarital affair, might she be motivated to leave?"

Ossoff considered and answered. "I would think that seeking a divorce would be the more commonly accepted way to deal with an adulterous spouse."

"Detective, let me try my question again. If a wife learned that her husband was involved in an extramarital affair, might she be motivated to leave?" *Repeating the question is a galvanizing technique.*

"Objection," said Wills. "The question calls for an opinion and has been asked and answered."

"Overruled." Walter looked at Ossoff. "Detective, do you have the question in mind?"

She nodded yes.

"Please answer." Walter said.

Ossoff nodded. "Perhaps."

"Is that a yes, detective?" insisted MacPherson.

"Yes."

MacPherson took a few steps back. "Detective, let's add yet another wrinkle to our equation. If the abusive husband threatened to kill his wife—should she attempt to end the marriage—would that be a motivation for the abused spouse to simply run away?"

"Objection, Your Honor." Wills was on his feet again. "Improper hypothetical."

Judge Walter looked at MacPherson, who smiled and said, "If counsel wants me to be more specific with my question, I'd be happy to."

Walter thought about it and then waved the objection away.

MacPherson, unrelentingly, went right back and repeated, "If the abusive husband threatened to kill his wife if she attempted to end the marriage, that could also be motivation for the abused spouse to simply run away?"

"Could be," was all Ossoff managed. *MacPherson was slowly beating Ossoff down.*

"Thank you for that, Detective. I want to briefly turn to the efforts to locate Ms. Cort's body in and around the radius of the residence. Now, did I hear you correctly, that the five-mile radius included the Cort residence?"

"That's right."

"And that also included the sheriff's station where Lt. Cort worked?"

"Also correct."

"You and your department determined the likely areas within that radius where a body might be buried, correct?"

"Yes. We virtually covered the whole area."

"And the search of those most-likely areas involved a grid search, isn't that right?"

"Yes."

"That search even involved ground-penetrating radar, didn't it?"

"Yes."

"And that search involved trained cadaver dogs?"

"It did."

"As to the reservoir, it was dredged for a body?"

"Yes, we used divers and dredged the reservoir."

"That's right. You employed divers to search the reservoir?"

"We did."

"Detective Ossoff, despite these extensive efforts, no body was found, correct?"

"The defendant did a good job of disposing of his wife's body."

MacPherson, inching ever closer to the detective, grinned at Ossoff improperly asserting an opinion, and she once again asked, "Despite the extensive efforts to locate a body, no body was found— isn't that true?"

A frustrated Ossoff conceded, "We never found her body."

MacPherson was right back at her. "Despite the best efforts of your department, no body was found, isn't that correct?"

"Yes."

That night, I reported to the Channel 6 audience that MacPherson's cross of the lead detective had been effective. I pointed out that MacPherson had a lot to work with, and she maximized the opportunity. I posed the same question to Lisbet and the audience that MacPherson put to Ossoff. "You can't tell these jurors whether or not Ms. Cort is living in Akron, Ohio, can you?"

Lisbet, always protective of the state's case, said, "But the burden of proof does not require absolute certainty."

"Of course, you're right, Lisbet. However, it's not up to us to make the call. Eventually the jurors will have the only say that matters. Merci MacPherson played her best card. How can we really know if Christie Cort is deceased?"

Trial Tip #2: Cross-Examination

Be cautious. Cross-examinations are a minefield. Given an opportunity, an opposition witness will attempt to hurt the advocate's case. More cases are damaged, some irretrievably, during poorly executed cross-examinations than were ever won during an excellent cross. Advocates must only ask questions about areas where they are protected, such as an earlier statement the witness made prior to trial or some physical evidence to support the cross-examiner's point. Should the witness venture from the earlier statement or from the undisputed physical evidence, the cross-examiner then has license to impeach the witness.

CHAPTER 8

SUZELLE

My Friday trial advocacy class had been canceled in favor of career day, which consisted of alums who had made good and were invited back to talk about their successes. I opted once again to go downtown and watch the trial in person. As I was driving to the courthouse, Suzelle Frost called. Suzelle, a former student, had sat second chair during the Durgeon trial. Now she was several months into her career as a deputy public defender. Once the pleasantries were exchanged, she said, "I'm enjoying your commentary on Cort. I feel like I'm back in your trial-ad class."

I chuckled. "I'm hearing that from a number of fronts. Am I being too pedagogic?"

"Oh no. You're helping people appreciate some of the subtleties of trials. I wouldn't change a thing. Keep it up. Even my parents in the hinterlands of Mandrake are making a point of watching your commentaries."

"How are they doing?"

"Ever since you helped them out, they've steadily developed a new dedication to each other. Seems as if that scare shook them enough to better appreciate what they've got." A year or so ago,

Suzelle's dad had been the victim of a mean-spirited, aggressive cop. Suzelle had recruited me to defend her dad at trial for allegedly striking the cop. Things had turned out okay for the Frosts.

"Give them my best. Now tell me, to what do I owe this call?"

"I wanted you to know that I got my first acquittal yesterday." I could hear the pride in her voice. Before I could congratulate her, she ran on, "It was a resisting arrest, a bit like my dad's case. The cop was over-the-top, and the jurors were able to figure that out."

"Wonderful news." *An aggressive cop. Imagine that.* "How'd your cross of the cop go?"

"Oh yeah!" She smiled through the phone. "Kept the white hat on and punched him out. You would have been proud, Jake. I used everything you taught me."

"I'm looking forward to hearing more about it. Right now, I'm heading downtown to the Cort trial." I stopped, and a spur-of-the-moment thought struck me. "Can you get the morning off and join me in the courtroom?"

She hesitated, but then replied, "Yeah, I think so. I don't have any court appearances this morning. Can you get me in? I hear it's a tough seat."

"You're talking to a TV star," I offered sardonically. "I've got priority seating courtesy of Channel 6. I'll meet you in front of the courthouse at 8:30."

We met at the front steps to the Clara Shortridge Foltz Criminal Justice Center, more commonly called CCB, short for "criminal courts building." It strikes me as ironic that pretty much everyone ignores the actual name. It minimizes Clara Foltz's considerable contributions to the legal profession as well as her place as a true pioneer for gender equality. Nearly a hundred and fifty years ago, Foltz sued Hastings Law School, California's original and only law school at the time, for denying her admittance. *What a silly notion, that a woman could understand, let alone practice, something as difficult as the law.* After arguing her own case before the California Supreme Court, she won—no small feat, since women were forbidden to even testify, due to their gender. Imagine that! Women couldn't even testify; they were considered incompetent. California's misogynistic history is startling. Foltz went on to not only become California's first woman lawyer but also spearheaded California's public defender system. While her contributions are not well known, her impact on women's equality and California's justice system are profound and should not be forgotten.

As Suzelle approached the steps, she looked great as always, ever the professional. She wore a dark-blue suit with her hair pulled back into a ponytail. We hugged. "Good to see you," I said. We had texted and emailed following the Durgeon trial but had not seen each other since.

"You too, Prof. Like I said on the phone, I've been following your commentary on the Cort trial. I'm still learning things from you. Looks like you're having fun."

"To an extent." I shrugged. "It's not all roses." *Lisa could testify to that.* "We've got an hour before we need to be in the courtroom. Let's get some coffee in the cafeteria and catch up. I want to hear about your acquittal."

With coffee in hand, we found a table. "How's Lisa?" Suzelle and Lisa had become friends during the Durgeon trial.

"She is up to her shoulders in adolescents, but otherwise doing great." I grinned and drank some so-so coffee. "I'll fill you in on her in a minute, but first, tell me about your trial."

She gave a humble shrug. "In the big scheme of things, it was a modest victory."

"Wait." I held up a hand and gave her a disapproving look. "Was it a modest victory for your client?"

Her face lit up in a bright grin. "No, he was very pleased and relieved. During pretrial discussion, the judge threatened him with three months custody if he went to trial and lost." She took a small sip. "It reminded me of the judge who threatened my dad during his trial."

I shook my head knowingly. "Always a subtle negotiating tactic. Judges are the same, no matter the case or circumstances—anything to avoid a trial. They have taken arm twisting, or should I say extortion, to an art form."

"Yeah, it's one of the things about being a PD. The judges try to push us around and do everything possible to scare defendants into pleading." She took another sip, made a face and pushed the coffee away. "I remember when you represented my dad, and the judge threatened him with six months. It's a crazy system. If my guy had pled, no jail time and one year probation. But if he had exercised his Constitutional right to trial and God forbid lost, three months." She blew out a breath. "On any level, that is unfair."

"Preaching to the choir," I said, nodding in agreement. "It's justice on an assembly line. Got to get cases to settle, or the whole system breaks down." I patted her hand. "Obviously you went forward. Did you have to talk your client into trial despite the threat, or was he ready to fight?"

Again a grin. "A little of both."

"Tell me about your cross of the cop."

"Jake, I learned from watching you. I was never a bully; I was the picture of polite earnestness. I got him to grudgingly agree that while my guy was mouthy, he was never physical or even threatening. The entire encounter was basically a contempt-of-cop situation. I hit that theme hard at closing, and the jurors agreed with me."

"Sounds like it was right out of our playbook." I smiled. "Any comments from the jurors afterward?"

"They were eager to talk, and almost to a person they focused on why so much time was wasted on the case when there are so many bad guys out there committing real crimes." She paused and added with a grin, "One juror, the age of my father, asked me out."

I had to laugh again. "Sometimes there is no excusing my gender." I shook my head apologetically. "I wish I could have watched you. Sounds like you did great."

She smiled, shrugged, and abruptly changed topics. "I've been enjoying your commentary. I take it you are not real high on the prosecutor." *Can't shake that rap.*

"Yeah, about that. Lisa thinks I've been too tough on the guy. I'm working to be as fair and objective as possible. The problem is that Wills is overmatched by MacPherson. She is as good as advertised. Her voir dire, in particular, was textbook. And yesterday's cross of the detective was solid. She's got a number of jurors eating out of her hand."

Suzelle took that in, then asked, "Is she as good as you?"

That was a question out of left field. Correction, that was from completely out of the stadium. I considered my answer. While watching the trial, I had mused about how I would have done some things differently from Wills. I sat back and studied Suzelle. "That's a hell of a question. The answer is I don't know. She's impressive. She has presence, she commands attention. She is the force in the courtroom, and yet you do not feel like she is bullying anyone. Like I said, her voir dire really shaped the focus of the trial. The prosecutor has been on his heels throughout. She's the real deal."

"I gathered all that from your comments, but you didn't answer my question."

"What?" I grinned. "Am I being cross-examined? I understood your question." I paused and gave her a what-the-hell look. "It's difficult to self-evaluate. I know my way around the courtroom, but to answer your question, I just don't know." I finished off my lukewarm coffee and added, "It would be a challenge to go up against such a talented trial lawyer."

"I know we're dealing with abstracts here since you are both defense lawyers, but a Clearwater–MacPherson trial would be something to see."

I gave a dismissive wave. "Let's not forget that little things like the facts, the evidence, play a role in the outcome. It's not all about the lawyers."

"Point taken," she said, nodding in agreement. "What does Lisa think of your commentary?"

"Like I said, she thinks I've been a bit hard on the prosecutor."

Suzelle gave me a knowing look. "Maybe lighten up on the poor guy."

"I'll keep that in mind." *How could I not?*

Court was not yet in session as we took our seats. Wills and MacPherson were standing and talking near the clerk's desk. Suzelle leaned to me and whispered, "Jake, she's even more beautiful in person."

"That she is," I said, as we both watched her talking to Wills. She was tall, almost as tall as me, with enormous blue eyes and platinum hair that fell loosely to her shoulders. She was dressed in a dark-blue skirt suit. It was like a fashion show every day. I idly wondered how the jurors felt about her upscale attire. Her posture was perfect, practiced, like she knew she was the center of attention. But, as I had learned from watching her, she was in no way defined by her beauty. Her intellect and charisma shared equal parts in forming her persona.

The lawyers returned to their stations as the judge emerged from his side door and the bailiff called court to order. Judge Walter nodded to the jurors, offered his stiff, perfunctory morning greeting, and looked expectantly at Prosecutor Wills.

Wills, in his off-the-rack ill-fitting suit and tie, made to look even more unfortunate next to the polish of MacPherson, called Caleb Ponce. Ponce was in his full sheriff's uniform with a sergeant chevron on his sleeve. He was a fifteen-year man with the department, and he appeared to be a no-nonsense type with a graying crew cut.

Wills worked Ponce through the preliminaries. He was second in command to Lt. Cort at the West Valley station during the time when Christie had gone missing. Ponce, in a Joe Friday delivery, testified that Cort, on four different occasions, left the station during the early morning hours of his 7:00 p.m. to 5:00 a.m. shift in the weeks leading up to Christie's disappearance. Ponce estimated that on those occasions, Cort would be gone anywhere from an hour to two hours and once for as long as three and a half to four hours.

Ponce was very careful to confine his answers to the precise call of the question. *Just the facts. Friday would have been pleased.* It was up to Wills to pull from Ponce what he needed. Under Wills's prodding, Ponce testified that when Cort left the station on those occasions, he did not sign out as per procedure but would orally instruct Ponce that he would be out. Ponce testified that Cort's pattern of leaving began on a Tuesday night shift in mid-January and continued on succeeding Tuesday shifts up until Tuesday, February 3, the evening before Christie disappeared.

On a document reader, Wills had his second, a rookie prosecutor, display a calendar depicting January and February 2015. Wills asked, "Are you certain it was always a shift that started on a Tuesday?"

"Counselor, that is what I testified to." *A little testy. No nonsense, indeed.*

"Thank you, Sergeant." Wills circled January 13, January 20,

January 27, and finally February 3. *Nice touch by Wills, giving the jurors something visual to latch onto.* "How can you be so certain of these dates?"

Anticipating the question, Ponce answered without missing a beat. "There was an event during that first Tuesday night shift, January 13, that needed his attention. I was concerned that if I took action in his stead, it would reflect negatively on both of us."

"What was the nature of the incident?"

MacPherson said, "Objection, Your Honor. I am hard-pressed to see the relevance of whatever the incident involved." *Sound objection.*

Judge Walter: "Sustained. Mr. Wills, move on."

"Sergeant, how can you be certain that it was always on a Tuesday night shift?"

Without any hesitation he answered, "After the first Tuesday, I was on alert." And then for the first time, Ponce embellished an answer. "It was peculiar to me. It just struck me that he was so flagrant about leaving and staying away so long."

"Let me stop you for a moment. To your knowledge, did Lt. Cort leave the station for a dinner or breakfast break?"

"No, he always brought food with him and ate at the station. It is customary for administrators to remain at the station throughout their shift."

"Let's zero in on the morning of February 4, the day Christie Cort disappeared. Were you and Lt. Cort working that same late-night shift?"

"Yes."

"Tell us what you recall about the early morning hours of that day."

"Pretty much the same thing. The shift started on a Tuesday

night, and I recall Lt. Cort leaving the station at approximately 1:00 a.m." Wills waited for more. He was disappointed.

"Please go on, concerning that morning." Wills maintained his composure, despite having to pull the information out of Ponce piece by painful piece.

"I noted that he was gone for a longer time, maybe three and a half, four hours." Then Ponce surprised everyone by adding, "I later learned that was the morning his wife went missing."

Wills paused, letting the answer settle in. "When you later found out that was the day Christie disappeared, did you make any connection between his absence and Ms. Cort's disappearance?"

MacPherson was on her feet. "Objection, counsel is asking the witness to speculate."

"Sustained. Mr. Wills, you know better than that," Walter said, as an aside.

Unabashed, Wills continued, "Sergeant, did you notice anything unusual about Lt. Cort when he returned to the station that morning around 5:00 a.m.?"

"No, other than he had been gone longer than the other times."

Wills drew a second circle around February 4. "Sergeant, did you inform anyone higher up at the sheriff's department of Lt. Cort's absences?" Wills recognized that MacPherson on cross would question the *convenience* of Ponce's testimony. Why did he only report this well after the events? Was he reliable?

"It is unusual to report negative conduct of a superior officer." I looked over at Cort. No reaction. Completely stoic.

"I understand. Eventually you did report it. How did that come about?"

"When Det. Ossoff questioned everyone at our station."

"Sergeant, did you and the defendant ever talk about promotions and such?"

"A couple of times. It seemed to me that he was obsessed with getting promoted."

"Objection, the witness is speculating." MacPherson was right on it.

"Sustained."

"Well then, let me ask you, what did the defendant actually say about promotions?"

"Objection, hearsay." MacPherson was doing everything she could to break up the examination.

"Mr. Wells?"

"Your Honor, this calls for a party-opponent admission."

"I agree," ruled Walter. "You may answer, Sergeant."

"He said promotion to central administration was the most important thing in his life. It was his life's goal."

Wills paused to let the response sink in. "Sergeant, as a fifteen-year veteran of the department, are you aware of whether divorce could compromise promotion?"

"Yeah, the sheriff's big on family values and frowns on divorce."

"Thank you, Sergeant." Turning to the judge, he said, "Your Honor, I have no further questions for Sgt. Ponce."

Wills retired to his table, and without waiting for an invitation from the judge, MacPherson jumped on Ponce. She established that there were strained relations between Cort and Ponce, that Ponce resented that Cort was superior to him. She also pointed out that if Ponce had concerns about Cort's conduct, he was derelict in failing to report. There wasn't much for MacPherson to work with; she made her quick jabs and moved on.

Following Ponce's testimony, Walter recessed for lunch, and I walked Suzelle to her office inside the Foltz Building. She observed that Ponce's testimony about Cort's absence on February 4 did leave a window of opportunity for Cort.

"What about the other three Tuesday shifts prior to the disappearance?" I asked, curious as to her take.

She shrugged and cocked her head, musing, "I guess he could have been getting things ready for the kill." She paused. "Or"—she drew out the *or*—"he was busy with his girlfriend."

"I'm sure the former explanation is part of Wills's grand scheme. After all, Cort had to grab his wife, kill her, and dispose of the body and her car, all in a short number of hours." I looked at Suzelle and added, "I've come to the same conclusion. Cort could've used the earlier absences to prepare for his kill."

"Boy, if that's what happened, how chilling and premeditated." Suzelle arched her eyebrows.

"But, as you also suggested, Cort could have been off canoodling with his girlfriend. And that Tuesday happened to be the time Christie departed for parts unknown."

"Canoodling?"

"Let's keep it clean." I grinned.

"Okay Prof, keep up the good work," she said with a smile. "I gotta get back to the office. I'll be watching tonight."

We hugged, and she was off.

That night on Channel 6, I reported on Sgt. Ponce's testimony describing Cort's absences from work on the three Tuesday night shifts leading up to the Tuesday before Christie went missing. Lisbet's face shone with surprise. Apparently she had not been updated on the day's developments.

"That would seem to be a strong point for the prosecution." *Nothing slipped by Lisbet.*

"I agree, it's compelling testimony. Unaccounted hours, including some on the early morning of Christie Cort's disappearance, creates a window of opportunity. Three and a half to four hours for Lt. Cort to allegedly kill his wife, dispose of her body, and get rid of her vehicle."

"I see," said Lisbet. "So, Jake, take us through your thought process as you work through this testimony."

I gave her an uncertain look and said, "I think the previous three Tuesday shifts when Lt. Cort left the station may be significant. Could he have used those times to prepare?" I asked rhetorically.

"What do you mean?" *Do I have to spell it out again?*

I went on, "I'm suggesting that there may have been too much for Lt. Cort to accomplish in one three- or four-hour stretch. Perhaps he laid some groundwork on those earlier nights."

"Now I understand." *I did have to spell it out.* She gave an acknowledging shrug and moved on to other events.

As I left the newscast, I called Lisa from my car. "How are things in the teenage wasteland?"

She gave a brief laugh. "I think the adolescent insurrection has quelled."

We both laughed. "I could drive up this early evening instead of tomorrow morning. Does that work?"

"Of course. I'll make a late dinner and then seduce you with my considerable charms."

"Maybe we'll skip dinner and just get to the seduction," I suggested. That elicited a soft giggle. She did not giggle often—it was delightful.

"Hey, big boy, you're going to need food to keep up with me."

"Is this turning into a dirty conversation?"

"I believe it is. I wish you were here right now."

"Save that thought; only two hours away."

Trial Tip #3: Voir Dire

From the French, literally meaning 'to speak the truth.' The process of questioning the prospective jurors. Never make a prospective juror look foolish. Jurors uninitiated in the trial process frequently ask questions or provide answers that are ill-informed or just plain foolish. Advocates must maintain a professional posture and respond as if the statement was plausible. Even in the event the juror may eventually be excused, the other jurors will look critically, should an advocate offer a disrespectful response.

CHAPTER 9

THE TASTE OF BLOOD

Monday, a challenging day was in the offing. Criminal law was from 10–11:00 a.m., followed by the makeup class—and in fact the first class meeting—for trial advocacy. Trial advocacy was an upper-division class limited to sixteen students. More than sixteen rendered the class unworkable, since we did weekly exercises. The class met once a week. I lectured on a component aspect of trial one week and the next week the students, utilizing the tools discussed, engaged in exercises using mock cases.

Today's class: cross-examination. It is the aspect of trial most often butchered by law students and lawyers alike. Too many lawyers attempt to win their cases on cross by going for gotcha points. Such a swing-for-the-fences approach often strikes out. Home runs are rare; strikeouts, common. Instead of trying to win the trial with a flashy but risky cross-examination, advocates should strive to put together a couple of singles. Witnesses on cross, of course, are hostile to the advocate's position and will strive to hurt the advocate's side of the case at every opportunity. Memorable concessions on cross, maybe once in a blue moon. *Perry Mason moments rarely, if ever, happen.* I had very exacting rules for cross-exam, and I expected them to be followed.

My sixteen students were sitting in the jury box in Pacifico's very elegant trial courtroom. I had ten women and six men in my class. I stood at the rail and, without preamble, began. "Cross-exam rule number one, always wear the white hat." I scanned the faces. "Grace, why?"

She was an attentive third-year student who had aced my criminal procedure class last year. She briefly hesitated. "I guess because you don't want the judge to come down hard on you."

Disappointed in her answer, I said, "Let's go a little deeper." I paused, then began again. "Of course, the judge is important, and it is rarely good practice to get on the wrong side of your judge. But the judge is not the audience you are playing to. It is the twelve in the box. That is your audience." I stepped back, taking in the whole group. "Great trial lawyers are always, and I mean always, assessing their jurors. It's easy during opening statement and closing argument because you're looking right at them while you're talking, but not so easy during examinations. You must have at least one eye on the jurors throughout trial. Project yourself into the jury box. Become that thirteenth juror. Read their body language, study their faces. Ask questions you imagine they would ask. Voice concerns they would voice. Treat witnesses with respect and kindness, even during cross-examination."

I was on a roll. I softened my voice for emphasis. "I want my jurors to like me and respect me, so if I treat a witness harshly, I will pay a price with my jurors. Likability translates into credibility, and if I've gained credibility, I am much more likely to succeed. Attacking a witness is not a winning strategy. Wear the white hat."

Lincoln, another third-year, who had already been offered a deputy district attorney position at graduation, jumped in so quickly,

I'm certain he did not hear my final admonition. "Professor, I've sat in on a couple of trials while clerking this past summer. Sometimes the attorneys encountered a difficult, even a dislikeable witness. Do you still wear the white hat with those witnesses?" That's the kind of question a gunner would ask.

"Thanks Lincoln, that allows me to dig into the exception to the rule. When I was a prosecutor, we had a word for witnesses you politely characterized as dislikeable. We called them assholes." That generated a lot of laughter. "Of course, I'm using that word as a term of art." More laughter.

I grinned. "Well, let's get into that. What to do with a witness who will not answer your questions or who is an extreme partisan for the other side or shows a lack of respect for you and your side of the case?" I paused to crystallize the question. "Once you feel or sense that the jurors have developed a disdain for a witness, you can take the gloves off and batter them. No more being nice. But, and this is a big but, make certain your attack is proportionate to the witness's attitude. Be careful not to overreach." I got appreciative nods all around. *The taste for blood was always appreciated by law students.*

I gave it a moment. "Rule number two, never ask a question." That caught some looks. I doubled down. "Never ask a question; only make statements." I paused again; I needed this point above all else to sink in. "Make a statement and put a question mark at the end." Some harbored skeptical looks, which in a way surprised me, despite my counterintuitive statement. They had all made an effort to get into my class over the other three trial-ad classes, so one would think they were all-in with me. Maybe my expectations for them hadn't been made clear, or maybe that was just my ego. "Instead of 'Did you then go into the house?' it should be 'You then went into the house, correct?' Any statement on cross that begins with a what, where, when, how, or why is out. If in your cross during our exercises, I hear any of the *w*'s, I will stop the exercise." The same skeptics leaned back in their seats, perhaps wondering if it was too late to get into another class.

"The difference is profound. A nonleading question allows, perhaps even encourages, the witness to elaborate, whereas a statement calls for a monosyllabic response. Cross-exam is about controlling the witness. At the end of the day, you are striving for a series of statements calling for monosyllabic ratification. Let me repeat that. Cross-examination is a series of statements looking for ratification." I slowly repeated. "Statements looking for ratification. No questions, ever."

Alexandra said, "Professor Clearwater, like Lincoln, I sat in on some trials this past summer and noticed that most of the lawyers seemed to be asking questions during cross-examination, instead of making statements."

"I'm not surprised. How did their crosses go?"

"Sometimes the questioning seemed a bit messy. The lawyers were trying to make the witness agree with their point, but the witnesses kept going beyond the question, and it would take a while for the attorney to make her point. Sometimes it got so confusing, I forgot what the point was."

"Your observations make my case. How do we avoid that messiness? We'll get there in a minute, but first let's tackle rule number three, which is a close corollary to rule number two." I moved over to counsel table and sat on the edge. "Always be protected. You've all heard the adage that you never ask a question unless you know the answer."

Nods all around.

"We are tightening that up a bit. Never make a statement unless you are protected." I nodded toward Earl, another student from last year's criminal law class. Coming into this class, I believed Earl would prove to be the class standout. "Earl, run with that."

Without hesitation, he replied, "It means that there is something this witness previously said or did to support your statement."

"For instance?"

He briefly looked down and then was on it. "Using your example. Make certain that the witness said, or wrote, on some prior occasion, such as in a deposition, that they went back into the house." *This guy was a keeper.*

"Excellent. We do not guess; we know. That protection can be in a statement that the witness made to an officer, or the witness's answer during a deposition, or even just common sense."

Abigail, an eager second-year student, pulled a face and asked, "What do you mean, being protected by common sense?"

"Earl, help me." *Go with the hot hand.*

"Sure." He thought for a moment and said, "If it developed that a woman just climbed out of a swimming pool, common sense tells us she is wet. Thus we are protected in assuming she is wet."

"On the fly, Earl, excellent." Turning to Abigail, I asked, "You good with that?" *Earl was already ahead of the pack.*

"I get it. Makes sense." She nodded.

"Earl"—*stay with the hot hand*—"what if the witness's answer varies from what she said or did in the past? What is the cross-examiner's response?"

Earl grinned and, without hesitation, said, "Impeach the hell out of them." His response elicited laughter and high-fives throughout the jury box. Earl jabbed his fist into the air.

Once again, drawing blood is a big hit.

Ja Lin tentatively raised her hand. "Ja Lin, don't raise your hand in this class," I mildly reminded. "Just jump right in." I wanted these hard chargers to be assertive without being aggressive. Fighting for class time was excellent preparation for thinking and responding on your feet during the pitch of battle. I was even okay, given the small class size, with them talking over one another, within limits. Welcome to the real courtroom. *Assertive, not aggressive, a fine line, but still a line.*

"What do you have, Ja Lin?"

"What if you have a question that is helpful to you, no matter which way the witness answers?" Good students are always probing and testing.

"Good question. Don't do it. Such questions are few, and even if you are okay with either response, it breaks the rhythm you have generated and implicitly gives the witness leave to elaborate. I want a stranglehold on the witness from the get-go. Control, control, control."

She nodded, but from her expression, it was clear she was not convinced. *Once we got into the exercises, she would become a convert.*

"Rule number four, control the runaway witness." I zeroed in on Brandon, a student that I had not had in class before. "Brandon, how do we do that?"

He was somewhat taken back and, without much conviction, stammered, "I guess you could just cut them off. Interrupt them."

I nodded. "That is the choice of many trial lawyers. We will discuss that option in a minute. How about the rest of you? Any other suggestions?"

Joanna spoke up. She was six months pregnant and informed me prior to class that later into the semester she may miss several weeks giving birth. If she was willing to work through class while pregnant, I was willing to accommodate her. I also didn't mind because, frankly, she was brilliant, and who doesn't appreciate brilliance? "If the witness is being nonresponsive, I might object and ask the judge to admonish the witness to restrict their answer to the question."

"Another acceptable answer. Let's examine both approaches. Brandon, let's start with your suggestion, the cutoff solution. How does such an approach play with the only audience we care about?"

He shrugged his shoulders as if the answer was obvious. "The jurors may hold the advocate accountable for being rude in cutting off the witness." He hesitated and added, "Or the jurors might also feel that the advocate is afraid of the answer, and that's why they cut the witness off."

"Great answer." I cocked my head. "Given your response, I'm surprised that you offered your earlier suggestion that you cut the witness off."

He grinned. "I couldn't think of anything else." Mild appreciative laughter.

"Fair enough." I laughed and continued. "Let's examine the jurors' reaction first. We are taught early in life that it is rude to cut someone off. It's almost an automatic response. As a result, we tend to hold someone who interrupts another as rude and disrespectful. Not good traits when we are trying to cultivate good will with our jurors."

Joanna had a quizzical look. "What say you, Joanna?"

"You are probably right, but I wouldn't want this hostile witness to go on and on during my cross, trying to hurt my case."

"Legitimate concern; nonetheless, you'd agree that alienating the jurors is not the best approach?"

"I would agree with that."

"Let's explore option number two, your elegant solution, that we go to the judge for help controlling the witness. Weigh in on any potential downside."

She shook her head. "Professor Clearwater, I don't see a downside."

"Anybody?"

No one offered. I let the silence hang for a minute. "Asking the judge for help seems as if I need help controlling the witness. That I am no longer driving the bus. When I'm in trial, I'm in charge. It is my courtroom. I don't need anyone's help. I'll fight my own battles." I studied the faces—everyone was tuned in. "Asking the judge for help has the same two downsides as the advocate cutting off the witness. The nonresponsive objection itself can seem rude because, again, I am cutting off the witness, and once again it looks as if I am in fact afraid of the answer."

"So what do you want us to do?" Joanna set me up for the solution.

"Ask the exact same question again." Confused looks across the board. My solution was not well received. *It never is.* "Let me explain. Let's assume your question-statement is very straightforward but the witness has decided to run off on her answer. Let her finish. Then come right back by responding, 'Ma'am, let's return to *my question.* Isn't it true that you *then* went back into the house?' There are a couple of advantages to this approach. First, you have repeated the question-statement with an emphasis on the phrase *my question.* Keep in mind that the question-statement is more important than the answer, and your repetition emphasizes that point. Second, you are pointing out to the jurors that the witness, for whatever reason, has opted to not answer the question-statement, which is in sharp contrast to the run-on nonanswer the witness just stated."

"But aren't you just giving the witness an opportunity to go off and restate whatever she wants?" Earl was back in the hunt.

"Earl, let's think this through. This witness has just testified on direct exam and has said her piece. After I finish my cross, opposing counsel is going to ask the witness to restate her position again on redirect examination. There is no way I can prevent that. She is going to tell her story. But by repeating my question-statement on cross, I can ensure my statement will stand out. The simple fact of repetition emphasizing the key point of my question-statement will draw the jury's attention. I'll even go a step further—if the witness refuses to answer a second time, I will once again repeat the question-statement, drawing even more attention to the point I am making." Everyone was focused. "Taking it even a step further, during closing argument I will point out that since the witness was not forthcoming in answering my straightforward question-statement on cross, what is she trying to hide? Can we trust her testimony?"

My solution to the dilemma of the nonresponsive answer scenario was a hard sell. To some, it was counterintuitive. However, situations would arise during the cross-exam exercises that would allow me to reinforce my point.

Again, no one spoke up; everyone was thinking things through. Time to move on. "Let's discuss how to impeach." That lit them up. *Impeachment, hostility, blood.* "There are multiple forms of impeachment, from pointing out some vested interest in the proceedings, to nailing someone who has suffered a prior conviction. But I want to start with the impeachment of a statement the witness made during her just-completed direct exam or during the ongoing cross-exam, specifically, impeachment by a prior inconsistent statement. For instance, let's say that because of your thorough familiarity with the case, you realize that in a deposition or in response to a police interrogation, the witness previously said something contrary to what she just testified to." I paused; everyone was keenly focused. "So how do we go about such an impeachment? There are four specific steps. First, do the calculation. Was the contradiction during the just-completed direct examination or during the current cross-examination truly worthy of impeachment? Impeaching on a trivial point is foolhardy and is a waste of the jurors' time. Earl, you started us on this impeachment business, so let's start with you. How do we know if a contradiction is egregious enough to impeach?"

He cocked his head in concentration and finally said, "I don't know, precisely. Is it just a feeling?"

I shrugged. "We need a little more clarity than that. Anybody?" No takers. "Here is how I know. Is the point important enough that it merits inclusion in my eventual closing argument? If it's a simple misspeak—no impeachment. It's got to be something that matters. Something that challenges the witness's credibility." I looked inquiringly at Earl. "What do you think, Earl, does that help?"

"It does."

"Second step. Firm the witness up with their current statement on which you want to impeach." I registered some confusion with several of the group. "Earl, you play along as the witness, while I play the advocate." *Showing was better than telling.*

Earl smiled and said, to the enjoyment of the class, "Don't hurt me, Prof."

"I'll try not to." More laughter.

"Let's assume Earl as the witness on the just-concluded direct exam said something that I believe is contrary to a statement he said at a deposition ten months ago. In a very non-confrontational tone, I'll ask, 'Mr. Hollister, help me understand a couple of points you made during your direct examination. You told us that you had never met Mr. X before the accident, correct?' That's it, that's the simple firm-up. We need the firm-up in clear, unequivocal terms, so that it stands in sharp contrast to his deposition statement that I am about to impeach him on. In getting the firm-up, I try to sound matter-of-fact, so as to not alert the witness that I am about to hurt him."

Earl pulled a face for the benefit of the class and cautiously answered, "That's right."

"If the witness is alerted, he may try to fend off the impeachment blow by offering some explanation, such as 'I forgot' or 'I was confused.' Ignore any of his excuses and stay on track.

"Now we move onto the third part of our impeachment. Mr. Hollister, you gave a deposition in this case, isn't that right?"

"Yes, I did."

"Just to be clear, I orally asked you some questions and you answered them, correct?"

"Yes."

"During that deposition, you swore an oath to tell the full and complete truth, didn't you?"

"I did."

"In fact, that is the same oath that you just took here today?"

"It is."

"After the conclusion of that deposition, you were given an opportunity to review your answers, isn't that right?"

"I was."

"And you did review those answers and you signed at the end of the deposition transcript that it was the complete truth, correct?"

"That's right."

"Referring court and counsel to page 23 of the witness's deposition transcript, lines 4 through 6. Your Honor, leave to approach the witness." I approached Earl with an imaginary deposition transcript.

"Mr. Hollister, I am showing you a deposition transcript. This is from your deposition, isn't it?"

"Yes it is."

"Turning to the back page of your deposition transcript, you recognize your signature attesting to the truth of your answers, isn't that right?"

"I do."

I paused and turned back to the class. "That is the play-around. I've established that the witness was fully aware of his prior statement. That there was no confusion or ambiguity. Once that is accomplished, I move in for the kill. Step four, the actual impeachment." I waited a beat and continued. "Mr. Hollister, I'm going to read page 23, lines 4 through 6 aloud. Please silently follow along with me to make certain I am reading correctly. Isn't it true that you were asked, 'Had you ever met Mr. X prior to the accident.' Did I read that correctly?"

"Yes."

"And isn't it true that you answered, and I quote, 'I met him briefly, several days before the accident'?"

With raised eyebrows, an incredulous tone, and a nod of my head, I asked, "Mr. Hollister, did I read that correctly?"

"Yes."

I stopped to gauge the class reaction. "Earl, what do I do now?"

"Seems to me there is nothing left to do. The witness has been impeached."

"Precisely." I scanned the faces. "Resist the temptation to go on and ask one question too many, which would be some variation of 'Were you lying then or lying now?' or 'How do you reconcile those two statements?' Going too far gives the witness an opportunity to attempt an explanation. Resist that urge." I studied my group. Lots of nods. "That's all for the day. Cross X exercises next class."

Joanna approached me as the other students began to leave. "I've been watching your commentary during the Cort trial."

"How have I been doing?" I grinned.

"You've been terrific. It's almost like you are teaching a trial-ad class to the TV audience."

I shook my head and laughed. "Too much so?

"Oh no, I think you are helping educate people on how the process works, while still providing commentary." She hesitated, pulled a face, and added, "Maybe lighten up on the prosecutor a little." *Damn.*

I nodded. "Okay."

"I want to thank you for steering me away from big-firm practice. I'm excited about a career trying cases, and I am seriously thinking of pursuing a job as a trial lawyer with either the US Attorney's office or the local DA."

"I am pleased to hear that. When I was a prosecutor, I felt like I was doing something important. Trying criminal cases and helping to ensure that the correct outcome, the just outcome, would happen was much more important to me than trying civil cases involving money. I know there are some civil cases where justice is achieved, but in criminal cases there are daily opportunities to work toward justice."

"Thanks, Prof."

Meanwhile, the Cort trial was at a standstill. We were in recess until the following Monday. Judge Walter was at a week-long session teaching newly appointed judges the intricacies of judging. Apparently Walter taught at the Judges' College every year. It was amazing to me that he was teaching other judges. While his rulings during the Cort trial were generally accurate, his judicial demeanor was lacking.

Trial Tip #4: Cross-Examination

Ask only leading questions. Cross-examination is about controlling the witness. Short, specific questions calling for monosyllabic responses allow advocates to control witnesses during cross-examination. This is no time to ask open-ended questions, which would cede control to the witness.

CHAPTER 10

INTO THE SURF

As I jogged to the pier early Wednesday morning, I was greeted by four young adults I didn't immediately recognize. "Hey Prof, we thought you could use some company on your swim." I was surprised as I realized the woman speaking was Maribeth, and these were first-year students from my criminal law class. Then I heard some cheering from up on the pier, and at least forty more students were watching from above, clapping and cheering. What the hell? How did they even know about my pier swims?

I shook my head in wonder and thrust out my arms in greeting to the crowd on the pier. Without a word, the four students standing near me stripped off their sweats and jogged into the surf. Still amazed, I again waved to the crowd on the pier then followed the swimmers into the surf. I ducked under a couple of small waves and caught up with the pack. The pier crowd was keeping pace and shouting encouragement. It was obvious that the four swimmers were all experienced and very fit as Maribeth took the lead, setting a strong pace. I had to work to keep up with them.

We neared the end of the pier, the crowd with us above. The few early morning fishermen looked on with smiles as the raucous group cheered us on. As we rounded the pier and began the last leg, Maribeth continued to pull away from us mere men and was the first to emerge from the cold surf. She was greeted by the cheering students, who had hustled down from the pier. After the rest of us trotted out of the surf, we were wrapped in towels.

I caught my breath, smiled, and said, "What is this? It's 6:30 a.m.—are you all nuts?"

William, one of the non-swimmers, explained. "We heard about your early swims and thought we would surprise you."

"Well, you did! I don't know what to say. Thank you all," I replied, as warmth slowly reentered my body under the towel. "Maribeth, you had to have been a collegiate swimmer."

"Stanford, four years, scholarship, butterfly and freestyle."

"Glen?" I asked.

"USC, scholarship. Same with Miguel. We won a national title in our junior year. Rudy swam for Long Beach State."

"I'm in the presence of swimming greatness." I grinned. "I've got at least a decade on you folks. I was pulling much harder than usual just to not be embarrassed." I turned to Maribeth. "Maribeth, you're a beast."

That drew an appreciative nod from her and a modest bow, to the enjoyment of the throng.

"Tell you what," I said to the assembled forty or fifty, "let us cold and wet swimmers do our beach change, and let's head up to Moe's Coffee. I'm springing for breakfast for everyone, swimmers and non-swimmers." Another round of cheers.

An hour and a half later, and with my bank account depleted by $280, we departed Moe's, the students to their dorms and me to my home. I am certain Moe's had never had such a lucrative or celebratory morning crowd.

Later that morning as I walked into my ten o'clock criminal law class, I was greeted by a multitude of smiles. It was apparent they were waiting for me to comment on the swim. I could feel a lump in my throat. *Really, Clearwater?* I steeled myself to not let my emotions carry the moment and opted to move on and dig right into the assigned materials. *Poor decision.* I called on Maribeth, and she closed her laptop and gave me a disapproving look. Other students were closing their laptops and staring at me. The silence was loud. Maribeth broke the uncomfortable silence and, in an incredulous tone, said, "You're not going to say anything about this morning?"

I looked at her and then scanned the faces. "You're right. All of you are right. I am still processing what happened this morning. You folks are really something. I don't think I have ever been so surprised about anything in my life. It was . . ." I hesitated, steadying myself; I could feel the emotion surging. I cleared my throat and said, "It was as wonderful as it was surprising. I thank you all."

It was still, very still. Maribeth broke the silence. "We think you're pretty cool," she said, smiling, "and wanted to show it." She shrugged. "Besides that, we need the exercise. This first year of law school is tough on our bodies." That broke things up as we all laughed.

Once again, "Thanks," was all I could muster. I tugged at my sport coat while pulling myself together. "Is it okay now to get back to criminal law?"

Laptops were flipped open, and we got underway.

After class, three of the swimmers came to my office. Once again, Maribeth was doing the talking—a natural leader. She seemed destined to have a memorable career. "Prof, there are others who would like to join in, but they're not as experienced as some of us. We were thinking that a couple of surfers and paddleboarders from class could come along, and if a swimmer needed help, they would have something to hang onto. Would you be okay with that?"

Once again surprised, I said, "Are you thinking this swim thing is going to be a regular event?"

"Speaking for the three of us, we do." She looked at the others for confirmation. Nods around.

Glen chimed in, "Like she said, it's an enjoyable way to get in our exercise. Working with a group is always motivating. It's inspiring."

"What can I say? This is not an official Pacifico event, and it's a free ocean. Good idea to open it up and keep it safe. A couple of boards out there is a good idea." Then looking at Glen, "You're right about camaraderie making it more enjoyable." Turning to Maribeth, "Try not to embarrass me out there."

With fist bumps, the swimmers smiled and stepped out.

Friday morning I was greeted by even more swimmers and a few paddleboarders. The crowd on the pier was as enthusiastic as before. No more springing for coffee though—too expensive.

Five minutes after finishing my Friday afternoon trial-ad class (cross-exam exercises), I was on my way to San Arcadia and Lisa. Walking through her door felt like coming home. It was right—the warmth, the lighting, the scent, the woman. Her greeting, her smile, her embrace.

She had made an artistic salad with shrimp and crab, and as we were finishing a bottle of Napa chardonnay, she stood, raised her glass, tapped for attention, cleared her throat, and with a huge smile announced, "My agent has secured a one-woman show at the Katharine Klart Gallery in San Francisco. Ta-da." She threw her arms up in triumph, as I stood to applaud. She shushed me down. "And you, my dear professor, are coming with me."

I rose and wrapped her in my arms. "I am so pleased for you. And I would be honored to accompany such a shining star. Tell me more."

Excitedly she said, "This gallery focuses exclusively on the work of contemporary artists and is considered the most discriminating gallery on the West Coast. Julia has been working on this for over a year."

I released her, retrieved my wine class, and saluted, "Here's to Julia, agent extraordinaire."

"Hear, hear!" Lisa raised her glass. "Jake, this opens my work up to a much larger audience. I know I shouldn't be so focused on commercial success, but this show validates me," she said, as she hunched her shoulders, looking for my understanding.

"Never apologize for success. You are a remarkable talent, and it's time the world knows." I cocked my head in question. "Your shows in San Arcadia and Los Angeles were huge successes, and from my limited perspective seemed to have already put you on the map. I gather from your joy that this is a significant upgrade?"

"This gallery has a more national prominence." She could not help grinning, and then to the tune of "New York, New York," she sang, "If you can make it there, you can make it anywhere." *Wrong city, right attitude.* We laughed as I pulled her tight. Celebratory sex can be transcendent. We didn't even make it to her bedroom.

Later that evening as things cooled, we were lying in bed. I stroked her bare leg and asked for more particulars about the showing.

"It's in May." She blew some hair from her forehead. "They want at least twenty pieces."

"Twenty pieces? Is that unusual?"

"Fairly typical. My other shows usually requested between twenty and twenty-five pieces."

The number of pieces surprised me. "Do you have that many already finished?"

She kissed my forehead. "What do you think I've been doing on all those lonely weekday nights when my lover has been down south?" Another kiss. "I've finished eighteen, and I'm about to finish with several others. I'll be okay." She tilted her head back and studied me. "There is one very special piece that is almost done. I'm hoping you'll be okay if we stay in tomorrow so I can work on it."

"Of course."

"Oh hell," she exclaimed as she suddenly jumped out of bed, "I can't wait any longer. Come on!"

She dragged me out of bed, as naked as we were, and pulled me into her studio. There it was, on an easel. It was one of her vivid signature watercolors depicting the view from my deck looking toward the Malibu Pier as dawn was breaking. A couple holding hands were walking toward the pier. Even though the faces were not revealed, I knew it was us.

I was blown away, speechless. The colors, the detail! It made me feel . . . warm. After studying the picture, I finally managed, "Lisa, I don't know what to say."

"I knew you would like it. This one has an added layer of love."

I pulled her naked beautiful self to me. "Love, the ultimate inspiration." Still staring at the picture, I said, "It looks finished to me."

"Just a bit more detail." She looked appraisingly at her work. "If I'm permitted to comment on my own work, this one is special." She then turned to study me, noted my aroused condition, and led me back to bed.

Inspired indeed.

CHAPTER 11

WILLS KEEPS GRINDING

Monday morning at 6:30, it was back to the real world. The sun was just emerging from the horizon. As I trotted to the pier, there were six students waiting. I shook my head and let out a small laugh and was greeted with fist bumps. One of the new volunteers was Helena from my first-year class, the other, a big guy I didn't recognize, but who I assumed was also a student. I stripped off my sweats, tossed them onto my towel, and we all jogged into the cold, calm surf. Before I dove under the first wave, I stopped and waved back at a dozen or so students waving from the pier. The onlookers had dwindled.

As we emerged and were handed our towels by the onlookers, I learned that Helena had swum for Cal State Northridge. Luke, the other newcomer, was of recent UCLA vintage. He was a third-year who had heard about the Friday swim and decided to join in. He offered that an ocean swim was more exhilarating than laps in Pacifico's Olympic-sized pool. "Laps are boring."

I figured the novelty of these early morning swims would quickly wane. I would be proven wrong.

Following class, I watched the recording of Monday's trial and was ready when Lisbet threw the camera to me in the early evening.

"Jake, it's been a week, and we're all anxious to catch up on the Cort trial."

"Bit of an unusual day today. As the prosecutor's DNA expert was preparing to take the oath and testify that the blood found on the rug leading to the garage was a DNA match with Christie Cort, MacPherson informed the court that she would stipulate that the blood was a match for Christie."

Lisbet jerked her head back in surprise. "Why would she do that? Did you see that coming?"

"No, I didn't see that coming. Frankly, I was braced for several days of tedious testimony concerning the DNA results. But as to your first question, Lisbet, I understand why MacPherson agreed to accept the results. I believe this was an effort to maintain her credibility. My guess is that she had retained her own expert to test that blood, and her expert determined it was Christie's. Given that result, MacPherson, realizing that her cross-examination would prove futile, opted not to expend her credibility on an issue where she could not prevail."

Lisbet thought for a moment and asked, "Does conceding on the blood evidence dispel the defense's runaway theory?" *Good question.*

"I don't think so. The DNA results don't tell us how long the blood had been there. The blood could have been left there weeks or even months before. I am sure the defense will offer up some explanation for that blood. I think this was a matter of Ms. MacPherson picking her battles. Don't fight battles you cannot win."

"Well, with that development, what else occurred today?"

"Not much. Like I said, everyone was thinking that the direct and cross-examination of the DNA expert would take up the entire day, if not several days. So when MacPherson offered her stipulation, the prosecutor had no other witnesses prepared to go. As a result, the courtroom went dark for the balance of the day."

"Going forward, what else do you expect from Prosecutor Wills?"

"Seems as if he has played all of his cards. I would not be surprised if he rested his case. Perhaps we'll find out tomorrow. If he does rest, it would then be up to Lt. Cort and Ms. MacPherson whether to put on a defense or to rely on the state of the evidence as it is."

"Any sense of how the jurors might be leaning?" *Terrible question, but I knew at some point Lisbet would go there.*

"I'm not privy to what additional evidence, if any, Mr. Wills has. Without that knowledge, I can't offer an informed opinion." I should have stopped there, but I felt compelled to add, "I'm concerned that the prosecution did not produce more evidence rebutting the defense theory that Christie Cort simply ran away."

"What specifically?"

"Seemed to me that there was a lack of thoroughness in establishing that Ms. Cort's body was not disposed of somewhere in the vicinity of the Cort residence."

"Professor, you mentioned that earlier. What else could the police have done? We've heard testimony about a grid search, cadaver dogs, that radar device . . ." She paused, thinking. "Yeah, and credit-card monitoring, social media, and phone pings. Seems pretty extensive to me."

"True. That being said, the search was too localized. It should have extended beyond the five-mile radius. Cort's a smart man and an experienced cop. If he killed her, he's not going to bury her in his backyard, so to speak. He's going to bury her as far away as possible, given the short window he was working within."

If folks, particularly Lisa, thought I was tough on the prosecutor before, I am really going to catch hell now.

"Thanks Jake, I guess we'll all have to be patient. Let's see what tomorrow will bring."

CHAPTER 12

WILLOW

I headed downtown Tuesday morning; the trial was coming to a head, and as expected, Wills stood and announced, "The prosecution rests."

Judge Walter turned to MacPherson. "Ms. MacPherson?"

"Your Honor, I have a motion to be heard outside the presence of the jury."

"Very well. Ladies and gentlemen of the jury, I must direct you back to the jury deliberation room."

Once the jurors had retired, Walter nodded at MacPherson.

"Pursuant to section 1118.1, the defense moves for a directed verdict."

No surprise there. At this juncture, the judge had the power to direct a not guilty if he remained skeptical about whether or not the prosecution had produced sufficient evidence to sustain a conviction.

"May I proceed?" MacPherson requested, looking at the judge.

Walter gestured for her to go ahead.

MacPherson pointed out the obvious, beginning, "Without a body, the state has not proven beyond any reasonable doubt that a murder has even been committed. And even if the court believes that Christie Cort has been murdered, there is insufficient evidence that Max Cort has killed her."

Walter was focused on MacPherson's argument and nodded solemnly.

Turning to the prosecutor, he invited Will's response.

Wills, anticipating MacPherson's motion, focused on what he described as the *overwhelming* circumstantial evidence surrounding Christie's disappearance: namely, Cort's abuse of her, his motivation to not allow her a divorce which would compromise his advancement within the sheriff's department, his unexplained absence during the time Christie went missing, and finally that Christie had been missing for nearly a year.

When Wills finished, there was a sense of expectancy and even dread from some in the gallery. Would the judge pull the case from the jury and end it right here? That would be a bold move and would subject Judge Walter to harsh criticism.

But the law was the law, and Judge Walter was a strict practitioner of his chosen profession. Walter, seemingly without deliberation or reflection, ended the suspense with a simple, "Motion dismissed."

MacPherson was nonplussed. She had to have known Walter was not going to take the case from the jury.

The jurors were called back in. I often wondered how the jurors must have felt, being sent away any number of times during trial. I imagined that they couldn't help wondering themselves what they were missing. Perhaps it's analogous to watching a movie with significant scenes cut. Just wondering.

Once they were settled, Walter asked MacPherson if there was to be a defense case-in-chief.

"Yes, Your Honor." She stood and confidently called Willow Merkle to the stand.

Merkle was escorted into the courtroom by MacPherson's investigator. From the various newspaper accounts, everyone who had been following the trial was aware that Merkle was not only Cort's *other woman* but also a dancer at a strip club. And indeed, she looked the part; she had long auburn hair and wore a very short skirt that showed off her long, shapely legs. Her crossover blouse, without benefit or necessity of a bra, displayed more cleavage and movement than expected in the staid courtroom environment. Given her role in the developing drama, one might suppose she would shy away from public scrutiny. Instead, she strolled into the courtroom like she owned the place, head up, with a steady stride. As a dancer, she was used to the hot white, although this time without the poles and with more than a G-string. It was just another performance. As she sat and took the oath, she carefully avoided eye contact with Cort. Cort was staring daggers at her. That made no sense to me. This was his witness. Maybe this was his form of intimidation to make certain she stayed the course.

Judge Walter, for his part, was keenly focused. I had to grin; the octogenarian was laser focused on Merkle. *Who was indeed someone to focus on.*

Merkle was sworn in, and MacPherson began. "Ms. Merkle, what is your relationship to Lt. Cort?"

Merkle looked directly at MacPherson and said, "I want a lawyer."

There was an audible gasp and then a stunned silence in the room. MacPherson's face paled. That was the first time I'd seen MacPherson unsettled, unnerved. I assumed, as apparently did she, that Merkle would provide an alibi for those early morning hours on February 4, when Christie went missing.

MacPherson quickly recovered and turned to the judge. "May we take a recess?"

Walter, staring at Merkle, asked her, "Is it your intention to invoke your privilege against self-incrimination?"

Merkle, maintaining her neutral expression, repeated, "I want a lawyer."

Following an animated sidebar dialogue with the lawyers, Walter sent them back to their stations and announced that the trial was recessed for the day. No one moved. Such an abrupt and disappointing ending for what was anticipated to be such a salacious examination deflated the room. *Sex and the surrounding drama were always a draw.* Merkle, for her part, rose and strolled down the middle of the courtroom without turning her head or responding to any comments. She didn't have to—her allure, very high heels, short skirt, and tight blouse commanded attention.

MacPherson had the rest of the day to evaluate her case. It had to be devastating to lose the alibi. She and Cort would have to confront some hard questions. How were they going to explain Cort's absence during that early morning? Did Merkle's refusal to provide an alibi mean that MacPherson would now be forced to put Cort on the stand to explain what he was doing that morning? His vulnerabilities (abuse, adultery, motives) would allow not only for Wills to crucify him during cross-examination but for the prosecution team to investigate and work to debunk whatever alibi the defense put forth. Two choices, both bad: put Cort on and see him get clubbed, or refuse to offer any explanation for his whereabouts and pray that the jurors would focus harder on the lack of Christie's body than on the lack of a Cort alibi.

Trial Tip #5: Mitigate Hurtful Evidence

Wherever possible, advocates should raise facts hurtful to their case before the opposition can exploit them. Raising such evidence first gives the examiner an opportunity to "prick the boil," mitigating the impact of the damaging evidence. Perhaps even more importantly, raising hurtful facts first enhances the advocate's credibility.

CHAPTER 13

WILLS LIGHTS IT UP

The next morning, I taught class, and later that afternoon I headed downtown to watch that day's trial video. As I had expected, MacPherson sucked it up and rested the defense case. I was not surprised she had opted not to call Cort. From her perspective, it was the least damaging choice. She made several perfunctory defense motions outside the presence of the jury, which were appropriately denied by Walter.

After the jurors were called back in and seated, Judge Walter turned to Wills. "Mr. Wills, are you ready to make your closing argument?"

"Your Honor, if I may have until tomorrow morning to present my closing argument?"

Walter glared at Wills. "Mr. Wills, you have delayed this trial on several occasions already; I would have thought you would be ready to proceed." *This was a screwup by Wills—he should have been ready.*

"My apologies, Your Honor; those previous delays resulted from unforeseeable circumstances. As for today, I anticipated the defense would call witnesses. I will be ready to offer my closing first thing in the morning."

Walter gave him a withering look, followed by a settling breath. "Alright, Mr. Wills, losing this day will just have to happen." Looking up from Wills, Walter declared a recess until 9:00 tomorrow morning.

That evening, I brought the Channel 6 audience up to speed. First, I discussed the decision by MacPherson to not put on a case. Lisbet asked for my opinion as to whether I thought MacPherson's decision was wise.

"The primary reason defense attorneys are reluctant to expose their case to the prosecution is the fear that their case, and in particular their client—should he testify—would be vulnerable under cross-examination. And given the circumstances surrounding Lt. Cort's conduct leading up to Christie's disappearance, MacPherson had good cause to be concerned. Beyond that, we don't know what else Mr. Wills might have in his back pocket to hit Cort with. Putting Cort on the stand would, in my judgment, expose him as a man who might well be capable of murdering his wife."

Lisbet countered. "But much of his disagreeable behavior has already come out. Was there much more that the prosecutor could use against him?"

"Like I said, I don't know. If nothing else, MacPherson may have just wanted to shield Cort from the glaring eyes of the jurors. His presence on the witness stand would serve to remind the jurors of his less-than-sterling character." I paused to see if Lisbet had anything to add. Apparently not. I went on. "Closing arguments are considered by some as the most crucial aspect of trial. But in my view, that notion is simply not true. The reality is that by most measures, voir dire and opening statements have more impact on verdicts than do closing arguments."

"I'd always thought that the closing argument was when the attorneys really went into persuasive overdrive to win their case."

"That is the popular perception, and in some cases that may be true. However, the empirical data suggests otherwise. By the conclusion of voir dire and opening statements, as many as 80 percent of jurors favor one side over the other. And the studies have found that once jurors favor one side, they will view the forthcoming evidence through the lens of the side they favor."

"That's remarkable. So you're saying that the jurors in this trial have already made up their minds, regardless of what they hear from the lawyers during the closings?"

"Not exactly. My point is that following opening statements, most of the jurors are predisposed, one way or another. And like I said, that predisposition colors how they will view the evidence. Now let me add, when I'm making my closing arguments, I not only want to reinforce those jurors who are predisposed to my side, but I want to give them the tools, the arguments, to carry my case back to the jury room. I want them to act as my agents during deliberations."

"I guess I never thought that deep into the persuasive process." Lisbet reflected. "How do you know whether particular jurors are with you? It always looks to me, at least from what I see on television, that the jurors are attempting to keep a neutral demeanor."

"Great question. Seasoned trial lawyers typically have a pretty solid understanding of where most of the jurors stand—from the answers the jurors gave during voir dire, to their body language during testimony, to their reactions to particular pieces of testimony, right down to the eye contact they make with counsel."

Lisbet paused and took that in. "Okay, thanks, Jake, for the primer. We eagerly anticipate tomorrow's arguments."

"Let me add one more thought to keep in mind, especially during the prosecution's closing argument. Since Cort didn't testify,

Prosecutor Wills must be very careful to not comment on his failure to testify. If he does, that's referred to as *Griffin* error and would lead to a mistrial."

Lisbet thought that over and asked, "Since the defense offered no alibi, can the prosecutor comment on the lack of an alibi?"

"Yes, but he must be careful and make certain his comments steer well clear of Cort's invocation of his Fifth Amendment right not to testify."

The following morning, I arrived at court early; there was no way I was going to miss watching the closes in person. Both counsel stood at their tables. John Wills, in a dark-blue suit with muted gray stripes and a red tie, was intently studying his notes. Merci MacPherson, wearing a light-tan skirt and jacket, was talking to one of her jury consultants. Max Cort was staring off at nothing, apparently not interested in MacPherson's conversation. I wondered what Cort was thinking. Were his thoughts of an innocent man wrongly accused, or of a guilty man wondering if his scheme had gone terribly wrong? The room was understandably packed with spectators, so many that some leaned against the back wall. The fire marshals would not be pleased. Folks would have given up their front row seats at Crypto Center for a Lakers playoff game in favor of the drama that was about to play out. *Maybe an overstatement. Probably not a playoff game.*

Jeremy Kaye, my Channel 6 boss, sat to my right, the other seat reserved for his station. He was pumped up. "Jake, your lecture last night about closing arguments was great television. We got a lot of favorable calls."

"Thanks Jeremy, I thought I went on a little long."

"Nope, the interaction between you and Lisbet was pitch perfect." *Pitch perfect?* He patted my knee. "You're a natural, Jake.

Let's do it again when another high-profile case comes up." He stopped when another idea had hit him. "Maybe we can give you a regular spot once a week to talk about trials and such."

"Jeremy, this is my one and only. It has been fun and instructive, but it's one and done for me."

"Yeah, let's think it over and get together after the trial. I'll be in touch." I don't think he heard a word I said. No never meant no, not with this guy.

It was 9:15 a.m. when the clerk and court reporter emerged from behind the judge's door. Five minutes later, Judge Walter appeared and ascended his throne. The bailiff called court to order, and our 9:00 a.m. call was only twenty minutes late.

Judges are never considered late, but if a lawyer shows up a minute late, there's hell to pay.

Walter gave his usual perfunctory greeting to the jurors and counsel. He then pre-instructed the jurors. Pre-instruction is designed to highlight the duties and responsibilities of the jurors and to remind them that counsels' remarks during closing arguments are not evidence. Rather, the only evidence is that which came from the testimony of sworn witnesses or from other evidence introduced during trial. Walter would give the final instructions following the closing arguments. The crowd and several jurors were fidgety, wanting to get on with it. But Walter was in no hurry to read the instructions, and he droned on. Forty minutes later, he finished. He finally looked at Wills and nodded.

As Wills rose, he thanked the judge and, turning to the jurors, thanked them. Without notes, he rounded counsel table and centered himself in front of the jury. In a slow staccato delivery, he began, "Max Cort is a calculating, scheming, premeditated killer." He gave a brief pause, letting his words resonate. "I chose those words carefully because the evidence supports each and every word. There are killings that occur in extreme situations, killings that happen in the blink of an eye, killings that arise out of chaotic circumstances, but we reserve premeditated murder, the most heinous of all murders, for those killings that arise as the result of the planning and the calculating of the murder of another human being in cold blood. That man"—pivoting and pointing at a seemingly nonchalant Cort—"schemed to kill his own wife." Turning back to the jury, he said, "Why? To further his own career! You heard the testimony: his career was the most important thing in his life. His life's goal. A divorce would jeopardize his career." Long pause. "A human life sacrificed to the altar of his career. The altar of his ambition." He took in a deep breath. "And maybe as a side benefit to further his adulterous relationship."

A brilliant start. I did not believe Wills had this in him. Wow!

Wills stepped back to his table, took a drink, picked up a controller, and displayed a PowerPoint photograph of Christie Cort's beautiful face. "Christie was loved and cherished, if not by the defendant, then by her parents and her sister, who are with us today, sitting over in the front row. Christie and Mary Lynn were so close, they talked every day and met up a couple of times every week. They shared their lives with one another. Murder is a mean, heartless business that strips and abuses so much more than only the person killed. It strips a human being from her loved ones. Mary Lynn and Christie's parents, Liz and Frank Holder, are victims here as well." Wills clicked off the photograph of Christie.

"Now, before the thirteen of us can have our intelligent conversation about the mountain of evidence we've heard, we need to pause and discuss the law that will guide you in your deliberations. Judge Walter has laid out the law, but we need to dig into some of those pieces of the law a bit deeper. The first is the burden of proof that I, as the state's representative, shoulder. Proof beyond a reasonable doubt. That is the burden I bear."

He nodded at the attentive jurors.

"That's right, a burden I shoulder, and that's as it should be in our justice system." Zeroing in on the jurors in the front row center, he continued. "Notice the placement of the word 'reasonable.' Not proof beyond all doubt, not proof beyond a shadow of doubt, but rather, my burden is simply proof beyond a reasonable doubt. A few minutes ago when the judge was giving the instructions, he cautioned that few things are subject to absolute knowledge. That word 'reasonable' is key to my burden of proof. Now, some will say that since Christie's body has not been recovered, that alone creates a reasonable doubt. That which we cannot see, we cannot know."

Wills gave a skeptical shake of his head. "Really?"

He made a brief pause before continuing. "No one came into this courtroom and said they saw Christie's body, so does it follow that her body isn't out there somewhere, well hidden from our efforts to find it? Do we in our everyday lives accept as true beyond a reasonable doubt, things we didn't see, or even that no one else saw?" Wills stepped back, taking in the whole jury. "The other day I found one of my eight-year-old daughter's favorite dolls torn apart in my fenced backyard. Now, I didn't see Charlie, my very territorial eighty-pound Lab, chew up Grace's doll, but since Charlie is our only dog and since he has access to the house and since the backyard is fully enclosed, I knew beyond a reasonable doubt that Charlie was the culprit. Now someone might come along and say, 'Well, no one saw your dog do it, so maybe some other animal, maybe a coyote or a possum, jumped the fence and chewed the doll.' But I live in the middle of a suburban neighborhood with a seven-foot fence, and I have a big territorial dog who constantly patrols the yard, so how probable is that? So, what did my wife and I conclude? Beyond any reasonable doubt, Charlie was the one. We did not see, but we knew." *Nice analogy. Well done.* Wills let that sit for a bit.

"The second piece of law I want to discuss is premeditated murder. This doesn't require much discussion. As Judge Walter instructed, we need to consider whether the killer reflected on the consequences of his killing act. Did the killer plan? Calculate? Scheme? You've heard the evidence. Did Lt. Cort carefully and methodically go about the business of killing Christie, disposing of her body, and then claiming she had run off? I am not going to elaborate on premeditation; you all heard the testimony, heard the motivations—you know the answer."

Wills walked over to his counsel table and took another drink. After glancing at his notes, he moved back to the jurors. "Now that we are squared away on the law, let's turn to the evidence we've all heard."

Pausing and turning to Cort, he said, "Let's start with Lt. Cort." He stared at Cort for a long heavy moment, then said, "He used the knowledge gained as a law-enforcement veteran to commit what he hoped would be the perfect murder. After all, he thought, no body, no conviction. He had learned from those killers who came before him— no body, no conviction. He schemed it well. Preparing a misdirection by staging a scenario in which she would run away, where she could have escaped, even while he kills her, even while he disposes of her body. Let's think about that. He has already projected the image of Christie as an unhappy wife. That is critical to his scheme. He's a bad husband, and that makes her by default an unhappy wife trapped in an abusive marriage. It makes some sense, given the circumstances, that she would run away. Working from that script, he carefully put the pieces together. Let's look at those pieces."

He clicked the controller and, in all caps, **MOTIVE–PROMOTION** appeared. "Some of you have got to be thinking, why didn't he just get a divorce? True? It's common. But we heard some enlightening testimony about divorce within the sheriff's department. If you have aspirations for advancement, your life should be squeaky clean. No divorces. The defendant made a choice between his wife and his career, and we all know how that went. What did Sgt. Ponce tell us? Cort's career was the most important thing in his life." He paused and just shook his head. "Did we hear any evidence to contradict the testimony that he was obsessive about being promoted?"

MacPherson was on her feet. "Your Honor, counsel just engaged in *Griffin* error. That was a comment about Lt. Cort's decision not to testify."

It was a close call. Just as I had earlier suggested to the television audience, prosecutors are absolutely forbidden from commenting on a defendant's failure to testify. Wills was walking a very fine line with a possible mistrial.

Walter overruled the objection without discussion. *The objection at least merited discussion.*

Since Wills had won the point, he reinforced its clout. "No one has contradicted that testimony." A brief pause to make certain the jurors understood its significance. "When you couple his motivation to never allow Christie to divorce with the rest of the evidence we've heard, it's chilling. A life for a promotion."

Wills clicked again. **MOTIVE–THE GIRLFRIEND**. "We did not get a chance to explore much about Cort's other woman. We did get an opportunity to see her, but unfortunately, we did not get a chance to hear from her. We do know that the Cort–Merkle relationship had gone on for a while. Were there promises made? Was she in Cort's long-term plans?" Wills arched his eyebrows and finished his point. "Perhaps we'll never know." A male juror in the back row shifted in his seat and shrugged.

Wills clicked again. **MYSTERIOUS ABSENCES**. "I hope you folks have been thinking about those three early morning Wednesday absences. What were those about? Maybe time with the girlfriend, or maybe time to prepare for the kill? The defendant had a lot to do during the three- to four-hour stretch the night of the killing. I challenge each of you to think about what those absences were about. And to think about the long stretch on the early morning of February 4, the morning Christie disappeared. Short drive home, kill Christie, put her body in her car, dispose of her body in a grave he had already dug, dump the car, ride his bike back home, and return to the station. Do we have any evidence to contradict that scenario?"

MacPherson again objected on *Griffin* grounds and again was shut down by the judge. Wills continued to walk a precarious line.

Click, **TWO YEARS GONE**. "No trace. Nothing. You heard the efforts the police went through, trying to locate Christie. Nothing." Wills took a deep breath. "Nothing, absolutely nothing. No sightings. No passport use. No credit or debit card use. No flights. No car rentals. Nothing. Even if she had run away, Christie had deep connections with her family. You heard how she and Mary Lynn spoke every single day, how they saw each other at least twice a week. How could Christie, after two years, let her loving sister and parents just wonder if she ran off, if she is even alive? Would she do that to them?" A woman juror in the back row, far right, closed her eyes and dropped her head.

Another click, **STAGING THE RUNAWAY**. "Could Cort have manipulated that? Made it appear that she ran off? How easy would that be? Let's see: the $1,900, her passport, her personal items, her car. They all have to disappear to make it look like she ran away. Now the money, the passport, and the personal items are easy enough, but the car is more of a challenge, and he did everything he could to get rid of that car. But cars are big and bulky, tough to destroy, hard to get rid of. And when that car surfaced, the schemer's *perfect* murder began to unravel. Before Christie's car turned up, Lt. Cort had to be thinking, I did it. I got away with it." He took a long pause, letting the point sink in.

Click, **THE NECKLACE**. "This might be one of the most compelling pieces of evidence. What did we hear about that necklace? It was precious to Christie, it was a family heirloom given to her by her mom. She never took it off." Wills stepped back and zeroed in on two front row women jurors. "If she ran off, why was the necklace found in the car? If she ran off, why leave the necklace behind? Wouldn't she take it with her?"

There were several almost imperceptible nods from the two women.

Wills gave them an imploring look. "When you go back into the jury room, please think about that."

Click, **CHRISTIE'S BLOOD**. "Christie's blood is the kicker, isn't it? Her blood, coupled with everything else we learned, is a clincher. Now, we don't know how he killed her. But we can surmise that perhaps Christie fought back. We can also surmise the killing was violent. Did he stab her? Again, maybe we will never know. That blood doesn't fit with the defense's runaway theory. Now, when defense counsel speaks to you, I expect she is going to offer some explanation concerning that blood. But I suggest that you think about that blood in the context of all that we have heard."

Wills turned to point at Cort. "The only person who saw the murder was that high-ranking police official. But even though we didn't see the murder, we know beyond a reasonable doubt that she was murdered, and that he did it. He is clever; he is meticulous. He was counting on committing the perfect murder by getting rid of the body. Call him out, do the right thing, and convict him of first-degree premeditated murder." Wills closed his eyes, dropped his head, and slowly made his way back to counsel table.

Judge Walter: "Thank you, Mr. Wills. We will be in recess until 1:00 p.m., at which time Ms. MacPherson will make her closing remarks."

As we were filing out of the courtroom, Kaye was right on my heels. He gripped my elbow and asked, "What did you think of the prosecutor's closing statement?"

"It was very good." Others near us heard my assessment and nodded agreement.

Kaye remarked, "Did you expect that? Did you think he would do such a powerful close?"

"He's one of the DA's top trial lawyers. He put together a very solid argument."

But Kaye was not finished prodding me. "Several times during your commentary, you were critical of him."

"That's right. There were occasions when I thought he could have done things differently and perhaps better," I replied. "Every trial lawyer has their own style. He displayed a lot of his style and substance during that close." I broke from Kaye and headed down to the cafeteria for a piece of pie, far from his presence.

Trial Tip #6: Closing Argument

Many closing arguments exceed the jurors' ability to remain focused. Shorter and tighter arguments are more apt to keep the jurors on point. Too often, closings veer off into a repetitious rehash of the testimony. Such arguments are condescending to the jurors. It's as if they are incapable of understanding the testimony for themselves. A closing argument that reasons through the evidence, leading the jurors to the advocate's position, is more effective than an argument bombasting the jurors with the advocate's opinions.

CHAPTER 14

MERCI'S CLOSING

"Ms. MacPherson, you have the floor," Judge Walter said, nodding at her.

"Your Honor, counsel," she said, as she dipped her head to Walter and then Wills. She slowly stood and touched Cort on the shoulder as she made her way behind the prosecution table toward the jury. She stopped behind Wills and began.

"You've just heard an excellent closing argument from Mr. Wills." She tapped the back of Wills's chair. "He mustered up everything the state has been able to produce. He did not miss a thing. And yet, as eloquent and comprehensive as his speech was, he was not able to cover up what is lacking." She continued to move toward the jurors. "What is lacking? What don't we know?"

The jurors were riveted by her; we all were—she was hypnotic, almost intoxicating in her confidence and beauty.

"Have we heard anything, other than the passage of time, to conclude that Ms. Cort is dead? Det. Ossoff and her department have done a remarkable job of trying to convince us that she is. Mr. Wills used his impressive list to set forth circumstantial factors. But do any of his points give us confidence that she is dead? And further, that Max Cort killed her?"

She moved to the jury and squared up front and center.

"You will recall when I had an opportunity to question Det. Ossoff. She had a difficult time responding to my question about whether Christie Cort was living in Akron, or, for that matter, Denver, or Salem, or Atlanta. Of course she struggled with that question, just like all of us in this courtroom are struggling with that question. We just don't know."

Several members of the fourth estate around me were arching their necks to keep sight of MacPherson.

"But before we get to the evidence, I want to pause here and comment on Mr. Wills's explanation of reasonable doubt. You all remember his story about his daughter's doll, right?"

Nods from several jurors.

"Did you notice the number of assumptions in his story? He assumed that no other animal could get into his backyard. He assumed that any other animal would have to jump the fence. Now, where I live, we have possums. They look like large gophers, and they like to walk along the top of my fence. If they see something in my yard, they are on it. But the prosecutor did not account for other animals, or even a neighbor's dog, who could have found a break in the fence, or simply dug under the fence. Did Mr. Wills check the integrity of his fence, or did he simply assume, assume, assume? Is it beyond the realm of reason that there could be some other way the doll was damaged? Now, that some other way doesn't even have to be that obvious, but if it could reasonably be found that that's what might have happened, then you have got to shake your head and think. That's what this reasonable doubt business is all about. Is there some other plausible way that doll got chewed up?"

MacPherson took a long pause as she locked onto the three male jurors sitting on the left side of the box in the front row.

"Is there some other way to account for Christie Cort's absence?"

One of the three men arched his eyebrows and gave the slightest of shoulder shrugs.

"I've got a confession to make. I don't know if she is dead. I don't know if she's out there somewhere, living what I suspect is a far different life than she had led before. I just don't know. The sheriff's department has done an admirable job of trying to give us an answer, one way or another. Looking for grave sites, scouring the internet for some evidence that she's alive. But at the end of all their hard effort, we know nothing more than we did when she first disappeared." She hesitated for emphasis. "Let me repeat that. We know nothing more than we did the very morning she disappeared. Nothing."

She worked her way from the three men in the left corner of the jury box to two jurors, a man and a woman, dead center in the back row. She stopped, took them in, and began again.

"I hope and pray that Christie found a way to start her life over. Maybe she connected with someone who helped her. Maybe changed her name, her hair, or the way she dresses. I hope she's out there, that she's happy. Happier than she was here."

There was faint sobbing coming from Christie's mother. With her arm around her mother, Mary Lynn gave MacPherson a steely look.

"I'm not going to go on and on about what else the authorities could have done in their difficult task of locating Christie. I'll leave that to the twelve of you when you have your opportunity to discuss the evidence. Frankly, with your collective wisdom, you will do a better job than I could. But"—she stepped back several feet—"one thing I want to caution you about is allowing any hard feelings you entertain against Max Cort to enter into your discussions. You will recall that during my opening statement, I told you that he is not a good husband. But being a poor husband, even an abusive husband, does not make him a murderer."

She stopped and settled her hands in a prayerful pose, and said, "I'm not going to make a long argument. I don't think it's necessary. You've heard the evidence. You know what is missing. Let me leave you with this. We just don't know. We just don't know if she ran off. She certainly had reason to. And if we don't know—we cannot convict."

MacPherson nodded at the jurors and slowly walked back to counsel table. She patted Cort's shoulder; Cort remained unresponsive, unreadable.

Judge Walter looked at Wills and said, "Mr. Wills, would you prefer to make your rebuttal now or in the morning?"

"I'm prepared now, Your Honor," he responded enthusiastically.

"Very well, Mr. Wills, you may proceed."

With a slap on the table, Wills hustled toward the jurors; he could hardly contain himself. His burst of energy was electric.

"We do know! We know beyond any reasonable doubt."

He had points to make, and he was determined to make them.

"I hope it occurs to you, jurors, that because a murderer is clever, he is more likely to get away with his vile deed. This defendant, a veteran cop, was fully aware that if he could be clever enough to conceal his wife's body, he'd have an excellent chance of committing a conviction-proof murder. We can't reward his carefully planned and executed murder by letting him get away with it!

"There are a couple of points the criminal-defense lawyer made that need to be answered. First, she praised the efforts by the sheriff's team in looking for Christie's body and for their efforts in establishing that she is simply in hiding. But did you notice she never offered, not one time, a comment about what the authorities could have done better? Did that strike you as unusual? This accomplished criminal-defense attorney knows that everything that could have been done, was in fact done. What you heard from her amounted to a concession as to the brilliant job the investigators did."

"Objection!" MacPherson was up. "Improper argument. I made no such concession."

"Overruled," said Walter. "Fair comment at closing argument."

Unruffled, Wills repeated in a commanding voice, "She conceded that the sheriff's department did a brilliant job. Ladies and gentlemen, Christie is not out there somewhere living her life. She is most likely in some unmarked hole in the ground. No marker, nothing to commemorate her life. No memorial service allowing her family and friends to give her a proper goodbye." He paused, and in a very low voice, repeated, "An unmarked hole in the ground."

"Objection!" MacPherson objected angrily. "Counsel is appealing to the jurors' passions; this is unduly prejudicial." *True, but it was also effective.*

Walter nodded and admonished, "Mr. Wills, reel it in."

Wills, undeterred, and without acknowledging the judge's admonishment, shifted to the left side of the jury rail. "Defense counsel tried to turn my daughter's doll story around. Let me just briefly point out that the sheriff's deputies, by going through their exhaustive efforts, were—in the words of counsel—looking for breaks in the fence and were looking for evidence that an animal had dug under the fence. They were systematically eliminating any doubts.

"The criminal-defense attorney said something else that I've got to question. She suggested that you shouldn't take a hard look at the defendant. Specifically, that any problems he had in the past shouldn't be considered against him." He shook his head and zeroed in on those same three men on the left corner of the box. "But why should you ignore it? You can consider his infidelity, his abuse. Isn't there something terribly wrong with a man who strikes a woman? Who cheats on his wife?"

Two of the three looked at Cort; the other looked off.

"Now, I'm not saying that every abusive husband is a potential murderer, but I am suggesting that you can factor in that kind of violence."

"Objection!" Again MacPherson was up. "Your Honor, improper use of character evidence. Move for a mistrial." Wills was on fire and pushing hard against the envelope.

Walter: "Overruled and denied. Mr. Wills, move on."

Wills, ignoring the objection, had not turned from the three men, and he continued. "Bad people are very capable of doing very bad things." He slowly scanned all twelve jurors. "I trust the twelve of you to do the right thing, the just thing. Thanks for your attention."

Walter nodded. "Very well. Members of the jury, I will give my concluding instructions." When he had finished doing so, the jurors left for the jury room to begin their deliberations.

That evening, I returned to the station to give my commentary on the day's proceedings.

Lisbet turned to me, her made-for-TV smile bright on her face. "I'm looking forward to hearing about today's closing arguments. Was Ms. MacPherson her usual brilliant self?"

"She was, but it was the prosecutor who stole the show."

"Really?" She registered genuine surprise.

"The two lawyers took decidedly different tacks in their arguments. Ms. MacPherson's remarks were short and leaned heavily on the no-body theme. She was effective as usual. However, it was prosecutor John Wills who wove together the various aspects of the state's case and tied them together with precision and passion. He called out Max Cort as a schemer, a manipulator, who sacrificed a human life for a promotion. A man intent on committing the perfect murder by cleverly getting rid of Christie Cort's body. Wills hit all the right notes."

Lisbet broke in. "This is the same attorney who you earlier called 'workmanlike?'"

I shrugged my shoulders. "His argument today was compelling. I would say that the highlight was his persuasive list of the incriminating factors pointing toward Cort's guilt."

"A list?"

"Yes, a list which he displayed on PowerPoint. It started with 'Motive–Promotion,' and we know what that was about. His second list point was 'Motive–The Girlfriend,' referring, of course, to Willow Merkle. He also displayed 'Two Years Gone.' And on that point, he not only discussed the length of time Christie has not been heard from, but also that Christie wouldn't leave her parents and sister wondering what had become of her, an excellent point. His list continued with 'Staging the Runaway.' Wills pointed out how easy it would be for Cort to take and dispose of Christie's personal items, making it look like she had run away. Then there was 'The Necklace.' He argued that if Christie had run away, she would have kept the necklace that was so precious to her. He finished with 'Christie's Blood,' as evidence of violence." I paused, then added, "Wills's closing did a thorough job of wrenching the maximum from the evidence produced at trial."

"Sounds impressive."

"It was. But, of course, we do have to factor in that there is still no body. Essentially, the state has two burdens to overcome. First, proving beyond a reasonable doubt Christie is dead. Second, proving beyond a reasonable doubt that Cort is the one who killed her. Despite today's closing argument, no one should underestimate the severity of those two challenges."

"Sounds like the jurors will have their hands full. Will they continue deliberations tomorrow morning?"

"Yes they will."

CHAPTER 15

WAITING

The following morning's swim was interrupted by a Channel 6 reporter and cameraperson. The reporter, dressed to the nines in heels and a pantsuit, was struggling to walk in the sand. She held a microphone while talking to Maribeth, who looked uncertainly in my direction. When the reporter saw me and beckoned me to her, I made no move. She relented and wobbled on her heels toward me.

"Professor Clearwater, good morning. I'm Marie Marney with Channel 6. We got word that you are leading a group of law students on morning swims around the Malibu Pier. How did this get started?"

I shook my head dismissively. "I am not leading anyone. These students found out about my swims and, on their own, decided to join me." My brusque tone should have made it clear that I resented this intrusion into our workout.

"How long has this been going on?" She was oblivious to my irritation.

"A while."

"It looks cold out there. Ocean swimming in March has got to be a challenge."

"Yes," I said, as I stripped down and trotted into the surf. The group, picking up on my cue, followed. When we emerged on the south side of the pier, Marney, or whatever her name was, was there to see us hustle in. She talked to a few more swimmers, and then she and her crew were off to cover some other hard-hitting news—*maybe a Girl Scout cookie sale.*

"Alright," I said, good-naturedly, "who squealed?"

"It was me, Prof." It was one of the student onlookers, a short young man with a bundle of towels in his hand.

"What's your name?"

"Nick Fuller."

"You in my crim class?"

"I am."

"Nick," I said with a grin, "you're up in class today. I hope you've done your reading."

That got an appreciative laugh, especially from Nick.

"I'll be ready, Prof."

The rest of the day dragged on as the jury continued to deliberate. I knew it would take a while to reach a verdict, if indeed a verdict was reachable. But even so, I got a call from the impatient folks at Channel 6 to provide an update.

As Lisbet turned to me that evening, she had a strange, almost mischievous gleam in her eye. She began, "Good evening, Professor. I understand our news crew caught up with you and some of your students this morning."

"Yep," I responded, with no enthusiasm.

When I offered no follow-up, she said, "Let's watch Marie Marney's report this morning from the Malibu Pier."

On the monitor above our heads, Lisbet and I watched a

three-minute clip of my students and me talking about our swims. It concluded with a shot of us jogging into the surf. *This was newsworthy?*

Lisbet smiled and said, "Impressive, Professor Jake."

I nodded but offered no comment.

Lisbet paused, expecting me to comment. When I didn't, she quickly segued. "Turning back to the Cort trial. Deliberations have now gone on for two days. Anything to report?"

"Apparently, one of the jurors fell while returning to court this morning and injured her leg. We were told she required immediate treatment. Fortunately, there are three alternate jurors. Judge Walter swore in one of the alternate jurors, and they continued their deliberations."

"In your experience, does replacing a juror have much of an impact?"

I smiled. "I guess it depends on the juror." I grinned, but when my quip fell flat, I continued. "When an alternate juror is brought in after deliberations have begun, the judge must instruct the whole jury to restart their discussions so that the new juror can catch up. Judge Walter gave that instruction."

"And so they will continue on through the weekend." She paused, then asked, "After allowing both closing arguments to settle in your mind, do you have any further reflections?"

"I've got a few thoughts. Some folks might have thought the closing arguments were too short. In my mind, the brevity by both advocates was in part what made them so compelling. Too often, lawyers at closing arguments go on and on ad nauseum. Too many arguments are simply repetitious and boring, with the jurors losing focus. These two lawyers recognized that most of us have limited attention spans. In my view, a tight, focused argument is most effective. Mark Twain once apologized to a friend for writing a long letter; he explained that he didn't have time to write a short letter.

"Beyond brevity, there were a number of aspects of both closings I appreciated. For instance, Prosecutor Wills's use of PowerPoint to underscore his key points was, in my view, very effective, by first displaying each point to focus the jurors' attention and then following up by discussing that point. Another positive aspect of both closing arguments was the effort by both lawyers to explain reasonable doubt. Reasonable doubt can be an elusive concept. Many people think that the state's burden is to prove the defendant's guilt beyond all doubt or beyond a shadow of a doubt. The prosecutor's use of a story involving how his child's doll came to be chewed up clarified his burden, that he's only required to establish guilt beyond a reasonable doubt. And then Merci MacPherson challenged the story by plugging in alternate scenarios, which crystalized that the defense has no burden whatsoever and is free to posit alternative scenarios. Both lawyers made the most of the evidence produced at trial.

"One last thought—MacPherson's concession that she doesn't know what happened to Christie was brilliant. By conceding, she built up credibility. Admitting her lack of knowledge concerning Christie's fate without playing into the prosecutor's hands placed the defense in a strong position. With that said, this is a tough case. I don't expect a quick decision."

"What can we tell by the length of the deliberations?" Lisbet asked.

"In criminal trials, it is commonly believed that shorter deliberations favor the prosecution. But I've seen it both ways, so I don't put any stock in it."

"Thanks Jake," and with a smile, she added, "keep up those swims."

An inspired motivational attaboy, indeed.

When I returned home, Lisa, Eve, Tony, and Howard were on the deck, sipping from copper mugs.

"Could these be Tony's infamous Moscow Mules?" I asked.

"Indeed they are," Lisa answered, as she rose and handed me a mug of my own. She pecked my cheek and turned to our friends. "Tony is a master mixologist. They do have the kick of a mule."

I gave Eve a cheek kiss and bumped fists with Tony. I took a tentative sip; I had learned to be careful with Tony's potent drinks. This was no exception—the cocktail did have the kick of a mule.

Howard saluted me with his drink. "Jake, you are a natural on TV. You should be doing the Sunday-morning shows instead of me."

"Thanks Howard, but you're so wrong. I know trials, but you, my friend, know pretty much everything else."

Howard grinned and said, "Not everything." *Ever so modest.* He would never admit it, but the historical piece he had recently completed on the relationship between George Washington and Benjamin Franklin was a true masterpiece.

Eve broke in. "We watched the interview with your swim buddies. Pretty cute bunch, fun story. I didn't realize your students had joined you for your ridiculously early and challenging swims."

"Yeah, the whole thing caught me by surprise as well," I said. "It won't last. I'll give them a few more days before they give up."

"I don't know, they looked pretty enthusiastic," she replied.

Howard brought us back to the trial. "I mean it, Jake. You're a natural. I gotta think you wish you were trying this case."

I grinned and asked, "From which side?"

"Either. But I'm thinking as the prosecutor. Cort comes off as such an asshole."

"If I were involved, it would be as the prosecutor. I wouldn't say as much on air, but my take is pretty much the same as yours."

"I figured. Yet, you have been able to thread the needle and not come off as biased toward the prosecution."

I looked at Lisa. *Not everyone is thinking I've been too hard on Wills.*

On Saturday, Lisa and I headed down to Marina del Rey and rented a kayak. We paddled several miles up the marina to Mounce's for lunch and drinks. On the way back, we had to work against the current, pumping our arms in tandem. Lisa pulled her weight the whole way, she was as strong as she was beautiful. On Sunday we slept in, then made slow morning love. We had breakfast at Marmalade and read our books while relaxing on the sand. We made love again that afternoon, and as the sun set, she drove back home.

On Monday morning, I noted the swimmers kept on coming. *Who would have thought?* Over the weekend, Dean Chauncey had sent me an email congratulating me for encouraging our students to exercise. He must have seen the telecast. I replied that this was not the result of my initiative. In a frivolous sidebar, I invited him to join us, but I received no response. When I got home, I called Judge Walter's clerk and asked him to call me with any news.

Tuesday and Wednesday drifted by with no word from the court, but on Thursday morning, I got a call from Judge Walter's clerk. The jurors had come up for air and wanted some testimony read back. The read-back was set for one o'clock that afternoon. I hurried down to the courthouse, curious as to what the jurors were focused on.

The courtroom was sparsely populated. Apparently, word hadn't gotten out about the jury's request, as only Cort and both counsel sat before a largely empty courtroom.

Walter ordered the jurors back into the courtroom. They

looked worn out. They had been deliberating for a week, and their efforts showed on their faces: no smiles, some determination, some exasperation.

Walter read the note the jurors had sent requesting Det. Ossoff's entire testimony be read back. It wasn't difficult to ascertain what they were looking for. They wanted to review the efforts to find Christie or her body. I could divine no clarity as to the tenor of the deliberations.

CHAPTER 16

UNFINISHED BUSINESS

Friday, I received another call from Walter's clerk.

"Judge wants everyone here at three this afternoon."

"Did he indicate if there was a verdict?"

"He was vague, but I don't think so."

Somehow the word got out this time, and the courtroom was packed. And once again I was sitting next to Jeremy Kaye. *My bad luck.*

"Jake, what's your take?" Kaye asked. *What a pest.*

"I have no idea."

"Come on Jake, you're the expert." *Did I mention he was a pest?*

I looked him right in the eyes and, with a note of finality, said, "Jeremy, I have no idea."

He put up his hands, surrendering. "Okay, okay!" *Sometimes you just need to swat the pest.*

We sat in uncomfortable silence for another ten minutes. Finally, Walter emerged and ordered the jury into the courtroom. As the jurors single-filed in, their faces were resigned and disappointed.

I leaned to the pest and whispered, "They're hung."

"What? Hung?"

"No verdict. They're hung up."

"You're sure?"

"Yep. Look at their faces."

When they were seated, Walter asked juror number eight, the engineer, "Madam Foreperson, I read your note. In your estimation, is there any chance that continued deliberation could result in a verdict?"

She stood and said, resignedly, "Unfortunately, Your Honor, we are unable to reach a verdict. We have tried and tried, and taken numerous votes, but we are convinced that we cannot agree on a verdict." There was an audible groan from the assemblage.

Judge Walter, who I suspect was a veteran of such impasses, asked, "Members of the jury, is that the consensus?"

The jurors, to a person, nodded their agreement. Juror number four, a retired postal worker, blurted out, "Judge, we've got several real stubborn people who wouldn't listen to reason! They're responsible for this failure."

Walter stared down the juror and, in a stern voice, chastised him. "Sir, your foreperson should be the only one speaking."

"Sorry, Judge." He dropped his head.

Walter then spoke to the jurors. "Occasionally this happens, that a jury can't agree on a verdict. That's part of the system. You have deliberated better than a week. It is now my duty to declare a mistrial." I snapped my head quickly to catch MacPherson and Cort's reactions. Their heads were together, so I couldn't see MacPherson's face; it was turned toward Cort, whose expression was impenetrable. I could discern no emotion. I would've expected some joy or at least some relief. *He was a cold sonofabitch.*

Walter thanked the jurors for their service and dismissed them with one final instruction: that they were under no obligation to discuss the matter with anyone, though they were free to do so if they so desired. Walter was aware that everyone involved would want to know the numbers for and against conviction.

After the jurors were dismissed, Walter announced that Lt. Cort would continue on bail, and he ordered both sides to return in on Monday, May 16. The time was to allow the district attorney an opportunity to assess whether or not to retry Cort. The ball was once again in DA Haines's court. Would he opt to try Cort again, or was this the end of things? An important factor would be how many of the jurors voted for conviction.

CHAPTER 17

LISA ON THE SAND

"Since it was seven to five for conviction," Lisbet asked that night on the newscast, "won't the DA retry Lt. Cort? A majority voted to convict."

A rival station's reporter got the scoop on how the jurors had split. Although I was sure Lisbet was disappointed to have not gotten to them first, she seemed to be making her peace with it and was incorporating their scoop into her own story.

I nodded. "I imagine the DA will try Lt. Cort again, even though seven jurors is far from unanimous. Seven is not a particularly encouraging showing for the prosecution. Beyond that seven-to-five result, there are a number of other considerations. The obvious and most important is whether prosecuting Lt. Cort could ever be successful. We've talked about the hurdles facing the prosecution throughout the trial. Without a body, a conviction is problematic. Frankly, that Prosecutor Wills got seven jurors to agree with him was rather remarkable."

"I understand it would again be a difficult trial, but what other considerations might factor into the decision?" Lisbet asked.

I hesitated, carefully considering my answer. "First, there is the issue of public perception. Even though it has been years since the DA's office lost some infamous, nationally televised trials, the public's opinion about their work back then has continued to plague how the public views the office. There is still a sense that they have failed in high-profile cases. Perhaps the anxiety that the DA's office might fail again, and in such a high-profile case, would further that negative perception and would reflect poorly on the DA's office. District attorneys are elected officials, and Mr. Haines is up for re-election in less than a year." *I suspect that observation may come back and bite me. But then again, truth is a powerful ally.* "I'm not saying that political calculations will or won't factor in, but it's something that should be part of the public discourse."

Lisbet naively observed, "Surely that won't be the deciding factor. What about Christie Cort? The DA wouldn't have filed in the first place if he didn't believe she was murdered by her husband."

"Lisbet, for what it is worth, I hope and think the DA retries Cort."

Lisbet gave a resigned nod. "Thanks, Jake, for being with us through the trial. Your insight and commentary have been appreciated. Speaking strictly for me, I've learned a lot. We are going to miss your nightly reports"—she paused and smiled—"and lessons."

"It's been my pleasure, Lisbet."

"One more question: if there is another trial, will you agree to provide commentary for us again?"

"Lisbet, as much as I've enjoyed this, I'm through with the commentary business." *A promise is a promise.*

"If there is a retrial, I hope you will reconsider."

What would the DA Haines do? Refile and try again? Or let the disappearance of Christie Cort eventually fade from memory? One look at any social media site would tell you there was strong public sentiment that Haines should order a retrial. If the numbers had been reversed, seven to five for acquittal, the call for a retrial might have been muted. But getting seven jurors left the door slightly cracked.

Could a better prosecutor have prevailed? In thinking through the various aspects of the prosecution's case that could be improved, I went back to the voir dires of both lawyers. MacPherson was personable and charismatic. Wills's effort was workmanlike (wasn't that the word Lisbet had used?). During jury selection, Wills, in my view, made some poor choices, leaving MacPherson with several jurors who seemed defense-oriented. And then there were the opening statements. Opening statements, when predispositions are formed, went decidedly to MacPherson. She planted her theme, largely took Cort's dislikeable conduct off the board, and charmed the jurors. *She* was the face of the defense, not her client. While Wills finished strong with his closing, the juror predispositions were most likely in place and difficult to dislodge. Going into testimony, MacPherson was in control of the trial. Everything triangulated through her. I preached to my students that you need to be the big dog in the courtroom. Merci MacPherson had been the big dog.

Tuesday morning, April 26, I received an out-of-the blue call from DA Haines's office requesting I meet with him Friday afternoon. I didn't know Haines, I had never met him. I asked the administrative assistant if he knew what this was about. He didn't. I agreed to the meeting; why the heck not? I was curious. Only thing I could figure, given the timing, is that it concerned Cort. Since I followed the trial so closely, maybe he wanted my take on whether or how to pursue a second trial. *Should be an interesting meeting.*

That evening, Lisa drove down. She was planning on taking

Wednesday off and spending the day with me. She was curious about my swims with the students and wanted to see for herself. In the morning, she watched as seventeen of us pulled ourselves around the pier, led by Maribeth. As we finished and trotted out of the surf, some of the watchers from the pier were talking to Lisa. She was laughing at the attention. I heard her say to the students, "I just wanted to see this wild pier swim for myself." She then approached Maribeth, the only woman swimmer. "I understand you're in the middle of this. I wanted to meet you."

"Thanks." Maribeth hesitated and said, "I'm sorry . . . I don't know what to call you."

"Lisa St. Marie. Please call me Lisa."

Maribeth smiled, saying, "Oh, you must be *that* Lisa. I can only assume you are the Lisa Professor Clearwater talks about in class from time to time?"

Lisa looked surprised and turned to me, asking, "Have you been talking about me?"

Spreading my hands, I replied, "Only in the most glowing and loving terms."

"It's true," offered Maribeth. "It's sweet what he says." Looking from me to Lisa, Maribeth added, "Nice to meet you in person."

Later that morning, Lisa and I walked into my criminal law class together, and Lisa took a seat off to the side. Despite her best efforts, she proved to be a distraction, especially for the male students. Class went well, and I resisted the temptation to call on her, just for the fun of it. *If I had, I would later pay for that moment of my own amusement.*

After class, we had a couple of eighteen-dollar hamburgers at Geoffrey's, took an afternoon nap, and capped off this memorable day with Tony and Eve at Spruzzo's Restaurant. A perfect day.

As I had promised Dean Chauncey, I spent the following

afternoon working with Pacifico's trial team in preparing for their upcoming tournament. The four members of the team had done a fine job of putting their case together. Over the next couple of days I judged several practice rounds to help polish their efforts. Two weeks later, they advanced from the field of twenty-two teams to the final round. They lost to a school from North Carolina.

CHAPTER 18

INTO THE BREACH

I was ushered into DA Gil Haines's office, located on the ground floor of the Foltz Building. It was spacious, its walls covered in photographs of Haines with recognizable persons, including a former president and three former governors. *Gotta have a glory wall.*

Haines met me at the door and greeted me as if we knew one another. It was Jake and Gil. He introduced me to Nancy Seah, his number two. Word around the campfire was that Seah made the important decisions. Haines was the DA and would occupy the office for several years, but Seah was the office's true constant, having served the last three district attorneys. Haines and Seah made a contrasting pair. He was short, with a Marine sidewall haircut and a polo shirt, casual and relaxed in his position. Seah was several inches taller than Haines and ten years older, with gray-streaked hair pulled into a tight bun at the base of her head.

We sat in a corner, grouped around a table with bottles of water, apples, and cookies. Haines smiled at me and began, "Thanks for coming in Jake. Nancy and I watched some of your commentary during the Cort trial."

"I hope I didn't offend anyone with my comments." I was thinking regretfully about my parting comment on the air about the retrial, when I asserted that the choice could become a political decision.

Seah shook her head. "On the contrary, we found your commentary refreshingly straightforward and honest."

I nodded but didn't speak.

Seah continued, "We also watched the clip of your closing argument up in San Arcadia on the death penalty trial last summer. Pretty impressive."

"Thank you, Nancy."

"Let's get right to it. Gil and I find ourselves in a difficult position. We are going to pursue a second Cort trial but are concerned that we may fare no better the second time around."

I nodded in agreement. "That's a real possibility. No-body cases are tough."

Haines jumped in. "And not just that, but it's a cop as the defendant, with Merci MacPherson. She's a formidable opponent."

"She's a force," I agreed.

Seah leaned toward me, and after a pause, she offered, "Jake, we think, with your presence and trial skills, you can successfully prosecute this case."

"What?" I said, collapsing back in my chair. My hands had shot up—I was stunned! Speechless! I figured I had been called in to offer my opinion on retrying Cort. Not this bombshell!

Haines and Seah shared a glance as they waited for my response.

Finally, I answered, "I'm sorry, but I'm at a loss here." I looked from Seah to Haines. "I thought we were going to talk about strategies for the next trial, if there was even going to *be* a next trial."

Seah raised her eyebrows and grinned. "I can understand your surprise. It is more than a bit unusual to bring in outside counsel."

"I'll agree with that," I said. Haines's and Seah's eyes were locked on my face, waiting for my response. No one spoke until I said, "You have more prosecutors than any DA office in the country. Why not Wills again, or another of your own? I don't understand."

Seah was ready for my reaction. "We have some brilliant prosecutors, John Wills being one of them. But this case, given the lack of a body, a high-ranking cop, and MacPherson, calls for something different. Gil and I think that something different might be you. Like I said, we saw your closing argument from last summer's trial. It was impressive. Further, your commentary during the Cort trial has convinced us that you understand MacPherson's strengths and can hold your own against her."

"I don't know what to say. You've caught me completely off guard." I paused. "You both know, I haven't been a prosecutor for close to five years. I'm a law professor now."

Haines was back, his hands reaching out. "That will not be a problem."

Seah followed up. "If you do come on board, the trial will be this upcoming summer and so shouldn't interfere with your classes."

These two were prepped and ready for anything I could ask. I waited for a moment before responding, "I don't mean any disrespect, and I appreciate the faith you have in my abilities, but this proposal is unsettling. To start with, there may be some resentment among your felony prosecutors about bringing in an outsider. I would be seen as a pariah, an interloper."

Seah retorted, "That's for us to handle, not for you to be concerned with."

"Besides that," Haines followed up, "it's just for one trial."

When I didn't respond, Seah kept pushing, saying, "I think we can make it work. And I appreciate your concern for office morale. But let's not lose sight of the bigger picture. Cort killed his wife, and we need to do something about that. It's our job, our responsibility, to make sure he doesn't get away with it."

Again I leaned back in my chair. "The case still involves all the same problems John Wills confronted in the first go-round. No matter who prosecutes, they could get their butt kicked."

Haines considered that for a moment before he answered. "True enough, but we think you give us the best shot at convicting this wife-killer." He was clearly making a pitch to my humanity, designed to soften my resistance.

I got up and walked across the room. Haines and Seah remained seated. As I paced, I said, "I've never heard of a provision that allows a non-prosecutor to prosecute."

Haines chuckled. "That's because it doesn't happen often."

Seah looked toward Haines, then back to me. "It's simply a matter of hiring you and swearing you into the office. You will once again be a deputy district attorney." She went on, "We think our best chance of success is with you. The areas where MacPherson really got the upper hand were during voir dire and opening statement. And as the three of us know, those are the most-likely times the jurors are forming critical impressions that they will carry throughout the trial. MacPherson got the jump on Wills, and I don't think he ever recovered."

Seah had shifted the discussion away from my decision whether to come aboard to analyzing the trial. Implicitly suggesting I had agreed to come aboard. *There's a reason she's the decision-maker here.*

I smiled, recognizing Seah's effort for what it was, and played along. "That was my take as well. I also think Mr. Wills made several questionable calls during jury selection."

Haines, apparently oblivious to the dance between Seah and me, put up his hands and asked, "Well, Jake, what do you think? Ready to jump onto the big stage?"

I shook my head at his bluntness. "I was on the big stage last summer with the Durgeon trial. Frankly, being a part of an ordeal like that again holds little appeal for me. But I do think Cort killed Christie, and I would like to see him convicted." I closed my eyes, looked down, and finally asked, "When do you need a decision?"

Seah considered my answer. "Let me turn your question around. How much time do you need to decide?"

I resumed my seat, considering. "Give me a week. I've got to think this all the way through."

Haines stood and put out his hand, offering, "You've got my number. I hope you'll come on board, Jake."

It was a Lisa-come-to-Malibu weekend. She called when she was a few minutes out, and I opened the garage door so she could pull her smart little Prius in. I opened her door and pulled her up into a full-body hug. It had only been since Wednesday, but so much had happened that it seemed longer. *Seismic shifts could distort time, and I had experienced a seismic shift.*

"I'm so glad you're here," I said, as we stood in the garage at her open car door. "Before we join Tony and Eve, I've got some startling news."

"What?" She leaned back, concerned. "Tell me. Startling is an ominous word."

"The DA wants me to prosecute the second Cort trial."

"What?" She pushed against my chest to better assess my face. "I don't understand." She was trying to make sense of my statement. "You're not a DA anymore," she said, stating the obvious.

"I know, but they want me to do this. They want to hire me just for this one trial."

She cocked her head, puzzling through the information. Her

hands rested on my chest as she asked, "Is that even allowed? The DA wants to bring you in, make you a prosecutor, and have you try Cort?"

"Exactly."

"When did this happen?"

"This afternoon, just hours ago."

"Just like that, out of the blue, they want you to come in and convict Cort?" She was having a difficult time getting her head around this. *Join the club.*

"That's the idea."

"What did you tell them?"

"That I'll think about it. I have a week to decide."

She grabbed my shirt and pulled me to her, and in an excited voice said, "If anyone can convict that vile, wretched man, you can."

"Now that's a ringing endorsement."

Nodding her head in confirmation, she looked up toward me and affirmed, "I've seen you in trial. I know your capabilities. You can get him. The DA, whatever his name is, is a brilliant person to bring you in."

"Thanks, Ms. St. Marie." I leaned down and kissed her. "Let's join our hosts and share the news." Her enthusiasm helped push me where I wanted to go.

Tony and Eve were equally surprised. Eve's face contorted in anger when she thought about Cort. "Cort is a vicious, murdering so-and-so. I'm glad they're going to retry him and I'm glad you're going to do it."

Tony, a bit more subdued, splashed some cold water on my enthusiasm. "Jake, I know you are good at this, but it's still a tough case. Wills, one of the DA's best, could only muster seven jurors. I worry about what you are walking into."

"Believe me, Tony, I have no false illusions that this will be easy.

But watching Cort's smug face throughout the trial, knowing that he killed his wife, left me unsettled. I have a chance to make this right."

Looking at Tony and Eve, Lisa wrapped her arms around my shoulders, and with profound confidence, said, "You heard him. He's going to make this right."

I tilted my head and kissed her.

Tony broke up the moment. "I caught some glimpses of his lawyer. Quite a looker, and from what you have said in your commentaries, she's a hell of a trial lawyer."

"She is a terrific trial lawyer, and it's not just in the technical aspects of trial. It's her charm, her likability, that sets her apart."

Lisa, not put off by talk of another beautiful, charming woman, responded, "You can be as charming and convincing as anyone I've ever known; you can match her across the board." *Gotta love your cheerleaders.*

Lisa smiled at me again. "Besides, there is one thing she is lacking: angels. There are no angels on her side. You, Jake, will have all the angels."

"Well said, honey," Eve said, and patted Lisa's arm.

"Thank you, ladies. I'm going to need all of those angels."

Tony asked, "When will this go public?"

"I don't know. I'll meet with DA Haines early next week and figure things out."

Tony, again the practical one. "We've got a few weeks of the semester left, and fall classes start in late August—I assume the trial can fit into your teaching schedule."

"I've thought about that. Most likely, the judge will set the trial for sometime in July, and I wouldn't expect it to last any longer than the first trial. Maybe two weeks. Three, tops. The logistics work."

Tony gave an affirmative nod. "Have you thought about what you will do differently than what Mr. Wills did?"

"Yeah, I have. But this whole business has only just begun to sink in. Some ideas occurred to me while watching the trial, and I'm certain others will start crossing my mind. But right now, let's give it a rest for the evening."

Everyone sat back on the spacious deck, with the sun just descending, and enjoyed the view and the wine.

Lisa and I stayed local over the weekend, straying no further than the walk to Marmalade for Sunday brunch. As I read Edward Larson's brilliant *Summer of the Gods* about the *Scopes* trial, I occasionally jotted down some ideas about the upcoming trial. My lack of focus did not do justice to the battle between Darrow and Bryant over evolution. I vowed to re-read the book when I wasn't so distracted.

Tuesday, I was back with Haines and Seah. A phone call wouldn't do—I needed a face-to-face. I think they were somewhat surprised when I accepted their offer. It was decided that Haines and I would appear in court together on May 16 to announce that there would be a retrial of Cort and that I would be the prosecutor. However, before things were formalized, I had some conditions: First, I would be permitted to bring on Steve Duke as my investigator. After I explained who Duke was, they agreed. Second, that I would be allowed to expand the search parameters beyond the five-mile radius surrounding the Cort residence. That was a money issue, but Seah said she could make that happen. Third, that John Wills would work the case with me.

That caught them both off guard. Seah looked at Haines, then pursed her lips. "I'm not so sure about that. Gil, your thoughts?"

Haines sat back and considered, looking at me. "We're turning this trial over to you. You make the decisions. We'll agree to your terms, with one caveat. You're lead, and you conduct voir dire and do the opening."

"Of course." I nodded. "And finally, I will need to hire a jury-consulting firm to assist with voir dire, jury selection, and case theory." That was also a money issue.

Seah, who I knew would be the one to answer, balked at the consulting firm. "Jake, we've never spent money on a consulting firm. I'm reluctant to do so now. Makes us look like we're stooping to defense tactics."

I was firm. "Nancy, MacPherson used one during the first trial and got five jurors. I understand your hesitancy, I know these outfits are expensive, but they can be extremely effective. I don't want to cede MacPherson any advantage. Besides that, without the firm, I'm out." *Hardball.*

She glanced at Haines with a resigned look and relented.

CHAPTER 19

LISA'S SHOW

The weekend before Lisa's art show, I helped her crate twenty-six watercolor paintings for shipping up to Carmel. It was an intricate process; we were dealing with paintings which would sell in the five figures. When we got to the painting of the two of us walking toward the pier, I asked how much she thought it would command at the show.

"Julia and I are thinking twenty thousand."

"Twenty grand, huh?"

"That's what we're listing it for."

"So some one-percenter is going to have this work, which is so precious to you and me, hanging in their home?"

Lisa stopped packing and turned to me. "Yeah, I guess that's the point. Jake, that's one of the reasons we are having the show," she said, as she cocked her head and gave me a questioning look.

"I'll buy it. Don't even ship it."

She put down her hammer and walked over to me. "You're the dearest man." She kissed me, and then, holding me at arm's length, said, "First off, that's a lot of money. Second, I will paint another and just give it to you."

"I don't want another. I want this one," I said stubbornly. "You told me it was inspired by our love. That can't be reproduced."

Another long kiss. "Okay, Jake, I'm giving it to you right now."

"No. The gift was your inspiration. Twenty grand is only money. Anything worth having is worth working for." *Maybe I could work out a payment plan.*

She relented and gave me a wrap-around-my-torso hug. "I love you, Jake."

The following Saturday morning, we drove the 101 to Carmel. A pleasant drive, it took us a bit over four hours. We arrived with plenty of time to check into our hotel, change, and then take the short walk to the studio before the show.

Julia, agent extraordinaire, was in charge, and everything was set. There was a three-by-four-foot placard at the entrance with Lisa's photograph and comments by several prominent art critics praising her work. The theme was oceanscapes, and the centerpiece was my painting, with a small card indicating it had already been sold. Since Lisa and Julia had planned on it being a focal point of the show, it still had to make an appearance, although a no-longer-for-sale appearance.

The show began at six, as a three-piece ensemble played subtly off to the side. There were servers passing through the crowd, offering champagne and hors d'oeuvres. There was a sizable crowd of art collectors, curators, and the curious, all of them talking and admiring Lisa's work. I walked and mingled as Lisa moved gracefully from group to group, from person to person. She was the star of the night, so everyone craved her attention. It was a well-turned-out crowd with loose checkbooks. Several of the guests were disappointed that *my* painting was already sold. One fellow, an old movie star who was still starring in and directing films well into his eighties, asked Lisa if the buyer of the painting would entertain an offer. She told him the buyer was not open to negotiation. He smiled and bought two other paintings.

Lisa found the recognition she was hoping for. One Bay-Area art critic pronounced Lisa's show a "resounding success." Another praised her as an emerging talent on the national scene. But I knew that no one loved her work like I did, because no one else could love her more.

CHAPTER 20

SWORN IN

As planned, I was sworn in as a deputy district attorney and made my first appearance with DA Gil Haines on May 16. Judge Walter's courtroom was once again at capacity. The decision to retry Cort had not been made public, and the public wanted to know. I caught a number of looks as I walked into the courtroom with Haines. Merci MacPherson noticed my appearance and gave me an appraising look. I suspected she knew who I was from my TV commentary.

Judge Walter called court to order and looked surprised to see Haines making a rare court appearance. District attorneys seldom go to court. In most large counties, they are represented by their deputies. A rare exception had been John Tice up in San Arcadia County. Tice had been my adversary in the Durgeon trial. I admit that I admired Tice's active involvement in actually trying cases. Might be the only thing I admired about Tice.

"Mr. Haines, it is a pleasure to have you in my courtroom," said Walter, at his most courteous.

"Thank you, Your Honor. It is a pleasure to be here. Let me introduce Jake Clearwater, who has just recently joined our office."

Walter studied me. "Mr. Clearwater, weren't you in the press section for the Cort trial?"

"I was, Your Honor." I was surprised that he had noticed me.

Turning back to Haines, Walter asked, "Mr. Haines, will there be a retrial in the Cort matter?"

"Yes, Your Honor, and Mr. Clearwater will be the lead prosecutor."

Walter paused and zeroed in on me. He wore his skepticism openly. He had to sense something was up when Haines introduced me. "I see." He looked down at his calendar and said, "Very well. I'm looking at July 18, which is a Monday, to begin trial."

MacPherson stood with her calendar in hand. "Your Honor, I'm conflicted on that date. I ask that we push the trial back a week until July 25."

Walter made a point of looking at Haines and avoiding me. "July 25 agreeable with the state?"

Haines replied, "Yes, Your Honor."

"Alright, I'll set July 11 for all motions to be filed, and July 19 to hear motions. Is that acceptable to both sides?"

Haines and MacPherson orally acknowledged the court.

"Then, we are adjourned. I will see counsel in chambers."

Walter took off his robe as we took seats. He turned toward Haines. "Gil, please explain to me what's going on." Without explanation, it was clear he was referring to my involvement.

With just a note of irritation, Haines replied, "Mr. Clearwater is an experienced trial attorney and a former prosecutor. He's more than qualified to represent the office."

Annoyed, Walter waved off the response.

"That's not what I'm talking about. How long has he been a

deputy in your office?" I didn't like being talked about in the third person. *But this wasn't my scuffle.*

Haines's voice dropped almost to a growl. "With all due respect, that is my affair and not the court's."

The pleasantries between Haines and Walter just moments earlier in open court appeared to have masked over some preexisting mutual disdain.

"Don't be impertinent." Walter leaned over his desk at Haines, jabbing his finger. "The whole city will once again be watching this trial. We don't need any shenanigans." *Shenanigans?* "And now you bring in a new deputy?" Walter punched the word *new* to drive home his point.

"Are we through here?" Haines said as he stood.

Following a deep breath, Walter conceded. "Very well, but I'll be watching your *new* deputy very carefully."

As we stood, MacPherson interrupted the heated exchange, asking, "May I speak, Your Honor?"

Walter heaved a sigh and worked to settle himself. "Of course you can, Ms. MacPherson."

"I'm putting the court and prosecution on notice that I may bring a change-of-venue motion. I don't want to surprise anyone."

"Noted. Anything further, Ms. MacPherson?"

And in a light, cheery tone, which did nothing to dispel the rancor in the room, she said, "Nothing further, Your Honor."

As we left the chambers and walked through the courtroom, I stuck my hand out to MacPherson. She smiled and shook my proffered hand firmly. "Mr. Clearwater, nice to meet you. I feel like I already know you from watching your commentary. You were very kind with your observations of my efforts."

"Ms. MacPherson, your efforts were worthy of my praise." I nodded and smiled.

She gave me a dazzling smile in return. "See you in court, Mr. Clearwater." *How civilized.*

As I exited the courtroom, I was met by several reporters curious about my status as the new Cort prosecutor. I referred the inquiries to Nancy Seah and climbed into an elevator.

Once word got out that I was to prosecute Cort, the LA media descended with interview requests. Lisbet Boget herself—not some intermediary or her boss, Kaye—called and asked me to come onto her nightly newscast. "Jake, it would be a boon to me professionally if you would let me interview you."

"Lisbet, I'm nearing the end of my semester. I've got final exams to write and grade. It just isn't practical to drive downtown right now." *And beyond that, I was through with the whole television thing.*

She didn't hesitate, and offered, "I completely understand. Instead of you coming to me, I will come to you."

She had me. I had given her an opening, and now I was trapped. "What do you have in mind?" I asked, suspecting the answer.

"My crew will come to Pacifico, and I'll interview you there."

I grudgingly laughed and told her to set it up with the school.

By Monday afternoon, Lisbet and her crew were already set up in Pacifico's trial courtroom when I stepped into the room. Word had gotten out, and the gallery was packed with students. Lisbet and I were perched on stools in front of the jury box as she got underway.

"We are inside the trial courtroom at Pacifico Law School with Professor Jake Clearwater. Professor Clearwater, though a full-time law professor, has agreed to step aside from teaching law to practice law. He will be the lead prosecutor in the retrial of Lt. Max Cort for the murder of his wife, Christie Cort."

She then turned to me. "Professor, just a few weeks ago you were doing commentary on the Cort trial right here on Channel 6. Now you find yourself as the prosecutor for the retrial. How did this come about?"

"It's not really complicated," I responded. "DA Haines contacted me and inquired about whether or not I'd consider coming on board for the retrial. I was, and frankly continue to be, a bit surprised, but after considering his request, I agreed."

"You say it wasn't too complicated. But I've learned from a number of sources that it is extremely unusual for an outside lawyer to be brought in to prosecute a case."

"It is unusual. But I'm pleased to be in a position to try and help out."

"I understand you are doing this without pay."

I gave a non-committal nod. "I have a full-time job which I'm very happy with. This is not about money. This is about doing something for my community." *How noble was that?*

"As I understand, you had to be sworn in as a deputy in the DA's office."

"That's right. So, to an extent, this is a return to my roots as a prosecutor. As you know, I began my legal career as a prosecutor up north in San Arcadia County."

Lisbet nodded and continued, "As a commentator during the first Cort trial, you had an opportunity to watch and evaluate the trial very closely. What will you do differently in attempting to convict Lt. Cort?"

I smiled at Lisbet. "It's too early to get into specifics. Let me just say, Mr. Wills and Ms. MacPherson both provided excellent advocacy during the trial. As for my preparation, I will study their efforts in an attempt to convince twelve jurors to agree with me."

"As a commentator, you were particularly impressed and complimentary of defense counsel Merci MacPherson."

"Ms. MacPherson, as those of us in attendance saw during the trial, is a superb advocate. It will be a challenge to go against her. But, this isn't just about the lawyers—this is about the evidence. I believe there is sufficient evidence on the prosecution side to get the job done."

There was a smattering of applause from the gallery. Then one student shouted, "Get him, Prof!" to further applause. I motioned with my hands for the crowd to be quiet, and they fell into whispers as we continued the interview.

Lisbet acknowledged the interruption. "Professor, you seem to have accrued quite the following here at the school."

I nodded in agreement. "This case has generated a lot of interest, not only with the public, but, as you can imagine, also with these law students. After the mistrial, there was some real frustration on campus, as I suspect there was in the general population."

"There's been some speculation that Judge Walter was not very pleased that an outsider was being brought in for the retrial. Can you confirm that?"

"Lisbet"—I pulled a face—"you know better than to ask such a question. Let me say this: Judge Walter is a consummate judge. He will go about his duties in a professional manner." *She deserved my rebuke.*

With a chastened look, Lisbet moved on. "Switching topics, this is a beautiful courtroom you have here at Pacifico. I take it this is where you train your students to become the next generation of trial lawyers?"

"It's state of the art. I'm fortunate to have such an amazing place to teach."

"Professor Clearwater"—she paused and smiled—"Jake, thanks for allowing me to interview you. We will be watching the retrial very closely. Good luck."

"It's been my pleasure. Lisbet."

CHAPTER 21

GATHERING MY TEAM

Classes had wound down. I had some fun writing my criminal law final. It involved a murder case without the victim's body and was chock-full of issues, it would serve as a real challenge for my students. Tough final-exam questions help separate the truly gifted from the merely capable and the "you should quit law school and pursue some other endeavor."

The final exam in my trial advocacy class was a full mock trial. Each trial was limited to four hours. Not surprisingly, Earl and Joanna were the standout advocates. Despite delivering her daughter three weeks earlier, Joanna didn't miss a beat. Her husband sat with the newborn in the gallery and watched.

Two weeks after my criminal law final, I had the exams graded. I had never before been so prompt. But then again, I had never before had to prepare to prosecute a no-body murder case before.

I assumed Judge Walter would make the same rulings as he had during the first trial. The one variable that could change our course was MacPherson's potential change-of-venue motion. Given the coverage of the first trial and the attendant commentary following the verdict, I was of the mind that Walter might be more receptive to a change of venue this time around. I wasn't particularly concerned; if the case was moved out of the county, I could live with that.

My first order of business was to retain the services of Steve Duke. Nancy Seah had reluctantly authorized $200 an hour for an outside investigator, plus lodging near the courthouse. She was reluctant because of the cost, yes, but more so because she feared that hiring an outside investigator displayed a lack of confidence in the sheriff's personnel who had been working the case. I countered by suggesting that since the defendant was with the LA sheriff's department, having an investigator from outside the department could dispel any concerns about this being an insider investigation. I also assured her that Det. Ossoff, in particular, would still be an integral part of my team. My argument proved persuasive, and our deal with Duke was set.

June 20, five weeks from trial, Duke was right on time. Same ol' Duke, with his buttons strained across his middle, his graying crew cut straight out of the '50s. His big smile and man hug greeted me around noonish at a Mexican restaurant roughly halfway between our homes. I had called Duke and told him that his $200 hourly rate had been approved, and I explained that I needed him in LA. We settled in, a Bud for Duke, a margarita for me. "How long's it been, Jake?"

"Too long. Not since Durgeon, last summer."

"We had quite a ride during Durgeon. I've been in tough trials before, but Durgeon was the one." He squinted at me, fighting the sun. "Speaking of that asshole, have you heard from him?"

"I get an occasional letter. You'll be pleased to know that our favorite felon informed me that he is keeping his nose clean while doing his four years in a Utah joint." Even though Durgeon had been acquitted of the double murder charges, he had been convicted of burglary. California had relinquished its hold on him, allowing Utah to violate his previous kidnapping parole and serve out his time in Utah.

"What a miserable excuse for a human being." Duke was not a member of the Duane Durgeon marching and chowder society. *Not many people were. In fact to my knowledge, no one was, and I think that might even include his mother.* "Let's hope that sonofabitch stays out of California after he's released and once again free to wreak havoc." Duke shook his head at the thought of a freed Durgeon. "There's no way he stays out of trouble." He took a healthy swallow of beer to wash away the foul taste of Durgeon. He set down his drink and refocused on me, asking, "How's Lisa?"

"Couldn't be better. She's the one, Duke."

He leaned back with an indulgent grin. "I hope you realize you are batting way above your average with her. You are a .220 hitter, and she's a Cy Young candidate."

"I'm keenly aware of that."

We drank to my wonderful fortune. "Give her my best." He hesitated, then with a questioning look asked, "How long have you two been copacetic?"

"Copacetic?" I grinned at the word. *We were far beyond copacetic.* "Better than a year and a half."

"I'm pleased for you, Jake." Then another change of direction— Duke's mind was kicking it. "What eventually happened to Dan Atwell?"

Following the Durgeon trial, we found out that Atwell had actually committed the murders for which Durgeon had been acquitted.

"Tice opted to not try him for the murders. Guess he figured that since he went all-in on Durgeon as the murderer, he would look bad if he went after Atwell for the same murders."

"Aw . . . a fragile ego." Duke chuckled. "The backbone of Tice's chicken-shit character." We both took long drinks, thinking through Tice's character. In our early days, Duke as a DA investigator and me as a DDA, we had worked under Tice, and we both had a hardened disdain for him.

"As I'm sure you can imagine, what a joy it was to be a witness for Tice in Atwell's trial for trying to kill Lisa, Suzelle, and me."

During the waning days of the Durgeon trial, Atwell had rammed his car into the one Lisa, Suzelle, and I were in. He had a gun but fortunately was thwarted before he could get to us. I reminisced with Duke how difficult we made Tice's life back then. The three of us refused to show up for witness prep. Tice threatened, yelled, and screamed, but we called his bluff. I smiled at the memory.

"We did show up for trial, though, and Atwell went down hard—fifteen years. I have to say, I was the most cooperative amongst the three of us. The fireworks were primarily between Suzelle and Tice. You should have seen Suzelle testify. She was barely able to be civil, and she made Tice work for every point." Duke belly laughed and almost choked on a loaded nacho. He recovered and gave a wicked grin. "Love that girl. Lots of spunk." He tipped his Bud to me. "I figure you're still in touch with her—she's a keeper."

"Of course I am. Saw her a couple of weeks ago. She got her first acquittal as a deputy public defender. It's a job she was made for, and she's very happy."

Duke loaded another nacho and leaned forward to avoid spilling any salsa on his shirt. "Love that girl." He repeated. "I need to give her a call." He put down his beer and pulled his chair closer to the table. "Now, let's get down to it. Exactly what have you gotten yourself into?"

"Like I told you during our call, I've been drafted to prosecute a cop for killing his wife."

"I get that, but what's so special about this case that one of the hundreds of LA prosecutors couldn't do it?"

"There's no body."

That made him sit back up. He knocked back half his beer and ordered another. After another overloaded chip, some of which landed on his shirt, he exclaimed, "No body! The sonofabitch cop got rid of the body?"

"Yep. Makes for a hard trial. First trial ended up seven to five for conviction."

"I'm surprised the prosecutor got seven. You sure there's a body out there somewhere?"

"I am, and Duke, I'm going to get him. But I need help."

"You got it. What do you need from me?" *Not even a pause to consider.*

"For starters, I need to turn the defendant's life inside out. I've got some dirt on this guy, but I need more." I sipped my margarita. "I can't think of a better guy to find anything we could use on this scumbag than you. But it's going to be a challenge—he's a ranking cop, so folks may be reticent to offer any dirt on him. I trust you can handle it, because after you dig up what you will, I'll need you with me."

"Sounds like I've got my work cut out for me." He smiled. "When do we get going?"

"I could use you in a couple of days, if you can swing it."

"I can."

Over a couple of combination plates, I filled him in on the case. He had lots of questions. Good questions. We then discussed hotel arrangements and agreed to meet up the following week. It felt reassuring to have Duke with me.

After Duke, the next person I contacted was Marge Abbott, the founder and CEO of Trial Advocates. Abbott's company was one of the premier jury-consulting firms in Southern California, and Abbott was not only a pioneer in the field, but, by the reckoning of most trial advocates, the best in the business. She and I had clashed while I was still a prosecutor in San Arcadia. It was toward the end of my first year as a deputy DA. I was still cutting my teeth on a steady stream of misdemeanors: lots of drunk driving, petty theft, and some domestic violence cases, the typical menu for baby prosecutors. Abbott had been retained by Todd Hatch, a character actor who was in Tom Hanks's platoon in *Private Ryan*. Hatch feared that a conviction for beating on his girlfriend would damage his career. *Probably true.* He authorized his lawyer to hire Abbott to fend off conviction. It was my first trial involving a jury consultant.

As with so many domestic violence cases, the victim, Hatch's battered girlfriend, was uncooperative and refused to testify against her abuser. She told my investigator that Hatch never laid a hand on her. She tried to convince him there had been a heated argument, but nothing more. She also explained that she and Hatch were still living together and that everything was fine—this, despite the body-worn video from the responding officer showing bruising on her face and her statements to the responding officer that Hatch had struck her and even threatened to kill her. I understand the reluctance of so many battered women to testify against their abuser; it was heartbreaking to witness their angst. Nonetheless, these abusing cowards are assholes, and as a prosecutor, I knew we needed to go forward with the prosecutions, often against the will of the victim. *Tough cases, but not impossible ones.*

Following the testimony of the responding officer, I called the victim. As anticipated, she denied that Hatch had struck her. She explained that she had been angry with him and made up the allegations. The bruises, she testified, were from several recent falls. *Mere coincidence that she kept falling right around the time of the Hatch incidents.* She sobbed and, through tears, told the jurors that she loved him and wanted to marry him. *It wasn't hard to figure how such a marriage would end.*

It was time to instill some plain old honesty to the proceedings. I started by confronting her with the video and her statements to the police. According to her, the police were lying. She doubled down on the "fall" scenario. When I questioned her about bruising on both sides of her face, she broke down again and cried. *Right on cue.* Under California law, her previous statements were not only admissible to impeach her testimony but could be used by the jurors as substantive evidence. In other words, the defendant could be convicted solely on the victim's prior statements.

Yet, despite the fact of her less-than-credible testimony, the jurors deliberated three days before calling it quits. They were eight-to-four for conviction. In speaking to several of the jurors following the trial, my concerns about their reluctance to convict were borne out. Some cited that the couple was not married ("So what did she expect?"), that the defendant seemed charming and likable ("He didn't even testify"), and finally, that the couple appeared to have mended their problems and were back together ("She loves him and didn't want him convicted"). I was not terribly surprised (though frustrated) by the comments and the hung jury. I had been warned by some of the veteran prosecutors that these kinds of cases were the most difficult to successfully prosecute. And Marge Abbott had brilliantly guided defense counsel through jury selection. My boss, over my protest, opted to not retry the case. Hatch was free to go about his career. I hoped that his film career would flop. He had earned my scorn, asshole that he was.

Curious, I called Marge Abbott several days after that trial and complimented her on her successful defense. I was impressed with how she had engineered a hung jury. I became a believer that there was something to this jury-consulting business. Abbott and I struck up a friendship and later, after I moved on to Pacifico, we coauthored a law review article on the benefits of jury consultants.

Abbott agreed to meet me next week to discuss coming on board.

I next reached out to John Wills. We set up a meeting in his office. He greeted me cordially, though a bit awkwardly. It would be no surprise if he had felt passed over and disrespected, now that he was not the prosecutor trying Cort again. Still, he understood that the decision was not mine, and so remained professional. I was impressed, because he was even able to ignore one of the rhinos in the room—namely, my TV commentary criticizing some of his efforts during the last trial. My hope was that he had been too engaged in the trial to bother with outside commentators. I complimented him on his fine closing argument.

He grinned, patted his hands on his desk and said, "Thank you. Though perhaps you weren't such a fan of some other aspects of my efforts?" *Perhaps he had been watching some television.*

I shrugged. "We've all got our styles. I would have done a few things differently, perhaps during jury selection."

Defensively, he answered, "Jury selection, especially in this case, was a crapshoot."

"Absolutely," I agreed. "The number of variables was difficult to figure. But everyone knew going in that you were in a tough spot—what with a cop defendant, no victim remains, and MacPherson."

"Yeah, you saw her." He grinned. "Pretty impressive."

I nodded in agreement. "Mr. Wills, let me tell you why I wanted to meet you. I'm hopeful that you will lend me your experience in trying Cort. Would you sit second chair with me? I'm going to need all the help I can get."

He gave me a peculiar look and finally said, "Second chair?"

I nodded.

"I've never sat second chair to anybody." He pulled a skeptical face. "Is Haines aware of what you're proposing? I didn't think they wanted me anywhere near this."

"He's aware but this is entirely my idea. Haines will have no problems, if you were so inclined."

He stood and walked to the window facing city hall. "How would that work, me being second chair?"

"We would work that out. I imagine we would split up the direct exams."

"You'd do the speeches and voir dire?"

"Probably, and we would consult on jury selection." I paused and shrugged. "And you handle all the media stuff," I joked. Some lawyers, maybe Wills, liked the media spotlight. I shunned it. There was a long stony silence. Wills didn't see the humor about the media comment. *Maybe it wasn't funny.*

"I've been trying felony cases for better than fifteen years," he said skeptically. "It would be strange to be second fiddle. And to be completely honest, awkward. Maybe even a little humiliating." Shaking his head, he said, "I don't think so."

"I get that. But, on the other hand, we both believe Cort needs to go down, and the chances of convicting him improve with your experience and knowledge of the case." I paused before admitting, "You would be taking one for the team."

"Taking one for the team," he echoed and cocked his head. "I don't mean for my ego to get in the way. But there it is, right smack dab in the way." Another long silence while the wheels were rolling around in his head. "I've dedicated my career to pursuing justice, doing the right thing. This guy Cort is an evil man. He needs to be in a cage." Musing aloud, perhaps only to himself, he continued, "And maybe the only way that is going to happen is if I take one for the team." He stood and stepped to the side of his desk, and with a determined look pounded his fist into his open palm. "You seem like a decent guy, Clearwater, and your appeal to my sense of justice really hits home."

"Does that mean you're in?"

"Yeah. Second fiddle."

I was astonished that he agreed. Had our roles been reversed, I'm not certain I could do what he was agreeing to do. Here really was a champion of justice, a person willing to sublimate his ego for the greater good. "It's a relief to have you on board."

He let out some breath and smiled. "It might take both of us to hang with Merci, who incidentally is a genuinely nice and thoughtful person."

"That's what it looked like from the gallery. We'll get deeper into things later on, but I'd like to start by you sharing what didn't come in during the trial, and more importantly, your impressions. As we both know, there is the public face of the trial, then there are the machinations behind the scenes that are not evident to those of us on the outside."

"Impressions?" He appeared to be reflecting as he resumed his seat and turned to put a K-cup into his Keurig. Still thinking about my question, he asked if I wanted a cup. I nodded.

"Impressions," he repeated. "Cort did it. There is no doubt in my mind that he killed her. That sonofabitch is clever and somehow managed to get rid of her body. As for other impressions, not anything that jumped out. The cross of the sister was rough, that's on me. She's got to be better prepared next time." He handed me a cup and inserted another pod.

"She got pretty beat up," I agreed. "We're going to have to work with her. We also need to suggest to Det. Ossoff better answers to the 'she's not living in Akron' question."

Wills laughed and said, "Merci's cross was pretty effective. And she stepped on it again at close." He retrieved his cup and took a sip.

"She did, but John, you more than held your own on closing."

He acknowledged the compliment with a shrug. "Wasn't good enough, though."

We sat and drank our coffees before I threw another wrinkle at him. "I've been authorized by Nancy Seah to hire a jury consultant for the retrial."

He looked impressed. "No way she would have greenlit that for any of us mere mortals."

"I know. I made it a condition of my employment."

"You've obviously got more juice than the rest of us. For my two cents' worth, jury consultants are bullshit." He picked up a baseball from his desk and began squeezing it. "Call me old school, but I'll take my chances with picking jurors built on years of trying cases."

"I hear you, but I figure this is the last shot at Cort. If this hangs again, Cort walks." I cocked my head. "MacPherson has a consultant. Let's fight fire with fire."

He continued kneading the baseball and then passed it from one hand to the other.

"Lucky ball?" I asked.

"Caught it while sitting in the left field pavilion. Justin Turner. A three-run shot."

"On the fly or after a scramble?"

"On the fly. No glove." He took another sip and smiled.

"Impressive," I said. He flipped the ball to me. I caught it with my free hand, nearly spilling my coffee.

Fingering the ball, I asked, "Would you be willing to sit through the recordings of the examinations of the witnesses? I would like for you, me, Ossoff, an outside investigator I'm bringing in, and our jury consultant to watch the exams, especially MacPherson's crosses. I figure we could better prepare our witnesses now that we know MacPherson's approach."

He considered that, nodded, and said, "Not a bad idea. Especially watching her crosses. Like you said, when she asked Ossoff if she was sure Christie wasn't living in Akron, Sherri was scrambling."

"Yeah." I said. "Since we are going to be in the trenches together, first names work."

"Okay Jake, I'm in. I better clear the time with Seah, so she can clear my trial calendar. Reviewing those exams is going to take a while."

"Oh, one more thing," I said. "Is there a vacant office near you that I can inhabit? I meant to ask Seah but forgot."

"I'll check and get back to you." We stood and shook.

That went better than I could've imagined.

CHAPTER 22

FANCY DIGS

I arrived at the posh office of Abbott and Associates on the thirty-second floor of the west tower in Century City for my lunch meeting with Marge Abbott. The expensive office was testament to the fact that jury consulting was no longer a fringe specialty but had evolved into an essential component of high-profile, high-stakes trials. Big firms trying multi-billion-dollar cases wouldn't dare go into the breach without a Marge Abbott on their side. Even so, consultants were not as frequently retained in criminal trials. Most defendants could not afford them, and prosecutors (present situation notwithstanding) rarely used them.

Abbott came to reception and guided me to her spacious corner office. Through the floor-to-ceiling fifteen-foot windows, I could see the Santa Monica Pier five miles off and Santa Catalina Island on the horizon.

Abbott was a petite woman with stylishly short hair and wearing a smart pantsuit. She was a pioneer in her business. She had five associates, and she was circumspect in the clients her firm agreed to take on. Her fees were otherworldly ($800 an hour), but the results typically justified the cost. I told Nancy Seah I would ask for the prosecutor discount, appealing to Abbott's sense that the Cort prosecution was in the public interest. Through emails, Abbott—who had watched the recordings I sent her of the voir dire, jury selection, and opening statements—had agreed to reduce her fees to $500 an hour. *Hell, practically minimum wage.*

"Jake, it's nice to see you in person. I'm tired of having our interactions reduced to texts and emails." She motioned me to a table at one of the windows, laid out with an assortment of sandwiches.

"I couldn't agree more." I took a seat. "Quite the view, Marge. I could get used to this."

She took in the view and pondered, "Isn't it strange? When something beautiful like this becomes an everyday part of your life, you tend to take it for granted."

"I hear that. I've got an ocean view from my office at Pacifico, and most of the time, I don't even bother turning around to glance at it."

"As you can see, I ordered some sandwiches from the deli downstairs. Chicken or beef?"

"Chicken works, thanks, Marge."

We sat, she poured iced tea, and I got right to my first question. "Have you ever worked a case involving Merci MacPherson?"

"No. But in addition to watching the recordings you sent me, I've called around to some other consultants to get a bit of a perspective on her. Apparently, she's quite a handful."

I nodded and grinned. "She's at least a handful."

Abbott took a delicate bite and dabbed at her mouth.

"So how do we beat her?" I asked.

She laughed. "So much for the preliminaries, Jake."

"I apologize, I'm just eager to hear your take."

"Okay. Let's get to it. I see four primary challenges. First, MacPherson is smart, gorgeous, and charming. It's a given that most of the men and some of the women on the jury will fall in love with her. Second, she is a very talented trial lawyer. Even without the looks, the clothes, and the charm, she knows her stuff. Third, Max Cort looks like a thirty-five-year-old Clint Eastwood. Looks matter, and as he seems to have the good sense to stay quiet, so far, his movie-star face is all our jury really associates with him. Finally, there is no body or victim we can point to. And that, my friend—I don't need to tell you—is the kicker."

"Lots of challenges. I'm not surprised that you zeroed in on the personal aspects of MacPherson and Cort. They make a handsome couple." I grinned and took another bite of my sandwich.

"I'm being serious, Jake; never underestimate the personal appeal of the primary players. Those two are going to be sitting and interacting in front of our jurors for days on end. Like I said, looks matter. Charm matters." She took another dainty bite.

I shrugged at the assessment, sipping my tea.

"Now that we've got a snapshot of the foe, let's focus on our assets," Marge continued.

"Okay."

"First, you are a very good trial lawyer." When I didn't respond, she went on, "Don't forget, I watched you try that domestic violence case years ago, and I came away very impressed." Nodding at me, she went on, "And correct me if I'm wrong, but you weren't even that experienced at the time. Your natural instincts were sound. You can hold your own against MacPherson."

"I hope you're right."

"Jake, no time for modesty. You know you are a superb trial lawyer. The DA wouldn't have brought you in if that wasn't true. So get over yourself." Abbott was direct. *At $500 an hour, direct was good.*

I put up my hands, fending off the admonishment. "Okay, so let's move along to the Cort/Eastwood concern. I gotta tell you,

Marge, it's difficult for me to see Cort as anything but an abusive husband and killer, not as some Adonis."

"Reality can be a bitch, Jake. He's a handsome man. We can't overlook the attractiveness factor." She took another contemplative bite.

"Probably not much we can do about that."

"I wonder." Marge cocked her head and mused. "Did the prosecutor focus much on his bad character? Can we dirty him up?"

"Well, his infidelity came in at trial and the victim's sister testified that Cort struck Christie and cursed at her."

"I see. What about other affairs?"

"I'm going to have my investigator look into that. Would be nice if we could establish that he is a serial philanderer. Would be even better for our case if he has abused any other women."

"Any psychological or other abuse of his wife?"

"He threatened to severely harm Christie if she tried to divorce."

"Seems an extreme reaction to divorce."

I filled her in on Sergeant Ponce's testimony about divorce being an evil word within the upper echelons of the sheriff's department. "Beyond that, when Christie brought up divorce, the vic's sister heard him threaten Christie in the most vicious terms—he promised that if she fucked his career, he would hurt her."

Marge's carefully cultivated eyebrows arched in question. "But a motive for murder?" She was skeptical. "What else do we have? How about on the job? Was he a bully? Any citizen or workplace complaints?"

"I don't know if the investigation even pushed into those areas. But I can guarantee they will be checked out prior to the next go-round."

"Good. This guy needs to be sullied with everything you've got.

We need the jurors to look beneath that handsome face to his cruel and despicable character."

"We can work on that."

"Good. That brings me to our biggest asset—your charm and charisma. Jake, you've got that in spades. That will serve as a counter to MacPherson." I sat back, but Abbott carried on. "I'm not blowing smoke, and that was not intended to flatter you. Facts are facts; you can hang with her. When I watched Wills, especially during voir dire and opening statement, he was overmatched by MacPherson's personality and charm. He was virtually invisible, almost a generic background character in a play staring Merci MacPherson. She had the stage from early on and never relinquished it. You may not be able to push her from the stage, but you can certainly share it with her."

"I watched the entire trial, and I agree she was the dominant force in the courtroom." The first half of my sandwich was nearly finished; Marge had barely touched hers. "That still leaves the problem of the lack of a body."

"And that needs to remain a work in progress for now." She held my eyes. "I've got to think you've got some ideas about why that challenge wasn't better explored at the first trial."

"I've been thinking about that. Nothing terribly specific yet, but I've got a few ideas beyond what developed at trial."

She smiled. "I'll bet you have."

"I'm inviting our entire team to watch the various examinations, especially the crosses, to brainstorm some additional ideas. You good for that?"

"It's your dime. I'm at your call."

"Great, I'll get back to you when it's set up." I hesitated. "One last thing. I want *you* for this soiree, not an associate."

"Jake, I wouldn't dream of missing this trial." She smiled again. "You've got me and at least one of my associates."

CHAPTER 23

CAMBRIA

With trial still several weeks away, it was time for a Jake-and-Lisa weekend getaway before I was buried, once again, in trial. That Friday afternoon, we drove up the Central Coast with the top down in my SLK 550. The sleepy little beachside town where we were headed was as far away from our busy lives as we could go during a weekend—both in mind and body—because it never changed. It's as if it, and the towns it slept beside, wait suspended in time for you to return and take up where you left off. Even the weathered and battered sign as you enter the town of Harmony has continued to report its population as eighteen since I was a kid traveling with my folks. Right across the street, there's the same gas station where, remarkably enough, an attendant stood waiting to pump the gas, check the oil, and clean the windshield. *Out of a different era.*

Along the way, Pacific Coast Highway veers to the left, goes over a little rise, and suddenly there is Pismo Beach, self-proclaimed clam capital of the world. *As if any other beach burg would want such a distinction.* There's the Old West Cinnamon Roll Bakery and the same old seedy but delicious Dick's Dive.

Just beyond Pismo Beach is Avila. As we got off PCH, we drove under a canopy of trees past Avila Hot Springs, where you could soak in a hot mineral pool, and Avila Farm, where you could buy greens to feed the animals in the petting zoo. We passed on a soak and the animals. As our drive broke free from the trees, the beach came into view. Another weathered sign that had been there for decades warned us to be aware of sharks, even though, to my knowledge, the last and possibly only shark attack here took place thirty years ago.

There were three piers in Avila. The northernmost one was a drive-on pier, with a harem of sea lions living next to it. We parked and, from the rail of the pier, watched them jockeying for position (I'm not certain what for) and barking orders at one another. On my last visit, which was pre-Lisa, I met a man who claimed to have been bitten by one. We maintained our safe viewing position, high above the action.

Further north was Morro Bay. The Great American Fish Company, which sat on a pier, was the place to eat when my dad and mom brought me here when I was a teen. From our window seat, Lisa and I could see momma sea otters with their furry babies playing on their bellies. *Cute, cute, cute!* We shared a clam chowder served in a hollowed-out sourdough loaf. Lisa had a crab and shrimp Louie; I had a fish sandwich. We drank a Central Coast white, which was more than passable. Our bill, under fifty dollars.

Going on up the coast, we came to Cambria and Moonstone Beach. Years ago, there were tons of moonstones, perfect for skimming into the waves. But as we walked the beach, not a one. I guess they had all been skimmed off. The restaurant to eat at in Cambria was the Sea Chest. It opened at five thirty, but I recalled from experience that the lines queued much earlier. They didn't take reservations, credit cards, "bitcoins or Spanish doubloons" (their wording, not mine), but, in their spirited language, "Classic baseball cards will be considered."

When we settled at our table, I leaned to Lisa and said, "Good thing I didn't bring my 1955 Roy Campanella card."

Surprised, she countered, "You collect baseball cards?"

"Since I was a kid. My dad got me started with a vintage Sandy Koufax card from 1962. Mostly I collect Dodger cards."

"You've never mentioned this before. I'd like to see them."

"Next time you're at my place." I squeezed her to me. "Speaking of baseball cards, I read recently that the Holy Grail of baseball cards, a Mickey Mantle rookie card, sold for something like $6 million recently."

"You're kidding. For a baseball card?"

I grinned. "Like I said, it's the Holy Grail of collectibles."

"That's ridiculous. It's a two-by-three-inch piece of cardboard."

"Incredible, right? They'll probably keep it in a vault and rarely look at it. What joy will that bring them?" I said, with a sardonic grin.

The half-hour wait was worth it. We both had sand dabs with creamed spinach, crusty bread, and a bottle of Central Coast chablis. We then took the short drive to Grace's Bed and Breakfast, our home for the weekend. The long, narrow drive was lined with thirty-foot hedges, which gave way to lush lawns as we approached. The place looked like a grand mansion, with white columns and an enormous wraparound porch. I knew from previous visits it had been built in 1876, and yet it was as fresh and clean as the sweet smell of jasmine in the air. The valet led us in, and we were greeted by Mrs. Cubbage, a high-energy middle-aged woman who I knew from my previous visits. She greeted me as an old friend. Her hug squeezed the breath from my lungs. I introduced her to Lisa, and she too was squeezed. "I've saved the Washington Room for you," she announced with a wink, adding theatrically, "Special people get the special room."

The room was beautifully appointed; the finishing touch was the gold and maroon wallpaper on the ceiling, set off by thick crown molding. After we settled in, we went back to the parlor, where bottles of port were set out. We helped ourselves and visited with several guests. As the evening began to wane, we took a moonlit stroll across the grounds and then retired early and enjoyed the luxurious bed.

In the morning we headed down to breakfast, where we were seated on the veranda at a bistro table covered with a white cloth. We were presented with personalized menus, welcoming Mr. and Mrs. Clearwater. Lisa gave me a look. Assumptions can lead to awkward moments. We were offered coffee, mimosas, and tiny muffins with nuts and raisins. Mimosas won out. Lisa ordered a blueberry waffle, and I had the bird's nest (eggs, cheese, beans, and salsa).

Following breakfast, and with fresh mimosas in hand, we strolled the grounds. One couple was playing croquet on a green lawn Augusta National would have envied. There were fountains and ponds, complete with lounging turtles.

Out of the blue, Lisa said, "Jake, thanks for bringing me here. This is"—she waved her hands—"magical. I love it here." And then without any change of inflection, "When we get married, we should spend our first night here."

Married! The topic had not surfaced before between us. The abuse Lisa had suffered at the hands of her ex-husband quelled any such talk, and I understood her discomfort . . . still, the idea had played in my mind since the early days of our relationship. But now the door had been jerked open, and I wasn't going to be left outside. The vision she had of us, here together as husband and wife, filled me with the kind of joy I had never known in anyone' s company but her own. I immediately dropped to a knee and, holding her hand, looked up into that beautiful face and asked, "Lisa, my perfect love, would you honor me and become my wife?"

She dropped to her knees and wrapped her arms around me. "Mr. Clearwater, I thought you would never ask. Of course, I'll marry you!"

We kissed, and a couple seated not far away stood and applauded. A life change as quick as the wings of a hummingbird. I'd always thought we would get married, but sometime off in the indefinite future. Before today, I had planned to pick a special place, have a beautiful ring, and make an eloquent speech. *Maybe this was the right time, right place. Who needed a ring?*

We spent the late morning celebrating our engagement on that king-sized bed. No one paid much attention to the ceiling.

That afternoon, with the top down, we took a meandering drive and stopped for lunch at Linn and Linn's, which advertised their "famous" olallieberry pancakes. Lisa was intrigued by the prospects of olallieberry pancakes, which she chose for lunch. (She thought the olallieberries tasted like cranberries.) I had a tuna melt. We smiled at each other like teenagers discovering first love. A mile further north, we passed Linn's farm (I'm not sure if it was Linn's or Linn's) where the olallieberries were grown, along with other organic produce for the restaurant. The route was lined with one after another of down-on-the-farm houses. You could easily envision Auntie Em on the porch calling for Dorothy.

The trippiest house along the way was Nitt Witt Ridge. *Is that a name or what?* Lisa had noticed a homemade sign advertising the place as a historic establishment, a "wonder of the world." In my earlier trips, I had never noticed the sign or the place, but when we saw the marker for the turnoff, we couldn't resist. *How could we pass on a wonder of the world?* As advertised, it was a wonder, a wonder that it was still standing. A wonder that it hadn't been condemned. A wonder that it had even been built.

It is difficult to describe Nitt Witt Ridge. I think that it had three stories, but I couldn't be certain. It was ambiguous. In places, it appeared to be three stories, but in other places, more like two. The window openings were lopsided, with no glass. The front door was partially collapsed and hung on one hinge. Random boards had been hammered onto the sides haphazardly, maybe to patch up gaps. The whole structure had an uneven feel that gave me a queasy feeling. There was a faded sign that read, "Tours today at noon." It was eleven thirty. What the heck, we were intrigued. There were no other takers. Another homemade sign, hammered into a nearby oak, advised that the building had been constructed by a man named Art Beal, who used "materials" found at the dump or along the side of the road. *Not hard to believe.*

At a quarter past noon, a man for whom the music of the 1960s had never stopped, rode up on a bike. He was at least in his seventies, with long, stringy hair and a scraggly beard down to his chest. His tie-dye shirt was clean, his jeans, not so much. Without preamble, he introduced himself as James, our guide through this wondrous house. James didn't acknowledge that he was late, and he went right into his spiel. We learned that Nitt Witt Ridge was *approximately* three stories. It was built with wire, odd pieces of lumber, discarded toilets, repurposed sinks, pipes, and seashells ("especially abalone"). James told us that he was restoring the place. *Restoration might entail a complete knockdown.* He explained that it was difficult to raise funds since the state would not let him charge for tours or sell souvenirs. *Interesting to speculate on the kinds of souvenirs James envisioned.* We nodded sympathetically at his plight as he led us inside. James's enthusiasm in showing off his treasure was joy to behold.

We never left the first floor, for the stairway looked like a broken leg ready to happen. Following the tour, James said it was okay to tip him, which would go to the restoration. The experience was worth the twenty-dollar tip, even though, as we walked back to our car, I googled Nitt Witt Ridge and learned that it was owned by a couple named O'Malley. There was no mention of James or of tours. James appeared to be a free agent.

About ten miles further north was Hearst Castle. I never got tired of seeing it on the hill. Lisa said she had taken a tour with her parents when she was a kid. Even though I loved to admire the property from the road, I had never taken a tour.

Lisa smiled as we stared at the magnificent testament to Hearst's ego and said, "Now, there would be a venue for a wedding!" That got us laughing.

The idea of it was so absurd. It didn't take much; we were still on a high from our engagement. We parked outside the grounds to fully appreciate the place and were rewarded when a dazzle of zebras, the descendants of Hearst's menagerie, strolled between us and the castle.

A few miles further north of the castle was the elephant seal viewing area. When those four-thousand-pound beasts were lying still, they looked like large boulders on the sand. The only color was when they opened their mouths, which were blood red. They roared like lions. We watched fascinated for better than an hour, and there was little movement; but then one bull tried to sneak up on another bull's female, and all hell broke loose. It was a spectacular fight, with moms and babies scrambling. It ended when the interloper, defeated, finally retreated down the beach.

Back at the bed and breakfast, as we were enjoying hors d'oeuvres and wine, Mrs. Cubbage brought out a small white cake to celebrate our engagement. Apparently Julie and Louie, the witnessing couple, had informed her of our eventful day. We shared the cake as far as it would go and informed Mrs. Cubbage we would return for our wedding night.

It was hard to leave Lisa at her home on Sunday night, but trial prep was looming.

CHAPTER 24

AN ATTITUDE

Monday morning I swam by myself. It was lonely out there. I'd grown accustomed to the students. They'd dispersed for the summer to judicial clerkships, jobs with firms—some large and prestigious, some small but prestigious—but most of all, just to have any legal-related job. Without the company, I was much slower around the pier. Some old-guy fisherman, who always seemed to be at the end of the pier, yelled at me to pick up the pace. I ignored him. But picked up the pace.

Bearing in mind Marge Abbott's advice to sully up Cort, I figured there were three potential avenues to pursue: the people Cort worked with and supervised; his personnel file, which would contain any citizen complaints; and Christie's sister, Mary Lynn Holder. Mary Lynn had been there to experience the couple's interactions. Maybe there was more there than came out at trial. I called John Wills and asked him to set up an interview with Mary Lynn.

"Jake, I'm not your secretary." *Touchy, touchy.*

"I know. I just figured you had rapport with her, but she doesn't know me. My apologies."

I got the number, made the call, and arranged for Duke and me to meet at her condo. I wanted Duke to be the primary point of contact with Mary Lynn after this initial meeting.

Her condo was in a mammoth Mediterranean-style complex in Encino, an upscale community twenty miles north of downtown LA. Mary Lynn was thirty-three, a year younger than Christie. Like Christie, she was blessed (maybe cursed?) with good looks: blond, tallish, nice features. I knew from Wills that she was divorced, no children. When I called to make the appointment, she didn't seem pleased that I was involved in the prosecution. Maybe that was out of some sense of loyalty to Wills. *Seemed to me that it might have occurred to her that I might accomplish what Wills failed to accomplish.*

She was dressed in sweats. Without much enthusiasm, she motioned us to a dining room table in the kitchen.

"I googled you, Mr. Clearwater," she began. "Your last trial was defending some dirtbag up north. That's not giving me much confidence that you can get Cort locked up." *An attitude. She didn't note that the dirtbag had been found not guilty.*

I ignored her remark. "It is unorthodox," I agreed. "But the DA thinks I can get the job done."

"He thought that about John Wills." *A serious attitude.*

Again, I shucked it off. "As you know, this is a tough case to prosecute. I think the DA was looking for a fresh approach."

"Yeah," she said with a bitter laugh. "I watched some of your TV commentary on the trial. I heard what you said about that bitch's cross-examination of me. That I was flustered and thoroughly defeated, and I quote, with my 'credibility in tatters.'" She arched her eyebrows. "Not real flattering." *This wasn't going well.*

"Ms. Holder," Duke said, "he'll get done . . . what needs getting done."

Mary Lynn slid Duke a look of annoyance, wary of promises.

"You're not the first to be beaten up by MacPherson," I said. "She's an effective lawyer. She saw your vulnerabilities and jumped on them."

"Well, I didn't know how to defend myself. John tried to prepare me, but it didn't help. It was humiliating."

"That's one of the things we are going to work on for the retrial. I promise we'll do a better job of protecting you the next time around."

"Right," she said sarcastically. "And how, exactly, could you protect me from her? John Wills couldn't. Besides, it seemed to me you were more on her side during your stint on TV."

"John Wills and I will have a better handle on dealing with MacPherson this next time around." I waited for her reaction to Wills's involvement, especially since she blamed him for not effectively prepping her.

"John's going to be involved?" Surprisingly, she perked up at the news. "I like John, he worked so hard. I only wish he had been stronger in dealing with that bitch." She practically spit out the word bitch.

"John's a very good lawyer. We will be working together. That gives us the best chance at a conviction."

"What do you mean, working together?"

"He'll be sitting at the prosecutor's table with me. We are going to co-try the case. Duke and Det. Ossoff are our investigators."

"I didn't know that. The paper only talked about you." With Wills aboard, her skepticism seemed to abate. "If John is such a big part of this, why isn't he here?"

"We agreed it was important for Duke and me to get a fresh perspective on you."

"A fresh perspective?" she said tentatively, as she bit into her bottom lip. "How's it going to be different this next time?"

"First off, since we're going to be working together, let's move to first names. Agreed?"

"Agreed." And with a nonchalant shrug, she responded, "What choice do I have, *Jake*?" She made a point of emphasizing my name.

"Okay, Mary Lynn." I smiled. "Let's get to work." She stood and began fiddling with the coffee maker. "We need to know more about Christie than what came out at trial. And after we exhaust that topic, I want to go deeper into Christie's relationship with Cort. And, I want to learn more about you."

"Anything to get that sonofabitch." There was some energy there, a certainty and passion that I could work with. "But I've gone over this with John and Det. Ossoff again and again."

"I know you have. But we're bringing fresh ears. It could prove helpful."

She nodded.

"Do you have time now to get started? This will take a while."

"Yeah. First, let me finish making us some coffee." *Maybe we were over the hump.*

She fixed us with coffee, settled in one of the dining chairs and said, "Okay, fire away."

I nodded. "Let's start with Christie."

She leaned back in her chair and exhaled deeply. "I know it's been what, a year and counting. But it's still hard to talk about her." She stared down at the mug of coffee in her hands as a memory played across her face. She smiled at the thought of her sister, and continued, "Since forever, Christie was our glamour girl. From middle school on, she was the prettiest girl. She was homecoming queen during both her junior and senior years. Voted most popular."

"Interesting. How did she perform in school? Not just socially, but academically?"

"Her grades were good—she got into USC. During her sophomore year there she tried out as a USC song girl. You know, those dancers up front at sporting events? And of course she got in."

"So she was athletic?" Duke asked.

"Our folks had put both of us in dance classes since we were old enough to walk. So yeah, making the team was no problem. She'd always been fit and strong."

"How'd she do in school?" I asked.

"She was living the college dream—lots of dating, lots of travel with the teams for the away games." Her voice trailed off. *Dark clouds in the dream?*

"Something went wrong?" I asked.

"Yeah, she started hanging out with this older guy, Chris something-or-other. I never trusted him. He kinda took over her life. Christie and I kind of lost track of each other for a while. It was mostly on her end. We used to talk every day, then it got to be every week . . . then just once in a while. I got tired of always having to be the one who calls. Next thing I knew, she was modeling for some other sketchy guy. Then, surprise, surprise, turns out she's one of *Playboy*'s Girls of the West, naked unto the world."

Duke said, "That had to be a shock for you and your parents?"

Mary Lynn looked off and shrugged. "My parents were mortified. They really had a hard time with it. It nearly ended their relationship with Christie."

"How'd Christie feel about the situation?" I asked.

"I don't think she got it at first. But when she got kicked off the dance team at school for what they labeled 'scandalous behavior,' I think the consequences started to sink in."

"Consequences?"

"She felt ostracized at school. Our folks weren't talking to her. She dropped out of USC. She felt lost."

"Tough times." I said.

"We started talking again. I was able to get her and my parents together. It took some time, but the four of us were able to work through it." Her eyes watered.

I gave her a moment before asking, "So what happened next?"

She wiped at her eyes and said, "She dropped her scumbag 'friends' and moved back home with my folks."

"Back home?" Duke arched his bushy eyebrows.

"Yeah, it was a real fall from grace."

"How'd that work out?" Duke asked.

"It took a while, but things settled down."

"Did she get a job? What'd she do?" I asked.

"Not much at first. She did eventually get into pottery." She paused and explained, "My mom is an artist. She's got a kiln and a wheel in the garage, and after a few months, Christie got really into it. According to my mom, Christie had a flair for it."

"Pottery?" *Seemed an odd choice for someone like Christie. Maybe part of the fall from grace.*

"Yep. Vases, lamps, coffee mugs, you name it. The mugs you're drinking from, they're Christie's."

"Okay, go on," I urged.

"After several months, she told me she needed more to her life than coffee mugs and flower vases, and pretty much out of the blue, she applied with the sheriff's department to become a dispatcher. And," with an insincere chuckle, "of course, got the job. It wasn't long after that she met The Once and Future Asshole." She stopped and composed herself. "They got married six months or so after. I had a bad feeling about him right away. I thought he was a really good-looking, smooth-talking know-it-all. And I sensed early on that he was a bully."

"What made you think that?" I asked.

"When things didn't go his way, everyone had to watch out. But Christie didn't see it. I think she felt like, after everything that went down with college and with *Playboy*, she needed to do the next right thing, to make a real change. So either she didn't see him, or didn't want to see him, for what he was."

"Let me take a step back. I recall there was pottery stuff in Christie's garage," I said.

"Yeah. Christie, even after she got the job and got married, was still really into her pottery. She told me that it gave her a creative outlet. Like I said, she was good at it."

"Okay, let's talk about the Christie–Max relationship."

"Max didn't like that she worked, and especially that she worked at the sheriff's." She shrugged. "I think he was jealous that she was around so many young cops. Eventually, he made her quit."

"What do you mean 'made her'?" I asked.

"Like I said, he's a forceful and intimidating guy. Even though Christie liked the job, and, I think, was good at her job, Max demanded that she quit." She leaned back and added, "From my perspective, the marriage, which had never been very strong, began seriously unraveling after that."

"How long had they been married when she quit?" Duke asked.

"Three, three and a half years."

Duke followed up. "Was Max a lieutenant when they first married?"

"No, he was promoted about the same time he forced Christie to quit."

I took a sip of my coffee and turned from Duke back to Mary Lynn. "Let's talk about your relationship with Christie during the marriage."

Her shoulders sagged. "Shit, we've got to go into that again?"

"I'm sorry," I said, as I leaned back and linked my fingers behind my head. "But MacPherson painted you as hostile and partisan. If we're going to protect you, we need the whole story."

She gave me a look but then went on. "I got divorced three years ago, and I was pretty depressed. Christie was really there for me. We talked constantly, probably a couple of times a day. We were each other's support." Her eyes watered again. She stood, retrieved the coffee pot, and quietly warmed our mugs.

"You testified that on one occasion, several months before February 4, you saw Max strike her. I heard your testimony. Is there anything you can add to that?"

"I wanted to kill him. Sonofabitch."

"So, you really went after him? Physically?"

Mary Lynn's eyes flashed with white-hot anger. "I wanted to hurt him like he hurt her."

"I understand. You also testified that you caught him in an affair."

"*Affair* is a nice way of describing it. He was slutting around."

"What tipped you off?"

"Christie suspected, after he quit having sex with her. Christie just knew."

"But you're the one who acted on it. Why?"

"If I could catch him at it, I hoped I could convince Christie to leave him."

"But you did catch him, and she still didn't leave. As I understand from your testimony, she couldn't leave because he threatened her?"

"That's right. I actually heard him say that to her."

"Do you recall his words?"

"I do, they were memorable. He said, 'A divorce would fuck my career. You fuck with my career, you fuck with my life, and I'll fuck with your life.'"

"Whoa!" Duke blurted. "You were there when he said that?"

"Standing right next to her. Max's face was flushed, he just lost it. He was so angry, I thought he was going to actually try and hurt us both."

"So, what did he do?" Duke asked.

"He stared at her, and then me, and punched the wall. He finally stalked off."

"He didn't hit either of you?"

She shook her head no.

I acknowledged her response and asked, "What do you think he meant when he told her he'd 'fuck with her life'?"

She looked at me like I had just rolled up on a turnip truck, and she shook her head.

"Okay," I said, putting my hands up defensively. I leaned back in my chair. "Thanks for going through all this again. You've filled in some gaps. I know that was tough. Thanks for bearing with us."

"Now that we've gotten through that, let's discuss how you can better protect me from that Amazon the next time around."

"I'm going to study your testimony. I'm pretty sure I can help. Give me a little time."

"Okay," she said, and forcing a smile, added, "I hope you're as good as advertised."

"Me too." I shrugged.

"He is," Duke added.

CHAPTER 25

BRAINSTORMING

I set up a meeting with Wills, Ossoff, and Duke in my newly requisitioned office in the DA's wing of the Foltz Building. The office was sparse. I didn't see any point in changing that—I wouldn't need it for long. I requested and received a PC, a printer, and two more office chairs. Earlier in the day, I had met with Wills in his office to discuss our meeting agenda; we were on the same page.

Duke arrived a half-hour early. He had on a short-sleeved button shirt with vertical stripes, blue jeans, and sandals with black socks. He looked ready for an umbrella drink at the Intercontinental's pool rather than a brainstorming session on a murder trial.

"Impressive digs," he remarked with a straight face, as he took in the bare walls, the battered desk, and the four hard-backed, experienced chairs.

"Yeah, they spared no expense. Right down to this office chair." I smiled as I jiggled the lever of my own seat. "It's stuck in the forward position. It's a back breaker."

He waved me out of the chair. "Let me take a look." I stood and slid the chair to him. He flipped it over, took off a sandal, and pounded on the release lever. Something popped. He stood the chair back up and sat in it. He leaned back and then forward. "Fixed." He slid it back to me. *All it needed was a little finesse.*

I sat and moved the chair through its range of motion. "Thanks, man." I was never surprised by anything Duke did. "Have you set yourself up in the Intercontinental yet?"

"This morning. Nice place. Only a quick walk from here." He settled into one of the stiff-back chairs. "So what's the plan?"

"Let's wait for Wills and Ossoff. I want the whole team involved. Collaborative decision-making," I said with a grin.

Duke shook his head. "Jake, sometimes I think you might be a bureaucrat at heart."

I turned my hands out. "Give me a break, Duke. I don't want anybody to feel left out."

"Your number two?"

"Careful referring to him as number two."

"Got it."

"Have you watched the trial tapes I sent you?"

"Yep."

"Thoughts?"

"Defense counsel is a beauty. And a hell of a lawyer." Slight pause. "She smoked your number two."

I had to laugh; Duke was irrepressible. "What did you think of the prosecution's case?"

"I don't know. I've never worked a no-body case, quite a challenge."

"Yeah, trying to prove a negative. Couple that with MacPherson and we've got our hands full."

"Jake, I never worry about you being out-lawyered."

I shrugged. "Before the troops arrive, I've got news."

Duke paused slightly, and then a knowing grin spread across his face. "You proposed, and she said yes." It was not a question.

"How'd you know?"

"I'm a trained investigator." He stood and gave me a hug. A very un-Duke-like thing to do. "Like I said before, she is way out of your league," Duke said against my shoulder. The joy in his voice surprised me even more than the hug. "But every now and then, a double-A hitter jerks a homerun off an ace. My friend, you've hit a grand slam."

We stood there together, my friend and I, basking in my good fortune, until a knock on the doorjamb announced that Wills and Ossoff had arrived. As they walked in, I made introductions, and everyone shook hands and took seats. I joined them on one of the uncomfortable straight-back chairs, passing on my mended desk chair. Didn't want to high-horse anyone, especially Wills. Our relationship was still a bit tenuous.

Sherri Ossoff took a hard, skeptical look at Duke. Duke ignored her and sat cross-legged, his hands in his lap. I filled the group in on Duke's background and added, "He's the best investigator I've ever worked with." Head nods, but no comments. I continued, "John and I have talked about expanding our efforts in proving Christie is dead. John, why don't you fill them in on what we discussed?"

"We want to expand the search radius from the five miles we've already done to ten miles."

Ossoff leaned back as far as her chair would allow. "That's a serious expansion. Gonna take lots of time."

"That's why we need to get on it now, Sherri. We've only got three and a half weeks to work with."

"It's also going to require a lot of overtime. Do we have the authorization?" Ossoff asked.

"We do. Nancy Seah talked to the sheriff. We are good to go."

Ossoff gave a surprised look and nodded. "Who do you want to run that?"

"Sherri, it's all yours," Wills said.

She nodded. "Same as last time? Search for any disturbances using ground-penetrating radar and the dogs on all open areas, and in particular, the orchards?"

"Yep." Wills nodded.

"How about the reservoir? Want to have one more look?"

Wills nodded again. His eyes locked on to Ossoff. "We've got to get on this right away."

"We used five of those ground-penetrating machines last time around. I'm going to need even more this time."

"You'll get them," Wills assured her.

I jumped in. "Moving forward, John and I have discussed another wrinkle which we think will play well with the jury." I hunched toward Ossoff and Duke. "We are going to make a video, tracking Cort's movements that morning."

Duke immediately caught on to what I was proposing. "A reenactment?"

"Pretty much," I said. "We are going to track what we believe were Cort's movements from the time he left the station through his return home hours later when he reported Christie missing. We are going to establish that he had sufficient time to kill his wife, dispose of her body, and dump her vehicle, all in the window of time he had."

Wills weighed in. "We want to rebut any concern that he couldn't have done it all in that three-and-a-half-hour window he had."

It was Duke's turn to sit back. He was not easily impressed. "Simulating his movements and activities during that morning? Good."

"We're going to do it in real time. Starting at 1:00 a.m. through to his eventual return home when he called it in," I said. "If a picture is worth a thousand words, then a film must be worth . . . well, plenty more. We want the jurors to *experience* Cort's conduct and to understand that the murder and the disposals of the body and the car were doable during the time frame."

Ossoff nodded her head in admiration. "I think you guys are on to something."

I nodded as well. "We're trying to eliminate from the minds of the jurors as many false scenarios as possible."

Ossoff was still thinking. "You two"—indicating Wills and me—"are the lawyers. Will the judge let something like this in?"

I looked at Wills. "John will figure it out and get it in. I will work with the folks we hire to get this made."

The room was quiet as everyone was working the film plan around in their minds.

I broke the silence. "Moving on to another front. We want to develop as much dirt on Cort as we can. Duke, you're the primary here; Sherri will help when she can. From what we heard from Mary Lynn, Cort has a mean streak. He's a bully, an intimidator. We need to work with that. Acquaintances, people he works with, supervisors, and especially the people he supervises, need to be contacted. Previous girlfriends. We need to know: Is he a bully? Intimidating? Violent? And while you two are digging up dirt, literal and otherwise, I'm going to try and get into his personnel file to look for anything negative. It's a delicate business, but if I can convince the judge that we have evidence that he struck his wife, that might give Judge Walter sufficient grounds to open his file."

"I can help with that," said Wills. "Since it's usually defense lawyers trying to poke around in the personnel files of cops, I've kept several good defense motions loaded with points and authorities I can share."

"That'll save me some work." I stopped and looked at my colleagues before venturing into an idea that I couldn't completely wrap my head around. "I haven't run this out-of-the-box idea by anyone yet, but it's stuck in my head. Maybe the three of you can help me shake it out. I keep thinking about MacPherson's point to Sherri that she couldn't testify for certain that Christie isn't living in Akron or Toronto."

That elicited a grimace from Ossoff.

"After talking to Mary Lynn, we learned that Christie had developed a passion for pottery. She learned it from her mom. I noticed from the police reports that she had a potter's wheel and a kiln in her garage. According to Mary Lynn, she constantly made vases, mugs, and more, and that her mother orders her pottery supplies online from a particular nationwide supplier. Would it make sense that if Christie was living in Akron, for instance, she would still be making pottery, and if so, would she be ordering her supplies online from the same supplier?" I was getting real skeptical looks from my comrades. But I was deep enough in that I might as well finish. "What if I got some of the DA's tech folks to run down the supplier and identify customers in the months following Christie's disappearance?"

Ossoff pulled a face. "Take me through this, Jake. I'm not following. Are you suggesting that we run down every customer from some nationwide supplier, and once Christie doesn't surface, we've got one more arrow in our quiver?"

"Like I said, this idea is not just half-baked—it's not even in the oven."

Duke weighed in. "Serious problem, Jake—since she would be in hiding, wouldn't she avoid using her real name?" *God, I hated looking stupid. But it was a stupid idea.*

I put up my hands in surrender. "Like I said, it was an 'unusual' idea. I was hopeful that her hobby might somehow be useful." I gave a rueful smile. "Trying to prove a negative is hard business. I'm thinking too much. Forget I even brought it up." I clapped my hands. "Moving along, anything other than my crackpot idea that needs discussing?"

No takers. As everyone stood, I asked Duke to stay behind.

We walked the four blocks to Philippe's. Duke had never experienced their remarkable sandwiches. We stood in line, then I ordered a lamb sandwich, cole slaw, chips, and a Modelo. Duke got a pork sandwich and the same sides but with a Heineken. We found a table. As I dabbed a small amount of horseradish on my sandwich, I warned Duke that the horseradish here is not to be trifled with. I had once taken a date to Philippe's before heading over to Chavez Ravine for a Dodger game. She had ignored my warning and slathered the horseradish on her food like it was mayonnaise. Her first bite sent her into a coughing spasm and then to the loo. We missed the first two innings. Duke exercised appropriate caution.

"Well, what do you think of our team?" I asked.

"Was it your idea to bring Wills in?"

"It was."

He gave me a look inviting an explanation. I shrugged and said, "He knows the case. He gave a helluva closing. Beyond that, I felt he needed a chance to vindicate himself. He's a good guy and a good lawyer."

Duke didn't require anything more.

CHAPTER 26

THE REENACTMENT

The following day, I contacted Julie Gold, a media professor at Pacifico's undergraduate campus, to get a recommendation for someone to film the reenactment. She was a friend of Eve's and had joined us for a few barbecues at Tony and Eve's. She invited me to come to her office down the hill from the law school. She was a bit of an eccentric, especially by Pacifico's staid standards. Her hair was currently purple, but I had seen it at various times dyed in shining blue or firetruck red. Her small, pretty face was framed by huge earrings. She wore blue jeans with strategic tears and a sleeveless tie-dye shirt.

She invited me to sit and, with one haunch on her desk, said, "Is this about the Cort trial?"

"Yes it is."

"How exciting. I love following murder trials. I watch *Dateline* pretty much every night, following investigations. I followed the first Cort trial, and I'm convinced he killed her. I hope you can get him."

"That's the plan, and I need some help."

"Tell me what you have in mind." Her enthusiasm was palpable.

"Okay, but you understand that this is confidential. I don't want word of what I'm doing leaking out before trial."

Julie was unfazed. "Come on, Jake, tell me how I can help."

"I want to film a reenactment of what I suspect was Cort's conduct on the morning of the murder."

"I see." She thoughtfully rested her chin against her knuckle.

I gave her a questioning look. "Julie, I'm only looking for a recommendation from you of someone who could do this for me on very little notice."

She waved my comment aside. "Okay, when do you need this done?"

"Within the next couple of weeks."

She stood. "How about me?" she declared, with her hands on her hips.

"Oh, Julie, I wasn't suggesting you should do it. I don't want to infringe on our relationship. I just need a recommendation."

"Jake, you're not going to get anybody on such short notice. Besides, these kinds of pseudo-documentaries are my specialty! I'm really good at this kind of thing, trust me. Besides, Cort is awful, and I would love to be involved in finding justice for that poor wife of his, even in a peripheral way."

Still surprised, I asked, "Are you certain about this? You haven't had any time to think it over."

"I'm finished with spring classes and have the next couple of weeks to myself. Let's do it. I'm your person. I've got the equipment. I've got the expertise, and I've got the time."

"You would be making my life much easier."

"When do you want to do this?"

I held my breath and said, "If possible, I'd like to film this coming Monday?"

"Yes." She clapped her hands together and continued, "I'll need to bring in two grad students to assist. We'll need to pay them, but I'll work without pay. Call it a public service."

I shook my head in amazement. "Julie, you are something. Thank you."

She grinned. "You can take me to dinner when you convict him."

"You've got a deal. I'll bring my fiancée, Lisa—I know she'll love to meet an artist like you." I'm not sure there was any agenda on her part, but I wanted things crystal clear. *What an ego, Jake. Not every woman is after you.*

Her face never changed. "Love to meet her." Then back to business. "Do you have a script or something I can look over before we film?"

"No, but I can get something for you in the next couple of days. Meanwhile, let me give you a quick overview of what I need: I want to stage a reenactment of what I believe were Max Cort's activities during the early morning of Christie's disappearance. We've narrowed down the window Cort was unaccounted for to about three and a half to four hours. I want to establish that during that time, he was able to drive from his station to his house, kill Christie, bury or otherwise dispose of her body, get rid of her car, and return to work. I have in my mind a running digital clock actually on the screen showing the elapsed time."

She offered a smug look. "Piece of cake. Do you want to do it during the same early morning hours?"

"That's what I have in mind. That would best simulate the same traffic conditions."

She jotted down a few notes. I was amazed at the good fortune of getting a pro like Julie. "I'll send you an email by Thursday with more detail about what we need to cover," I said, as I headed out of her office. "Maybe we can meet in my office Saturday to work out the details?"

"That works. I'm looking forward to this, Jake. It will probably be the most exciting part of my summer!"

"I doubt that." I grinned. "I sure appreciate your jumping in like this."

I still needed someone to be Cort for the reenactment. The first name to pop into my head was Earl Hollister, my trial advocacy standout. Earl was tall and muscular like Cort. Hopefully, his summer clerkship was local and left him with some free night and weekend time. When I called him, he was not only available but eager to be involved. He agreed to meet with Julie, Wills, and me on Saturday morning to work out the logistics. On Saturday afternoon, Julie and her two students met in my office. Working from the outline I had prepared, Julie laid out how we would proceed.

Everyone was present in the parking lot of the sheriff's station at 11:00 p.m. Monday night. Julie was very much in charge. Filming started at one that morning; she kept the clock running as she filmed. When we were done, Julie said she would review the footage and let me know if anything needed cleaning up. Everyone exchanged hugs and went home to sleep. Two days later, Julie played the film for Wills and me. We were pleased. Using the script I wrote, Julie had one of her crew do the voiceover.

Trial Tip #7: Communication

Advocates should eliminate barriers between themselves and their jurors. Lecterns, counsel tables, and even legal pads impede the direct communication between counsel and the jurors. The goal is to be an immediate presence with the jurors. Eye contact during voir dire, opening statement, and closing argument helps ensure that the jurors stay engaged. Counsel reading from a legal pad or buried behind a lectern will find it difficult to work eye contact with the twelve jurors.

CHAPTER 27

MORE BRAINSTORMING

July 12, just under two weeks from trial. I joined Sherri Ossoff in the field, working with her crew. She had seven deputies working with the ground-penetrating radar and two deputies with cadaver dogs working the same turf. Like the initial five-mile-radius search, this search was of horse country, and the residences were spread out: lots of citrus and avocado orchards, very little in the way of houses.

Ossoff reported that she and her crew were about halfway through the expanded search. The GPR machines had so far identified two anomalies. One produced the remains of a human, which the coroner determined to be some poor soul who had been buried approximately twenty years ago. The remains were handed off to the cold case detectives. The other alert was a false positive. Nothing else of note had been revealed.

"Finding that old corpse was eerie," Sherri said. "When I heard someone shout 'remains,' I thought we had Christie, but it was immediately clear that it wasn't her." She shook her head and mused, "I wonder where Cort got rid of her."

"Don't we all," I agreed, and asked, "How many more days?"

"A week, maybe a week and a half. The open areas go pretty quick. It's the orchards where it's slow going."

"That makes sense," I said, as we watched a deputy operating one of the radar devices carefully working his way around an avocado tree. "Who would have thought that even ten years ago we'd have machines that could penetrate into the ground?"

"It is amazing, and they're relatively easy to operate. One of the company's techs trained my guys in about an hour."

"How about the reservoir?"

"Nothing, we've scoured it. She's not there."

We watched in silence as another deputy worked his device around another tree.

Ossoff asked, "How'd the filming go?"

"Good. It's going to be a powerful exhibit. My colleague did a really solid job."

"Glad to hear it." And then, giving me another skeptical look, she said, "Here's hoping the judge will let it in." She wasn't a lawyer, but Ossoff had been involved in a number of trials and was fully aware that judges occasionally thwarted plans.

"I hear you. John's working on the motion for inclusion. He likes our chances."

"Hope he's right."

On Thursday, I secured one of the DA's conference rooms. The room was set up for the five of us to watch the direct and cross-examinations from the first trial. Ossoff and Wills were seated when I arrived shortly before nine. I brought a box of donuts, a large takeout container of coffee, and cups. I figured that this would be a long meeting; sugar and caffeine would have to sustain us. Duke and Marge Abbott arrived within five minutes.

When we were all assembled, I introduced Marge to everyone. I had no concerns about her fitting in. Her charming demeanor won over the group in minutes. She had also thought to bring in refreshments: a mixed box of pastries from Gelson's, which rendered my donuts as trash fodder.

"Here's the plan," I said. "We are not going to watch the voir dires, jury selection, and opening statements. Marge, John, and I will look over those later. Right now, we want to cover the examinations, with an eye toward what we can do better on the direct exams and how we can best diffuse MacPherson's crosses. John recognizes that some of his work will be criticized, and to his credit, he is willing to self-examine and listen to the group dialogue. John, anything to add?"

"No. Our goal here is to put on the best case possible, so to that end, I welcome your thoughts. Blast away!" he said good-naturedly.

"Let's start with the direct exam of Mary Lynn," I said, and Ossoff started the video.

Midway through the direct exam of Mary Lynn, Abbott asked Ossoff to stop the recording. "John, I like how you established the bond between the sisters at the time of Christie's death. I like it so much, I'm wondering if we could start discussing their relationship earlier in the exam. Maybe go back to before Christie married the defendant. We could show the jury how the sisters had been each other's support well before the defendant came on the scene."

"Good point," Wills said. "That would deepen their relationship, since they were always there for one another."

Abbott then added, "What concerns me is that it is noticeable from the beginning of the exam that Mary Lynn harbors hard feelings toward Cort. That really paints her as a partisan whose testimony is tainted by her disdain for Cort."

"Marge is right," I broke in. "She understandably hates Cort, and she wears it on her sleeve. She comes off as a bit untrustworthy in describing what she knows about him." Wills and Abbott nodded agreement. "We need Mary Lynn to be as objective as possible in relating the facts about Cort. Let's try to keep her feelings about him to a minimum. Just the facts. Since she was convinced from the time of the murder that he killed her, everything she said is viewed through that tainted lens. We need to separate the facts she can relate about Cort before the murder from her thoughts after the murder." Everyone was with me. "Let's draw a hard line from before and after. Let's be as factual as we can be and give the jurors an opportunity to dislike Cort on their own, even before Christie goes missing."

Wills said, "I agree. I didn't do enough to separate pre-murder facts from post-murder events."

"Let's start from Mary Lynn's initial thoughts about him," I said. "She described him to me as a good-looking, domineering know-it-all. She told me that when he didn't get his way, those who crossed him had to watch out. She witnessed him hit Christie. She said that he forced Christie to quit her job at the sheriff's department, a job she enjoyed. Mary Lynn witnessed his affair, and perhaps most tellingly, she has relayed his statement concerning a possible divorce. I wrote down his threat: 'A divorce would fuck my career. You fuck with my career, you fuck with my life, and I'll fuck with your life.'"

Abbott said, "Those words have to be showcased. 'You fuck with my life, and I'll fuck with your life.'" It was odd hearing an F-bomb coming from the mouth of Marge Abbott.

Nodding, Wills said, "I should have laid out those facts and better showcased the actual threat prior to moving on to the murder. That would have given the jurors compelling reasons to despise him before we ever moved into the murder itself. And Mary Lynn doesn't look nearly as biased."

"Right," I said. "So, after we cover the relationship between the sisters, we need to go into a whole factual segment. Perhaps we can start that segment off by saying, 'It is important for the jurors to understand the underlying facts before we turn to Christie's disappearance. So I ask you to be as completely factual as you can; put your feelings aside, and just give us the facts that my questions call for. Can you do that?'"

I didn't mean to lecture, but Wills had not set up his direct as powerfully as he should have. Wills looked at me but didn't voice his feelings. *Getting critiqued is tough on the ego.*

The room went silent until Abbott said, "I agree. Credibility is everything. By laying out the undisputed facts early on, Mary Lynn is not so vulnerable to attack on cross-examination."

To his credit, Wills quickly agreed. "Since I assume that MacPherson will once again not put Cort on the stand, Mary Lynn's account of the pre-murder relationship will go undisputed and give the jury every reason to hate Cort."

Duke spoke for the first time. "Jake, I've seen you use PowerPoint effectively. Would you be able to put up the key facts as Mary Lynn is testifying? Especially that threat about leaving."

"Excellent idea," I responded. Duke wasn't just an investigator. He, like Ossoff, was a veteran of the trial wars. I trusted his instincts as much as my own. "I was thinking along the same lines, Duke. Judge Walter is pretty conservative on what we can do at trial. We could catch a cumulative objection. But, nothing ventured . . ." I shrugged.

"Worth a try," said Wills. "I have another thought about Mary Lynn's testimony, especially the cross. I felt she was too assertive. She needs to keep to the undisputed facts when MacPherson leans in on her. I could see her responding, 'I'm just reporting what I saw and heard.'"

"Good," I said. Then, after a moment, "I think we've worked

through Mary Lynn's exams. Unless anyone has something more to add, let's turn to the examination of Sherri."

"Yes, please," Ossoff said with exaggerated enthusiasm, eliciting laughs. "I certainly need a better answer to MacPherson's question that Christie could be living in Akron. I would like to be better armed next time around."

"We'll work on that," I said. "Meanwhile, your direct exam will have an entirely different feel if the reenactment comes in."

I looked at Wills, who was studying his notes. He looked up at me and said, "I've done my research and written the motion for inclusion. I think it's a fifty–fifty call," he declared, demonstrating the odds by wiggling his hand side-to-side. "I'm not sure. Is it too speculative, prejudicial? It will come down to Walter's discretion. I sensed during the first trial that the judge was with me and realized what a difficult task we had with no body. He may lean to us. But again, that is only my gut feeling."

"Hold onto that thought, John." I grinned. "Since the judge was hostile to me when Haines told him I was coming in, you are going to have to carry the water on that motion, and it seems to me you should conduct Sherri's direct exam."

Wills said, "I figured that, and I think you should do the direct on Mary Lynn." *Maybe there was a little dig there. Since I lectured him about Mary Lynn's direct, I should just do it myself.*

Abbott said, "I haven't seen the reenactment. How did it come out?"

Wills answered, "It's pretty powerful. It does what we hoped in establishing that Cort had time to do what we think he did." He then added, "It has a feeling of authenticity—makes you visualize what Cort must have been doing that night."

"I'm looking forward to seeing it. How long is it?" Abbott

asked. "I'm always worried about juror attentiveness. We certainly can't play a four-hour film."

"It's about thirty minutes," Wills answered. "We had to truncate those parts when Cort is driving from place to place. Our filmmaker was able to edit out the drive times and still convey how much time was elapsing. Marge, you'll be impressed with the job. Like I said, if we can get the judge to sign off, the defense's argument that Cort didn't have enough time is debunked."

Ossoff let the point settle and said, "Now back to my particular problem. How do I fend off MacPherson's cross about Akron?"

Abbott smiled. "Sherri, when I watched the recording of her cross of you, I had to admit that her question was quite clever and effective. Part of the reason it was effective is because it was surprising and caught you off guard. However, with that said, I thought you handled the question quite well."

"I agree, Sherri. I know you feel you got hurt, but you held your own," said Wills.

"You did fine," I said, weighing in. "When and if MacPherson hits you with that Akron-type question again, you need to respond with some version of the following: 'Because her abusive and controlling husband wouldn't let her get away.' And MacPherson may respond, 'But you can't tell us that she didn't run away, can you?' Your response would be, 'I can tell you that Lt. Cort had an intimidating and iron grip on her. As we all heard, he wasn't going to let her, excuse my language, fuck up his promotion.'"

The room nodded agreement. Wills said, "We fight fire with fire. The idea of jamming Cort's vicious words down the defense's throat in response to MacPherson's question turns that question into an opportunity for us."

Ossoff took in the exchange and looked pleased. "Thanks.

Let me think this through. I feel better armed." Ossoff's relief was palpable.

I said, "Other than the examinations of Mary Lynn and Sherri, I don't think there's much else to review. Everybody agree?" There were affirmative nods around the table. "Okay. Let's get updates on everyone's progress. We've heard from John concerning his work on the inclusion of the film. Duke, were you able to find anything on Cort that we can use to show he's abusive?"

Duke sighed. "It was a dead end. He was with a Missy Albright for almost two years before he married Christie. She made it very clear she would not testify against him. I think she's afraid of him, but there is no chance of getting her here to testify. As for officers who have worked with Cort, no one other than Ponce, his second in command, is talking. The Blue Wall is still a thing."

I banged my hands on the table. "Isn't that something? I can understand cops sticking up for one another under some circumstances, but not here. It was his wife. He murdered his wife."

"I hear you, Jake. It is what it is," Duke said, commiserating.

"Yeah, I know," I said, resigned to such a foolish reality. "Sherri, how's the search going?"

"We're closing in on it now," she said. "Should be finished in a couple of days. So far, we've come across five anomalies. One human corpse from decades ago, two canine remains, and two alerts where nothing turned up."

"Good work, Sherri." Turning to Marge, I asked, "How's the profiling on what we're looking for from jurors this time around?"

She opened a file folder. "We've been able to interview eight of the jurors from the first trial, plus the alternate. I'm still working through the interviews. Nothing terribly concrete at this time. General observations indicate that gender may have been a factor.

But it's still early. I'll have a lot more to say in the next couple of days."

"Okay, Marge. I've finished the motion to get into Cort's personnel file to see if there are any incidents of citizen complaints involving abuse or excessive violence. We'll argue that during motions. No idea if the judge will let us take a look and see if there is anything there. I'm also going to take a run at Merkle, the girlfriend. Maybe there is something there."

"What are you looking for from Merkle?" Ossoff asked.

"I don't know. But she did have a relationship with Cort," I said, with little conviction. "Most likely I'm grabbing at air. Even though she refused to testify the first time around, I need to get a read on her. We don't know her plans for this next go-round."

I looked at Wills. "John, anything else we need to cover?"

"Nope. Good work, everybody."

We filed our motions. Our first was to allow us to use the reenactment. Wills would handle the oral argument for that motion. In the second, we requested access to Cort's personnel file. That oral argument would be mine. In return, we received MacPherson's motions seeking approval from the judge to use juror questionnaires. Juror questionnaires were developed by mutual assent. Both sides met and conferred on the questions being asked. They could run anywhere from thirty pages to fifty pages and ultimately had to be approved by the judge. Once the judge approved the questionnaires, they would be distributed to the prospective jurors prior to voir dire. A questionnaire gave the lawyers much more information than during typical oral voir dire. Questionnaires were cumbersome and time intensive, and with rare exception, were reserved for capital cases. MacPherson had requested questionnaires before the first trial and been denied. She was trying again, arguing that following the mistrial and the extensive news coverage of the trial, she felt it was necessary to gather more information from the prospective jurors than was typical during voir dire. She had a point. I wasn't of a mind to disagree: it would aid us as much as it would aid her. But we were not the decision-makers here. My sense was that Judge Walter would not be so inclined. Questionnaires slowed things down because they provided so much more to cover during voir dire.

MacPherson also wanted a sequestered voir dire of each prospective juror, for many of the same reasons she had asked for the questionnaires. Sequestered or individual questioning, as the name implies, was conducted with no other prospective jurors present and, like questionnaires, was typically reserved for capital cases in which the jurors were carefully examined for their views regarding the death penalty. It was also a slow, deliberative process, which I'm certain the judge would deny. Surprisingly, she did not move for a change of venue, even though she indicated earlier that she might. That was hard to figure out. This case has been saturated in the news. A fresh start somewhere else made sense, but I wasn't going to fight for it. Considering that she was a brilliant advocate, she must have had her reasons.

The hearing on the motions would take place in a week, on July 19. Wills and I didn't file written responses to either defense motion. Frankly, if they were granted, we could live with them. The real battle would be over our motions.

Trial Tip #8: Direct Examination

Advocates should compartmentalize their direct examination by subject matter. Every direct should be broken down into distinct segments. Each segment should have a headline introducing the material to be covered during that segment. As each segment is concluded, a new headline should introduce the next segment. For instance, the examiner might say, "Now that we understand where you were situated prior to seeing the accident, let's focus on what you actually witnessed." Such a transition signals the end of the previous segment and allows for the introduction of the next. Such a roadmap allows the jurors to more easily follow the examination.

CHAPTER 28

INTO THE ROCKS

Meanwhile, there was one aspect of the first trial that was unresolved: Willow Merkle. The strip club dancer, Cort's other woman, was an X-factor. She was the only person MacPherson had called as a defense witness. Wills told me that he had been concerned, prior to the first trial, that she might provide an alibi for Cort, and he had instructed Ossoff to interview her. Merkle refused to be interviewed, and her dramatic refusal to testify during the trial left question marks for us, as I'm certain it did for Cort and MacPherson. She was a wild card. I don't like trial surprises. I needed to get some kind of a handle on her, for better or worse. I called the strip club and, using her "club" name, which I got from Wills, learned that she was working that evening. I figured showing up unannounced and catching her unawares might be my best opportunity to learn more about her possible involvement in this second trial.

The Rocks, where she danced, was, appropriately enough, located in a strip mall in a predominately industrial area. It was lit up like a garishly decorated Christmas tree. A neon sign as large as a triple garage door read "NUDE, NUDE, NUDE," leaving little doubt as to what the Rocks was selling. The parking lot behind the club was nearly full. I parked and walked in. A man the size of an RV told me the cover charge was fifteen dollars. I paid, brushed aside the curtain, and walked into a wall of music. It took a moment for my ears to adjust to the deafening sound and my eyes to the low lighting. Dozens of men and a couple of women were seated in chairs, watching three women gyrating on an elevated stage. The women were down to their G-strings, which were themselves in the process of being slowly removed and tossed off stage. A couple of guys sitting at the stage were waving bills at the dancers.

I found a seat fifteen feet or so from the stage and was immediately approached by a topless woman asking if I wanted to buy a drink. I ordered a beer and took in the surroundings. There were booths shielded by curtains on the far wall. Several of the customers had partially clad women sitting on their laps. When the music momentarily paused, a voice announced that lap dances during the next music set were two for one. Soon after my fifteen-dollar beer arrived, another topless woman, who couldn't have been more than twenty, approached and asked if I wanted a lap dance. "Two for one," she enticed. I begged off and sipped my expensive beer. She shrugged, "You're missing a great dance, handsome."

I scanned the room for Merkle and saw her working her way to the stage with two other women. She was beautiful in an exotic way, and by the third song she was completely nude and slightly perspiring from her exertions. I could appreciate Cort's interest. But then, it occurred to me that Cort already had a gorgeous woman waiting for him at home. *Hard to figure.*

After her dance, I watched Merkle leave the stage to muted applause and disappear into the back. Fifteen minutes and two other entreaties for lap dances passed before she reappeared. She was wearing high-cut shorts and a see-through bra. I waited and watched.

Instead of taking the stage again, Merkle worked the crowd, looking to get a drink or a lap dance. She eventually got to me and asked if I wanted to buy her a drink. I nodded and motioned to the chair next to me. She pulled the chair closer, sat, and raised a finger to one of her colleagues for a drink.

"My name is Dee Dee, what's yours?"

"I thought your name was Willow."

She looked at me suspiciously. "Do I know you?"

"No, I'm involved in the Cort trial, and I'd like to talk to you."

She leaned back and gave me an appraising stare that worked its way to mean. "How dare you come into my work! See that huge guy over there?" She gestured. *It would have been hard to miss him.* "I could call him over and he would thump your ass and make you eat asphalt."

I looked at the RV disguised as a man and put my hands up defensively. "That, I imagine he could do. But I'm only here to talk. I'm prosecuting Max Cort, and I was hopeful you would spare me some time."

She took a couple of beats to consider whether I should be tossed. "Listen, I want to make this clear so people will quit bothering me. I haven't seen Max for a long time." She paused and then added, "Once I figured him out, I cut him off."

"What do you mean, figured him out?"

She hesitated, not sure she wanted to engage me. Grudgingly, she said, "Things started to get a little tense. He got too physical and started to scare me. He was a cop, and I knew he could disappear me." *Disappear me?* There was another long pause before Willow half-whispered, "He killed her, didn't he? I followed the trial."

"He did. And I'm going to try and convince a jury of that." Her stare was intense. "I would appreciate you talking to me about him."

She looked at me as if that was the most foolish request anyone had ever made. "He finds out that I talked to you, he'll come after me."

"Not if he is in prison for the rest of his life."

Merkle gave a dismissive chortle. "Good luck with that. You couldn't convict him the first time, what makes you think you're going to get him this time around?" She looked up and caught a stare from that same huge bouncer. "You need to buy a lap dance, or I have to move on."

I agreed. She took my hand and led me back to one of the curtained booths. It was dark. She sat right next to me and took off her top, explaining that the bouncers check on the booth activity, so it had to look legitimate. *Legitimate being a relative term.*

"To answer your question, I wasn't the prosecutor at the first trial. But I was brought in to convict this time around. It would help me to know if you are planning to provide an alibi for him."

Merkle gave me another scrutinizing look. "I need to get this thing behind me. He finds out I talked to you, I'm dead. I mean really dead."

Maintaining strict eye contact, I made my pitch. "Willow, he's probably been abusing women his whole life. If he gets away with this, he'll just keep going." Through the dim light I could see her considering. I gave her time, and when she didn't respond, I lowered my voice to a whisper. "Don't let him get away with it."

Suddenly she pulled on her top and stood. "I'm off at one. How about you buy me breakfast at Denny's over on Devore?"

I stood, trying to conceal my surprise. "Thanks, Willow. See you there."

By the time Willow arrived, I was wired on coffee. She was dressed in leggings and a bulky pullover sweater, covering as much of her body as she could. As she sat, the server, an elderly woman who looked as if she had been working the graveyard shift for years, asked her, "The usual?"

Willow nodded. "Thanks, Margaret."

"Your after-work haunt?" I asked, and got a tired nod. "Thanks again for agreeing to talk to me."

She gave me a *I'm not so sure this is the right thing to do* look. "Like I said, Max can be a scary guy. I'm not exactly pleased to be here. But if this is the only way for people to quit bothering me, to get this all behind me . . ." She waved her hand distractedly.

"I understand that."

She got up and went to the restroom, and when she returned, her breakfast had arrived: three eggs over medium, bacon, hash browns, pancakes, and orange juice. She chuckled weakly as she registered my surprise at her mountain of food. "I burn a lot of calories doing what I do. This is how I keep my weight up."

"Bon appétit." I grinned.

She started with the eggs. "I know what you're looking for."

Between bites, she set out the story of her relationship with Cort. Cort had been a regular at the club, and following his persistence, they began "dating." She was drawn to his commanding presence. The relationship lasted about five months, oftentimes with late-night "dates" at her place when he left the station.

"Around New Year's, a year and a half ago, I broke it off. He had become increasingly obsessed with talking about his wife. He referred to her as the bitch trying to ruin his life. Sometimes it got pretty explicit about what he would do to her. Finally, I had enough. I was tired of his rants, and like I said, he was getting scarier and scarier. When I told him it was over, he lost it and grabbed me by my neck. I thought he was going to kill me. I must have lost consciousness, because I remember that he slapped me awake. I don't know how long I was out." Her sentences were coming in bursts. "He told me that he was the one who ended things, not me." She paused, taking in some deep breaths. "To this day, I'm not certain what he meant by that—whether he ended relationships, or lives. Then he grabbed my arms so hard it left bruising, jerked me to my feet, and told me he could have me anytime he wanted. It would always be his choice." She paused again, looked down at her food, and pushed the plates away. "He scared the shit out of me. As we are sitting here right now, a year and a half later, he still scares the shit out of me. I have panic attacks that he could burst in wherever I'm at and kill me." She wiped her eyes. "Wherever I'm at, I always sit where I can see the door and know where the exits are."

Neither of us spoke. With shaky hands, she sipped some water.

"Has he come near you since you broke it off?" I asked gingerly.

"No."

"Christie was killed in February 2015 and you haven't seen him since?"

She nodded in agreement. "But before the trial, he sent one of his guys to give me a subpoena and a note."

"A note?"

"Yeah, instructing me to testify that he was at my place the morning of February 4."

"I don't suppose you kept the note?"

"Course not."

"Have you gotten a subpoena for the second trial?"

"No, and I hope I don't get one."

"Let's back up. So you haven't seen him since New Year's before Christie's death?"

"Right. I told the bouncers at the club to keep him out."

"How about at your apartment?"

"After he left that last night, I became paranoid. I moved out the next day. He scared me that bad. I also told my club manager to bar him from coming into the club. For months, I had one of the bouncers escort me to and from my car." Another long silence before she added, "When I heard that his wife had disappeared, I didn't want to admit it, but I just knew that he'd finally done it. He'd made her disappear."

I sipped some more coffee. She pinched off a bite of pancake and slowly chewed.

"You showed up at the trial but then refused to testify. What was that about?" I asked.

"Cort sent me a text promising that if I testified that I was with him the night his wife disappeared, he would never bother me again. I thought I could do it. But when I saw him sitting there in the courtroom that fear hit me again, and I didn't believe he would let me be. I thought, 'What the hell am I doing?' I did my best to maintain my composure. I just needed to get out of there."

"I was in court that day, and you didn't appear upset or nervous."

"What's your name again? I'm sorry, I forgot."

"Jake. Jake Clearwater." *I didn't mean to channel Bond, it just came out.*

"Jake, I'm an entertainer. I can usually control my emotions. How do you think I get through some of those lap dances with some asshole drooling all over me while he's grabbing my tits? I might be the best actor you've ever seen."

I grinned at her. "Quite a life you've got, Willow."

"It pays well." She gave a halfhearted smile. "I figure I've got another two years before the tits start to sag, and then I'll have to move on to a real job."

"Will you testify for me?"

She looked at me in stark amazement. "Testify to what?"

"That he threatened you, that he wanted you to testify for him, to give him a fake alibi."

"You're kidding. Aren't you listening? I'm telling you this stuff so that you'll leave me alone."

"Willow, he's a predator! He's going to hurt other women unless we can cage him."

"Damn right, he's a predator! And I don't want him coming after me."

"Can you at least assure me that you won't testify for him this time around?"

"I want to stay as far from him as I can."

"I understand. I know you're in a tough spot." I handed her my card. "If there is anything I can do, call."

"Listen, Jake, you seem like a straight-up guy, but I've got to watch out for myself."

"Okay." I dropped two twenties on the table and left.

I told Lisa about my evening at the Rocks. She sat back and gave me a Mona Lisa smile. "Tough duty, Clearwater. I've never been to a strip club. Tell me about it."

I leaned back and grinned. "It wasn't as raunchy as you would imagine. The bouncers keep things pretty tight. The place advertises nudes, and it delivers on that."

"Was it worthwhile? What do you think she'll do?"

"I just don't know."

CHAPTER 29

THE MOTIONS

Later that week, Wills and I sat down to finalize which of the various parts of the trial we would each have primary responsibility for. I would take voir dire. We would consult and make final decisions regarding juror selection. I would make the opening statement and conduct the direct exam of Mary Lynn. Wills would direct Ossoff and conduct the direct exam on Sgt. Ponce. And if necessary, he would also take Dr. Simone, the DNA expert. MacPherson had stipulated to Simone's testimony during the first trial, but that didn't mean she would stipulate this time around. We agreed that, should MacPherson call any witnesses, we would make a decision on who would do the cross-examination. Though Will's closing in the first trial was excellent, we decided together that for the sake of continuity to the jury, closing argument was all mine.

Tuesday, July 19, six days from trial. The date set to hear the in limine motions. It was a full house. It had been five months since the conclusion of the first trial, and once again the Cort trial would be a media spectacle. The news trucks with their cables and antennas virtually took over Second Street fronting the Foltz Building. Since I was now a government employee, I was able to park in the underground garage along with the rest of the county employees and avoid the media crush, as well as the onlookers. I met Wills and Ossoff in Wills's office, and the three of us walked to the courtroom together. As I entered, some odd-looking man grabbed my arm, asking for an autograph. I shook him off. *Autographs were something Clayton Kershaw and LeBron James did.*

When we arrived in the courtroom, Cort and MacPherson were already seated with their investigator. Wills and I went to her and shook hands. She was dressed in an elegant cream-colored dress, one that would have been well-suited for an executive board room. I noted that she had cut inches from her blond mane. If anything, she was more attractive than ever.

"Welcome to the show, Jake." Nodding at Wills, she said, "John and I have been here before."

"Perhaps we'll get some closure this time around," I said, with a grin.

She smiled graciously. "My closure would be different from your closure."

"You're right about that." I nodded and walked to my table. It felt familiar to be at the prosecutor's table. It had been better than five years since I had last had that honor. Since the judge had yet to appear, I went over to the bailiff and clerk and introduced myself. They were friendly and gracious. The clerk, an older woman with '70s-style hair, leaned over her desk and whispered, "Nail that guy. He's evil." *Too bad she wasn't on the jury.*

I leaned back to her, feeding the conspiratorial tone between us. "That's why I'm here. I'm going to give it my best shot." After a beat, I said, "Your judge wasn't real friendly with me. Why's that?"

"I don't know." She gave me an apologetic face. "I think he's irked that the DA felt he needed an outsider. Keep in mind that *he* was the DA, back in the day. He's always been protective of the office."

I nodded my understanding and retired back to my table. Wills and I sat side by side. Ossoff sat behind us.

At 9:10, Judge Walter ascended the bench. The bailiff called court to order, and we all stood.

Walter immediately zeroed in on me. "Counselor, is this how you show your respect to this court?"

Puzzled, I asked, "I'm sorry Your Honor, what are you referring to?"

Before Walter answered, Wills looked at me and noted that my tie was not knotted tight at my neck. He reached over and pulled the knot taunt.

Walter clarified in a stern voice, "I expect counsel to be properly attired and demonstrate their respect for the court. Am I clear, counselor?"

I hesitated and cocked my head. *What the hell?* Finally I muttered, without thinking, "No disrespect intended." The exchange was surreal. I had never been called out like that. It was extraordinary. I'm certain my face flushed, not with embarrassment, but with anger. I had to figure that it was Walter's pique over DA Haines's decision to bring me in that inspired that kind of ire. Apparently, my presence continued to be a sore point for the judge. As I continued to stand, my anger only grew, and I struggled to maintain my composure. Wills reached over and pulled me down to my seat. I regretted not responding immediately. However, letting my anger lead the way was not prudent or practical. I'd bide my time; I'd have opportunities to dig back. I didn't know when, I didn't know how, but an opportunity would arise. *It was a rough start to what was sure to be a rough trial.*

Satisfied that he had asserted control, Walter called the case, looked at MacPherson, and smiled. "Ms. MacPherson, welcome back to my courtroom. I trust the past couple of months have been productive."

"Your Honor, it's good to be back in beautiful Los Angeles, and in your courtroom." *What a bullshit lovefest.*

Addressing MacPherson, Walter said, "I read your motions, so let's start there. You're requesting a juror questionnaire." He shrugged apologetically. "I typically reserve those for capital cases; I'm not inclined to burden my jurors with a questionnaire in this matter. But I'm willing to listen."

MacPherson stepped to the side of counsel table and gestured to the full house. "As evidenced by this full courtroom and the media activity outside the courtroom, this case has generated intense attention. I'm concerned that potential jurors have been exposed to the coverage and may well enter into this trial with preconceptions. I believe a questionnaire would allow the state, me, and this court to identify if, and to what extent, the jurors have been influenced by the coverage."

Walter turned to Wills, pointedly avoiding eye contact with me. "Mr. Wills, what is the state's position regarding questionnaires?"

"Your Honor," Wills responded with grace, "I agree with counsel concerning the media coverage, but I'm indifferent as to the benefits of a questionnaire. We're okay either way."

"Mr. Wills, you are not being particularly helpful regarding the matter." Clearly, Walter was looking for Wills to challenge MacPherson's request for questionnaires. Walter didn't want it to look as if this was an arbitrary decision on his part.

Wills cocked his head and put out his hands, "I'll submit to the court's judgment."

Walter turned to MacPherson. "Counsel, I think during voir dire we should be able to address any concerns regarding juror preconceptions." He looked at her, giving her an opportunity to respond. When she didn't, he denied her motion.

"Your second motion, Ms. MacPherson?"

"I'm requesting a sequestered voir dire. I realize that's a bit unusual in a non-capital case, but as I mentioned earlier, the people of this county have been saturated with information regarding this case. The publicity has been intense. In light of this court's ruling regarding questionnaires, I think the opportunity to sequester and individually question each prospective juror is necessary to ensure that we get a jury as free of preconceptions as possible." She paused before adding, "Mr. Cort has been demonized in the media, and I'm concerned about going forward under such a specter. More specific scrutiny of each prospective juror would alleviate some of my concerns."

"Thank you, counsel." Again turning to Wills and avoiding contact with me, Judge Walter addressed the prosecution: "Mr. Wills?" *I remained a nonentity.*

"Your Honor, my position as to sequestration is largely consistent with my view on questionnaires. I believe our standard voir dire will be sufficient to address defense counsel's concerns, and I'll point out the obvious: individual questioning is laborious and time intensive. It could stretch jury selection from days to weeks."

"I agree, Mr. Wills." Walter nodded. "Ms. MacPherson, I will allow counsel additional time for questioning to alleviate your concerns. Motion denied. Anything further from the defense?"

"No, Your Honor."

"I understand the state has two motions. Mr. Wills, you may be heard."

"Actually, Mr. Clearwater will speak to our first motion."

I stood and locked eyes with Walter, holding my look through the uncomfortable silence to make a point. *I'm in this trial, you asshole, whether you like it or not.* "Judge, as you know, we filed a *Pitchess* motion to examine Lt. Cort's personnel file."

"I'm aware of what such a motion is, counselor," he said with an edge. "I've also read your brief on the matter. It is woefully lacking as to sufficient cause supporting your motion. In my mind, there are inadequate facts supporting your request for digging into such files. I believe such files should remain confidential, unless a strong showing of cause has been made."

Without waiting for his invitation to respond, I was at him. "As this court is aware, when there are allegations of police use of excessive force or any other acts of violence, that officer's files can be reviewed confidentially by the court for any such instances. I'm asking you to undertake such a review."

"You list, as a basis for your motion, one alleged incident, that being Lt. Cort's alleged, one-time battery of his spouse. The justification for such a claim is that an officer under the color of authority physically abused that authority. I don't read that as sufficient basis for your request."

"May I respond?"

"Go ahead." His voice was uninviting.

"I believe you are reading the requirements too narrowly. When officers of the law engage in acts or an act of violence, it is appropriate to examine their past and determine whether there is a pattern of abusive conduct. We heard during the first trial that Lt. Cort struck his wife. That opens the door into his past conduct."

"I don't share your understanding of the law." In a condescending voice he continued. "Perhaps in your previous county, judges are less vigilant in protecting confidential files, but here in this court, we take that concern very seriously. Such motions refer to conduct under the color of authority." He pounded his gavel. "Motion denied."

"May I be heard?"

"No, I've made my ruling. Move on." His hostility, palpable.

There was an uncomfortable silence. I remained standing, staring at Walter. Walter broke contact and needlessly shuffled some papers. Having made my unspoken statement, I sat as Wills rose and broke the impasse. "Our second motion concerns the admissibility of a demonstrative aid. I believe it is in the best interest to have the court review our aid prior to discussing its admissibility."

"Okay, Mr. Wills. We will stand in recess while counsel and I review the prosecution's offer."

As we assembled in Walter's chambers and everyone took seats, I addressed Walter. "Your dressing down of me was inappropriate and displayed a hostility toward me which I find compromises your judicial temperament." My words felt out-of-body, as if spoken by someone else.

Walter appeared momentarily taken back by my verbal slap in his face, but he quickly recovered and leaned over his desk and angrily responded, "I resent your insinuation, and I will brook no further insolence from you."

"Insolence?" I responded, leaning over his desk, my anger on full display. "It is not insolence to speak the truth. You made it clear when DA Haines appointed me that you were concerned about his decision. I understand your misgivings. But that was his call to make, not yours. I demand to be treated with respect and dignity throughout this trial!" I briefly paused. "If you cannot conduct this trial fairly, perhaps you should consider recusing yourself."

Walter stood, his face white. Heart-attack white. He very deliberately took a breath, composing himself. "Counselor," he said bitterly, "I'm going to let your comment go unaddressed, since there is no merit to your claim, and further, I'm not going to cite you for contempt at this time. But with that said, you very well should understand that any further outburst or attacks by you will result in severe consequences."

We stared at one another until Walter resumed his seat.

The room was graveyard silent until Wills broke the impasse. "May we show the demonstrative?"

Had I squelched our chances of getting the video in? *Shit!*

Walter nodded, and Wills set up his laptop where everyone could see. We watched in silence. Everyone in the room was still replaying the acidic confrontation between Walter and me. As we neared the conclusion of the film, MacPherson was slowly shaking her head. *Was it at the exchange with Walter or at the film?* When the film was concluded, Walter, looking at Wills and me, asked, "Which of the two of you are making the argument for inclusion?"

Wills said, "I am, Your Honor." *Thank God for that. I could have been arguing the benefits of sliced bread and been trampled.*

Walter looked at MacPherson. "Let's start with Merci's take on the film." *First name for Merci, last names for Wills and me.*

"Thank you, Your Honor. As I was watching, I was amazed at the state's audacity. This, whatever you call it, is patently speculative and prejudicial." She paused, organizing her argument. "Let's start with speculation. Without any foundation, it presumes Lt. Cort's conduct: what he did, where he went, and how long it took. Again, without any basis. That alone is sufficient to exclude this"—she groped for the word—"spectacle." She continued, her voice smothered in incredulity. "Furthermore, the prejudicial impact on the jury would be profound. The state is in essence offering their version of how Lt. Cort could have done what they are alleging. This thing tramples the requisite balancing test between the probative value and the prejudicial impact required under section 352 of the California Evidence Code." *Well argued.*

Walter nodded and turned to Wills.

"Your Honor, we've all had the benefit of seeing how the first trial played out. One of the takeaways from the defense is that there was insufficient time for the defendant to accomplish what we believe he did during that unaccounted three-and-a-half- to four-hour window. Our demonstrative aid is simply putting before the jury what we could have our investigator testify to. Det. Ossoff, using a map of the area encompassing the residence, the sheriff's station, and the reservoir, could testify to the distance and the travel time from point to point. She could also testify that within the time parameters there was sufficient time to engage in other conduct. This is not speculative but rather a demonstration of feasibility, and as such it would assist the jury in the search for the truth." *Well done, John.*

Walter arched his long gray eyebrows, inviting MacPherson to respond.

"This is nothing short of an incredibly prejudicial speculation of Lt. Cort's conduct that early morning. This demonstrative aid, as the prosecution likes to refer to it, is anything but innocuous. This puts Lt. Cort behind the wheel as he allegedly goes about disposing of his wife's body." She drew in a breath. "The entirety of this so-called aid is speculative, and its overwhelmingly prejudicial impact compromises my client's right to a fair trial."

Without waiting for the judge, Wills responded. "This is simply another way of putting before the jury what we have every right to do." He paused. "We have a heavy burden to prove the defendant murdered Christie Cort without the benefit of her remains. Our demonstrative is simply offered to explain feasibility. The fact that we've chosen to use film to demonstrate what we have every right to put before the jury is not speculative or unduly prejudicial."

Walter leaned back in his chair. "I'm going to take the matter under advisement. I'll let everyone know of my ruling within the next few days." He scanned the faces. "Anything else to take up?"

There wasn't, and we were dismissed.

Wills and I retreated to Wills's office. The moment he closed the door, Wills unloaded on me. "Dammit Jake, that was terrible timing to take on Walter, given the tenuous nature of our demo!"

I put my hands up in a defensive posture. "You're right. But I couldn't just let him run roughshod over me before we even got underway. His hostility couldn't go unanswered. Otherwise I think it would have just gotten worse." I let out a breath, and continued. "I know the timing was unfortunate, but his conduct had to be checked."

Wills slumped in his chair and blew out some breath. "I understand why you did what you did, but we have enough challenges without dealing with a hostile judge."

"John, my response was not entirely out of anger. I truly felt I needed to call him out. I was willing to take a contempt citation to make my point. Now that he understands that I won't tolerate his crap, we have a better shot at getting a fair trial." I grinned, adding, "Or just the reverse, that he will do everything he can to screw us."

Wills shook his head in amazement. "Dammit, Jake. It's going to be quite a ride."

"Your argument for admissibility was clean. I think we are going to get it in. If for no other reason than for Walter to show how he is not hostile to our case."

CHAPTER 30

ABBOTT'S COUNSEL

Thursday, four days to trial. It was time to have a serious sit-down with Marge Abbott about voir dire and jury selection. Voir dire is about the lawyers questioning and indoctrinating the prospective jurors, and jury selection is the actual selecting of jurors. Actually, *selecting* is the wrong word. Jury selection is not so much about picking the *right* jurors, but rather about deselecting the *wrong* jurors. Bearing in mind the unanimity requirement for conviction, we couldn't afford even one wrong juror. The pressure is always on the prosecutor. Eleven-to-one for conviction is not a win.

Wills and I met with Abbott in her office at ten o'clock in the morning. Too early for lunch, but there was very good coffee and fresh pastries. We coffeed up and took seats at her conference table.

Marge was all business. "Before we even get to jury selection, we need to set the stage with some preconditioning of the prospective jurors. I watched both MacPherson's and John's voir dires. MacPherson was very good and certainly set the stage for the defense. John, your effort was okay, but lacked the energy and clear focus I think we need."

Wills interjected, "Marge, I realize that my effort was a bit flat, so I appreciate your candor. My goal is to win this thing. I'm a big boy, and I can handle the critique."

"Thanks, John," she said. "You were up against an accomplished opponent who presents us with a number of challenges. While MacPherson didn't paint a false narrative of Cort, she played on the edges, and she emphasized his law-enforcement service. Her personalization of Cort somewhat mitigated his negatives and focused on his long career in law enforcement. As I previously suggested to Jake, we've got to recast the personal narrative of this guy. He's not a good guy—he's a mean, abusive adulterer." She looked at Wills. "You lost the personalization, or should I say, the depersonalization battle."

"I agree, I should have hit him harder."

"Yes," she nodded. "By the conclusion of voir dire, the jurors had a favorable impression of MacPherson, which mitigated much of their negative impression of Cort."

"John, you were up against it," I said, commiserating. "I told Marge when we first met that MacPherson's voir dire was as good as I had ever seen."

Marge drank some coffee and continued. "Her presence and easy banter with the jurors was off the map. She did what the great lawyers do: she facilitated a group discussion by using open-ended questions. As both of you know, one mark of a good voir dire is that the jurors are talking more than the lawyer. It always amazes me that so many lawyers screw that up. Voir dire is about the lawyers listening more and talking less. MacPherson was superb at incrementally escalating the jurors into the deeper issues. By the conclusion of her voir dire, several jurors were ready to walk through fire for her."

She turned to me. "Jake, you saw what I saw. When you get up to follow her voir dire, you must be completely aware of the spell she casts. You've got to break the spell and spin things back our way.

You need to refocus the jurors on his abuse and on his motivations."
She broke off a piece of pastry and chewed.

"Point taken," I responded. She was stating the obvious. "Now
share with us what we need on our jury."

"Gender, age, occupation, and sophistication are my starting
points. Let's start broad and then narrow our focus. Gender?" She
took a breath. "With the understanding that this is an unrealistically
simplified binary and heterosexual analysis . . . women over men.
MacPherson's physical presence and charm will, in a very general
sense, play better with men than women. Half of the men will
fantasize about her and want to please her. Conversely, as I mentioned
to you last time, Jake, you present an attractive package that most
likely will carry more weight with women."

She looked at her laptop. "From the eight jurors we were
able to interview from the first trial, four of the five who voted to
acquit were men." She gave us a knowing look. "So let's move on
to age. Again, I'm only talking in generalities here. But when a cop
is in the picture, age can factor in. Older people tend to be more
supportive of cops. However, that dynamic is dependent on cops
being witnesses, not defendants. I'm still thinking through how
Cort's status as a cop defendant plays out. Older people might be
turned off by Cort, feeling that he violated his badge. On the other
hand, he's still a ranking law-enforcement officer and carries the
imprimatur of his job."

"But when they learn that he had an affair and abused his wife,
being a cop who is a bully cuts our way," I added.

"Agreed," said Abbott, nodding. "Age, in my view, doesn't figure
to be a factor. And that was borne out in the after-action interviews
of the first trial. We couldn't tell one way or another."

"Occupation—how do you see that playing out?" I asked, as I
sipped my coffee.

"I don't see that a person's occupation will factor in here. Again, having a cop as the defendant turns the generalized notions on their heads."

Wills spoke up. "People are not used to cops in the docket. I struggled with that during the trial. It was hard to see how the jurors would react to what they must have thought of as an anomaly."

"You're right, John," Abbott said. "A person's generalized perception of law enforcement doesn't help here." She pushed back in her chair. "Let's slide over to my last general category: level of sophistication, particularly as viewed through their education. I realize that education and sophistication are not in lockstep, but that's the crude connection we are stuck with here. So, do we want college grads and bosses, or high school diplomas and employees?"

I looked at Wills. "John, you first."

"Cort's murder scheme was pretty sophisticated, and our theory involves the jurors following our train of thought. Further, the jurors have to believe that Christie didn't run away. We need the jurors to think things through." He paused and mused, "I guess I'm inclined to go highbrow."

"Probably," I said, nodding in agreement. "We need thinkers to act as leaders in the jury room to help guide the group. But to be honest, I'm not real big on this generalization."

"Gentlemen," Marge added, "I'm also conflicted on this one. I don't see us getting much traction with it."

I sat back and gave a halfhearted laugh. "Not much to work with here. Maybe gender, but only maybe."

"You're right," she said. "Jury selection will come down to the questioning of each juror. How they react to you and MacPherson. Body language, level of sincerity, leader or follower." She got up and paced. "No easy answers. However, in my experience, every voir dire comes down to an evaluation of each individual called into the box.

That's when we can get our best handle on who we are dealing with, and along with my most trusted colleague, we will be sitting in the courtroom and evaluating. The questioning regarding their views on cops and domestic violence will help make some decisions." She paused, then said, "Jake, while we focus on their views on cops and domestic violence, you've got to dive into circumstantial evidence. That has to overcome the lack of a body. Even if we can't see her body, that doesn't mean she wasn't killed."

"I've got some ideas on that." I nodded. "The lack of a body is and will remain our biggest challenge." Then I added, to lighten things up, "MacPherson has her own consultants." I grinned, looking at Abbott. "We're counting on our experts being better than her experts."

"We won't let you down," Abbott assured us. "But our analysis can only go so far. This is far from an exact science. Keep in mind, a huge component is the impressions formed as to each side during voir dire—your likability and credibility versus her likability and credibility." She tapped the table with her index finger. "Let's talk themes and approaches."

Our discussion went on as lunches were brought in. As we worked through lunch, we determined we wanted to associate Cort with words like "bully," "manipulative," "ambitious," and "misogynistic." With Christie, we would associate "victim," "trapped," "fearful," and "intimidated."

CHAPTER 31

THE CALM BEFORE . . .

Friday, three days out. Lisa offered to pass on our weekend, thinking I needed the time to prepare. But I wasn't about to lose a Lisa weekend. She arrived at six that evening and joined Tony, Eve, and me on the deck. She had come straight from work and had on a beautiful navy dress. Not typical vice principal attire, but then again, she was not anybody's idea of what a vice principal would look like. We hugged, and I got the kind of kiss a fiancé would get. Tony had chicken on the barbecue. Eve had a pitcher of sangria with strawberries and nectarines made from a recipe she found in a magazine. The recipe was worthy of publication.

Lisa and I had not told anyone about our engagement except Duke. It was the second time around for both of us. We wanted to keep it low-key and private. As Eve was pouring everyone a glass of her concoction, I took Lisa's hand and brought her to her feet. I dropped to a knee and pulled a small box from my pocket. I opened it and showed her the ring, a silver band set with diamonds. She gave a radiant smile as I slid it onto her finger.

Eve exclaimed, "Oh my God, Tony, he's finally doing it!" She grabbed her phone and took a photo of me putting the ring on Lisa's finger. I stood and we embraced with watery eyes. Eve hugged Lisa and then me. Actually, I got a full mouth kiss from Eve. Tony was all congratulations and handshakes. As we gathered ourselves and sipped sangria, I explained that this was already a done deal, and I told them about my earlier proposal at the bed and breakfast. Lisa explained about our decision to be low-key, and then she asked our gracious hosts if we could have a small wedding on the beach in front of their house.

"Of course, of course!" Eve was excited and pleased.

I asked Tony if he would do us the honor of officiating.

He smiled and echoed his wife. "Of course, of course." Everyone laughed.

Eve said, "Since you are doing this on the down low, I assume there will not be many guests. If you'd like, we can do the reception here."

Lisa hugged Eve again. "Eve, that would be special. We're only going to have a handful of guests, and this would be perfect."

To celebrate, the next evening, Tony and Eve insisted on taking us to Nobu Malibu, a very, very upscale Japanese fusion restaurant on the south side of the Malibu Pier. We walked barefoot along the hard packed sand and arrived right on time for our seven o'clock reservation. We rinsed our feet, slipped on sandals, and were seated against the floor-to-ceiling window, virtually hovering over the dark surf.

Nobu was the place to see and be seen. Lisa was interested in celebrity gazing. Maybe we would catch a glimpse of Bruce Springsteen or Sting. Maybe a Dodger. The rest of us had lived in Malibu long enough to not bother.

The menu was extensive; the variety and uniqueness called

for careful decision-making. We laughed when our drinks, colored bright red and blue and dotted with tiny umbrellas, arrived at our table. Then things got serious. Eve, a Nobu veteran, ordered a seaweed salad, followed by king crab tempura. *Not my choice.* Tony chose an artichoke salad and two lobster tacos. Lisa and I agreed to share the seafood ceviche, and for her entrée she ordered spicy snow crab. I had the lobster sweet and sour. *How could anyone pass on lobster sweet and sour?*

Dinner was brilliant—all that hubbub about Nobu's was well deserved, and all the hubbub about their ridiculous prices was also well deserved. Lisa thought she saw a Laker, although she didn't know which Laker. I caught a brief glimpse; I think it was James Worthy. Following several more cocktails, we opted to Uber for our short drive back home. The drinks had taken the measure of us.

Sunday, I was up dark and early. I couldn't sleep much with the trial, and in particular the voir dire, looming. I let Lisa sleep and took my coffee on the sand, sitting on a towel watching the sunrise. There was a slight invigorating chill. I worried through the different approaches I could take at voir dire. I couldn't seem to settle. I finally decided to wait and observe how MacPherson would proceed during her voir dire. I did have the advantage of going second, so I could pick up the discussion she had initiated and bend it back my way. It was a plan, though a bit loose.

Lisa broke my reverie as she snuggled up to me. She handed me a fresh coffee and gave me a good morning kiss. We watched the surf in companionable silence. Lisa leaned into me and said, "I've been thinking that if it would not be too distracting for you, I'd watch the trial in person. It's my summer and I have some time off." As she spoke, she was intently studying my face. "I'm caught up at work. I'd like to be there to support you."

I grinned and wrapped my arm around her. "You are always a distraction. And the answer is yes, I welcome your distracting presence."

That afternoon, we made sandwiches and cut up some watermelon and ate on my deck. Lisa was admiring her ring and wanted to know where and when I had purchased it. I refused to give details, figuring the mundane details of my shopping trip would diminish the mystical appeal. We talked through a date: August, after the trial and before fall classes. It was incredibly short notice, but it was going to be an incredibly short guest list. Lisa's list included her father; her best friend from her school; her agent, Julia; and her principal. My list was Duke, Suzelle, Howard, John and Edie Chauncey, and, of course, our hosts, Tony and Eve. It's too bad my dad had passed; he would have enjoyed all these people.

Trial Tip #9: Simplify the Language

Plain words and simple sentences help ensure that there won't be an intellectual gap between the advocate and the jurors. For instance, "cut" is a better word than "laceration." Likewise, "bruise" is better than "contusion." When expert witnesses testify, they often lapse into speech and jargon peculiar to their calling. It is the advocate's responsibility to translate any such speech into easily understood language.

CHAPTER 32

VOIR DIRE

Monday morning, Lisa was seated in one of the two press seats reserved to Channel 6. I had pulled some strings. The downside was that Jeremy Kaye, the overbearing station manager, filled the other. By late morning on Monday, Merci MacPherson had finished her voir dire. As anticipated, it was brilliant. Proceedings had gotten started on time at 9:00 a.m. Fifty prospective jurors had been ushered into four reserved rows in the gallery. Judge Walter had graciously welcomed them to the courtroom. *He could play nice when he chose to. After all, he was an elected official and had to answer to the good folks once every four years.*

Walter introduced Lt. Cort and MacPherson, and then John and me. He read the charge, and he told the assembled venire that the trial was scheduled to go no longer than three weeks. He explained that if any of the jurors had a hardship serving, they should stand and voice those concerns. This was the best opportunity for folks trying to escape jury duty to plead their case. However, this had become a celebrated case, and the typical reluctance to serve might be muted. Indeed, some people craved to be part of a headline-generating trial. Nonetheless, there were more than a handful of hardship claims, ranging from previously scheduled and paid-for vacations to childcare concerns to employers who would not give paid leave for as long as three weeks. Walter was, for the most part, accommodating, and fifteen of the fifty were granted hardship leaves and sent back to the jury assembly room.

Walter's clerk then randomly pulled twelve chits, and the prospective jurors with those numbers were seated in the jury box. Starting in the back row, from left to right, were one through six, and then the front row, also from left to right, seven through twelve. The judge explained that for security reasons, the names of the jurors would not be used. Each of the seated jurors were assigned a number by the seat they now occupied.

Walter's clerk powered up the projector, and a PowerPoint flashed across the screen, which called for basic biographical information. Walter called on each of the seated jurors to supply the requested details. He then engaged in the appropriate follow-up. By the time he concluded, it was time for the midmorning recess. When we were reassembled, Walter invited MacPherson to inquire. Dressed in an impeccably tailored midnight-blue pantsuit, she rose and stood behind Cort and, with a hand on his shoulder, introduced him. Cort was more animated than I had noticed during the first trial. I suspected some coaching had taken place. Cort nodded in sync with MacPherson's words. She then walked toward the jurors but stopped behind Wills and me. "These two gentlemen will be representing the state. Jake Clearwater and John Wills are both talented trial lawyers. I have the utmost respect for them."

I had never experienced opposing counsel doing that before, though I remembered she'd done the same when it was just Wills. *Nice, nice, nice, charming, charming, charming.* She then continued on to the jury box.

"Ladies and gentlemen of the jury, this is a hard case. A

beautiful young woman is missing, and Mr. Clearwater and Mr. Wills are going to try and convince you that Lt. Cort killed her. They," she continued as she turned to Wills and me, "are going to dig into Lt. Cort's life, looking for some evidence that he could kill his own wife. They are going to suggest that because he has done some things that call his character into question, he murdered his Christie." *His Christie, how galling.*

"But we are going to save them the trouble of delving into Lt. Cort's past problems because he"—MacPherson nodded at Cort—"has encouraged me to tell you about himself, even the difficult parts." *Boil pricking at its finest.* The jurors were with her. Every eye was riveted on her. She was once again taking over the courtroom.

Motioning at Cort, she continued, "He's not been a good husband. He's cheated on his wife." She paused. "Shameful. And once, when arguing with her, he struck out at her. He's ashamed of his conduct, and even now he wishes he had been a better man, a better husband."

She leaned into the three prospective jurors in the front row center.

"His hope, as he endures the anxiety of this trial, is that Christie would forgive him and return home. That's right, return home. For, you see, he is convinced that she ran away." She paused for emphasis. "That's right, she ran away."

I stood and looked at MacPherson. "My apologies for interrupting, Ms. MacPherson." Then turning to the judge, I declared, "Your Honor, this is voir dire, not opening statement. I have yet to hear a single question asked of the prospective jurors." I hated to object, but there are limits, and she was way over the line. I had to reel her in.

Walter looked inquiringly at MacPherson. "Counsel?"

Unfazed, she responded, "My apologies, Your Honor." Turning to me with a gracious smile, she said, "Thank you for the heads up, Mr. Clearwater. I was just getting to my inquiries."

Dammit, she made me feel like I was the bad guy, even though she was the one who had pushed beyond what was appropriate.

She turned back to the jurors. "This is where I want to start." She slid over to face juror number seven, front row far left. "First off, I want to apologize for not addressing you by name, but you and the rest of your colleagues here understand we can't use your names, for security purposes." Number seven, a retired firefighter captain, nodded. "This questioning process can be a bit intrusive. Some people resent that intrusion. I get that." She shrugged and smiled. "My goal is to help get the fairest group of jurors possible." The firefighter nodded understandingly. "Let's talk a bit about your background. We learned a little about you when Judge Walter was questioning you, but your answers provided only the most basic information. I'd like to probe a little deeper into the whole group, but you are first." That elicited a smile from the firefighter. "We learned that you are a retired fire captain, that you are happily married, and that you are a world traveler. Did I get all that right?" No notes, perfect recall.

"You did."

"You told the judge that you didn't follow this case in the media, why was that?"

"I wasn't that interested."

"And now you're here." She gave him a bright smile, which he returned. "As you sit here, and based on what you've heard so far, have you formed any early impressions?"

"No, I haven't."

"So the fact that Lt. Cort has been charged with murder doesn't prejudice you against him?"

The fire captain paused, considering the question. "Since he was arrested and the DA brought charges, I have to assume there must be pretty good evidence of guilt." *Ouch! That's not what MacPherson was looking for.*

Nodding agreeably despite the unexpected response, MacPherson said, "Fair enough. However, you would also agree that as Lt. Cort sits before you, he is presumed innocent." *A so-so recovery; she had to move away from his remark. She didn't want him tainting the rest of the prospective jurors.*

"I understand and agree," he answered in a neutral voice.

She gave him an appreciative smile. "Thank you, sir." The lack of a follow-up confirmed that she was worried about him contaminating the panel. He was too sure of himself and, if given leave, might expound on the scrutiny a case receives from law enforcement and the prosecution before it is brought to trial. He did not present a cause challenge for MacPherson, but she would surely exercise a peremptory challenge on him.

She turned to number ten, a young woman who was a student at Cal State LA. "How about you?" MacPherson tilted her head at the woman. "What does the presumption of innocence mean to you?"

In a hesitant voice, tinged with an obvious fear of public speaking, she managed to get out, "I agree with the fire captain about the presumption of innocence." *A follower, whichever way the wind was blowing.* Despite the woman's obvious discomfort, MacPherson stayed with her.

"Let's probe a little deeper. What if during the trial, you learn that Lt. Cort was unfaithful, and maybe even an abusive husband? Would that cause you to rethink the presumption of innocence?"

"That would bother me," she managed, shrinking from the spotlight and MacPherson's full attention.

"Of course it would," MacPherson said, nodding understandingly, "but would you be inclined to believe that because of his past conduct, he might be someone who could murder his wife?"

Fortifying herself with a deep breath, she replied, "Not necessarily. I might not like him, but I would want to hear all the evidence one way or another." MacPherson was using this compliant juror to soften the impact of Cort's past abuse. No doubt she would continue to prick that boil throughout trial. Repeated often enough, its impact was increasingly mitigated. I flashed to the Rodney King trial in the midnineties, when the attorneys for the accused officers who beat King played the eighty-one-second videotape of the horrific beating by the four cops of King over and over for the jury. The shock, revulsion, and anger at the beating eventually lessened in the minds of the jurors, and as a result, the officers were eventually acquitted. To this day, it's difficult to reconcile that verdict.

"So you would agree that because he is not a good husband, that doesn't lead you to believe he is a murderer?"

"No, it doesn't."

"Thank you," MacPherson said, with an encouraging smile. "I want to direct that same question to you, sir." Looking at number six, who had revealed he was an orthodontist in the process of a divorce. "Does being a bad, even an abusive husband lead you to believe he could commit murder?"

"Of course not." He answered with the confidence of a man accustomed to being in charge. "I may not like him, but that doesn't mean he's a murderer. There's a huge gulf between bad behavior and murder." Number six was a strong presence, perhaps with the potential to lead the jury. *He was on my endangered list.*

"Let's change directions." She was staying with number six. "There may be evidence that Lt. Cort's wife, Christie, simply ran away and is in hiding. Can you imagine a situation where an abused wife might simply run away?"

He nodded thoughtfully. "I guess so, but I would want to hear some compelling evidence of that." *No shit.*

"That makes sense." She nodded. "Thank you." Putting out her hands to the entire group, she asked, "How about the rest of you? Would you find it believable that an abused spouse might just run away?"

Number one spoke up. She was a middle-aged executive with a research firm. "Running away seems an odd choice. Divorce would seem more likely to me. I've been there. I was once in a difficult marriage and decided to end it by getting a divorce. It never occurred to me to run away." *MacPherson had hit another speed bump.*

Unfazed, she nodded agreeably at number one and continued. "I appreciate you sharing your personal experience. Let's add another layer to my question. What if you learned that the woman had been threatened to not leave the marriage?"

Number one exhaled audibly. "That may be all the more reason to leave. But again, there are options short of running away." *This was my kind of juror. Tough, no nonsense, a leader. No way MacPherson would leave her on the jury.*

"Thank you for your thoughts." MacPherson understandably moved off the woman and turned to number four, an older man, who had raised his hand. "Yes sir."

"My daughter was briefly in a relationship with a dislikeable man. But she had the good sense to get out."

Nodding her understanding, MacPherson said, "Thank you for sharing that, sir. Will that experience carry over to your deliberations in this trial?"

"Nah, that was a long time ago. She found the right guy and has been happily married for fifteen years."

"Glad to hear that. Thank you for letting us know."

Juror number eight, a twenty-something who was dressed

far too casually and was slouching in her chair, raised her hand. MacPherson nodded for her to speak. "For a short time, I was in an abusive relationship. It got so bad, I seriously thought about just running away. But then he left and saved me the trouble." *Flaky, an attention seeker? I couldn't trust her on the jury.*

"Sorry for your troubles." MacPherson commiserated. "Hope things are better for you now."

She nodded and smiled. "They are. Got a good solid one this time."

MacPherson gave her a warm smile. "I'm glad." *Talk about connecting.*

She then centered herself in front of the jury. "Anyone else have thoughts on this difficult subject?" No one responded. "Okay, let's change topics. One of the more difficult decisions during a criminal trial is whether the defendant, the person accused, should take the witness stand. As you all know, the Fifth Amendment to our Constitution states that it's acceptable for an accused person to not take the witness stand." She paused and emphasized, "That's perfectly okay. There could be any number of reasons for such a decision. But despite the fact that it's a Constitutional right, that doesn't sit well with some people." Again she paused, letting that sink in. "As I stand here now, I don't know if Lt. Cort will take the stand in his own defense. But if, on my recommendation, for any number of reasons, he doesn't, will you hold that against him?" She held everyone's looks, and then moved over in front of number eleven, a retired police sergeant formerly from a Northern California county. "Sergeant, what do you think of this right to not testify?"

He was a big man who had grown a beard in his retirement. He cocked his head and responded, "I know it's his right not to testify—that's part of the game of trials." *Game of trials?* "We've got to accept it. I don't like it, but there you go." *Odd to raise this delicate issue with a former cop. Strange call.*

"Sergeant, I appreciate your candor. You said we've got to accept it. Does that mean you would not hold it against a person who exercised that right?"

"I would try very hard not to."

"You recognize that sometimes the lawyer has a lot to do with that decision. You also recognize that there can be concerns not known to the jurors that affect that decision?"

"I do."

"As you sit here now, would you hold it against Lt. Cort if he didn't testify?"

"Like I said. I would do my level best not to."

"Sergeant, that's all we can ask. Thank you for your thoughtful response." *She wouldn't dare leave this former cop on the jury. He may even present her a cause challenge. She could argue that he may not be able to follow the law. If her cause challenge was unsuccessful, she would have to use one of her precious peremptory challenges.*

MacPherson slid to her right and centered in front of number twelve, a middle-aged woman. "Ma'am, what did you think of the discussion about the Fifth Amendment right not to testify?"

"I understand a person not wanting to testify. I'm okay with that." She shrugged, "I read a lot and I know there can be a number of reasons why a person wouldn't testify. I wouldn't hold it against him."

Nodding approvingly, MacPherson said, "I appreciate your thoughtful response."

MacPherson's questioning went on for nearly an hour. During that time, she involved all twelve of the prospective jurors. She continued to masterfully employ open-ended questions. Her plan played out beautifully, just like Marge had said: one sign of a successful voir dire is if the jurors are talking more than the lawyer who is asking the questions. She certainly accomplished that.

At the conclusion of her questioning, she asked to approach. "Your Honor, I've got a cause challenge as to numbers one and eleven." We both had unlimited cause challenges, but only five peremptory challenges. Cause challenges had to do with some bias or conflict a potential juror might have, whereas peremptory challenges were, with few exceptions, discretionary with each lawyer. MacPherson, of course, wanted to save as many of her peremptories as possible, hence trying to burn numbers one and eleven for cause.

Her challenge of number one, the woman who had opted for divorce without considering running away, made sense. Completely apart from the merits of the challenge, number one had a commanding presence, which would make her a foreperson candidate. MacPherson couldn't take a chance on that. Judge Walter, without asking for my response, sent us back to our respective tables and asked number one, "Ma'am, despite your personal experience, would you be able to set that aside and judge this matter on the law and facts produced during the trial?"

Without hesitation, she replied, "I can, Your Honor."

Walter denied the motion and turned to number eleven, the retired cop. "Sir, would you be able to follow the law as I instruct despite any personal feeling you might have?"

Number eleven, nodding his head agreeably, answered, "I can, Your Honor."

And with that, Walter denied the challenges and dismissed us for the lunch recess.

I huddled in an attorney conference room with Wills, Abbott, and Abbott's associate, Murielle Pierce. Abbott checked her notes and said, "I would love to keep number one; she really fought back on the runaway theory. But there's no way MacPherson is going to leave her on. Likewise, she'll want to eliminate number eleven, the retired cop."

Wills said, "I agree, no way MacPherson doesn't kick those two. Conversely, number eight would be trouble for us. She considered running away instead of just breaking off the relationship. Beyond that, she's odd. I don't trust her."

Pierce jumped in. "Number six is also a problem. His responses about running away seemed feigned, like he was courting MacPherson. I don't trust him. Beyond that, he's an orthodontist, and medical professionals are always candidates to end up as forepersons." I shared Pierce's concern.

Abbott passed out water bottles and energy bars and said, "I like the retired cop. A straight shooter. I liked the way he worked around the Fifth Amendment issue. He wasn't buying it for a second. But she's going to kick him." She paused and scanned her notes again. "Jake, what did you think of number seven, the fire captain?"

"A sophisticated man. His comments about the scrutiny of cases showed a thoughtful, smart guy. I like him. He also has the potential to be a leader."

"MacPherson is going to absolutely kick him," Wills said.

"You're right," said Abbott. "Let's circle back to number eight, the strange little attention seeker. What kind of read did you get from her, Jake?"

"Hard to read," I said. "She kept looking over at me. I'm not sure what to make of that."

Abbott pulled a face. "Be careful with her. I couldn't get a strong feel from her."

Pierce zeroed in on number ten, the hesitant college student.

"She's a follower; she'll go along with the crowd. I wouldn't waste a peremptory on her."

When no one had further comment, Wills looked at me. "Jake, MacPherson wove her magic. Even when she caught some rough responses, she kept smiling as if everything was smooth as glass."

"He's right," said Abbott. "You've got to out-charm her without looking like you're trying to out-charm her."

We still had a half hour. I found Lisa in the hallway, cornered by Jeremy Kaye. "Hey Jeremy, thanks for keeping Lisa company." Turning to Lisa, "Let's head up to my office." In my office, she handed me an energy bar. "Gotta keep your strength up, counselor."

I chose to not tell her I'd already had one when I met with the others. "How are you getting on with Kaye?"

"He surely knows a lot about courtroom procedure and isn't afraid to mansplain with his vast knowledge, but I'll endure him to witness you in your element."

I had to laugh; he was such a pest. "Moving forward, what did you think of the defense lawyer?"

"Very pretty and very smooth, maybe a bit too smooth. I'm not sure if she's putting on an act."

"Interesting take. I'm afraid the jurors would disagree. They looked pretty enthralled."

She winked at me. That's right, winked. "Those jurors haven't seen charm yet. You're going to bowl them over."

Trial Tip #10: Voir Dire

Have ready explanations for frequently confused legal concepts, such as beyond a reasonable doubt and preponderance of the evidence. Prospective jurors often have ill-informed ideas concerning legal concepts. For instance, many jurors have the idea that beyond a reasonable doubt means beyond all doubt or beyond a shadow of a doubt. Misconceptions about the prosecutor's burden of proof could harm the prosecutor's case. A simple illustration focusing on the "reasonable" in "reasonable doubt" can assist in clearing up any confusion. Even though at the conclusion of the evidence, the judge will instruct on the various concepts, it is ill-advised to allow jurors to go through the trial laboring under a misunderstanding of the law.

CHAPTER 33

CHARMING, CHARMING, CHARMING

At 1:40 p.m., Walter took the bench, and his bailiff called court to order. Walter looked at Wills, and Wills looked at me. When I stood instead of Wills, Walter's shoulders visibly tightened, inching up toward his neck as he pursed his lips. *What a jerk. Suck it up, judge—we all suffer disappointments from time to time.*

I nodded to him. "Thank you, Judge." *Judge wasn't quite as dignified as "Your Honor."* The slight was intentional.

I turned to MacPherson. "Thank you for your thoughtful questioning, Ms. MacPherson." Stepping toward the jury, "And most of all, I want to thank you folks for answering your call of citizenship by being here today. As you already know, my name is Jake Clearwater, and along with my friend and co-counsel John Wills, I am here on behalf of the State of California in this important trial. This is an unusual matter, because the body of Christie Cort, the defendant's wife, has not been found. There is no body for Christie's family and friends to grieve over. There is no body to enable the forensic technicians to tell us how she was killed. While John and I will not be able to point to Christie's body during the trial, we will be able to tell you that the defendant is a veteran police officer who has investigated numerous murder cases, and that he understands the significant incriminating evidence an examination of a body can provide. Because of his experience, he also understands the difficulty of prosecuting a murder case without a body."

MacPherson stood, already aggravated so early into my voir dire. *Was this in response to my objection during her voir dire?* "Your Honor, is there a question in there somewhere?"

"He's leading up to it, Ms. MacPherson." *Walter cut me some slack—surprise, surprise.* I nodded at him. "What we will be able to also show you is that the defendant abused Christie, that he was having an adulterous affair, and that he threatened Christie with violence if she ever dared to divorce him and ruin his career."

"Again, I must object, Your Honor," MacPherson said, looking imploringly at Walter.

"Mr. Clearwater, confine yourself to inquiries," Walter admonished

I nodded graciously. "Pardon me, Judge." Turning back to the jurors, "I would like to follow-up on some of the areas you folks have been asked about. Let's start with your thoughts about Christie's body being missing." I looked at number five, an older man who had what appeared to be a perpetual frown, ringed by more wrinkles than a map that had been balled up and crammed into a glovebox. "Sir, I understand from the answers you supplied to Judge Walter that you served on a jury in a murder case a while back, correct?"

"Yes, I did. That must have been five or six years ago."

"I assume in that case there was a body?"

He grinned through the scowl, not an easy thing to do. "There was."

"Simply because in this case the victim's body was never recovered, would that fact alone prevent you from convicting?"

"No, but I would need to hear a lot of evidence that she was killed."

"Fair enough. I appreciate your answer. Let's open that question up to the rest of you folks. Any volunteers?"

There were several volunteers. Number two, a young man who was self-employed as a computer programmer, was the first to raise his hand. "I agree with the older guy's answer," nodding at number five. "I could convict without a body, if there was sufficient evidence to believe she was murdered."

Number nine, a semi-retired real estate agent, jumped in without being called upon. "A veteran officer would seem to understand that without a body, his chances of conviction would be reduced. I can see that. But like the previous answers, I would want very strong evidence that a murder had occurred."

I smiled at her. "Thank you, ma'am. I appreciate your enthusiasm and candor." I turned to number three, a self-employed web designer. "Your thoughts, sir?"

"I would want to be convinced beyond a shadow of a doubt that she was gone. There couldn't be any lingering questions."

"I'm glad you went there. Let's talk about the burden my colleague and I shoulder in this trial. Judge Walter, at the conclusion of all the evidence, is going to tell you that our burden is to convince you beyond a reasonable doubt that the defendant killed his wife. Now that's a phrase we've heard repeated on TV and in the movies for our entire lives. And I'm going to suggest to you that 'beyond a reasonable doubt,' despite the similar phrasing, is not the same as 'beyond a shadow of a doubt' or 'beyond all doubt.' Judge Walter will explain that when we are dealing with human affairs, it is difficult to be absolutely certain about pretty much anything. So through the centuries of lawmaking in this country, we have refined the legal standard to reflect a need to provide evidence beyond a *reasonable* doubt, not absolute doubt. So, if the evidence convinces you that there is no *reasonable* doubt, would you be able to follow the judge's guidance?"

"Thank you for that explanation. I guess I never really thought about the difference." He nodded. "I can follow the law."

"Your candor is refreshing. If my partner and I put on sufficient evidence establishing that Christie Cort was murdered by the defendant, would you be able to convict him, even without seeing Christie's body?"

"Yes, if you prove it beyond a reasonable doubt," he said with a smile.

I returned his smile, appreciating his comment, and moved on. "How about the rest of you? If we put on sufficient evidence to convince you beyond a reasonable doubt that Christie was murdered and that the defendant killed her, would you be able to convict?" I scanned the faces and got nods of assurances across the board.

I turned to number twelve, the woman who stated she had no concerns about a defendant invoking the Fifth Amendment not to testify. "If you are convinced beyond a reasonable doubt that the defendant murdered his wife, would you be able to convict?"

"I most certainly would."

I nodded and turned to face the twelve and said, "This prosecution presents some significant challenges beyond a missing body, as we—"

"Objection!" MacPherson stood again. "Your Honor, the counsel's comment presupposes a body. That is merely counsel's speculation. I ask that you admonish counsel and so instruct the jury."

Walter nodded. "I agree, Ms. MacPherson. Mr. Clearwater, please rephrase."

Third interruption; perhaps she was concerned. *Good.*

"Certainly. As I suggested, there are other considerations in this case. One is that a law-enforcement officer is the defendant. That could prove a complication for some people. Many of us view law enforcement as generally trustworthy—as upholding the law." Looking at juror number nine, who had volunteered a response earlier, I asked, "Since the defendant is in law enforcement, are you presupposed to believe that he wouldn't kill his wife?"

She was caught a bit off guard. "I don't know." She paused. "I trust the police. I think sometimes they are unjustly vilified. I want to believe the best of them."

"I completely understand. Many of us were raised that way." I nodded at her. "But will you be able to put those preconceptions aside and consider all the evidence in this case?"

She offered a faint head nod. "Yeah, I think I could." Still nodding, she rephrased her answer. "I will try my best."

I grinned at her reassuringly. "That's all we can ask."

I turned to number eleven, the retired cop. "Sir, will it be difficult for you to sit in judgment of another law-enforcement officer?"

"I don't think so. I firmly believe I can impartially evaluate the evidence."

"Thank you, sir." Stepping back and taking in the whole panel, I asked, "How about the rest of you? Will you be able to evaluate the evidence fairly without any preconceptions concerning law-enforcement officers?"

Again, I got affirmation from the jurors.

Acknowledging the group's assent, I stepped directly in front of juror number five, the fire captain. "Defense counsel spent a lot of time questioning you folks about the possibility that Christie Cort might have just run away. I want to dig back into that line of questioning. Can you assure me you will carefully consider the efforts by law enforcement to search for her body, even if their search couldn't exhaust every single possibility?"

He paused and considered before answering. "Well, if I understand your question, you're asking if I could reasonably conclude she was dead without one-hundred-percent conclusive evidence. Did I get that right?"

"That's exactly what I'm asking."

"Okay, then my answer is yes, if I conclude that the efforts to find the body proved to me beyond a reasonable doubt that she is dead."

"Thank you for that thoughtful answer." I stepped back and surveyed the assembled twelve. "The discussion the captain and I just engaged in is going to be central to this trial. How about the rest of you? Even if the sheriff's team didn't turn over every single stone, would you be satisfied if their efforts to find Christie's body convinced you beyond a reasonable doubt that she was killed, and that her body was out there somewhere?" I received a number of nods. I came back to number one, who had challenged MacPherson's position that running away was a reasonable response to an abusive spouse. "Ma'am, your reaction to my dialogue with the captain?"

"Seemed reasonable to me . . . law enforcement was in a difficult position, trying to essentially prove a negative. If I'm convinced that their efforts to find a body proved that she was killed and her body was missing, I could convict if I believe the defendant was the one who killed her."

Scanning the rest of the faces, "How about the rest of you? This is going to be one of the central questions in this trial." Once again, I moved methodically from juror to juror and received assurances. "Your Honor, I have no further questions and I have no challenges for cause."

"Thank you, Mr. Clearwater." He turned to MacPherson. "Ms.

MacPherson, do you care to exercise a peremptory challenge?" Judge Walter seemed intent on hurrying the proceedings along.

"Your Honor, may we have a brief recess?"

"Of course," Walter said, relenting. "We will take our afternoon recess at this time."

CHAPTER 34

DESELECTING A JURY

Wills and I again huddled with Abbott and Pierce in an attorney conference room to review our options. We decided quickly who we wanted to keep and who to challenge. When we reconvened, MacPherson stood, and began, "May I make a peremptory challenge on behalf of Lt. Cort at this time?"

"Please." Judge Walter nodded.

"We thank and excuse juror number one." Locking eyes with number one, MacPherson said, "Thank you, ma'am, for your service." *No surprise there. She was too smart and too sophisticated. Beyond that, MacPherson had to be concerned that she could have been the foreperson.*

Walter excused her and asked her to return to the jury assembly room. She stood and gave MacPherson a disapproving stare. *It's hard not to take it personally.*

The clerk pulled another chit, and a new juror assumed seat number one. Walter worked him through the biographical preliminaries. He was an elementary teacher, fifth grade. Walter then turned him over to MacPherson for follow-up questioning.

"Sir, were you able to hear the questions that were asked by me and the prosecutor?"

"Yes, I followed the questions."

"Would your answers be substantially different from those given by the other jurors?"

"I don't think so. As I sat and listened, I had time to reflect on the Fifth Amendment right against self-incrimination. And I agree with you that it is an important safeguard that we all need to respect." *This guy was drinking MacPherson's Kool-Aid.*

Nodding agreement, MacPherson said, "Thank you for your thoughtfulness. Any other reflections come to mind during the questioning?"

"No, I guess I'm pretty squared away."

Smiling, she said, "I think you are squared away." *There is a distinction between charming and flirting.* Turning to Walter, MacPherson said, "No cause challenge for this gentleman." *Not hard to figure MacPherson would like this guy.*

This guy's apparent infatuation with MacPherson was concerning. There was no way I was going to let him sit. However, I had to respond quickly to mitigate the obvious crush factor between this juror and MacPherson.

Walter looked quizzically at me as I rose to address the new number one.

"Sir, you heard my discussion with some of the folks sitting with you concerning reasonable doubt, correct?"

"I did, and I thought you made the concept very clear. I appreciated that." *He is sucking up, trying to convince me not to exercise a challenge on him. He was fighting to be part of the jury.*

"Thank you, sir." I turned to Walter, "No cause challenge."

Walter looked at me. "Mr. Clearwater, a peremptory?"

"Yes, the state would thank and excuse number one." *He wasn't going to pollute my jury with his obsequious presence.*

The number one seat was next occupied by a middle-aged engineer who worked for a research lab. He was somewhat introverted, and during questioning, no flags were raised.

We went back and forth. MacPherson exercised her second perempt on number eleven, the retired cop who wasn't buying the right not to testify. That seat was then taken by a high school history teacher. The teacher felt compelled to comment on the significance of the right of the accused not to testify. Despite that, I was okay with her.

I exercised my second challenge on number eight, the odd young woman who thought the runaway theory viable. Her seat was taken by a real estate broker, who complained that time on the jury impeded her sales opportunities. Judge Walter made short work of her complaint and reminded everyone in the courtroom of their civic responsibilities. Nevertheless, I noted her self-confidence and her leadership potential. She was a bit of a wild card.

It was MacPherson's turn. Before she stood, Cort motioned for her attention. They briefly conferred. She rose and looked at number seven, the fire captain, and excused him. No surprise. I hated to lose him—smart and a leader.

That seat was assumed by an unemployed actor. In responding to MacPherson's questioning, it was clear he was enthralled by her. *Hell, but for the trappings of formality, he would have asked her to dinner and a movie.* He clearly had to go, but could I burn one of my three remaining challenges on him? Instead, I bit the bullet and burned my third challenge on number six, the orthodontist. He gave off an odd vibe. Abbott had been adamant about kicking him.

That sixth seat was filled by a manager of a Barnes and Noble. She was an enthusiastic young woman who seemed delighted to be seated. During Walter's questioning we learned that her deceased father had been a highway patrolman. She felt cops walked on water. But, of course, under questioning, she promised to not give undue deference to police officers. *She was a potential landmine.*

I looked over my shoulder at the remaining prospective jurors and tried to divine, just by looking, who would be a good prosecution juror. Abbott caught my eye and briefly and discreetly held up seven fingers. Wills leaned to me and whispered, "You've got that actor character. I think he's in love with MacPherson."

I whispered back, "I know, but we've only got two challenges left. What if someone worse pops up?"

MacPherson then threw me a curveball. "Your Honor, on behalf of Lt. Cort, we accept the jury panel as presently constituted." She knew I would be forced to kick number seven, the unemployed-wannabe actor. MacPherson knew that everyone in the courtroom had picked up on the obvious chemistry she had with him. Her acceptance of the jury accomplished two things. First, it signaled to the jurors that she was not playing games with the jury selection, while I was still trying to manipulate the process. Second, it saved one of her five precious peremptory challenges, knowing I had to utilize my fourth precious challenge on the wannabe. But I had no choice. I kicked the wannabe.

The replacement was a car mechanic. During questioning by Walter, he indicated that he had some negative experiences with law enforcement. He was of the opinion that some cops abused their power. *Now there was a revelation.* Yet when MacPherson challenged him for cause, Walter denied the challenge. MacPherson was forced to excuse him with her fourth challenge. And onto the jury came a doctor of internal medicine, the final number seven. He was in his midfifties and did not appear pleased to be a juror, although he came across as pleasant and perhaps resigned to his fate. No alerts.

There was a better than even chance that if the doctor survived, he would be the eventual foreperson.

It was my turn. We each had one peremptory left. The jury currently seemed to be balanced by gender. I didn't want to burn my last challenge for fear there might be a defense-oriented juror lurking like a shark in the shallows. But I was not comfortable with number two, the self-employed computer programmer. He seemed too eager to please MacPherson. As the prosecutor, I needed all twelve. MacPherson only needed one for a hung jury. Given that this was the second go-round, a hung jury was tantamount to an acquittal. There was no way the DA would opt for the third trial.

"Your Honor, may we take a brief recess?" I needed to get this right.

Walter reluctantly ordered a fifteen-minute recess.

Back in the attorney conference room, both Abbott and Wills felt we should accept the jury as is. I voiced my concern about number two. They were not as concerned about the mechanic. I reluctantly agreed.

When we resumed, I said, "The prosecution is satisfied with the present composition of the jury. We have no challenges."

It was MacPherson's time to decide. Would she burn her final challenge on number seven, the internist? She had to feel as I did, that if he remains on the jury there is a good chance he will be the foreperson. Given his profession and age, we both knew he fit the classic prosecution profile. As she stood, Cort pulled at her sleeve. She paused, and asked, "Your Honor, may I have just a moment?"

Walter nodded.

She sat as she and Cort engaged in what appeared to be a heated, albeit whispered, tête-à-tête.

Finally she rose and stated, "Lt. Cort and I are pleased with the jury as constituted."

I accepted the jury as well. And with that, we had our jury. The clerk swore them in. It had been an excruciating process. In the UK, they don't bother with the intricacies we had just gone through during jury selection. For the most part, they summon people to court and put twelve in the box, and absent extraordinary circumstances, that's their jury. Maybe our English cousins have got it right.

The clerk then selected another chit and, following questions, a grocery clerk was sworn in as the alternate. It was nearly four by the time Walter adjourned. We would resume tomorrow with opening statements.

Trial Tip #11: Voir Dire

Avoid "blue-sky" questions, those for which the relevance is not readily apparent to the jurors. In transitioning from topic to topic during voir dire, offer the prospective jurors sufficient context to understand why you are inquiring into a particular topic. Give some context. A question that seemingly comes out of the blue may confuse the jurors, and they may even believe they are being manipulated. Context is critical.

CHAPTER 35

WILLOW REDUX

"I'm still keyed up," Lisa said on the way home to Malibu. "That was intense. I was thinking along with you about who you should excuse. I agreed with your decisions. I wish you could have kept the firefighter. He was smart and confident."

"I liked him as well. There was no way Merci was going to leave him on."

"And what was the story with the actor? Could he have been more obvious?

"Probably not. The problem with a person like that is that it appears obvious he will side with one side and there is nothing he said that I could base a cause challenge on."

"That had to be frustrating."

"It was. Hated to burn a perempt on him. But no choice."

Following a contemplative silence, Lisa said, "I'm exhausted. The whole day I was on the edge of my seat. It wore me out."

"Me too. Jury selection is like playing high-stakes poker. You're trying to find tells with the jurors while also analyzing the moves of your opponent. And since I need all twelve jurors, one mistake could cost me the whole shootin' match." I grunted. "No pressure."

She reached over and squeezed my thigh. "Jake, you are so good at this. You handled the pressure well." She paused, "and so did your opponent."

"She's good, very good."

"Not as good as you." I squeezed her hand.

As we had left the courtroom, MacPherson had handed me her witness list, and once again Willow Merkle was listed as the only defense witness. After my earlier visit with Merkle, I was surprised. Apparently MacPherson wasn't yet aware that Merkle would not be a cooperating defense witness. Yet, I was still concerned that she might change her mind. That evening I called her—only to find that the number was disconnected. Before I made my opening statement, I wanted to be certain about Merkle; I needed to account for her. Even though she had assured me she was completely out as a witness, I had to know for certain.

I explained to Lisa my concern and drove back down to the Rocks. (She didn't ask to come.) The same enormous bouncer stood at the entrance. I asked if DeeDee was working. He told me she was no longer working at the club, and, with an insolent smirk, volunteered that he had no idea how I could locate her. I explained that it was important that I contact her. He was unmoved and repeated that he had no idea where she might work or live. I thought about tipping him fifty dollars and pulled out my wallet. Wrong move. He started coming around the counter. Out of deference to his size, I turned back and hit the door.

Back in my car, I called Duke and explained the situation.

"Let me see what I can do."

I gave him her last known residence and the location of the Rocks. It was for situations like this that I brought Duke on board. He would find her. I knew that with absolute conviction.

I returned home and had a light dinner with Lisa. Later that evening, Duke called. "She's working at a place called the Elite Gentlemen's Club on Roscoe Boulevard in the Valley."

"What took you so long?"

"Had to stop for dinner," he deadpanned. "When are you going to take a run at her?"

"You free now? Maybe we can catch her at work."

"You want me along?"

"Yeah, if we get anything from her, I want both of us there. We need to be ready, in case she testifies at trial and goes sideways on us." I had erred earlier when speaking to her. Since no one else was there and since I couldn't testify to anything she said, her statements were worthless. If I could now get some helpful information from her, or at least assurance that she wasn't going to testify for Cort, I'd need Duke with me to verify her statements.

Forty-five minutes later, Duke and I met in the parking lot of the club, paid the cover, and entered. Duke quipped, "You and me, Jake, always in the finest of company." We were dressed casually. Duke sported a porkpie hat. *Yeah, a porkpie hat.* We fit right in, just a couple of working stiffs looking for beer and naked women. The club was smaller than the Rocks and a bit seedier. The stage could accommodate only two dancers, and one of them was Willow. Our lucky night. She couldn't see us, the light was on her, but we could certainly see her. When I pointed her out, Duke was impressed. We sat toward the back, ordered our beers and politely brushed off the lap-dance solicitations. Twenty minutes later, Willow, making her rounds, came upon us. She saw me and went rigid. She hesitated, and seemed as if she was planning to ignore us, but soon realized that since we had run her down, there was little use in avoiding us. She was wearing some odd top that didn't leave much to the imagination, and bikini bottoms. She reluctantly sat, eyeing Duke.

"Okay, you found me," she said in a resigned voice. "I already told you I don't want any part of this. You should have figured that out when I quit the Rocks and moved from my apartment."

"Things haven't changed, Willow. You might end up being an important part of the trial. You're on the defense's witness list."

Motioning to Duke, Merkle addressed me. "Who's this, your bodyguard?" she said sarcastically.

Duke doffed his hat. "I'm Duke. Pleased to meet you. Enjoyed the show."

"Fuck you, Porkpie."

Duke laughed it off. Willow sat and said, "So much for changing jobs and moving out of my apartment. You found me, and Max found me."

"Cort contacted you?"

"Damn straight!" She held out her arms to show some bruising. "He came in here two nights ago, got me back behind a curtain for a dance, squeezed my arms, and threatened to kill me if I wouldn't testify for him."

"Willow, I'm sorry you're in the middle of this. What are you going to do?"

"He didn't leave me with a lot of choices."

"So you're going to perjure yourself for Cort?"

"It's as simple as that stupid hat he's wearing," she said, nodding to Duke's hat. "If I don't, he will kill me, sure as he killed his wife."

A long silence before I said, "We can offer you protection, but I assume that's a no-go?"

"He's a sheriff's lieutenant," she hissed. "Give me a break." She was right; his job made him a threatening presence.

"Willow, I don't know if you realize this, but if you do decide to testify, I can use the statements you just made about Cort threatening to kill you."

Duke pulled his recorder out of his pocket.

She cocked her head in anger. "What a shitty thing to do!"

The recording was just for show. If push came to shove, I couldn't use it. But she might not know that. I hoped it would make her more compliant. However, there was nothing that could stop Duke from testifying about her statements.

It was a shitty thing to do. I felt bad about resorting to such a tactic, but I had a bigger picture in mind.

I shook my head. "I'm prosecuting a first-degree murder case. The man I'm prosecuting needs very much to go down, to be locked up, for the rest of his life. I can't play games here. I'm trying to protect the integrity of the trial."

"And I'm what?" She looked around the room. "Just a piece of trash left on the side of the road?" She was on the verge of tears.

A bouncer suddenly appeared. "DeeDee, you good? These guys a problem?"

"Yeah, these guys are a problem. I want them out of here."

The human steroid gestured to the door. "Gentlemen."

We stood as Willow got in her frustrated jab. "Fuck you, counselor, and fuck you, Porkpie."

Duke doffed his hat once again and flashed Merkle a sardonic grin.

I didn't sleep well that night. I felt for Willow, despite her anger at us. I guess I hoped she would just take off—get out of Dodge, maybe even out of the state. Las Vegas was only hours away. She could hide in a big city like that, with lots of places to get lost in, and lots of strip clubs where she could dance.

Beyond concerns about Merkle, I flashed to my opening statement. I hadn't settled on how I wanted to approach it. I knew I had to anticipate where MacPherson would go and blunt her defense.

But I also knew I had to take the initiative. I bore the burden of proof. This wasn't about defending my case, but rather about slamming my case in the faces of the jurors. As I tossed and turned, my brain kept rolling, but I couldn't shake the knowledge that my case was pretty much a do-over of the unsuccessful case Wills had put on. We had added a few bells and whistles, but nothing substantive. And lurking on the edge of it all was Merci MacPherson. It was a fitful night, the kind of night when you're relieved when the alarm finally goes off, forcing you to shake yourself into another day.

Lisa and I had coffee and toast while I filled her in on the late-night visit with Merkle. I wasn't much for conversation on the drive downtown. I was still reworking my opening statement in my head. Lisa gave me space. When we pulled into the underground garage, Lisa handed me a thin narrow box that I hadn't noticed. The box said "Gucci." It was a beautiful understated maroon tie.

"Thanks. It's perfect."

She reached over, removed my tie, and tied her gift around my neck.

CHAPTER 36

GETTING THE JUMP

I stood in my dark-blue lightly pinstriped suit, sporting my Lisa-se-lected Gucci tie, and from counsel table, in a firm voice, began, "No body."

Then in a softer voice, I repeated, "No. Body."

I paused, and began making my way to the jurors. "You are going to hear that over and over from the defendant's lawyer. But the twelve of you already know that from our discussion during voir dire. It's a reality of the trial. We may never know where Christie Cort's body is, or how she was killed. But by the conclusion of this trial, you will be convinced beyond any reasonable doubt of two things." I paused and locked up with number one, the middle-aged engineer. "First, that Christie Cort is dead. Second, that the defendant murdered her." Juror number one kept a stoic expression. Not a facial muscle moved.

"Murder is ugly and gruesome. We are going to be spared some of that ugly and gruesome." Number eleven, the history teacher, looked off when I locked on her. "There will, of course, be no photographs of Christie's body lying in blood. No graphic autopsy photographs and clinical discussions concerning her injuries and the cause of her death." I stayed with eleven. I wanted to bring her front and center and imagine the ugly. "No, we are going to be spared all that. Why? Because he," I said pointing and looking at Cort, "knew that without Christie's body, it's hard to convict." Cort quickly turned his face at me with his jaw locked into a sneer. I held his stare until he looked off. "No blood, no gruesomeness, no photographs, no body."

I nodded at eleven and eased to my left in front of eight and nine, the two real-estate women. "However, the evidence is going to prove that there was blood, and gruesome acts, and ugly truths. That a human life was brutalized." Motioning to Christie's parents in the gallery, I continued, "That a daughter was taken from them." Long pause. "As we go through this ordeal together in this sanitized courtroom, with everything pristine and orderly, the underlying horror must not be overlooked. The testimony will establish that the defendant is a violent man. A cheating man. And a murdering man."

"Objection!" MacPherson was up. "Your Honor, this is not the time for closing argument."

"Sustained. Mr. Clearwater, confine yourself to discussing your case instead of embarking on closing argument." *You don't object during opening. MacPherson knew better than that. Even if the statement is a bit argumentative, there's a professional courtesy at play.*

I ignored the judge and didn't turn from the jurors. *You want my case, Merci? I'll give you my case.* I moved right up close to the jurors, irritation on my face and in my voice, my thighs brushing the jury rail, and in a firm voice bordering on mean, said, "The evidence presented here will establish that the defendant is a violent man who struck Christie in the face. That same evidence will establish that he was having an adulterous affair. The evidence will establish that he was obsessively ambitious, that he feared, above all else, that a divorce would ruin his career. The evidence will establish that he threatened Christie in the most vile terms when she dared mention divorce."

. I stopped and stepped back, my tirade spent. In a calmer voice, I went on. "We will prove that Christie didn't run away, that she and her sister had planned a cruise together just weeks before she was killed. And finally, we will prove that *he*"—I pointed at Cort—"had ample opportunity to kidnap Christie, kill her, and conceal her body during the very early morning hours when she went missing."

Continuing in an up-tempo cadence, I stepped further back, angling my head at Cort and said, "We have a direct statement from the defendant that will shine a damning light on his character. His *character*," I repeated the word disdainfully, directing my hard stare at Cort. This time he didn't look up. "When Christie mentioned divorce, he got in her face and said, and I quote: 'A divorce would fuck my career. You fuck with my career, you fuck with my life, and I'll fuck with your life.' His words." I let that resonate as I turned back to the jurors. "That threat provides us some insight into his *character*." That generated some wide-eyed looks from some of the jurors.

"From what you've heard during voir dire questioning, you have most likely already figured out that Christie and Cort's marriage was a mess. Divorce was inevitable. But Cort couldn't accept that. Couldn't accept not getting that next promotion. That next step up the ladder. So, in the absence of the acceptable, he did the unacceptable, the unimaginable. We will prove that he staged what he hoped would be the perfect murder. A no-body murder. He's a seasoned law-enforcement officer. He knows without a body, my job as a prosecutor is much more difficult. He knows full well that without a body, without all the forensics the body of a murder victim reveals, the investigation and prosecution is more difficult. Without a body, he knows there may be some who, despite all the evidence, will not believe there even was a murder. And that's why you folks have been selected to be on this jury, to recognize his cunning and his motivation and hold him accountable."

The juror's eyes were riveted on me as I stepped back a couple of paces, now imbuing my voice with calm, calculated sincerity. "So how did he go about this terrible business? How did he attempt to commit the perfect murder? First, he needed to make certain that it was clear to everyone that Christie was an unhappy wife." I locked onto number seven, the internist. "Cort calculated that would give her a reason to just run away. That was critical to his plan. Should there ever be a trial, he could just claim she was unhappy and simply took off. That first part of his plan was not complicated. He was a terrible husband, he hit her, he cheated on her, he threatened her. Unhappy wife.

"Next, he needed an alibi for the hours of time that it took to commit the murder. His alibi, a rendezvous with a stripper. That's right, a rendezvous with a stripper." That caught some raised eyebrows. "The evidence will establish that he left work for nearly four hours on the early morning of February 4. He arranged for his girlfriend, a stripper, to provide an alibi for those very hours. The evidence will establish that instead of that rendezvous, he undertook a well-calculated plan. First, to return home and kill Christie and throw her body in her car. Next, to drive several miles to an isolated area and dispose of her body. Then, to drive to the reservoir, remove the bike he had stashed in the car, push the car into the water, and ride the bike home. Then he drove back to his job to check in before leaving for breakfast and eventually returning home. Once he was home, he called the sheriff's office and reported Christie missing."

I took a breath to let my words sink in.

"My co-counsel and I are convinced that once you hear all the evidence, you will see through to the very soul of the defendant. He can conceal Christie's body, but he can't conceal his character. He can't conceal his monstrous acts." I held my spot and nodded toward the judge.

"Thank you, Mr. Clearwater. Let's take our midmorning break. Court will reconvene at 10:45."

Wills greeted me as I returned to our table. "Good job, Jake. The jurors were locked on you. You sullied Cort up pretty good. I like our start."

"Thanks, John. Now we watch as Merci spins her magic."

I looked over at Lisa and caught her eye. She gave me a discreet head nod.

Trial Tip #12: Opening Statement

Opening statements should begin with a compelling grab or hook to capture the jurors' attention. Jurors quickly decide whether to remain engaged. If not engaged, they tend to lose attention. However, if they are hooked, there is a greater chance they will hear the advocate out. Empirical studies indicate that most jurors favor one side or the other at the conclusion of the opening statements. Consequently, evidence favoring "their" side will be more readily accepted as true, whereas evidence contrary to "their" side will be viewed with skepticism.

CHAPTER 37

MERCI'S MAGIC

When we reconvened, Judge Walter tilted his head toward MacPherson.

She stood, nodded at Walter, then at Wills and me, and walked behind counsel table where Wills and I sat, and then on to the jury box. She was wearing a perfectly fitted light-brown corduroy skirt suit. Resting her hands on the jury rail, she began in a low, solemn voice. "There is a world of difference between speculation and evidence." She slightly cocked her head, her left hand lifted to the jurors. "For the last half hour, you have been subjected to speculation, not evidence. The prosecutor's entire opening statement was built on speculation. He was speculating that Christie Cort is dead. He was speculating that Christie Cort didn't just abandon her life and run away." She gave a small admonishing shake of her head.

"During my examination of the prosecution's lead detective, I'm going to ask her the question that goes to the very heart of this case. I'm going to ask her whether she is certain that Christie Cort is not living under a new name in Orlando or Stillwater or anywhere else in our great nation." A significant pause, letting her words resonate. "My question will be direct and straightforward.

And I urge you to listen very carefully to her answer." She paused again, thoughtfully taking in the twelve. "The detective won't be able to tell you no. She won't be able to say that she is certain that Christie Cort is dead."

"Objection, Your Honor. Counsel is misstating the burden of proof." *Fair's fair.*

"Overruled, Mr. Clearwater. However, I will instruct the jurors on the law and on the burden of proof at the conclusion of the evidence." Looking at MacPherson, Walter stated, "Counsel, you may proceed."

"Thank you, Your Honor. As I was saying, the lead detective will not be able to look you twelve in the eye and testify for certain that Christie Cort is dead. She will not be able to say whether or not Christie just up and ran off. Christie, as you will learn, is a smart, sophisticated woman who certainly is capable of starting over somewhere else." *I noted the present tense in referring to Christie.* MacPherson lifted her shoulders in a nonchalant manner, continuing, "And who can blame her? She was in a bad marriage. Max Cort is a lousy husband. He's unfaithful, and once, during a heated conversation, he even struck her."

Stepping back from the rail, MacPherson moved slightly to her left and locked onto numbers two and three, the two computer guys I was a bit concerned with. "As we get ready to listen to testimony, it is important to keep in mind that Lt. Cort is not on trial for being a bad husband. The evidence will establish that he is a good cop, a decorated cop. And that on the night and early morning that Christie ran away, he was off to his friend's place. Not the best of alibis, but nonetheless the truth." *Apparently MacPherson still believed that Willow Merkle would testify. Had they gotten to her since I had spoken to her?*

"He then returned to check into the station, left the station shortly after five o'clock, and grabbed some breakfast on his way home. The evidence will establish that when he returned home, Christie was gone. He searched the house for her, beginning to fear the worst. He called Christie's sister Mary Lynn, hoping Christie was with her. No Christie." Looking directly at number seven, the internist, she continued. "He then immediately called the station, looking for help. Does a guilty man call law enforcement?" *Poor rhetorical question, from my perspective. A guilty man trying to spin a murder alibi would do exactly that. I hoped number seven was on my wavelength.*

MacPherson moved to her right, zeroing in on four, five, and six in the back row. "Christie's sister arrived shortly after the deputies and immediately, without knowing any of the circumstances, accused Lt. Cort of hurting Christie. The evidence will show that was a key point in the investigation. From the time of the sister's accusation, the sheriff's department viewed Lt. Cort as a suspect. And that investigation never turned away from him. In fact, the evidence will establish that it infected and prejudiced the entire investigation against Lt. Cort."

Taking a beat and stepping back from the jurors, she then began again. "There is a phenomenon called confirmation bias. This bias occurs when an investigator has a predetermined suspect and views the evidence in a way that confirms the suspect's guilt."

"Objection, Your Honor. This is way out of bounds." A legitimate objection.

"I agree, counsel. Ms. MacPherson, reel in your statement. We are nowhere near closing arguments as of yet."

She nodded her head, but then surprisingly went right back into an argumentative mode. "Instead of the facts driving an independent investigation, the biased investigation made the facts fit the suspect."

I was up again. "Judge, apparently counsel didn't understand your admonition, as she continues along a very inappropriate path."

Walter ordered us to the bench. Switching off his microphone, he turned to MacPherson. "Merci, what part of my admonishment didn't you understand?" Without waiting for her response, he went on. "I'm holding you in contempt and fining you $500." *Well done, Judge.*

MacPherson had the good sense to remain quiet. She had rung an important bell for her case. It was well worth the $500. She knew that bell could not be unrung. She had once again, as she had during the first trial, set the tone for the defense. She had them wondering if the fix was in. Cort's investigation was biased against him from the get-go. The investigation was perfunctory and had Cort in its crosshairs from the morning of Christie's disappearance. $500 was a gnat quickly swatted away, and worth every cent.

I returned to my seat. MacPherson returned to the jury and stood for several seconds without speaking, perhaps allowing the jurors to think back to her last sentences. When she began again, she was focused on eight and nine, the two real-estate people. "The evidence will establish that the investigation never even considered another suspect. They had their man. Why bother looking any further?"

In disbelief, I stood to object again, but MacPherson was done and walking back to her table.

Walter sustained my objection, but MacPherson's point was well made.

Trial Tip #13: Opening Statement

The purpose of opening statement is for counsel to offer a factual overview of the case from the advocate's perspective. Counsel are generally prohibited from arguing their case during opening statement. Yet despite the rule, nearly every opening statement to some degree or another slips into argument. Most often, opposing counsel and the judge will tolerate some degree of argument. However, when the opening pushes too far over the line, an objection is appropriate. It is the general practice that counsel refrain from objecting during the opposing counsel's opening.

CHAPTER 38

FREAK OUT

As I was leaving the courtroom for the lunch recess following opening statements, Duke grabbed my arm and gestured for Wills and me to join him in an attorney conference room. I spotted Lisa near the courtroom doors and held up a give-me-a-minute finger. She nodded. In the conference room, Duke said, "Mary Lynn is in the wind. I went to her place to pick her up this morning, and she wasn't there."

A quick burst of nausea hit me. She was not only our first witness, but our most important witness. "Some kind of mix-up, a miscommunication?" I asked.

"Don't think so." Duke answered. "We had dinner last night." I gave him a confused look.

"Dinner?"

"It's not what you think. I'll explain later. I was to pick her up at ten from her condo this morning. But she was a no-show. Pounded on the door. Questioned the neighbors. Gone. Phone goes to voicemail."

"Did you have any indication when you were with her last night that there might be a problem?"

"She seemed a little hinky, but I wrote that off as nerves. During dinner she finally relaxed; maybe that was the wine. I thought she was okay to go."

"Duke, you need to find her," I said, maintaining my composure while stating the obvious. I turned to Wills. "The judge is expecting us to call witnesses this afternoon. He's going to chew us up if we are not ready to go."

"Dammit!" uttered a frustrated Duke. "I thought she was squared away." It was rare to see Duke rattled.

I again looked to Wills. "If Duke can't locate her in the next hour or so, can we call another witness and buy some time until we can locate her?"

"I could probably get Sgt. Ponce to come in this afternoon," Wills said. "But then our order is screwed up. She is our cornerstone witness, so without her going first, the context of the other witnesses' testimony is a bit awkward."

"Awkward or not, I'm not sure we have a lot of choices here. Asking Walter for the afternoon off is not going to play well with him. He's looking for an opportunity to rip into us, or should I say, into me?"

"Let me see if I can get Ponce in here by two."

"Do your best. Meanwhile"—I looked at Duke—"find Mary Lynn."

As I finished my sentence, he was already out the door. This is precisely why I brought Duke onto the team. The expected unexpected—there are always hiccups. I don't think I've ever tried a case without some hiccups. And here, we had a bigger problem than a hiccup. Without Holder's testimony, our case would wither and die.

Lisa and I had an unsettling lunch in the court's cafeteria. The coffee hadn't improved. My stomach was in a knot.

Wills was able to reach Sgt. Ponce, who graciously agreed to come in on his day off. Duke called at one-thirty. He had been unable to find Mary Lynn. When court reconvened, Wills took Ponce through his direct examination, focusing on the three Tuesday nights prior to Christie's disappearance and the early morning of February 4, when Cort was out of the office for that extended period of time. There was very little variance from the examination Wills and Ponce engaged in during the first trial. Ponce confirmed his understanding that divorce could prove an impediment to promotion within leadership positions in the sheriff's department.

"Sergeant, did you and Lt. Cort ever talk about promotions and such?"

"A couple of times. It seemed to me he was obsessed with getting promoted."

"Objection! The witness is speculating."

"Sustained."

"What did he say about promotions?"

"Calls for hearsay, Your Honor." MacPherson was doing everything she could to block Ponce's statement. She knew her objection would be overruled. The statement fell within the party-opponent exception to the hearsay rule.

"Overruled."

"Go on, Sergeant."

"That his career was the most important thing in his life." He paused and added, "It was his life's goal."

MacPherson used her cross-examination to establish that Ponce resented Cort being his supervisor. She established that Ponce believed he was better qualified to be in a leadership position at the West Valley Station. She also attacked his veracity by establishing that since the two did not respect one another, Cort would never have confided his thoughts about promotion to him.

Ponce was dismissed at three-thirty, and Walter looked expectantly at us to call our next witness. I stood. "Your Honor, I beg the court's indulgence, but the witness we anticipated calling this afternoon has experienced some difficulties. I anticipate she will be here first thing in the morning."

"Counsel," Walter looked incredulously at me, his voice low and menacing like acid burning holes into me, "are you telling me that with at least an hour and a half of available time, you are not ready to proceed?"

"Again, my apologies. We didn't expect this delay. But we will be prepared to resume our case in the morning." Walter motioned us to the bench. Glaring at me, he said, "This is unacceptable. This is valuable time you are wasting." His jaw clenched tightly as he ground out his words. "This shall not happen again. You've got your delay today, but not going forward. Understood?"

Wills and I offered assurances that I hoped we could keep. Walter motioned us back. "Members of the jury, we will take the rest of the afternoon off and resume in the morning at 9:00 a.m. We are adjourned for today."

Duke ran Mary Lynn down as Lisa and I were driving home. He reported that she had driven around aimlessly for hours before finally retreating to her parents' home. Duke was waiting outside the Holder residence when Lisa and I arrived. We were let in by Frank Holder, Mary Lynn's father. Mary Lynn was on the couch and looked a mess. Her face was flushed, her eyes bloodshot. She was curled in a fetal position under a quilt. Her mother was stroking her hair and making soothing sounds. Mr. Holder guided the three of us into the kitchen. "When we got home from court today, we found her pretty much like this. As you can see, she's had a major anxiety attack. She suffered from these kinds of attacks as a teen, but not since then." He shook his head. "Going through another trial might be too much for her."

I nodded. "It's understandable. The stress of trial and being asked to again testify about Christie has got to be rough on her. We are asking her to relive those last days with her sister," I paused and added, "and Cort's presence has got to exacerbate the stress."

"She and Christie were so close." He spoke slowly, his concern for Mary Lynn obvious. "Frankly, that she was able to testify during the first trial was pretty amazing to her mother and me."

"I get that," I said. "When I watched her testify, it felt to me that her anger was driving her. Maybe the anger overcame some of the anxiety."

Holder nodded in agreement as he fiddled with an old-style coffee machine. "She had worked her way into a lather for the first trial. But afterward, she felt she had been humiliated by the defense attorney, and then when Cort wasn't convicted, she wondered what the point of putting herself out there had been in the first place." He poured coffee and handed us mugs. "Frankly, I don't know if she can go through all that again. As you just saw in there, she is pretty fragile."

"Is she on any medications for anxiety?" Duke asked.

"I'm pretty sure she is, but check with my wife on that. She can tell you exactly what medications."

"Would it be okay with you and your wife if we talk to her?" Duke asked.

"I guess. Let's see what Liz thinks."

Back in the living room, I asked Mrs. Holder if we could talk to Mary Lynn.

She nodded. "I think she's calmed down." Then, looking at her daughter, she asked, "Honey, are you up to talking with them?"

Mary Lynn pushed away the quilt and sat straight up. She

nodded as I introduced her to Lisa. Putting on a resolute face and looking past Lisa and me to Duke, she said, "I'm sorry, Duke. After you left last night, I freaked out. This morning, I got in my car and drove off. I don't even know where I was going, but I finally ended up here."

Duke moved past me and sat next to her, replying, "I completely understand. This trial resurfaces so much of the pain and loss you and your parents have suffered. Last night when we talked, you were nervous but determined. I sensed you were working up that anger at Cort once again. I think you just had a bad night, and it spilled over into today."

Mary Lynn nodded, and unexpectedly pulled Duke toward her. Duke nestled her into his shoulder. The familiarity between them seemed the most natural thing in the world to them. "The freakout is behind you now," Duke murmured. "That tough, determined woman I talked to last night can do this." She leaned back, wiped at her eyes, and smiled at Duke.

Duke was the secret ingredient. I knew he was a superb investigator, but this side of him was new to me. Clearly, he and Mary Lynn, in the short time they had been together, had built a bond, an understanding. *Not exactly patient–therapist. Maybe just human to human.* At any rate, I began to relax. Mary Lynn would be alright. She was in Duke's good hands. Our case would hold together.

The plan was for her to spend the night at her parents' house, and Duke would pick her up early, take her to breakfast, and get her to the courthouse by 9:00 a.m.

On the drive home, Lisa looked exhausted. "Once again, I didn't do anything today except watch you, and I'm wrung out. First the tension of you fighting off objections during your opening, and then her statement and the controversy. Then no witness and the judge's anger. It was a brutal day."

I patted her on the knee. "And we're just getting started." I caught a look.

We pretty much drank our dinner as Tony played bartender on their deck.

CHAPTER 39

MARY LYNN IN THE DOCK

The following morning, Judge Walter emerged from the side door and assumed the bench, as the bailiff called court to order. Walter settled onto his throne and looked expectantly at me.

I stood and said, "The people call Mary Lynn Holder." Duke escorted her into the courtroom and then took a seat directly behind me. As Mary Lynn was sworn in, I noticed that her eyes were locked on Duke. Apparently, Duke was to be her anchor. Good. Much better than hard looks from Cort.

She had some butterflies during the first few minutes of the direct, but as we progressed, she became more relaxed, and we established a rhythm. The jurors were acutely focused on the woman who had lost her best friend and sister. As planned, I began by spending time developing the relationship between the sisters. During her testimony, Mary Lynn's eyes would occasionally have an overwhelmed, almost panicky look, but then I could see her focusing on Duke, and that seemed to resolve her ability to go on.

As we continued, I transitioned to Christie's problems during college and then onto Christie's retreat to her parent's home. We discussed the *Playboy* interlude. I didn't see that as a hurtful fact, but

I wanted to bring it up on my terms rather than have MacPherson try to exploit it as a way to question Christie's character or her poor decision-making. After we addressed her early years, Mary Lynn and I were now ready to move to the deep end of the pool, where the trouble began: Christie's job at the sheriff's department, and her early days with Cort.

"It is important for the jurors to understand the underlying facts before we turn to Christie's disappearance. So I ask you to be as completely factual as you can; put your feelings aside, and just give us the facts that my questions call for. Can you do that?"

"I'll try my best. But it's hard."

"Just do your best. After you had met Lt. Cort on a number of occasions, what was your impression of him?" I asked.

"Objection, irrelevant!" MacPherson was on her feet. I think she just wanted to break up the flow rather than seriously questioning my right to dwell here.

Walter waved her down. "Overruled." Looking at Mary Lynn, "Ms. Holder, do you have the question in mind or should Mr. Clearwater repeat it?" Walter being kind.

I've got to pause here and comment on Judge Walter's fair, even cordial treatment of me. Maybe I had earned it during the trial or he had rethought his earlier attack. I was almost on equal footing with MacPherson. *Almost.*

Mary Lynn again looked past me to Duke. "I understand the question."

"Please answer," Walter gently prodded.

"I thought he was overbearing. He struck me as someone who always needs to be right."

"What do you mean by that?"

"It seemed to me that he always wanted to impose his will on others . . . especially Christie."

I paused and moved a little closer to her, mindful not to block her view of Duke. I wanted the jurors to take in that last answer. I noticed number seven, the internist, had picked up on Mary Lynn's eye contact fluttering between Duke and me. I wondered what that bright man thought of that.

I transitioned to Mary Lynn's observations of the interactions between Cort and Christie. Mary Lynn took a moment to think, before answering, "For the first couple of years, the relationship didn't appear volatile to me, as long as Max was in charge. From what I observed, Christie deferred to him."

"What do you mean by that?' I asked, folding my arms as I stepped back and leaned against the edge of counsel table.

"He called the shots. He made the decisions. Where they went on vacations, what restaurants they ate at, what car they bought—he was the decider."

"From your knowledge, prior to her relationship with the defendant, was Christie a woman who typically deferred to others?"

"Not at all." She offered a pale grin, recalling her sister. "Until Max came along, she was a bit of an alpha. It was a noticeable change in her."

"Now, I understand Christie was working for the sheriff's department when she and the defendant met. From your observations, did Christie like her job there?"

"Your Honor," objected MacPherson. "I don't see the relevance of this line of questioning." I took a few steps toward the bench.

"Mr. Clearwater, help me here," Walter urged.

"Judge, it is critical that the jurors understand the full nature of the deteriorating relationship as a precursor to murder."

Walter nodded. "Overruled. Proceed." Once again, an accommodating ruling.

"Let me repeat my question. To your knowledge, did Christie like her job?"

"Oh yeah. And I think she was good at it." Another slight smile snuck across her face.

"And yet at some point, she quit. Did she ever tell you why?"

MacPherson was up again. "Calls for hearsay."

Walter looked at me. "Counsel?"

"This is not offered for the truth of the matter asserted; rather it is offered to show Christie's evolving state of mind." *The hearsay rule is loaded with exceptions, and proving someone's state of mind is one of them.*

"Overruled."

"Did she tell you why she quit?"

"He made her. She told me he didn't like her being around so many young cops."

"So, just like that, she quit?"

"That's right, she didn't want to cross Max." Mary Lynn was getting stronger and bolder as we went on.

"I want to turn to the time period around Thanksgiving, that would be a bit over two months before Christie went missing. Tell us about a physical incident you observed between the defendant and Christie."

She hesitated ever so slightly, locked onto Duke, took a deep breath and continued. "I had just arrived at their house to pick up Christie. The two of us were going out to dinner. Max pulled up as we were walking to my car. He got out of his car and demanded to know where we were going. She told him that we were going out for dinner, and he just lost it."

"Lost it?"

"He yelled at her and accused her of trying to avoid him. I don't know if it was because I was there, but Christie just stood her ground for once. She stood there with a defiant grin, and then he struck her in the face. He knocked her down." I took a couple of steps back, letting the jury absorb the testimony. I wanted to park here, stretch this out as long as possible.

Finally, I continued. "After he struck her and knocked her to the ground, what happened next?" This was a double direct, incorporating a critical phrase from the previous answer into my question. *Like I said, I wanted the jurors to dwell here.*

"I went after him, but he grabbed me and pinned my arms. Christie got up and pulled me away from him." Mary Lynn hesitated, locked on Duke, and went on. "We were both crying. We got in my car. Max just watched us drive off." Mary Lynn's eyes were glistening.

I walked back behind counsel table for no reason but to let the testimony resonate. And from the looks of the jurors, it was resonating; they were staring hard at Cort. Cort for his part was staring hard at Mary Lynn. The somewhat nonchalant aloof Cort that had played out throughout most of the trial was replaced by his intimidating presence.

Good; let some of Cort's mean shine through.

"Did you or Christie call the police?"

"I wanted to, but Christie wouldn't let me. She said it would only make matters worse."

Again I let that answer linger, before asking, "Let's move forward to December, a few weeks later and a couple of months before Christie went missing. Relate to the jurors what you did."

She hesitated, took a hard look at Duke, and steadied herself. "I spied on him."

I nodded, encouraging her to go on. "Tell us about that."

"I suspected he was having an affair."

"Why did you believe that?"

"Any number of reasons. Just who he was. And Christie told me they were no longer having marital relations."

"How did you spy on him?"

"I knew he worked the graveyard shift three nights a week. I figured maybe that was when he might be carrying on. So I camped in my car for three consecutive nights across from the sheriff's parking lot. On the third night, I saw him drive out of the lot around 1:00 a.m. And I followed him."

"Go on," I urged.

He drove a mile or so to an apartment complex on Douglas Road and entered an apartment."

"What did you do?"

"I sat in my car and waited. After an hour or so, I saw him come out and stand just outside the door of the apartment with a woman who was wearing a bathrobe. They hugged and kissed, then he drove back to the station."

"Did you tell Christie what you had observed?"

"I did. She said it didn't matter. She said things couldn't be any worse than they already were."

I stepped closer to her and went on. "Okay, Mary Lynn. Let's move to February 3, the night before Christie went missing. Did you talk to her that evening?"

"I did. We talked most nights after he went to work."

"Tell us about that call."

Mary Lynn's confidence all of a sudden began to waver. I walked back to counsel table and stood next to Duke. I wanted her to lock up with him again. She needed his reassurance. I repeated my question. "What did the two of you talk about?"

Duke gave her a slight nod.

Mary Lynn swallowed before she answered, in a quieter voice,

"We talked about just the two of us getting away." Her eyes had drifted off Duke.

"Getting away?"

"We were planning on taking a cruise, one of those weekend cruises down to Cabo."

"Just the two of you?"

"Yes." She was steadying herself.

"To your knowledge, was the defendant aware of your plans?"

"No. Christie was afraid to bring it up. But I kept encouraging her. She needed a break from him. I thought we could just relax, have some drinks, watch some shows, and walk around Cabo."

"When was this planned for?"

"Sometime in March."

"What else did you and Christie talk about that evening?"

"She surprised me. She said she was going to file for divorce when we returned."

"Divorce?"

"Yeah. I was so pleased for her." Mary Lynn brightened. "She needed to start over."

"Had you ever heard Christie broach the topic of divorce before?"

"Between the two of us we had discussed it."

"To your knowledge had she ever mentioned divorce to the defendant?"

"Oh yeah!"

"Tell us about that."

She leaned back in her chair and seemed to compose herself. "We were in their home when Christie got up the nerve to tell him that the marriage wasn't working and that they should consider divorce."

"What was the defendant's reaction?"

"He went ballistic and screamed at her and then threatened her."

"Do you recall his words?"

"I'll never forget them. It's full of expletives which could offend some people here."

"I appreciate your concern, but we need to hear what the defendant said."

She steeled herself. "'A divorce would fuck my career. You fuck with my career, you fuck with my life, and I'll fuck with your life.'"

My eyes sidled over the jury box and caught the internist's look. His heretofore placid demeanor cracked as he turned to look at Cort.

"To your knowledge, why did Christie ask him about divorce with you present?"

"Objection, calls for the witness to speculate."

"Overruled. The witness may answer."

Without repeating the question, Mary Lynn answered. "Because she was afraid he would hit her."

"Okay, Mary Lynn, now that we have heard about the defendant's reaction to divorce, let's return to the last phone conversation you had with your sister. Do you recall what time you and Christie finished talking that evening?"

"Around eight or eight thirty."

"Mary Lynn, have you heard from Christie since that call?"

"No, because that's when he murdered her."

"Objection! Personal opinion, speculation." MacPherson was adamant.

"That's no opinion, that's God's honest truth." Mary Lynn blurted out before Walter could rule on the objection. *It appeared that anger had once again supplanted anxiety.*

Walter quickly interceded. "Ms. Holder, I'll have no more of that. You just answer the questions asked of you." Looking over his glasses, "Do I make myself clear?"

Mary Lynn nodded agreement, her eyes malevolently pinned on MacPherson.

"Is that a yes, Ms. Holder?"

"Yes."

"The objection is sustained. The response is stricken from the record, and the jurors are admonished to disregard the statement." Turning to me, "Mr. Clearwater, you may resume."

"Thank you." Moving away from my counsel table and assuming a position halfway up the jury rail, I asked, "From that evening's phone call forward, have you had any communication with your sister?"

"No," she said, and stared defiantly at Cort. That was the first time I noticed that she looked at Cort.

"Not a text, an email, nothing on social media?"

"Objection, Your Honor, she already said she had no communication. This question has been asked and answered."

I waved off the question without waiting for Walter to rule. "Very well. I want to move to the next morning, February 4. Tell us what happened."

The brief uncertainty that had haunted Mary Lynn earlier had evaporated under the heat of her rage. She looked directly at Cort now. No fear, no hesitancy, just anger. "He"—staring at Cort—"called me, asking if Christie was with me. And, of course she wasn't. I knew right then that he had killed her."

"Objection again," MacPherson interrupted. "This witness doesn't seem to be able to refrain from her personal asides and opinions."

"I agree," Walter responded, clearing his throat. "Mr. Clearwater, we are going to take our midmorning recess at this time. I suggest that you speak with your witness. She must confine her answers to the question being asked and refrain from offering her opinions."

"I'll speak to her, Your Honor."

Wills, Duke, and I took Mary Lynn into one of the attorney conference rooms. She went directly to Duke. "Too much?" she asked him.

Duke grinned. "You're doing great. We definitely don't have to worry about that anxiety anymore. You're mad as hell." He paused, then cautioned, "That's good to a point, but you can't spill over into becoming too partisan. You need to dial it down a bit." Of course, her testimony had already lost any sense of objectivity.

She sat back and gave him a questioning look. "Of course I'm partisan. The sonofabitch murdered my sister!"

I joined the dialogue. "But the concern is that you're losing any sense of being a reporting witness. You're coming off as a biased witness."

Duke rested a hand on her shoulder and said, "We need the jurors to believe you. If you are too over-the-top, you lose credibility. You've got to reel in the anger. Especially since the cross is coming. You can't let MacPherson goad you into losing it. When you feel the anger taking hold, look over at me and take a breath."

"I understand," she said. "It's just that I get so angry at him. I hate that he's just sitting right there, watching and glaring."

"I understand," I said. "But like Duke said, you've got to dial it back."

She closed her eyes and took a long breath through her mouth, then looked at Duke. "I'm okay." Wills and I were pretty much invisible. This was about Mary Lynn and Duke.

Duke clapped his hands. "Time's up. Let's go get 'em."

Walter looked at Mary Lynn as she once again settled into the witness chair. "I'll remind you that you are still under oath."

Mary Lynn's eyes darted up briefly toward the judge. "Yes."

I stepped toward Mary Lynn and began again. "Let's pick it up with the phone call you received from the defendant on that morning. What did you do after you received his call?"

"I threw on my clothes and immediately drove to their house." She was calmer as she answered.

"What happened when you arrived?"

She paused and looked at Duke. "Max was on the front lawn, talking to an officer. I ran at him, screaming, accusing him of hurting Christie. I ran at him, but the officer restrained me."

"After you were restrained, did you have an opportunity to discuss your concerns about the defendant with the investigating officer?"

Maintaining composure, she responded, "I did. I told her about his abuse of Christie and about that business he was having with that woman."

"Mary Lynn, thank you. I know that was difficult." Turning to Walter, "Your Honor, I have no other questions for Ms. Holder."

Trial Tip #14: Direct Examination

Showcase the emotional aspect. The testimony of many witnesses involves strong, even intense, emotions. Allow the jurors to vicariously experience the devotion, love, surprise, pain, stress, grief, or disappointment of the witnesses. Courtrooms are staid, clinical environments; it is incumbent on advocates to assist their witnesses in bringing their testimony to life. Bear in mind that it is often intense circumstances in the lives of the witnesses that are at the heart of the trial.

CHAPTER 40

THE CROSS

Walter nodded to MacPherson. "Counsel, you may proceed." She slowly stood and almost casually walked behind my table to find a comfortable place mid-jury box, and in a soft voice began, "Ms. Holder, you very much want Lt. Cort convicted, don't you?"

No hesitation. "Of course I do." Mary Lynn's voice was wary, flat, devoid of emotion.

MacPherson cocked her head and in that same almost soothing voice, "And you will do everything you can to see that he is convicted, won't you?"

"I'm here to tell the truth." Steady and emotionless.

"Ms. Holder, we've heard you voice your opinions during your direct examination. In fact, Ms. Holder," she asked ruefully, "you disliked Lt. Cort from the first time you met him, isn't that true?"

Holding steady, Mary Lynn maintained her eye contact with MacPherson. "My first impression of him was that he was a person who insisted on being right all the time. That he needed to be the dominant person in any relationship."

"So that's a 'yes.'" A bit more volume and just a touch of heat, yet far from confrontational. "You disliked him from the first time you met him?"

"Yeah."

Maintaining that same cadence and tone. "Let's move beyond your impressions and opinions into the actual evidence. After your call to your sister on February 3, the night before, you didn't have any further contact with her later that night or that early morning, correct?"

"Correct." Mary Lynn bit her lip, resisting the urge to go beyond the question. She stole a look at Duke.

"And you didn't have any contact with Lt. Cort during the early morning hours of February 4, did you?"

"No."

"So, just to be clear, you have no direct knowledge of the whereabouts of either Christie or Lt. Cort during those early morning hours, correct?"

"That's right. No direct knowledge."

MacPherson's pace and volume picked up as she changed direction. "Christie is a smart, resourceful woman, isn't she?"

"You're talking about her as if she is still alive, but we both know she isn't." Mary Lynn's retort was tinged with just a trace of devilment.

MacPherson ignored the comment. "Let me ask my question again. Christie's smart and resourceful, isn't she?" Ever patient.

"She was." Mary Lynn wasn't budging.

"And according to you, she was being abused by Lt. Cort."

Nodding affirmatively, Mary Lynn snapped, "As I've already testified."

"You are aware that there was never a call to law enforcement reporting any abuse?"

"He wouldn't let her make that kind of call."

MacPherson cocked her head in mock puzzlement. "And are you aware that you are the only one who claims that he abused her?"

Mary Lynn made direct eye contact with MacPherson before responding, "In Christie's words, 'It would have only gotten worse.'"

"My point, Ms. Holder, is that there is no corroboration of any kind for your claim that she was being abused."

"He kept her on a tight leash." She gave a quick snap to Duke who discreetly gestured with his hands for her to maintain control.

"Returning to my question, no corroboration, right?"

"I don't know." Resignation tinged her voice, but she was hanging pretty tough.

MacPherson continued. "According to you, when Christie brought up the idea of divorce, Lt. Cort wouldn't hear of it, would he?"

"He threatened her if she even brought up the subject."

"But again, you're the only person that claims he threatened her."

"Like I said, he kept a tight leash on her. Apart from our parents, I was pretty much her only contact." Again she flashed to Duke.

"Alright, let's go with your assumptions about their relationship. Factoring in those assumptions," MacPherson said in a skeptical voice, "I'm surprised that you've never entertained the idea that she simply ran off."

Mary Lynn put up her hands and gave an incredulous look. "She would have let me know. I know that for an absolute certainty. She would've reached out to me."

"But by reaching out, she might have run the risk of Lt. Cort using the resources of his office to find her. True?"

"She never contacted me because she couldn't."

"You are aware that Christie's passport and some $1,900 in cash went missing?"

"That's what he claimed." Mary Lynn's voice began to take on a sharper edge. The anger lurking just beneath the surface.

"Let me ask you this, Ms. Holder. If Christie had run away and then somehow reached out to you, you would keep that secret, isn't that right?" MacPherson's assertiveness had picked up, in response to Mary Lynn's edge.

"She hasn't reached out because she can't. How many times must I say that?"

"Even if she had contacted you and you knew she was alive, you would still want Lt. Cort to be found guilty of her murder, because you hate him that much?"

Leaning forward, Mary Lynn responded angrily, "She hasn't contacted anyone because she is dead."

"You haven't answered my question. You would cover it up to help convict Lt. Cort, wouldn't you?" MacPherson was insistent.

Mary Lynn took a controlling breath and contemptuously answered, "I wouldn't lie."

"Yet you took extraordinary steps to expose Lt. Cort. You went so far as to spy on him." MacPherson's questions were coming faster and harder.

"I did, and look what I found out," she retorted, not bothering to control her anger. She had abandoned Duke. "That he was not only an abuser but an adulterer."

"Let's return to my question. You would cover up any contact you had with her in order to see Lt. Cort convicted of a murder that never happened."

"Objection. Counsel has asked the same question several times." I wanted to buy Mary Lynn some time to check her emotions.

Without waiting for Walter to rule, Mary Lynn spat out, "I'll give you the same answer, I wouldn't lie. I haven't lied about anything I've said today."

MacPherson looked at Mary Lynn and then at Walter. "Your Honor, I have no more questions for this witness." MacPherson gave the jurors a curt smile and returned to her table. It wasn't the warm MacPherson charm we had seen earlier.

"Mr. Clearwater, will there be any redirect examination?"

I quickly thought through a possible redirect but didn't find it necessary. Mary Lynn had held her own. MacPherson's accusation about Mary Lynn covering up any contact would ultimately be for the jury to decide. I thought Mary Lynn had made her case. "Judge, I see no reason for a redirect," I said, for the benefit of the jury. I wanted to communicate that MacPherson hadn't laid a glove on Mary Lynn.

Duke walked Mary Lynn out of the courtroom. I figured I wouldn't see either of them for the balance of the day. She had hung tough, and Duke had been her rock throughout.

As we were leaving the courtroom for the lunch recess, it took me two attempts to stand up. The stress of Mary Lynn's direct and cross had caused my thighs to tighten up. I hadn't realized how stressful her testimony had been.

I shook some life into my legs and met Lisa at the elevator. "Let's get lunch across the street. You up for a hot dog?"

She gave me a look. "You're kidding, right?"

"I am," I lied. "There's a Thai restaurant nearby. Does that work?"

"That works."

Lisa was anxious to discuss Mary Lynn's examinations. "She was too strident. She didn't show enough sorrow for her sister."

I nodded in partial agreement. "But keep in mind, she was under tremendous pressure, and for the most part, I think she accomplished what we needed her to accomplish. She painted Cort as an abusive, domineering husband. That's what we needed." I paused, then said, "It was far from perfect, but given her earlier freakout, it was good enough."

"I'm glad. So what's next?"

"Sherry Ossoff. MacPherson beat her up at the first trial, but I think she'll do better this time around."

"I take it you and John have worked with her?"

"We have. But the bigger question right now is whether the judge will let us show our demonstrative aid to the jury. If he lets it in, we'll play it during Sherri's exam."

"Will the judge let it in?"

"I hope so. Fifty–fifty whether he will."

Returning from the lunch recess, we were informed by the clerk that Judge Walter wasn't feeling well and that the trial would be in recess until Thursday morning at nine. Later that afternoon I received another call that Judge Walter was still ill and that the trial was pushed over to Friday.

CHAPTER 41

CORT ON THE LOOSE

Friday morning, we were summoned to chambers. Walter looked ill, fragile. *Maybe he needed another day or even the weekend before returning.* Looking directly at MacPherson, he announced, "I'm going to allow the prosecutors to use their demonstrative aid." Wills suppressed a smile, leaned to me, and gave me a discreet low fist-bump. What a relief to get this in.

MacPherson was not pleased. "Your Honor, may I be heard?" Her voice had an urgency to it.

"Merci," Walter said, leaning back in his chair, expecting her pushback. "This doesn't cover any turf that they don't have a right to cover. It's fair game."

MacPherson wouldn't let go. "It creates a false and incriminating narrative of Lt. Cort going about the business of murder. It's remarkably prejudicial. The appellate court will not be sympathetic to your ruling."

That last comment dug under Walter's skin. He sat up straight and looked over his glasses at MacPherson. "I've made my ruling. If the appellate court doesn't like my call, they can have at me. Most likely I'll be retired by then anyway." *Whoa! What a startling comment. Judges are usually very concerned about their rulings being overturned. And maybe just as startling, the shine he had accorded MacPherson wasn't quite as bright.*

Surprisingly, MacPherson persisted, despite the judge's adamance. "With respect, it's the wrong ruling. And seriously compromises the integrity of this trial."

"That's enough, counsel." Walter's voice broached no further comment. "Let's get back in the courtroom and resume trial."

The jurors were brought in and we were once again underway. Wills called Det. Sherri Ossoff. They ran through the preliminaries, establishing her professional training and experience. As he had done during the first trial, Wills first questioned Ossoff about her investigation. Her narrative followed the same arc as the first trial, but with the addition of the extended investigation performed between trials. Wills then turned to the making of the demonstrative aid. Ossoff confirmed that the distances and travel times were accurate. In particular, she explained that the elapsed time displayed on the screen was accelerated during the travel periods to remain in sync with the action displayed. And with that, the screens—one for the witness's benefit and the other for the jurors—lit up.

The jurors, not to mention the gallery, were keenly focused as the display began with an individual exiting the sheriff's station at 1:00 a.m.

Ten minutes into the screening, there was a guttural sound from the judge's bench. I saw Judge Walter's head drop to the bench and then jerk back against his chair. I pushed back from counsel table and ran to him, unclear as to the nature of his distress. As I came around the bench, the bailiff was just behind me and he shouted a command to the jurors and visitors to remain seated. Walter had slipped from his chair. We pulled the chair away and laid him on his back. The bailiff yelled for the clerk to call court security for medical aid. The judge was breathing but unconscious. I took off my jacket to make a pillow for his head.

A commanding voice was suddenly at my side. It was juror number seven, the internist. "I've got it, Mr. Clearwater." To those pushing in, he commanded, "Give me some room," and he proceeded to tend to the judge, unzipping his robe and removing his tie. Ten minutes or so later, EMTs arrived, and after conferring with the doctor, they gurneyed the still-unconscious judge from the courtroom.

Meanwhile, the bailiff had called for additional backup. Two more sheriff's deputies arrived and secured the jurors back into the jury deliberation room. The people in the gallery were ushered out of the courtroom. When the dust settled, Judge Coines, from a neighboring department, had been called in. She summoned the lawyers back into Judge Walter's chambers. After we gave her our accounts, she nodded her understanding. I was still amped up and replaying the scene, wondering if Judge Walter would survive whatever had befallen him.

MacPherson, however, was already moving forward. "I think it important to speak to the jurors right away and give them some idea of how things would progress, going forward."

Coines looked at me. "I agree," I said. *If Coines or MacPherson weren't going to dwell on Walter's condition, then perhaps I shouldn't, either.* "I suggest we bring them back into the courtroom."

Coines agreed and instructed the bailiff to bring the jurors back into the empty courtroom. Once assembled, Coines thanked the internist for tending to Judge Walter and asked him whether he could make an assessment of the judge's condition.

"It looked to me like he suffered a stroke. Given his age, it could be a lengthy recovery."

Juror number two piped up unexpectedly and asked the internist, "Do you think he'll survive?"

Without looking back to his fellow juror, the internist answered, "I don't know."

Coines ignored juror two's interruption and said, "Obviously, we are going to need to adjourn for the day. I suggest that the jurors go home, and we'll keep you posted on how we will move forward with the trial. We have your contact information and will let you know when trial will resume. We are now in recess. I will see counsel in chambers."

Juror two chirped again, "I think we would all like to know how Judge Walter is doing. Will we be contacted about his condition?" Coines responded that there might be some confidentiality issues involved, but she would see what could be done.

Back in chambers, Coines advised that she would discuss the situation with the presiding judge, who would determine how to proceed. She was skeptical that Walter would be back anytime soon and ordered us back Monday to map out the way forward. *I hoped the crotchety old judge would pull through. I didn't much like him, but I felt for him.*

That evening, Lisa, Duke, Howard, and I joined Tony and Eve for drinks on their balcony. I was eager to hear everyone's take on today's events; Mary Lynn's cross and the judge's collapse had created quite a stir. Just as we settled down to talk, Duke received a call, and after listening for a moment, said, "We'll be right over." Sliding the phone quickly into his pocket, he looked at me. "Mary Lynn just got a threatening and abusive call from Max Cort. She's afraid he's coming for her. She's pretty much hysterical."

"Let's go," I said, already on my feet.

When Duke and I arrived at Mary Lynn's condo, she threw herself into Duke's arms. *They had indeed bonded.* She was a mess, sobbing with a runny nose. Duke ushered her to a couch, offered his old-school hanky, and made soft reassuring sounds. I went to the restroom and dampened a washcloth before handing it to her.

When her breathing had evened out, Duke, with his arm wrapped around Mary Lynn's shoulders, asked her to tell us about Cort's call. She gave a small nod. "He said that I had ruined his life and that I would pay dearly." She took in a ragged breath and continued, "He called me every foul name you can imagine before I hung up." She ducked her head into Duke's chest and mumbled, "He said he was going to kill me."

Duke rubbed her shoulder gently. "There's no chance of that. You're going to be with me going forward."

She blinked away her tears, focused on Duke, and gave him a wan smile before nuzzling into his chest.

Duke asked, "Did he sound like he had been drinking?"

She thought that over and slowly nodded. "Yeah, he did. He slurred some words. But his threats that he would kill me came through loud and clear." Again, she collected herself. "I've never been more afraid. I didn't know what to do. Duke, I'm going to need some protection. He wasn't kidding."

"Like Duke said, you're going to get a lot of protection," I said, reassuringly.

She sat up and looked hard first at Duke and then at me. "I don't just mean tonight or this week. I need protection from him for as long as he is out there."

Duke assured her, "Nothing's going to happen to you."

"I don't know how you can say that. He's a killer!"

"Let me see what I can arrange," I said. "Duke, would you stay with her tonight?"

Duke looked at Mary Lynn. "Can I sleep on your couch tonight?"

"Thank you, Duke, of course. I'd feel a lot better." She gave him an appreciative smile, then redirected to me. "What about tomorrow? This weekend? Beyond that? What about then?"

"I'm going to work on that," I said.

"He's a high-ranking sheriff's-department guy. What can you do against that?"

"I understand. Let me work on it."

I called Wills and had him request a patrol car outside the condo complex and a deputy outside her door.

She tucked her head down and again nuzzled into Duke's chest. *Was there something romantic going on here? Wouldn't that be something? Duke was probably twenty years her senior. What the hell, if there were sparks, there were sparks.*

In twenty minutes, Wills called back, confirming there would be a patrol car at the curb and a deputy outside her door. "We could also get a restraining order," he suggested.

"Yeah, but to a determined person, a TRO provides little protection." I paused, frustrated with our lack of good options. "How in hell is this guy not in custody? This is a murder case, and he's out there doing this shit. It's not just Mary Lynn; I know he's been hovering around Merkle's life as well."

"When Walter set bail at $2 million," Wills said, "I thought that would keep him in custody. I didn't know at the time that his mother was loaded. She lives on the harbor in Newport Beach. From what I understand, she fronted the $200 grand for the 10-percent down and put her property up as collateral."

"Shit. We've got to revoke his bail and get him back in custody. This jackass has murdered once already, and now he's out here intimidating a witness."

"Since Walter is out of the picture, which I assume is permanent, we need to go to the presiding judge and make our case to revoke his bail," Wills said. "Given this incident, that shouldn't be a problem. I'll contact the presiding judge over the weekend and see what he is willing to do. It may take until Monday, but we can get the wheels rolling."

"Meanwhile, we are going to keep Mary Lynn under wraps," I said to Wills. Then suddenly, a cold, startling reality hit me. "What about Merkle? She's still in play." *Why had that taken so long to hit me?* "Cort wants her to alibi him. If he lashed out at Mary Lynn, who is no longer a factor, what more will he do to confirm Merkle will be testifying?" *Dammit Clearwater, start thinking!*

"Especially if he's been drinking," Wills added with alarm.

"We've got to get to Merkle."

"I agree. How do we find her?"

"She works at the Elite Gentlemen's Club on Roscoe in North Hollywood. I'm on my way. Can you meet me there?"

"Should we call the police?"

"It's a short drive. We can be there in minutes. I'm on my horse."

CHAPTER 42

TO THE RESCUE

When I arrived at the parking lot of the club, Wills was waiting for me. We entered and learned that DeeDee was working. We paid the cover, and I pushed back the curtain. We took tentative steps, acclimating to the dim lighting. Willow was not on the stage. I scanned the room and didn't see her. We took seats and ordered our fifteen-dollar beers. We passed on lap dances and waited. Minutes later, Willow emerged from one of the lap-dance booths followed by Cort. Cort was right on her heels. They hadn't seen us. Willow was rubbing her neck. Cort had a hand on the small of her back, hustling her toward the exit. I stood, followed by Wills, and stepped over to block their path. They both recognized us. Willow looked terrified; Cort stunned. In a flash of panic, Cort pushed past us and ran for the exit. He was holding a gun. Wills started after him, but I pulled him back, "He's got a gun. Dammit!"

Willow collapsed against me. *Where were the damn bouncers?* I half-carried, half-walked Willow to a chair. A bouncer suddenly showed up and asked Willow if she was alright. *Stupid question.* Merkle stared at him with a venomous look and screamed at him,

"I told you assholes to not let him in! He was trying to kidnap me. And you dumbshits conveniently disappear?"

"Sorry, DeeDee. I wasn't at the front. I told Mel to be aware, but obviously it didn't work. Was that the guy you warned us about who just ran out?"

"Sure was!" she screamed at him, and slumped back in her chair. "Did you hear what I said? He wanted to kidnap me! You and the other two clowns are worthless."

"Sorry, DeeDee," he said again, contritely. "Anything I can do now?" *Stupid question number two.* He gestured to Wills and me. "How about these two guys?"

"They're the reason I'm not in his car going to some back alley or hole in the woods where he could dump my body." She paused, her hysteria abating. "Get me a drink, Benny, and one for my two rescuers—and make it a real drink!"

Benny went to retrieve our drinks. One of the other dancers handed Willow a T-shirt to cover her breasts. She pulled it on. I took a seat next to Willow.

"You alright?"

"No! But I'm trying to get there. Damn, that was scary." She grabbed at my shoulder. "Thanks."

Meanwhile, the music was still pulsing, and the stage show continued unabated.

"Did he say he was going to kill you?" I asked.

"Yeah, though not in so many words. He told me he was going to 'impress upon me the importance of my testimony.'"

"He didn't know that you've talked to us and that your testimony wouldn't do him any good?"

"He does now. I told him. He was livid. He tried to choke me." She tilted her head, and finger marks were already visible on her neck. "If I hadn't been in a public place, I think he would have killed me."

Wills asked, "Any idea where he was going to take you?"

"I don't know, but who cares? He's been drinking—I don't know if he had a clear plan. He said without my testimony, he was going to be convicted, but he would never go to prison. He was desperate. I don't know what he was going to do. Like I said, I felt like he was going to kill me."

"I'm sorry Willow, we should have provided you some protection." She gave me a penetrating look but said nothing. I shrugged apologetically, even though the last time I had seen her, she refused protection before kicking Duke and me out of the club.

"I think you've had enough of this place for tonight. Let's get you out of here. Let's go someplace, call the police, and you can make a statement to them."

"No! Don't call the police. This place finds out that I've brought the police here, I'm out of a job."

"He tried to kidnap you at gunpoint!" Wills was perplexed at her refusal.

"Dammit, this is my job! I can't afford to lose it. Just let me be."

Wills and I exchanged looks and relented.

She nodded as if that had been settled. "Let me get dressed." Benny returned with the drinks. Willow grabbed one and headed to the dressing room. I knocked mine back. Wills passed.

She returned, dressed in leggings and that same bulky sweater I had seen her in before. "How about we go to that same Denny's?" I suggested.

"That's fine. Can I ride with you? I don't know if he's still out there, hanging around."

"You can ride with me. We'll pick your car up later. John can follow us."

Margaret, the same server we had last time, greeted Willow, Wills, and me as we settled into a booth at the back of the restaurant. We ordered coffees all around. Willow didn't order the mountain of food she had during our previous visit. *I guess a kidnapping scare tends to dry up one's appetite.*

After the coffee arrived, I said, "Fill us in."

She took a tentative sip. "I think you two saved my life." Her hand started shaking, and before she could put down her cup, some coffee shook free. While I mopped it up with a napkin, she stuffed her hands between her knees, trying to steady herself. Wills and I gave her time to compose. She tried another sip, this time with two hands; it went better. "When I told him that you had gotten to me, he lost it. He said that without me testifying about where he was, he was going to be convicted."

"I don't understand," said Wills. "You didn't alibi him during the first trial, and he wasn't convicted. Nothing's really changed. Why would he risk coming after you now?"

"He said you guys showed something—a film? I'm not quite clear. Apparently, he thought it was over for him."

I looked at Wills. "Apparently, our reenactment really got to him. And he only saw the first ten minutes before the judge collapsed."

"Whatever you did, he thought he was sure to be convicted unless I alibied him."

"Let's back up," I said. "Did he show up tonight to make sure you were going to testify for him?"

"Yeah," she said, nodding. "He was hell-bent on it."

"But when you told him that you had already talked to us, that's when he lost it?"

Merkle scoffed, a hollow, bitter laugh. She gestured vaguely toward a growing lump on her cheekbone—"See this welt on the side of my face?"—and raised one of her sleeves up to her forearm—"See these bruises on my arms and neck?"

"I thought the steroid grunts at the club were there to protect you," Wills said.

"Those losers knew he's a cop," and then added, "A lieutenant." *She said the last part as if that explained their failure to act.* "But I really thought they would protect me," Willow said, through a sudden rush of tears. "Worthless sonsofbitches." She looked down, trying to compose herself, and sipped some water. "I think he was going to kill me and then himself. He had enough booze in him to do it." Another long pause. "I thought I was dead."

"Where were the bouncers when he had you back in a booth? Aren't they supposed to protect you women when you're isolated back there?" Wills insisted. He was stuck on that point.

Willow groaned. "It's like I said. He's a cop, and it seems like they knew that. Maybe he flashed his badge when he came in."

"I think we should call the sheriff's department and have you make a report. We need to get all this down," Wills suggested.

"Screw that!" She flashed her angry, bloodshot eyes at us. "I already told you, that would cost me my job." She then reasoned, "You two were there and saw what happened. If it comes to it, I'm sure you would corroborate what happened. I don't want to see or talk to anybody from the goddamn sheriff's."

"Okay, we're not going to push it," I said, placating her. "But we need to at least make sure you're safe tonight. Do you have someplace where you can stay until we can get Cort back in custody?"

"I've been staying with a woman I worked with at the Rocks. Max doesn't know about her."

"Are you sure? Cort seems to find things out."

"I've been living with her for a while. It's safe."

"I'd feel a lot better if we put you up in a hotel with cops at the door."

"I'll be okay at Clarice's place. He doesn't know about it. I'll be fine."

"Willow, you don't know if he's been following you. I don't like the idea of you not being protected, at least until we can get him in custody."

"Like I said, I've been living with her for a while. There's been no problems." She gave me a thank-you look and said, "I'll be okay."

"It's a bad idea, but I can't make you," I said, with a sense of impending regret. "At least let us take you there? Leave your car at the club?"

"Can we just sit here for a while? I need to catch my bearings."

Wills tried to lighten things. "We can stay here all night if you want. In fact, I'm hungry. Let's have your friend bring a few Grand Slams."

That brought a meek smile to Willow's pretty but battered face. She reached for Wills's hand and then mine, and gave us each a long, lingering stare, mixed with fear and relief. "I mean it. You two guys showing up probably saved my life." She threw me a questioning look. "Why tonight—why did you show up tonight?"

I answered, "Cort was tanked up and called Mary Lynn, Christie's sister, and threatened her. Once we learned that he was drinking and making threats, it occurred to us that you may also be on his list."

She closed her eyes and in a barely audible voice said, "I *was* on his list."

We dropped her at Clarice's condo in Reseda. Clarice mothered Willow into her place.

When I returned home, I was keyed up. Lisa was waiting; I filled her in. "This guy is a real threat. He was going to take her out to God-knows-where and do God-knows-what. He had already scared Mary Lynn down to her soul. We could very well have had another murder or murders on our hands, and still might."

She handed me a glass of wine and motioned us to the deck.

I sucked in some of the salty warm air, trying to unwind.

"The fact that he is out there, with his cop authority, his access to weapons, and his willingness to intimidate, threaten, and even kidnap . . . is daunting. Hell, he defines a loose cannon."

Lisa rubbed my shoulder. "I understand, you're upset. I don't blame you. But it seems like you've taken the best precautions you could with Mary Lynn and Willow."

"I hope so. Cort's very dangerous, and desperate. From what Willow told us, he's convinced he's going to be convicted, and for a guy like him, a cop, to go to prison? That is definitely the worst-case scenario for him." I paused. "He may even be suicidal. And a suicidal man has little to fear. Who knows what he is capable of?"

"Jake, I don't know what to tell you. Seems like you've done what you can do for now." She offered a reassuring grin. "I know you're keyed up, but try to relax."

"Okay, but first I want to call Duke and check in, and then I'm going to call Willow and make sure she's secure."

Lisa spent that worrisome weekend with me. I suspect I wasn't very good company. I called Duke and Willow several times Saturday and Sunday. Duke had moved Mary Lynn to a room in the Intercontinental.

Wills had been unsuccessful in his attempt to get Cort's bail revoked and secure an arrest warrant from the presiding judge. He said we would have to wait until Monday morning with our new judge.

CHAPTER 43

CORT IN THE WIND

Monday morning rolled around, and we were back in session. No Cort. No surprise there.

Her Honor, Joyce Coines, was once again on the bench. The jury had not been called. The gallery, however, was full. Coines gave MacPherson a questioning look. "Counsel? Your client?"

MacPherson stood. "Your Honor, I've not been in contact with Lt. Cort over the weekend. I'm at a loss to explain his absence this morning. As this court may not be aware, Lt. Cort has been out on bail since his arrest and has never failed to make a court appearance. May I indulge your patience and attempt to contact him? I'm hopeful that he will be present as soon as possible."

I slowly stood. "Your Honor, may we retire to chambers? I believe Mr. Wills and I have some knowledge concerning the defendant."

We settled into our seats in what was, at least temporarily, Judge Joyce Coines's chambers. Coines looked comfortable and confident behind Walter's desk. She appeared to be in her midforties. She wore her dark hair in a severe no-nonsense ponytail. Wills had informed me that she had been a deputy public defender for ten years before being appointed to the bench. According to Wills, who had tried a case before her, she was a very capable trial judge. Coines, cognizant of making a complete record against the possibility of an appeal, had the clerk and court reporter present. Speaking for the record, she said, "I've been assigned by the presiding judge to assume the Cort trial. Judge Walter took ill on Friday, and it appears that he will not be able to complete the trial. On Friday past, I ordered the defendant and counsel back this morning to discuss resumption of the trial. This morning the defendant, who is out on bail, failed to appear. Counsel for both sides are in chambers, and we are discussing going forward in the wake of defendant's failure to appear."

Coines, having made the record, turned to me. "Mr. Clearwater, you indicated that you have information related to Mr. Cort's absence. Please proceed."

"Thank you, Your Honor. This past Friday night, I received word that the defendant, perhaps in a state of inebriation, telephoned Mary Lynn Holder, a prosecution witness who had previously testified, and made dire threats and directed abusive language at her."

MacPherson sat back in her chair, surprised and speechless. It was clear from her response that she had had no contact with Cort. Sometimes the lot of the defense lawyer is mean.

Coines considered my statement and asked, "And if I understand correctly, Ms. Holder has already testified?"

"That's correct. When Mr. Wills and I learned of the defendant's threats to Ms. Holder, we were concerned that the defendant might also direct his anger toward Willow Merkle, a potential defense witness."

Coines, looking confused, asked, "Why would he threaten a defense witness?"

"It's my belief from speaking to the witness that when the

defendant approached her, she informed him that she would not be testifying on his behalf."

"Your Honor," interrupted MacPherson, "this is the first I'm hearing of any of this. I've not been informed by either prosecutor of these events." *Was she accusing me?*

Turning to her, I said, in a bitter tone, "Mr. Wills and I attempted to contact you. But it was over the weekend, and our efforts to reach you or your office were unsuccessful." *So shut up, Merci!*

Brushing MacPherson's concerns aside, Coines said, "Do you have more information to share about the situation, Mr. Clearwater?"

"I'm speculating here," I answered. "But I had contacted Ms. Merkle a week or so ago when I learned that the defense might call her to provide an alibi for the defendant. In my conversation with Ms. Merkle, I learned that she was not with the defendant during the critical time, and further, that she would not perjure herself on his behalf and would testify accordingly if called to the trial."

MacPherson started to speak but abruptly stopped.

Coines looked at MacPherson and then back at me. "I think I'm getting the picture. So what happened, Mr. Clearwater?"

"Our concerns about Ms. Merkle's safety were borne out. John and I immediately went to Ms. Merkle's place of employment and fortunately interrupted the defendant in the process of spiriting Merkle against her will into his car at gunpoint. When Cort saw us, he fled the scene. Other than some bruising administered by the defendant, Ms. Merkle was shaken but relatively unharmed."

Coines shook her head and asked, "I assume you and Mr. Wills have had no further contact with Mr. Cort?"

"That's correct."

Coines turned to MacPherson. "Ms. MacPherson, what do you know of all this?"

"Nothing, Your Honor. This catches me by surprise." She

paused and considered. "I would like a day or two to ascertain where Lt. Cort might be."

Before the judge spoke, Wills interjected, "In light of Friday's events, I contacted the presiding judge and requested that the defendant's bail be revoked and that he be returned to custody."

"His response?" asked Coines.

"He put the matter in your hands, Judge. It's your call."

MacPherson spoke up. "Before any further action is undertaken, I request twenty-four hours to get to the bottom of what happened, and to try and locate my client."

Coines ignored MacPherson while considering. "Mr. Clearwater and Mr. Wills, to your knowledge, are the two witnesses you spoke of secure? Such that you believe that they are under no immediate threat?"

"We have made arrangements in the short term for Ms. Holder. As for Ms. Merkle, she insisted on staying with a friend. I have reservations as to whether she is secure."

Coines, turning to MacPherson said, "From what I hear, this sounds like an individual who should be in custody. Any further thoughts, Ms. MacPherson?"

MacPherson, ever the defense lawyer, made her pitch. "These are very sketchy facts that we've been presented with. We have no testimony. No corroboration. Neither of the women who claimed to have been harmed by Cort called the authorities. I think any action curtailing Lt. Cort's freedom is premature. There may be some extenuating circumstances at play. I ask the court to not take any action until we know more."

"If I may, Your Honor," I shot back. "Mr. Wills and I were there to see the defendant in what certainly appeared to be a kidnapping attempt at gunpoint. We were both there—we saw this. This is a dangerous man doing dangerous things. He needs to be in a box."

MacPherson started to speak, only to be cut off by the judge. "Counsel," Coines began, directing her comment to MacPherson, "I can't have this conduct by your client. And especially now that he has failed to appear. I am revoking his bail and issuing an arrest warrant."

MacPherson slumped back in her chair, resigned.

Coines sat forward. "Now, let's get this trial back on track."

"Before we do that, Judge, have you learned anything about Judge Walter's condition?" I asked.

"My apologies, I should have said something when we first came into chambers." In a grave tone, she said, "He's in critical condition. They're not certain he'll survive."

"That's difficult to hear," I said. "Thanks for letting us know."

We paused for a moment in deference to Judge Walter's condition. Coines broke the silence. "It makes sense to me to resume trial tomorrow morning, whether the defendant is present or not." She was taking charge. "Any concerns?"

MacPherson responded, "I could use some additional time to ascertain my client's whereabouts."

"Ms. MacPherson, I've got a jury waiting. We start up tomorrow morning with or without your client."

"If my client isn't present tomorrow, what do we tell the jurors about his absence?" MacPherson asked.

"What would you suggest?" Coines asked.

"I would ask that you instruct them that due to unforeseen circumstances, he will not be present in court. Further, that they draw no inferences from his absence."

"Mr. Clearwater, Mr. Wills, your thoughts?"

Wills took the lead. "Seems a bit lenient, especially the language about 'unforeseen circumstances.' This guy absented himself and should get no benefit from that. We don't need to elaborate. I think it would be more appropriate that the jurors draw no inferences from his absence and leave it at that. I would further request that you find on the record that Mr. Cort, of his own accord, absented himself." He paused. "I don't want defense counsel to later raise a confrontation issue." He shot a glance at MacPherson.

"Understood," said Coines, tipping her head toward Wills. "I agree, Mr. Wills. In the event Mr. Cort is not with us tomorrow, I will so instruct as per Mr. Wills's suggestion. The trial will proceed with the defendant in absentia. Is there anything else we should discuss?"

"So we resume testimony tomorrow?" Wills asked.

"Yes, my clerk will contact the jurors. Meanwhile, I will read the reporter's transcripts in order to catch up." She looked at all of us, gave a smile, and said, "I will see everyone bright and early tomorrow morning."

Add "terrified" to "bright and early." Coines's sense of obliviousness belied the dread hovering over the trial. Cort was out there. He wasn't in Mexico or back East. He was here. It wasn't in his nature to run, to back off. It was in his DNA to strike out, to strike back, to avenge—to make his perceived enemies pay. He was a creature always moving forward, not backing off. He was a dangerous man whose desperation and anger made him a lethal threat. It wasn't a matter of if, only when, he would strike out at those who he believed had hurt him, betrayed him. Willow Merkle? Mary Lynn Holder? Sgt. Ponce? Could it extend to Merci MacPherson? John Wills? Me?

The trial would go on, but I felt there were targets on too many backs, too many people he might come after. I felt certain he would not go to prison. A high-ranking cop in prison was out of the question. He would take action compelled by his anger and desperation for as long as he could and, when cornered, take as many people with him as he could.

CHAPTER 44

OSSOFF—FRONT AND CENTER

Tuesday morning, to no one's surprise, Cort was again a no-show. It occurred to me that this started off as a murder trial without a body, and it was now a murder trial that lacked both a body and a defendant. Judge Coines had already done what she had promised. Cort's bail had been revoked, and an arrest warrant had been issued. Coines had the jurors brought in, and she instructed them concerning Cort's absence. Scanning the jurors' faces, I read their reactions, which ranged from puzzlement, to concern, to a healthy dose of skepticism.

Juror number two, as he was wont to do, voiced his thoughts. "Your Honor, so how are we to deal with this?"

"Respectfully, sir, I have given you all the guidance you will receive concerning Mr. Cort's absence. Is that clear?"

Undaunted, number two persisted. "But, I don't understand how we can have a trial without the defendant."

Coines, the model of patience in dealing with this dolt, replied, "I understand your concern, but like I just said, we will proceed with the trial under the guidance I have provided."

And with that, number two was shut down, and we were once

again underway. Det. Ossoff was called back to the stand. Wills went back and covered the preliminaries Ossoff had testified to on Friday. MacPherson didn't object, recognizing the passage of time and the confusion concerning Judge Walter's collapse.

When Wills asked Ossoff to start the film, however, MacPherson objected. "Your Honor, may we approach?"

Coines motioned us up. "I renew my objection to this film."

"Ms. MacPherson, I read the transcripts, including your motion to exclude. Judge Walter heard your arguments and, following what I'm certain was thoughtful deliberation, allowed the demonstrative aid. Are you suggesting that I reverse his decision?"

"Judge, I would ask you to watch this demonstrative aid, as they're calling it, before it is shown to the jury and then make an independent decision as to its appropriateness."

"I understand your fervor, counsel, but I disagree with your request that I second-guess a colleague jurist." Coines gave MacPherson a hard look and motioned us back to our tables. "Deputy, you may activate the film."

From the reaction of the jurors, the film was impactful. Without question, it took away a significant defense argument that there was insufficient time for Cort to do what we as the prosecution were alleging he did. It also had the effect that MacPherson was concerned about, as it allowed the jurors to viscerally imagine Cort doing precisely what the film depicted.

Following the film, MacPherson, still visibly upset at the playing of the film, began her cross-examination of Ossoff.

She struggled to put on a pleasant smile. Some of her charm had wilted. "Detective, let's start with this little demonstration we just watched. To be clear, this entire *thing* is speculative, isn't it?"

Ossoff, careful of traps, considered and chose her words

carefully. "No. We were careful to be as accurate as possible. Especially moving from place to place."

"Maybe my question was not clear. You and your colleagues who made this *thing*, have no actual evidence that when Lt. Cort left the station around one that morning, he immediately drove home, correct?"

"No direct evidence, but pretty good circumstantial evidence."

MacPherson acknowledged the equivocal answer with a subtle grin and continued. "Let's take each of those in turn, starting with direct evidence. There is no direct evidence that Lt. Cort drove to his residence right after he left the station, is there?"

"No direct evidence," Ossoff admitted.

"So you are only speculating that he drove to his residence from the station?"

"Given the whole picture from those early morning hours when Mrs. Cort went missing, I believe we have compelling circumstantial evidence of what the defendant did."

"Detective, as you sit here, you can't even say with any degree of certainty which direction Lt. Cort took when he left the station, can you?"

"No one saw him driving."

"I guess that's my point. For instance, your so-called demonstrative aid later showed Lt. Cort driving Christie's car from the residence and proceeding along Route 51, correct?"

"Yes it does."

"Yet once again you and your colleagues are just speculating, aren't you?"

Ossoff was calm, holding her own. "Counsel, it certainly seems like a reasonable assumption."

MacPherson seized on the word assumption. "Let's cut to the most egregious assumption. Your film," she spat out the word, dripping sarcasm, "depicts Lt. Cort stopping miles from his residence and dumping something into a pre-dug grave, correct?"

"Objection, Your Honor." Wills was up. "Counsel is mischaracterizing the depiction by referring to it as *egregious*."

Coines nodded at MacPherson. "Please rephrase."

"Certainly." MacPherson seemed a bit frazzled. With Cort in the wind and the reenactment just concluded, she wasn't her usual graceful self. "You would agree with me that depicting Lt. Cort dumping something into what appears to be a grave is a speculative hypothesis, wouldn't you?"

"He had to get rid of the body."

"Please answer my question. You and your colleagues are once again speculating, drawing assumptions, about Lt. Cort's conduct."

"I'll agree that no one saw the defendant dump his wife's body."

"You personally led the team in the efforts to determine if Ms. Cort's body was buried."

"I did."

"And yet, despite hundreds of worker hours and using sophisticated equipment, you didn't find the body you were looking for, isn't that right?"

"No, we didn't."

"Yet this aid of yours suggests that he buried her body."

"That's one possibility."

"So, taking a step back, the depiction of burying a body is rendered false by the very efforts you undertook?" *Score one for Merci.*

"We couldn't cover every square yard. That's true." *Ossoff had to back down a bit.*

"So you would agree that the depiction of Lt. Cort burying a body is actually refuted by your own efforts?" *MacPherson, pushing her advantage.*

"Like I said, we couldn't cover every square yard."

MacPherson gave a satisfied grin. "Since you have been so bold as to offer such assumptions and speculations, perhaps you'll indulge me. It's possible that Christie herself drove her car to the reservoir?"

"I don't understand your question."

She cocked her head. "I think it's straightforward enough, Detective. Let me try it again. It's possible that Christie drove her car to the reservoir, right?"

"I guess anything's possible."

"It's also possible that she drove her car into the water, isn't it?"

"Why would she do that?"

MacPherson gave a shrewd look. "Maybe to set her husband up for murder."

Ossoff grinned. "Now *you* are speculating, counsel." *Score one for Sherri.*

"It works both ways, Detective. Let's play this out a bit. When Mrs. Cort went missing, you confirmed that her passport was missing?"

"That's right."

"And that at least $1900 was missing."

"That's what the defendant told us. So take it with a grain of salt." *Ossoff was battling.*

"And that some personal items were missing."

"Again, that's what your client told us."

"You would agree with me that Christie could have taken those items."

"Not if she's dead."

"Returning to my question, it's possible Christie took those items before she dumped the car and ran away."

Ossoff blew out some breath. "Like I said, not if she is dead."

MacPherson smiled at the nonanswer and continued. "Let's

focus on Christie's necklace found in the car. You learned that necklace was precious to Christie, right?"

"That's right."

"And you would further agree that if Christie ran away, it would make sense that she would take the necklace with her?" MacPherson nodded, looking for agreement from Ossoff.

"Perhaps."

"But, if that necklace was intentionally left behind by Christie, that would be inconsistent with her running away, correct?"

"I guess."

"That would look bad for Lt. Cort, right?"

"I guess."

"And would focus another damning piece of evidence against Lt. Cort, wouldn't it?"

"If you insist."

"That could help incriminate Lt. Cort, correct?"

"Like I've said a number of times, there is no evidence that she ran away."

"Very well, detective. Your partisanship is noted."

"Objection." Wills was on it. "Counsel's comment was inappropriate."

Coines was quick to respond. "Counsel, please confine yourself to appropriate questions."

Ignoring Coines's admonition, MacPherson was right back at Ossoff. "Let's switch our perspective a bit. Let's assume Christie dumped her car and rode the bike back to the residence. In order to run away, she would need to use a taxi, or an Uber, or some other rideshare company to flee, wouldn't she?"

"Counsel, I'm not buying your hypothesis."

"As the lead detective, you never checked any of the rideshare outfits to see if she got a ride, isn't that correct?"

"No, we didn't."

"Yet she could've used a rideshare outfit, correct?"

"She could've."

"Detective, let's talk about Christie's motivations to run away. You knew her husband was abusive, right?" *MacPherson's jumping around from topic to topic was calculated to keep Ossoff off balance. It was sound strategy.*

"I did."

"You knew he had an adulterous affair around the time of her disappearance."

"Yes, I knew that."

"You also knew that he had forbidden her to initiate divorce proceedings, correct?"

"Yes."

"In fact, you learned from Ms. Holder that he threatened her in the most abusive language about divorce."

"Yes."

"Yet even under those harrowing circumstances, it never occurred to you that she just up and abandoned her life?"

Ossoff shook her head. "She wouldn't leave her family in such an awful state of not knowing. She didn't run away."

"Detective, you can't look at these good people sitting in the jury box with any degree of certainty and tell them that she isn't living a much better life under a new name somewhere else, can you?"

Here it was, the "Akron" question.

Wills was ready this time. "Objection! Misstates the burden of proof." *Indeed it did, and indeed MacPherson's question was effective.*

"Sustained. Ms. MacPherson, you have leave to explore the area."

Looking at the jurors and then back to Ossoff, MacPherson

exhaled and wiped her palms across the fabric of her pantsuit. She gathered herself before flashing one last brilliant smile at the jurors, and concluded, "I am through with this witness. Detective, you have been most helpful." *Always put on a game face.*

On redirect, Wills had Ossoff clear up any questions about how the demonstrative aid was made. "All the distances and the drive times from place to place were accurate. If anything, we erred on the side of giving the defendant more leeway." Wills also asked Ossoff about not finding a body despite all the effort to locate a grave site. "Like I said, there was no way we could completely cover every yard within the radius. And frankly, the site could have been a bit beyond our coverage."

Coines recessed for lunch. Ossoff insisted that we join her during the break in the attorney conference room. She was angry at Wills. "You didn't protect me enough during cross. I could have used an advocate to get her off my back. So many of her questions were argumentative and cumulative."

I was the intermediary. "Actually, Sherri, most of her cross was in bounds. MacPherson's a very good cross-examiner. But with that said, you handled yourself very well. I don't think we lost any ground. And the tradeoff between her cross and our film went decidedly in our direction. You did great."

"Okay," she said, somewhat mollified. "John, I'm sorry. Guess I'm a little keyed up."

"Don't worry about it. You held your own," he acknowledged.

"Sherri, would you please call Mary Lynn and Willow and check that they are staying out of sight?" I asked.

"On it, Jake. Though I'm not too concerned about Mary Lynn, since Duke is with her. Merkle's the one most likely to get back out there."

"I hope not. Not after almost being kidnapped," I said.

CHAPTER 45

BRINGING IT HOME

That afternoon, it was time to put on the balance of our case. That meant bringing forward the forensic scientist, who would testify that the blood found on the rug leading to the garage belonged to Christie. During the first trial, MacPherson had stipulated to the scientist's opinion concerning the blood. Wills and I believed she would once again stipulate and save everyone from the tedious nature of examining the expert. It made sense for her to stipulate. Clearly she had hired her own expert to perform a DNA analysis, and that expert had come to the same result as our Department of Justice analyst. However, even when I inquired about it during the break, she wasn't prepared to stipulate. I think the absence of Cort influenced her decision. She was playing for time, hoping he would either voluntarily come forward, or he'd be arrested. In my mind, she very much wanted Cort sitting at counsel table when she made her closing argument. *Couldn't blame her for that.*

Wills called Dr. Ron Simone, the criminalist who had analyzed the DNA samples from the blood found on the rug leading to the garage.

His direct examination went on for much of the afternoon. It was indeed tedious— full of lots of graphs and charts. Very few of us fully understood what Dr. Simone was talking about. Wills did the best he could to keep the exam lively, but he was fighting the material. Most of the jurors, with the exception of number two, the dolt, and number seven, the doc, had mentally checked out, and looked on with glazed eyes.

MacPherson took the analyst on a perfunctory cross during the afternoon with a very predictable and checklist cross-examination. Her heart wasn't in it, but she was buying time, hopeful that her fool of a client would materialize. The judge called it a day at four fifteen when the cross-examination concluded. I believe she had had enough of the DNA testimony, as had everyone else.

During the drive home, Lisa and I talked about anything but the trial. We were both trial exhausted. We talked about our upcoming wedding and maybe a delayed honeymoon to Mooréa or the Bahamas over winter break. A room over or near the water, soft breezes, leisurely afternoons, brilliant food and drinks, and thousands of miles from an American courtroom.

When we got home, I checked in with Willow Merkle, who complained, "I'm bored sitting around this dumpy little apartment by myself."

"Isn't your roommate there?"

"She's working. I'm sitting around going stir crazy, watching TV, eating junk food."

"I understand you're bored, but Cort is still out there. Being bored is better than being attacked again."

"No word on him yet, I guess?"

"No, ever since he tried to grab you, he's been on the loose."

"Damn him, anyway!"

"Yeah. Sit tight, Willow. This ugly episode in your life has got to come to a close pretty soon."

"God, I hope so."

I then checked in with Duke at the Intercontinental. "What's up, Duke?"

"Mary Lynn and I haven't left the hotel. Haven't seen the sun in days."

"How's she holding up?"

"She's solid. Wondering how long she'll be in hiding. What if Cort doesn't surface?"

"I don't know. It's just got to be one day at a time."

"I hear you. We're doing fine." He hesitated just a touch. "Mary Lynn's something. It's light duty." Was there a smile in those words?

It was my turn to hesitate. "Stay with it, Duke. I'll check in if I hear anything."

Wednesday morning, I called Liz Holder, Christie's mother, to the witness stand. I didn't want to end our case-in-chief with the DNA testimony. I wanted to finish with an emotional appeal. The mother's testimony would allow us a strong emotional finish. I had asked her permission to put her on several days before. She was nervous about testifying, but when I explained why I wanted her, she was willing.

As I posed my first question, Sherri Ossoff slipped through the courtroom door. She pushed through the gate and knelt next to Wills. I paused. Clearly something of note was underway. Wills looked at me and then at the judge and stood and asked, "May we have a moment, Your Honor?"

When I returned to our table, I leaned in as Ossoff was whispering to Wills. She grabbed my arm and pulled me to her.

"Merkle has been murdered. Stabbed and strangled. Her roommate is in intensive care."

"Oh God, no!" I stammered. Ossoff gripped my arm tight as I groped for my chair. "When? How?" *As if when or how made a difference.*

"Sometime early this morning. The roommate was finally able to call 911. But Willow had already bled out."

Sucking in air, I asked, "Cort?"

She nodded. "From what little the roommate said, Cort broke in and stabbed Willow over and over. He also severely injured Clarice, the roommate."

I was having a hard time processing. Last night she was fine, safe. She was even *bored*, that's how safe she had felt. She had assured me Cort didn't know about the roommate's place. I should have insisted. Dammit!

Wills looked up at the judge, who was staring at us. "Judge, may we approach?"

"Certainly."

MacPherson, Wills, and I gathered in front of the bench. Coines covered her microphone. "What's the disturbance, Mr. Wills?"

"We just received word that Willow Merkle, the defense witness spoken of earlier, has been murdered, and her roommate seriously injured. It appears that the attacker was Max Cort."

MacPherson lurched forward, off balance, and grabbed onto the judge's bench. I reached for her arm to help steady her. Her face drained of color. "You okay, Merci? Do you need to sit?" I asked.

She took in some air through her mouth. "Give me a moment, I think I'm okay."

Wills addressed the judge. "Your Honor, may we recess to chambers? Ms. MacPherson, Mr. Clearwater, and I need some time to gather ourselves."

Coines, hunched forward, said in a subdued voice, "Yes, I imagine you do." She looked at MacPherson. "Do you need some assistance?"

MacPherson shook off the request. "I'm okay." Somewhat recovered, she asked Coines to recess to chambers. She hadn't caught up to Wills's request. Coines nodded agreement.

Wills escorted Ossoff into chambers with the rest of us. She reported the tragic news to Coines as we sat silently.

In chambers, MacPherson fidgeted with a bottle of water and worked to calm herself, taking in deep breaths as the color slowly returned to her face. She wasn't alone. I thought about Willow and her roommate, and the horror they must have gone through. *Damn Cort to hell! If I had gotten the police involved the night Cort tried to kidnap Willow, would she have been killed? Should I have insisted that we put her in a hotel with an armed officer? Would that have made a difference?*

MacPherson had gathered herself and broke the silence. "Judge, in light of this terrible news, we've got to immediately sequester the jurors. If this gets out, there is no way my client will be able to receive a fair trial." I sat back. MacPherson had managed to think through the implications of this seismic jolt quicker than the rest of us. *I was still reeling from the shock.*

Coines looked at me, surprised as I was at MacPherson's suggestion. I sat back, put up my hands, and nodded. "She's right," I said. "Something like this is too big to hope the jurors won't learn of it. Admonitions won't be sufficient."

"Sequestration is a pretty radical step," Coines said. "We are very near the end of trial. Probably only a couple of days."

"Judge, this will be a big news story," I said. "I agree with Merci—there's a real chance of something this big getting through to the jurors. And if that happens, everything we have done, everything we have said in this trial, has been for naught. We need to preserve the integrity of the trial." *I felt guilty discussing the "integrity" of the trial with images of Willow being butchered racing through my head.*

MacPherson and Wills nodded. Coines slowly nodded agreement.

No one was in a hurry to return to the courtroom. We sat in silence for a while, thinking through the raw reality of what we had learned.

Finally, back in court, Coines explained to the jurors that for the balance of the trial, they were to be sequestered. She acknowledged the surprised faces of the jurors, as well as the stunned silence of the overflowing gallery, as she explained that sequestration was essential. "I can't go into specifics, but it is my determination that you jurors will need to be kept in virtual isolation pending the completion of trial and into your deliberations." She drew a deep breath. "I profusely apologize for the inconvenience. We will, of course, arrange for any necessities you require."

Juror number two, no surprise, had questions. They went unanswered. The jurors were ushered back to the jury deliberation room and waited as arrangements were made for them to stay in a nearby hotel. Coines recessed and ordered everyone back in the morning.

I went to an attorney conference room and called Duke. Without waiting for a greeting, I asked, "Are you and Mary Lynn okay?"

"Of course, what's up?"

When I filled him in, there was a long silence followed by a "*Sonofabitch!*"

"Are you two safe there?"

"Yeah, just the two of us tucked away in our cozy room."

"She's in your room?"

"Yeah, it made sense."

"Made sense?" I questioned. *A dawning suspicion blossomed into full realization.*

Duke, always a quick study, picked up on my question. "Don't be an ass, Jake. Two consenting adults. And as another benefit, I'm much better able to handle any security issues, having her in my room."

I took in the information and stifled any comment. "Keep her tucked away and safe. Apparently Cort has completely lost it. Can't be too careful."

Duke paused. "That goes for you and our team. Everybody is a potential target."

"Message received. Stay in touch."

Along with Wills and Ossoff, Lisa and I returned to Wills's office. Wills rolled his Dodger baseball over and over in his hands, while Sherri angrily shoved a pod into the Keurig so hard, she punctured the lid before it could close and spilled grounds across the table. I collapsed in a chair, my worry for Duke and Mary Lynn and sorrow for Willow briefly overwhelming me.

Lisa walked over and massaged my shoulders. "Sorry Jake, I know you were concerned for her."

"Yeah, a lot of good that did. I should have insisted."

"What now?" Ossoff asked.

Wills shrugged. "We go forward." And with just the slightest hitch of his voice, added, "Should we even think about trying to get Cort's murder of Willow before the jury?"

"Not a chance," I said. "And even if Coines would allow it, it's a terrible idea. We'd have to do a trial within a trial to prove he killed Willow, and then somehow beat back the overwhelming prejudicial impact of her murder. No." I shook my head. "We go forward like you said. From the perspective of the trial, nothing has changed."

"Except another woman has been murdered!" Ossoff was barely able to contain her anger at the murder of Merkle.

"Yeah, except for that," I said.

A tight silence was broken by Wills. "There might be a lighter side to this news. If we can't convict this miserable excuse for a human being at this trial, we can try him again on Willow's murder." *Tasteless comment. Was the stress getting to Wills?*

"John, you're sick," Ossoff said. "I'm out of here." She brushed the coffee grounds onto the carpet and walked out, slamming the door behind her.

I raised my hand for Wills's Dodger ball, and he tossed it to me. "Yeah, John, she's dead." We drank coffee in silence. I finally got up to leave. "Lisa let's go home." I tossed back the ball. "Would you do me a favor and call Liz Holder? Tell her the news, and let her know that we will resume her testimony in the morning?"

"Will do."

Wills probably didn't need to inform the Holders. The news of Merkle's murder was already splashed across the media outlets. KNX, LA's twenty-four-hour radio news station, had the story on every ten minutes. A manhunt was underway. And since Cort was very obviously still local, I felt it only a matter of time before they would catch up to him. I firmly held to my belief that he wouldn't allow himself to be arrested.

Cort's actions had blown this local trial into regional attention.

Lisa asked as we were driving home, "Are you and your team in jeopardy?"

"I don't think so. If I were to guess, I would say either Mary Lynn or Merci MacPherson would be the ones he might hunt."

"I understand Mary Lynn, but the defense lawyer?"

"It is not uncommon for defendants to attack their lawyer, believing their lawyer let them down."

"But she got him a hung jury the first time."

"I understand, but I've seen it a number of times. When things don't go well for a defendant, they blame their lawyer."

"For what? She didn't do anything wrong."

"It's hard to climb into Cort's head right now, so who knows what he's thinking. Maybe he blames her for allowing us to get in the reenactment. According to Willow, that really got to him."

"That he might be angry at his lawyer didn't even occur to me. Especially someone who you have raved about."

"I know, it's pretty counterintuitive."

"Are you and John potential targets?"

"I don't think so. We are more or less just generic prosecutors."

"Jake." She smiled. "You are anything but generic."

I laughed through the tension. "Glad to hear that."

The following morning, the media coverage amped up from regional to national. A cop on trial for murder in 2016 was rare and always generated coverage, and now a cop who allegedly killed a possible witness gave the story running legs. I learned from the bailiffs that people had begun lining up for seats in the gallery at two in the morning. *To think that they were treating this murderer's trial like a Black Friday sale!* Wills, MacPherson, and I were ushered into Judge Coines's chambers prior to getting underway. Coines wanted to know if any further developments had surfaced overnight. No one had anything further to report. Cort was still out there. Willow was still dead.

As we returned to the courtroom, MacPherson had a serious-looking man sitting directly behind her, next to her investigator. My guess was a bodyguard. *Merci wasn't taking chances.*

Waiting for the judge to take her bench, I looked out over the packed gallery. There was a hum of anticipation. In the front row, Lisa was talking to Jeremy Kaye. Or rather Kaye was talking to her. *Tough duty for Lisa.* Several rows behind them, I was surprised to see Joanna and Earl from my trial advocacy class. I walked over to them through the gate and asked, "What are you two doing here?"

"We're both clerking in the building and wanted to see you in action." Joanna smiled.

"I'm surprised you were able to get seats. This apparently is the place to be."

"We were in line at two thirty this morning." She then added, "This is indeed the place to be."

"It's good to see you both. Let's catch up when this trial is over."

"Will do," said Joanna.

"Knock 'em dead, Prof," from Earl.

I returned to my table as the bailiff called court to order and we watched the jurors file in. With the exception of number two, they didn't appear to be in a jocular mood. Number two looked refreshed and eager to go. *What a piece of work. I could kick myself for not challenging him during jury selection. He was such a loose cannon.*

The judge settled in and looked to me to recall Liz Holder. After she took the stand, Coines reminded her that she was still under oath.

"Mrs. Holder," I began, "I want to talk with you about your relationship with Christie."

"Objection, Your Honor. Irrelevant."

Coines looked at me with a cocked head.

"May I make an offer of proof?"

"Certainly."

"Defense counsel, during her cross-examination of Mary Lynn Holder, questioned whether Christie might have made contact with her sister or her parents. Counsel, by her questions, has put this area of inquiry into play. It is now my intent to explore that area."

"I agree," nodded Coines. "I have read the direct and crosses of Mary Lynn Holder and Det. Ossoff. I think the door to this testimony has been breached. The objection is overruled."

"May I ask my question again?"

"You may."

"Mrs. Holder, please describe your relationship with Christie."

Mrs. Holder took a breath. "We were very close. I spoke with her three or four times a week, and Frank and I would meet with her at least once a month or so for lunch or dinner."

"Would Max Cort typically join you for lunch or dinner?"

"Very seldom."

I nodded understandingly.

"Based on your relationship with Christie, do you believe she would fail to contact you if she was still alive?"

"Objection, Your Honor. This is base speculation."

"Overruled, for the same reasons I previously indicated."

I nodded for Mrs. Holder to proceed.

"I know my girl—she would have reached out. I know that for certain."

"Thank you, Mrs. Holder. Your Honor, I have no further questions of Mrs. Holder."

"Ms. MacPherson, would you care to inquire?"

"Briefly. Mrs. Holder, you hate Max Cort, don't you?"

Mrs. Holder shook her head in dismay at the question. "He killed my daughter."

"In fact, you hate him so much that you would perjure yourself to see him convicted."

Shaking her head again, "I would not do that."

"Isn't it true that even if your daughter had reached out to you, you would withhold that information from the authorities?"

"I would not do anything of the kind."

"Nothing further, Your Honor."

I met Mrs. Holder as she was walking from the witness chair and escorted her through the gate into the gallery. I turned to Judge Coines and said, "Your Honor, the people rest their case."

I usually experience a sense of accomplishment when resting my case. I didn't experience that here. Willow's murder cast an ominous gloom over the trial. I felt a sense of foreboding, knowing Cort was out there. Things felt unfinished, at loose ends. Intellectually, I knew that made no sense, but in my gut, I couldn't shake my dread.

Coines looked at MacPherson. "Ms. MacPherson, will there be a defense case?"

"Your Honor, the defense is satisfied with the state of the evidence and is prepared for closing arguments." *No surprise there. Who could she possibly call? Merkle was dead and Cort was out there, hunting.*

"Very well. Mr. Clearwater, who will be making the prosecution closing?"

"I will, Your Honor. May I have until this afternoon?"

"Certainly." Turning to the jurors, Coines instructed, "We'll recess until two this afternoon, at which time I will preinstruct you on the law, and then we will move onto closing arguments."

I hoped Joanna and Earl wouldn't lose their prized seats.

CHAPTER 46

CLOSING

As I continued thinking through how I was going to approach my closing argument, I had to be wary of inadvertently referring to Cort's absence. Doing so was tantamount to commenting on his Fifth Amendment right against self-incrimination, which would lead to a mistrial. Coines, in her instructions, would warn the jurors that they were not to consider that the defendant had absented himself and accordingly opted to not testify. Of course, once the jurors retired and began their deliberations, I suspected Cort's absence would be a robust topic of conjecture and speculation, despite the judge's admonition. How could they not ignore the court's directive?

I hadn't written out my closing. I never do. Closings needed that spark of spontaneity. No notes or scripts allowed for the freedom to establish maximum contact with the jurors. I wanted that immediacy. I needed to watch their eyes, study their faces. No barriers. Canned speeches are seldom memorable and rarely move an audience to the speaker's point of view. Of course, throughout history there have been a few notable exceptions—Lincoln, for example, read his 272-word Gettysburg Address verbatim from his handwritten notes. There were exceptions to every rule. (Although, perhaps it should be noted that Lincoln's iconic speech received less than enthusiastic acclaim as he delivered it. It was only later that it ascended to immortality.) I used my iPad to outline, organize, and craft out some phrasing that I thought would resonate, but I didn't carry it in with me that afternoon. Once I had my thoughts organized, I was ready to go.

The large courtroom was quiet and expectant as Judge Coines read the jury instructions. As is usually the case, the instructions were tedious and seemed to go on forever. I could sense the jurors trying to stay focused, not an easy task. Coines's delivery was in a monotone that could put heavily caffeinated folks to sleep. My stomach churned as I waited for my cue. Coines finally ended the misery, to the relief of all, probably including herself, and called on me to begin.

As I rose from my chair, I turned and nodded to Mary Lynn and Duke, as well as Frank and Liz Holder, all sitting in the front row. Duke had told me that Mary Lynn and her parents insisted on being there. Standing at counsel table, I took in the jurors, and began: "She's dead. That's a hard, cruel fact. She's dead. No funeral, no memorial service for her loved ones to mourn her. To say goodbye." I began slowly making my way toward the jurors. "She's dead because the person she married, and who swore to care for her in sickness and in health, killed her." I offered a faint, distasteful shake of my head. "Why? Because she was inconvenient. She was just an obstacle the defendant had to clear away as he was climbing the sheriff's promotion ladder. A life for a promotion. Christie's life for a promotion. Damn, what a tragedy. What a stupid, senseless tragedy."

I paused and moved to my left, toward the internist. "Let's take a step back before the thirteen of us undertake a thoughtful discussion of the evidence. To do that, we need to have a clear understanding of the law, the rules to guide you in your deliberations. Judge Coines, who has done an exemplary job filling in for Judge Walter, has laid out the law. She carefully set forth all the law, but what I want to do right now is focus on just two pieces of the law, so we can have that intelligent discussion of the task ahead of you. Okay?"

I got a couple of faint nods. I moved back to my right and centered myself in front of the jury box. "First, reasonable doubt. You'll remember during voir dire, we talked about the burden that John and I have as prosecutors. Our burden is not beyond a shadow of a doubt, or beyond all doubt, but only beyond a reasonable doubt."

I received a grin from number eleven, recalling the explanation I had offered him during voir dire.

"The word *reasonable* is critical here. Judge Coines instructed you that there are few things we can know absolutely, or beyond all doubt. For instance, if you see something with your own eyes, you can be absolutely certain of that. But what about those events that we don't actually see? How do we determine whether those events happened?" I stepped back and looked at jurors eight and nine, the real-estate women. They were focused.

"We use our common sense, our understanding of how the world works. We fit together what we've learned of the events to inform us of what happened. We consider the source of those facts. We consider the surrounding circumstances. We consider the motivations of the involved individuals. And we even consider if there is some other reasonable explanation for what happened. And when those facts paint a compelling picture, we know. We are confident as to what the picture depicts. We are confident beyond a reasonable doubt, even if we didn't see it with our own eyes."

I took in the whole group. "You've got a difficult task before you today." I shrugged. "No one saw Cort kill Christie. Does that mean we throw up our hands and say we just can't be certain? In that case, let's just call it off. Trial over. Let's all go home. Or, instead, do you folks do what juries have always done? You carefully put together the compelling pieces of evidence to determine what happened. That's the job ahead of the twelve of you." I locked onto the internist. "I'm confident you folks are up to the job."

I stepped back from the group and glanced up to the judge. "The second piece of law Judge Coines instructed you on is the definition of first-degree murder. She told you that not only must John and I prove that Cort intended to kill Christie, but also that he premediated her murder. You will have to ask yourself, do you believe he premeditated?" I leaned to the jurors. "Did he plan out the murder? Or was it just a spur-of-the-moment thing? I'll leave it to you good folks to apply your collective common sense to that question.

"Now that we have a sense of the job ahead of you, let's take a look at the pieces of evidence we've heard and examine how they fit together."

Behind me, Ossoff took her cue and clicked on to our PowerPoint presentation. The words **UNHAPPY WIFE** flashed across the projector screens.

"Why was this important in understanding Cort's plan?" I left the question unanswered for a moment. I wanted the jurors to think it through. I could read the answer on several faces. "That's right." I nodded to several responsive faces. "He needed a reason for Christie to be unhappy so that after he killed her, he could claim she ran away from her abusive husband. That was a big part of his grand plan. And oh my, did Cort give her reasons to be unhappy." I shook my head, with chagrin playing across my face. "Let's see: adultery, physical abuse, vicious threats." I put up my hands. "Job one accomplished."

I looked at Ossoff. She advanced the presentation, so now it read **PREPARING FOR THE KILL**.

"Let's step back and think about Cort's conduct during the weeks leading up to Christie's murder. What, do you imagine, could have been going on during those three Tuesday night shifts before the fatal Tuesday night shift, after which he reported that his wife was missing? We know he had up to an hour, maybe even an hour and a half, unaccounted for during each of those previous nights. What was he doing during those unaccounted-for hours? Could he have been setting things up? You folks heard the same testimony I heard; you talk that through back in the deliberation room." *Pose the question, recall critical facts, and then let the jurors' collective common sense do the rest. Never, never foist your opinions on them. That invariably engenders pushback. Let the jurors make that final jump.*

I nodded at Ossoff, who clicked once more. **TIME ENOUGH?**

"You saw the demonstrative aid. Did he have—"

I stopped midsentence as several clap-like sounds emanated from outside our courtroom. I froze. The whole room froze. Gunshots? I, along with everyone else, instinctively turned to the courtroom doors. One of the bailiffs ran to the doors as a sheriff's deputy with his service weapon drawn burst through, almost knocking the bailiff down, and shouted, "We have an active shooter on this floor!" His voice was harsh with adrenaline. "Everyone stay in place and shelter under the benches. Bailiffs, I want these doors closed and locked until you receive an all clear."

Before he finished his directive, Sherri Ossoff, gun drawn, slipped through the doors and out into the hall. She was running to danger. My already high regard for Sherri soared.

Our two bailiffs locked the doors and ordered everyone to get down between the benches. Stunned and frightened, people complied. I ran to Lisa and helped her over the rail. She was going to shelter with me. The jurors crouched beside their chairs. MacPherson and her investigator worked their way under their counsel table. Her bodyguard crouched next to the table. Wills huddled against the gallery rail, Lisa and I under our table. Judge Coines was nowhere to be seen.

Minutes passed . . . two, three, four. We all hunkered down in eerie silence, our hearts and bodies flooded with adrenaline. What if the shooter gets in? Who would he go after? How would I react? I hoped I would act like Sherri Ossoff. The quiet of the courtroom was suddenly punctuated by the horrible, bright sounds of shots ringing out in the hallway. This time, there was no doubt they were gunshots. They sounded like they were just outside our courtroom doors.

Tense minutes passed before someone out in the hallway yelled, "All clear!"

No one moved. We needed more than a disembodied "all clear" to believe the danger was over. One of the bailiffs, standing at the closed doors, was intently listening to his earpiece. The room was looking at him for confirmation. He finally announced that the shooter had been neutralized. *Neutralized? God, we love euphemistic words.* He went on to tell us that apparently the shooter was stopped just outside our courtroom. We were told we could resume our seats but otherwise remain in place while the investigators and forensic technicians secured the scene.

Wills whispered to me, "You think it was Cort?"

"Of course it was!" Lisa croaked.

"It wouldn't surprise me," I said. My throat was still tight with fear and twisted in anger as I thought about Cort hurting or killing others.

"But how could he get a gun into the courthouse?" Wills asked, still whispering, eyes still wide.

I was thinking through that same question. I took in lungfuls of air, working to consciously control my breathing. "He's a sheriff's officer. He's got essentially the same uniform as the bailiffs. He's familiar with the courthouse. He knows the entrances. He doesn't need to clear security. He doesn't need to check his gun," I speculated. "We may have left a gaping hole for Cort to walk through."

"Shit, Jake, we should have thought of that," Wills groaned.

"Yeah, a whole bunch of us should have thought about that." I then posed my own question. "What I want to know is how someone alerted to him before he got to our courtroom."

"My God, Jake! If he managed to get in here . . ." Lisa said.

"Let's hold on a bit," I said, without much conviction. "We don't know for certain it was Cort."

"Who else would be trying to get into this courtroom?" Lisa said. She was working to calm herself down.

I heard sobbing from MacPherson. I looked over at her and saw her frantically rocking in her chair. Her bodyguard stood, stony and silent, next to her.

"Lisa, are you okay if I check on Merci?"

"I'm good. Go ahead. She looks hysterical."

I nodded and walked over to her. "Merci, it's over."

She managed to choke out, "He was coming for me!" She stopped rocking and intensely scrutinized my face. "He was coming for me."

I put my hand on her shoulder. "Hell, Merci, if it was Cort, he could just as easily have been coming for me or John."

She shook her head. Her sobbing had subsided. "No. He was coming for me. When things start to go bad, they blame their lawyer. You know that. It's an occupational hazard." She offered a wan smile while wiping her face with her hands. "Maybe I've been in this business too long."

I offered a sardonic grin. "I don't think so. You love the courtroom, the drama, the rush. This is what you do. And you do it better than anyone."

"Thanks, Jake." She was still working to regain her composure. "But I'm sincere; maybe it's time to turn to civil trials. No more murder cases. They're too exhausting and dangerous."

"Now's not the time to make big decisions."

Her thoughts jumped at lightning speed. "You know Jake, if that was him and they killed him, this trial is over."

That hadn't yet occurred to me. But, of course, she was right. You can't try a dead man.

One of our guardian bailiffs opened one of the doors to let Ossoff enter. She came directly to me as I stood by Merci. She looked at Merci and then to me. "Okay to talk?"

"Yeah, go ahead."

"It was Cort. He's dead. Two deputies have been shot. Neither fatal."

MacPherson closed her eyes and bowed her head. She whispered just loud enough for me to hear. "Last night he called and threatened to kill me." She looked up, her eyes watering with relief. She grabbed my arm. "When you and John talked Walter into your so-called reenactment, he thought he was as good as convicted." She wiped at her eyes. "Maybe he was right. I don't know. But it was me he blamed for letting that damned thing in." She nodded. "You know Walter should never have let that in."

"Well, he did. No point discussing that again."

"You're right. Water under . . ." She was still pulling herself together.

It was my turn. "Now that this is over, did he ever tell you where Christie's body is?"

She looked up at me and said, "Of course not." Then, with a suddenly mischievous grin, she added, "Maybe she's in Akron."

EPILOGUE

No body fitting Christie Cort's description has ever been located. And no evidence ever surfaced that Christie had run away and was leading a better life in Akron or anywhere else. I don't believe Cort ever revealed to Merci where he had disposed of the body. (If, indeed, there was a body.)

Duke and Mary Lynn's relationship wore out after several months. I suspect that the angst brought on by the trial as well as Cort's threats brought them together but wasn't enough to sustain a long run. Duke was philosophic about the short romance. "Hey, it's better to have taken a shot than sittin' on the sidelines." Gotta love Duke.

Lisa and I married a week after the trial. There was no time for a real honeymoon, but we did drive north and spent the weekend in Cambria. We had decided that our deferred honeymoon would be a week in the Bahamas over the winter break. Classes resumed Monday morning, right after the morning swim.

Suzelle had gotten her wished-for confrontation matching MacPherson and me. I guess it was a draw. Had the trial gone the distance, I believed juror seven, the internist, would have gone with me. Whether he could have corralled the other eleven will remain an open question, especially considering that number two, the dolt, was one of the eleven.

ABOUT THE AUTHOR

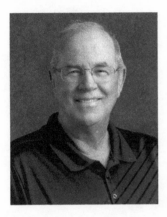

HARRY CALDWELL is a law professor at Pepperdine/Caruso School of Law. He teaches criminal procedure and trial advocacy. Professor Caldwell routinely represents death row inmates appealing their convictions before the California Supreme Court. He is the author of the legal thriller, *Cost of Arrogance*. He has co-authored several trial advocacy textbooks as well as the critically acclaimed *Ladies and Gentlemen of the Jury* series of books. He resides in Southern California.

CPSIA information can be obtained
at www.ICGtesting.com
Printed in the USA
BVHW040128210323
660674BV00005B/13/J